Thomas Allen Reed

Leaves from the Note-Book of Thomas Allen Reed

Volume 2

Thomas Allen Reed

Leaves from the Note-Book of Thomas Allen Reed
Volume 2

ISBN/EAN: 9783337396602

Printed in Europe, USA, Canada, Australia, Japan

Cover: Foto ©Andreas Hilbeck / pixelio.de

More available books at **www.hansebooks.com**

LEAVES

FROM

THE NOTE-BOOK

OF

THOMAS ALLEN REED.

Printed in the Reporting Style of Phonography.

VOLUME II.

LONDON:
FRED. PITMAN, 20 PATERNOSTER ROW, *E.C.*
BATH:
ISAAC PITMAN, PHONETIC INSTITUTE.

1885.

PREFACE.

In the course of my professional life as a shorthand-writer, reporter, and teacher of Shorthand, I have contributed to the press numerous articles with reference to the theory, the history, and the manifold uses of the art I have practised, and also a number of sketches and personal reminiscences connected with my daily occupation. Most of these are scattered through the pages of phonographic and other periodicals, including my own magazine, the "Phonographic Reporter," which I edited and lithographed for thirty years. It has often been suggested to me that many phonographers would be interested in having, in a convenient form, a collection of these contributions, many of which are not now easily accessible, the periodicals in which they appeared having long since ceased to exist. Mr Isaac Pitman was good enough to endorse the suggestion, and he further recommended that the articles, when collected and revised, should appear in consecutive numbers of the *Phonetic Journal*, and then be republished in a separate volume. This method was adopted, and for the last two years these "Leaves" have appeared week by week in the Journal in shorthand characters, together with a printed key in the common type. In the summer of 1884 a volume was issued containing all the contributions that had appeared up to that time; and the reception it met with at the hands of my shorthand brethren and of many non-professional readers who, notwithstanding the smallness of the type, took the trouble to read the printed key, was very gratifying to myself. The book answered the double purpose of giving information on matters of interest to shorthand practitioners, and of serving as a reading-book for students. The "Leaves" have been continued weekly during another year, and now, on their completion, they are re-issued in a second volume, which I hope will not be less favorably received and kindly judged than the first. It includes one or two addresses delivered before the Shorthand Society and other kindred associations, which, if not of so light a character as some of the sketches and reminiscences, will not, I trust, on that account prove less interesting.

CONTENTS.

LEAVES FROM THE NOTE-BOOK OF T. A. REED.

—:o:—

THE SHORTHAND WRITER "ON CIRCUIT."

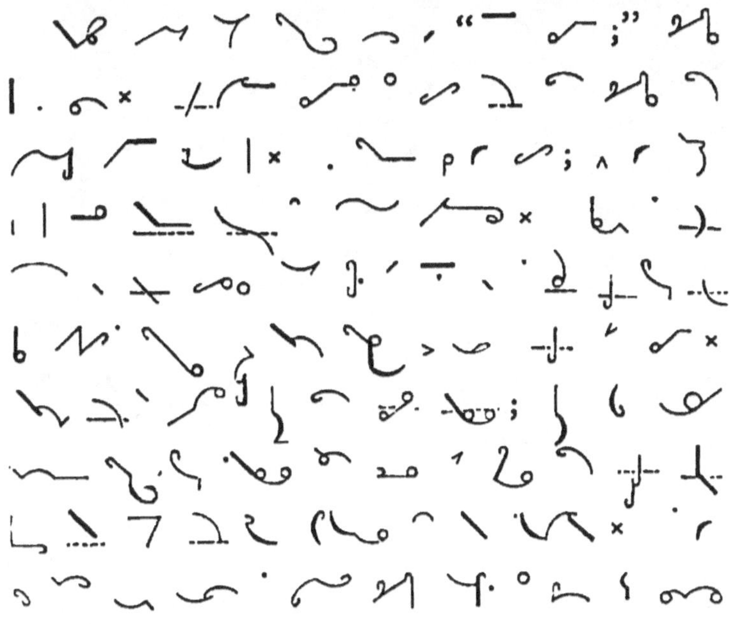

Barristers are not the only professional men who "go circuit;" shorthand writers do the same. Each of the legal circuits has one or more shorthand writers from London regularly attending it. The practice is an old one; how old I cannot say, but it goes back far beyond my own recollections. It is now an easy matter to put onesself in the train and go to an Assize town for a few days, returning perhaps to London before proceeding to the next town on the circuit. Before the era of railways it was a more serious business; it was then necessary to make provision for an absence of some weeks, and the journeys from town to town had to be taken by coach or whatever other conveyance might be available. An old friend of mine, now no more, a well-known shorthand writer in his day, has told

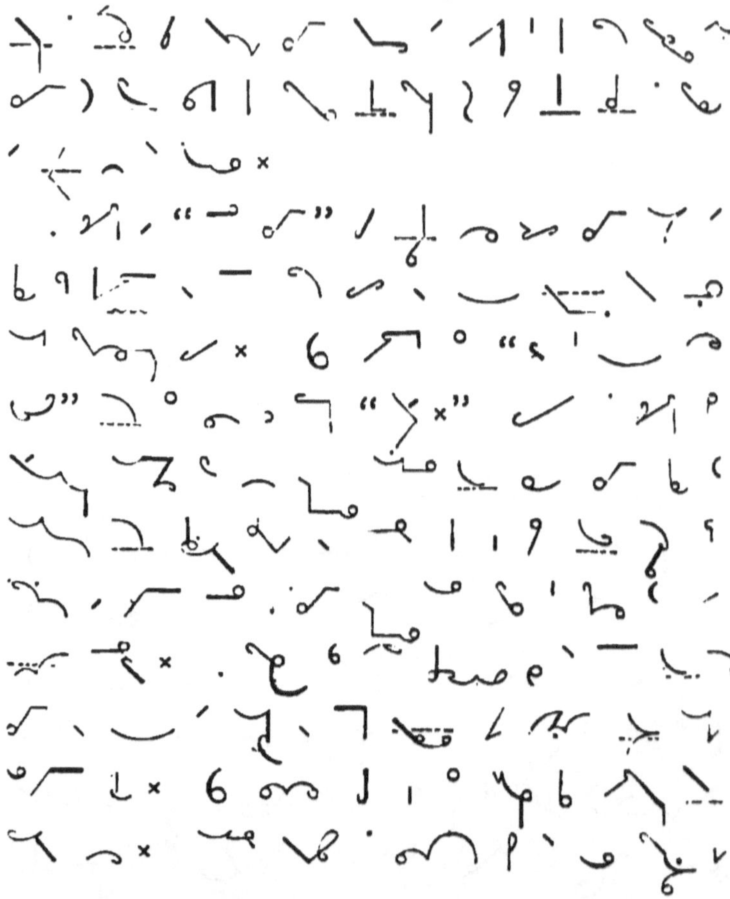

me that he sometimes bought a horse just before the circuit began, and rode on it from place to place, and after the circuit was over sold it, perhaps at a profit, so that he had at once a pleasant and cheap mode of conveyance.

The shorthand writer who "goes circuit" generally attaches himself to one circuit only, and it is not considered *de rigeur* to go from one to another picking up cases in a promiscuous way. This is regarded as "building on another man's foundation," or, as some would call it, "poaching." Where a shorthand writer has a *bonâ fide* engagement offered him to take notes in a case off his own circuit, it is not thought unfair or dishonorable on his part to accept it, but he often arranges with a *confrère* who regularly goes the circuit to take notes in his place on terms that are mutually acceptable. The proceeding that is most discountenanced is that of going off your own circuit to another and endeavoring to get business which should legitimately fall into the hands of the regular attendant. This is sometimes done, but, as I have said, it is reprobated by honorable men. In the case of barristers a similar state of things prevails,

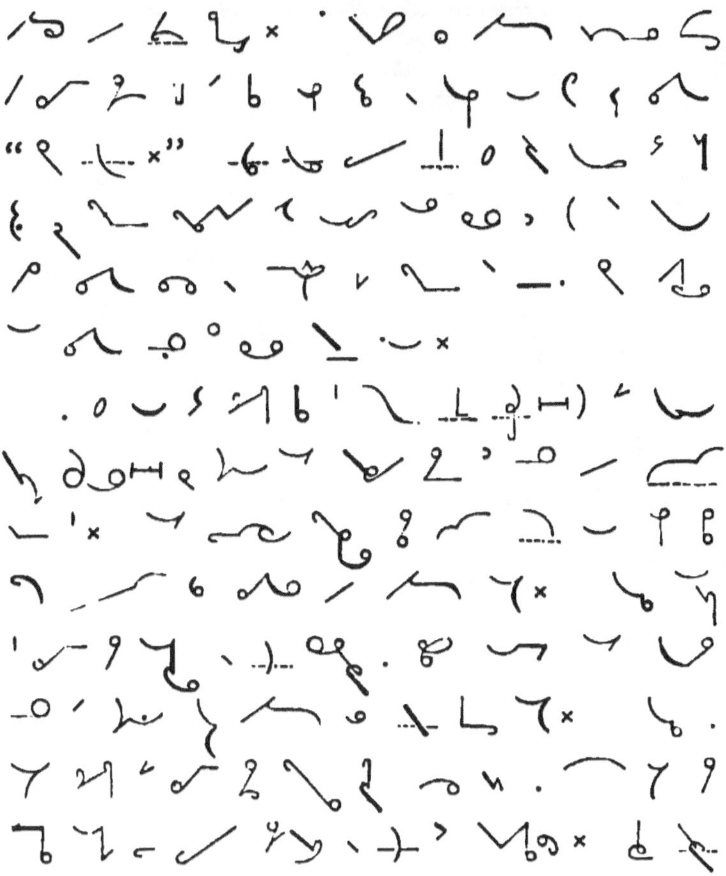

but the regulations are much more stringent. A barrister is required to make his election which circuit he will attend, and it is understood that he is to visit no other without a heavy "special fee." These fees were at first, I believe, fixed with the idea that they would be practically prohibitory, and that no one in his senses would think of paying such heavy sums to counsel, but the practice of giving special retainers in heavy cases has since become common.

The first thing that a shorthand writer does on arriving at an Assize town—say on the evening before the Assizes commences—is to ascertain in the best way he can what causes are likely to come on. In the criminal proceedings he has little or no interest, as it is very rarely that his services are required in them. If he has any competitor on circuit he endeavors to see as soon as possible the solicitors engaged in the various causes, and ascertain if they require notes to be taken in them. If he is the only shorthand writer on the circuit, he may not perhaps trouble himself about the matter until he gets into the court, where he will be sure to see all the parties concerned. It is quite possible that he has received some instruc-

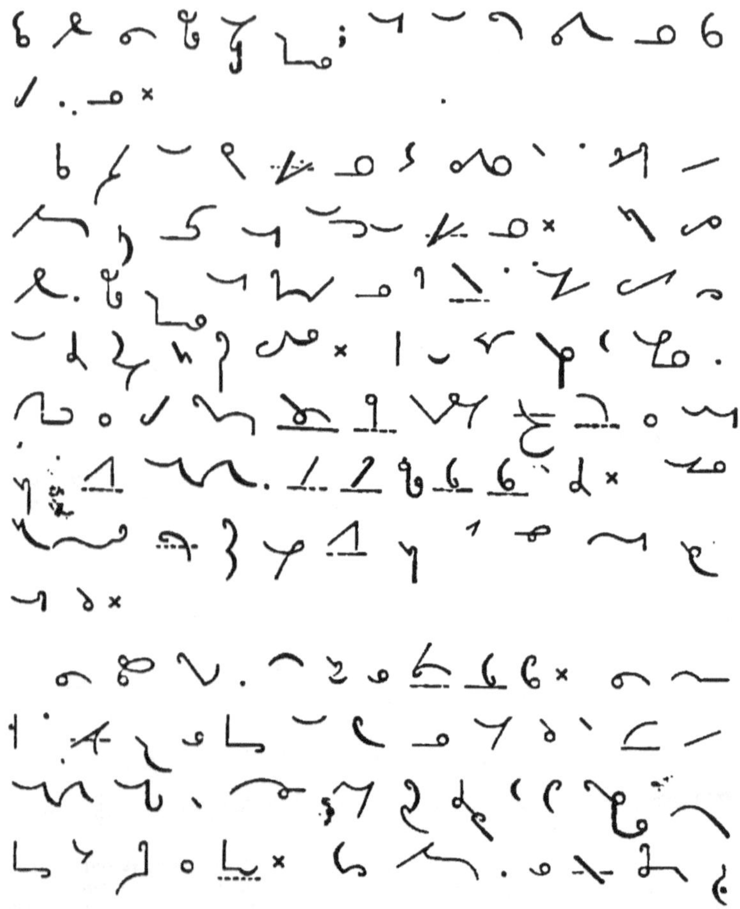

tions in London to take notes; indeed in very heavy cases this is generally the case.

It is chiefly in special jury cases that the services of a shorthand writer are required, but they are occasionally needed in connection with common jury cases. I remember once receiving instructions to take notes in a trumpery case tried by a common jury where the amount in dispute was only about thirty shillings. It need hardly be said that in such cases the litigation is generally prompted by some strong personal feeling, or is intended to try a right involving much larger considerations than those of the particular dispute. In the case I have mentioned, however, there was no such right to try, and the costs amounted to several hundred pounds.

Some solicitors appreciate the importance of shorthand notes much more than others. Some make it a rule to have notes taken in every case in which points of law are involved, in addition to matters of fact, and in which, therefore, it is possible that other proceedings may be taken after the trial is at an end. They may not require the notes to be transcribed,

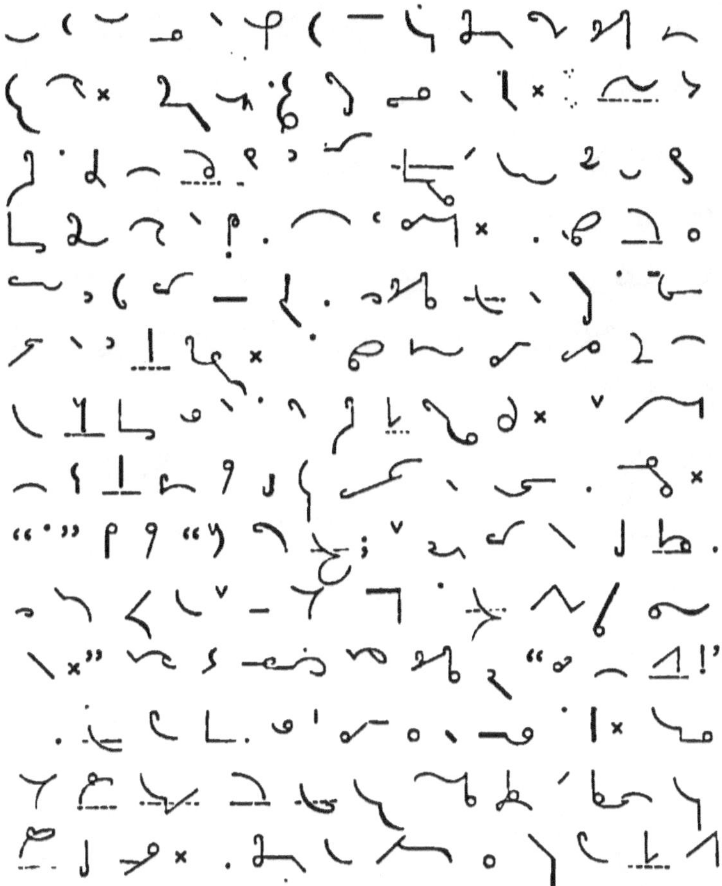

but they know that in case of necessity they can have a transcript from the shorthand writer whom they have employed. There can be no doubt that this is a prudent course to adopt. Long after the trial a dispute may arise as to what actually took place, and if no shorthand note has been taken there is no method of settling the matter with certainty. The solicitor or his client would then gladly give double the amount of the shorthand writer's fee to obtain an authentic record of what had transpired. A solicitor on my own circuit once asked me if I had taken notes of a particular trial at the previous Assizes. I reminded him that he had told me he did not think it worth while to incur the expense. "Ah," said he, "I was very foolish, I would now gladly pay ten times the amount of your charge if I could only get a full report of the Judge's summing up." I am afraid that the exclamation of most shorthand writers would be "served him right!"

The fee for taking notes on circuit is two guineas a day. If a case only lasts half an hour or even five minutes it is the same, and it is no more if it lasts ten hours. The transcript, if required, is paid for at the

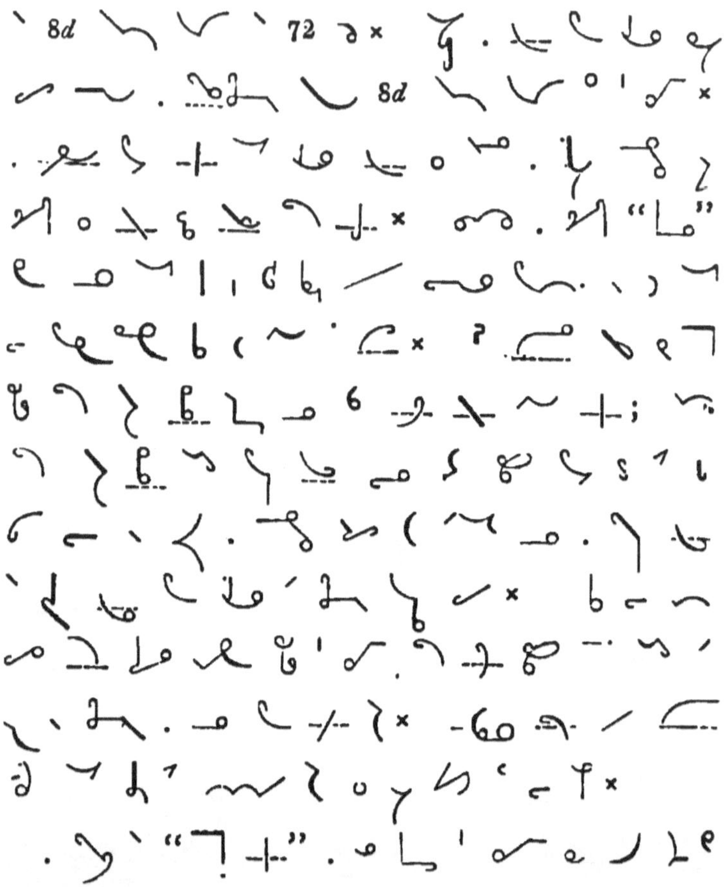

rate of 8d. per folio of 72 words. In London the fee for attendance is only one guinea, the price of the transcript being 8d. per folio as on circuit. The reason for the difference in the attendance fee is of course the additional expense to which the shorthand writer is put when he is absent from town. Sometimes the shorthand writer "takes" several cases in a day, but on the other hand it is not a rare occurrence for him to sit in a court for several successive days without writing a line. What he likes best is to get instructions from both sides to take a case that is sure to be written out; I mean from both sides independently, for it often occurs that the solicitors for the plaintiff and the defendant will agree to share the expense between them, and in that case the bright vision of double fees for attendance and transcript fades away. It has occurred to me once or twice to receive instructions on circuit from three solicitors acting independently, and to have to transcribe the case for each of them. These cases, however, are like oases in the desert, and the memory of them is naturally cherished with great interest.

The pressure of "getting out" the notes taken on circuit is not usually

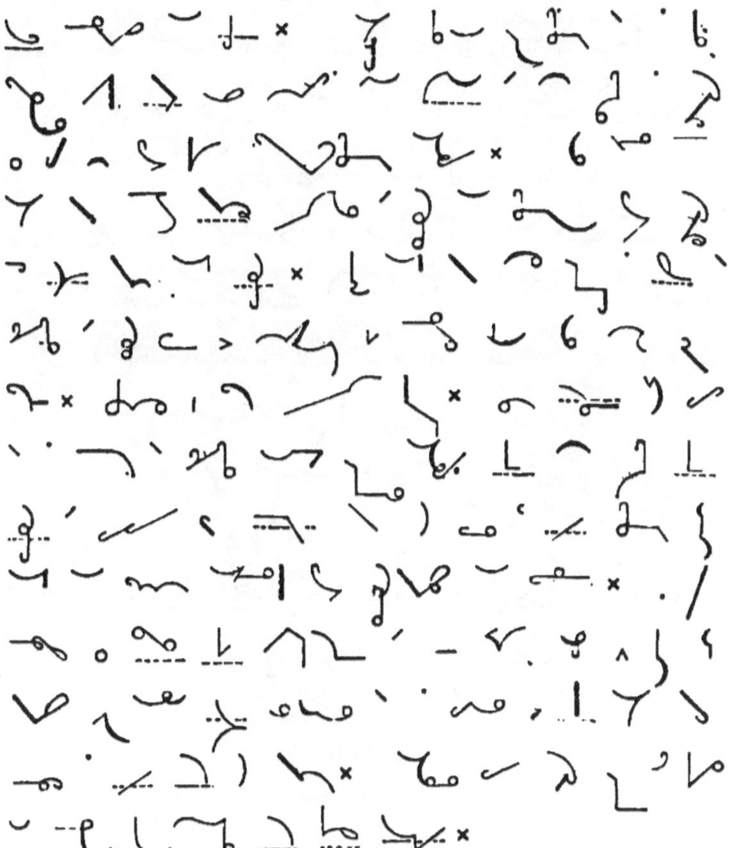

so great as that often experienced in town. In London it is common to have tbe transcript of a day's proceedings ready by the next morning, and in long and important trials an arrangement is generally made for the daily preparation of the transcript in this way. This of course can only be accomplished by means of reliefs and assistance in transcribing, for which arrangements cannot easily be made in an Assize town. It would not, indeed, be impossible to take down a staff of shorthand writers and assistants equal to the emergency, but the expense attending tbis method would be very great. It is sometimes, but very rately adopted. Some years ago I was one of a corps of shortband writers engaged to take notes in this way at an important trial at an Assize town, and we were able to keep up so close witb our transcript that it was handed in from time to time in the course of the day for the assistance of the barristers in cross-examination. Tbe Judge expressed his surprise at tbe rapidity of the work, and could hardly understand bow it was that a barrister should have in his hand full notes of the evidence of a witness who had only been examined an hour or so before. In this case we arranged to take short turns not exceeding twenty minutes, or at most half an bour.

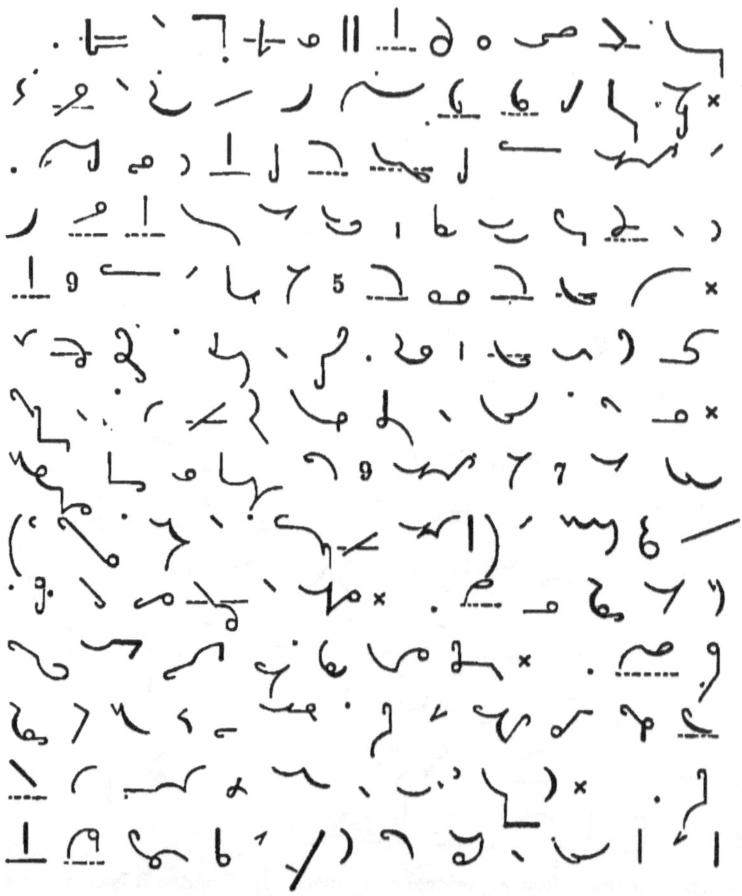

The difficulty of getting out the notes from day to day at assizes is increased by the fact that the hours of sitting are usually longer than those generally adopted in London. The London Courts sit at 10 or half past 10 o'clock in the morning, and usually rise at 4 in the afternoon, but it is not uncommon for an Assize Court to sit at 9 o'clock and continue until 5 or 6 or even later. Of late years there has been a tendency to shorten the sittings, but even now they are occasionally protracted to a late hour, especially if there is a desire to finish a particular case. I have several times taken notes continuously from nine in the morning until seven in the evening, (with perhaps an interval of a quarter of an hour in the middle of the day,) and I need not say that this is rather a strain upon one's powers of endurance. The last case of this kind in which I was professionally engaged, yielded nearly a thousand folios transcript. The longest stretch of this kind of which I have heard, occurred in the case of a trial on the Northern circuit, presided over by Lord Campbell, who seemed never to know what fatigue was. The trial had lasted for some days, and the Judge was very anxious to finish it on the day to which I refer. The evidence did

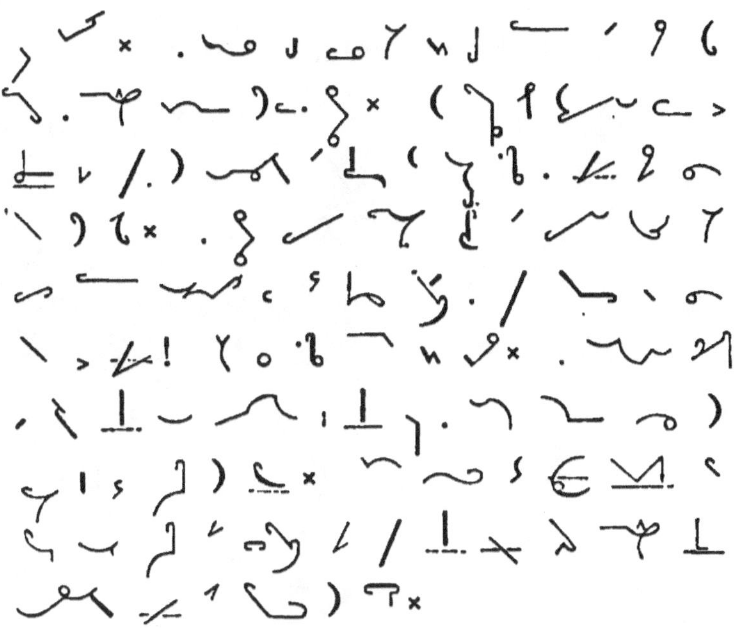

not close until about ten oclock, and he then called upon the counsel to make their concluding speeches. They protested, and said they were not equal to the task, but the Judge was inexorable, and declared that if they did not address the jury, he should sum up there and then. The speeches were accordingly delivered, and were not finished until one oclock in the morning, when, with the utmost composure, the Judge began to sum up to the jury! I think his address occupied about two hours. The unfortunate shorthand writer, who, I believe, had no relief, but had to do the entire work himself, was nearly dead when the trial was over. I may mention that the losing party applied for a new trial on the ground of the pressure which the Judge had put upon the counsel at an unreasonable hour, and the application was granted.

REPORTERS AT PUBLIC DINNERS.

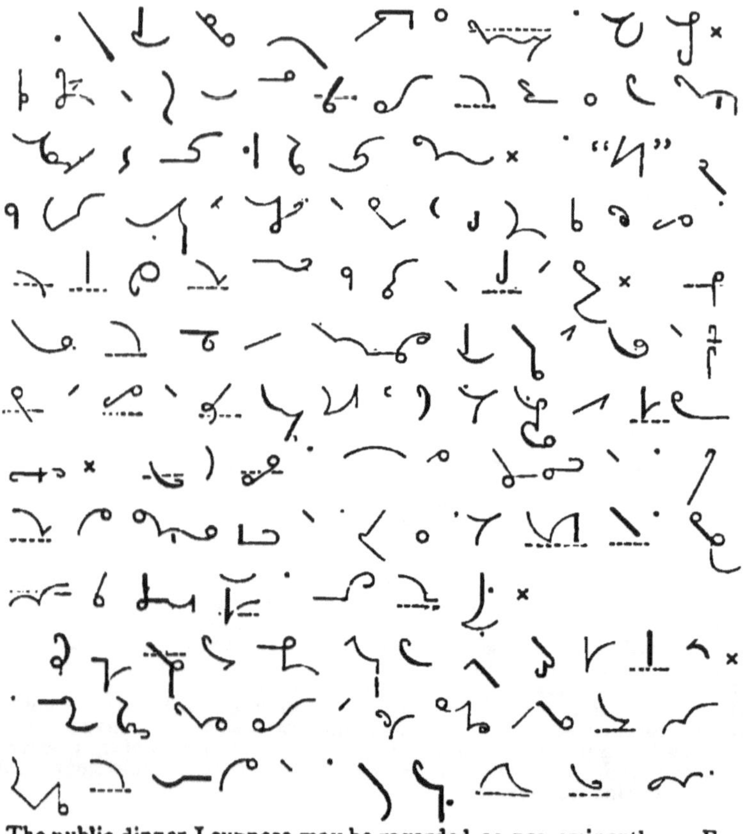

The public dinner I suppose may be regarded as pre-eminently an English institution. It is a truism to say that no cause, religious, social, or political, is ever promoted in this country without the occasional aid of this national ceremony. A "charity" would be considered thoroughly unorthodox and undeserving of support that did not assemble its friends once a year at Willis's, or the Cannon Street Hotel, to dine and speechify. City Companies or Guilds are *par excellence* dining bodies, and the visions of turtle-soup and wines of choicest vintage associated with their annual festivals are the delight of the civic *gourmand*. Even so serious a matter as the episcopal consecration of a church, or the less ceremonious dedication of a chapel, is commonly followed by a substantial meal which is designated indifferently a collation or a *dejeûner*.

There is a good deal to be said for the custom, and if it ever should be abandoned it will die hard. A gathering of this kind promotes social and friendly sentiments, rubs off the little asperities or angularities of a busy every-day-life, often stimulating charitable feelings which might otherwise

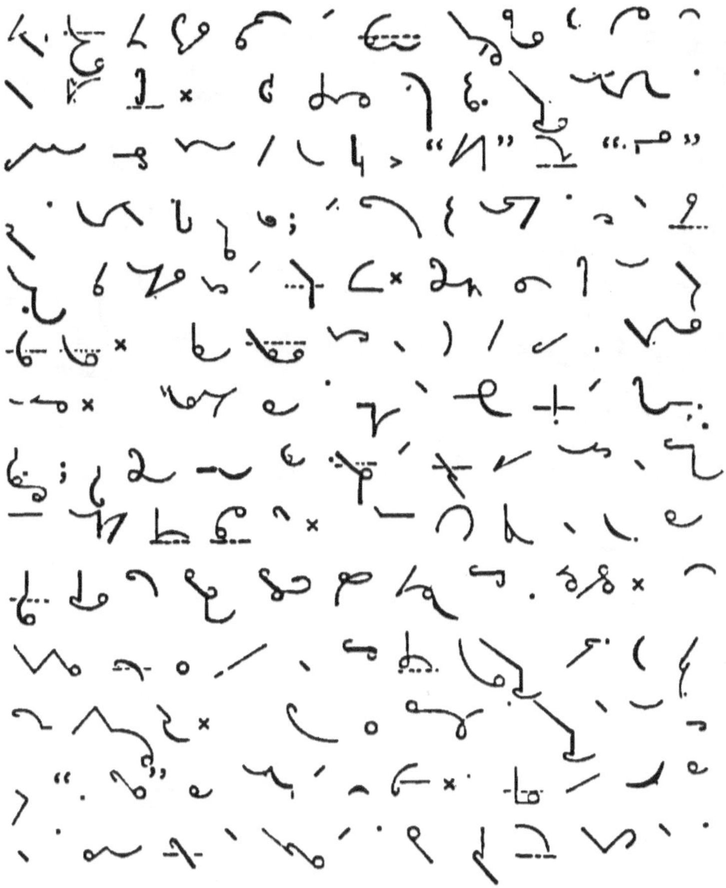

slumber, and loosening purse-strings that else might be tightly drawn. On the other hand it is sometimes urged that these public dinners involve a wanton expenditure of money, which if devoted to the "charity" or the "cause," would be a valuable addition to its funds; and further that they encourage an amount of high feeding which is injurious to mind and body alike. There is, no doubt, some truth in both these views. It is no business of mine to say which way the balance inclines. I have certainly seen a good deal of excessive eating and drinking on these occasions; but then there is no good thing that is not abused, and people who are inclined to gluttony can indulge at home as well as abroad. I can also testify to having seen at these dinners very substantial subscription lists which must have gladdened the hearts of the recipients. My purpose, however, is rather to glance at some features of the public dinner, regarding them chiefly from a reporter's point of view. For there is scarcely a public dinner of any account to which "the Press" is not invited and made welcome. Tickets are usually sent to a certain number of papers, and a special table or portion of a table is set apart for the reporters who

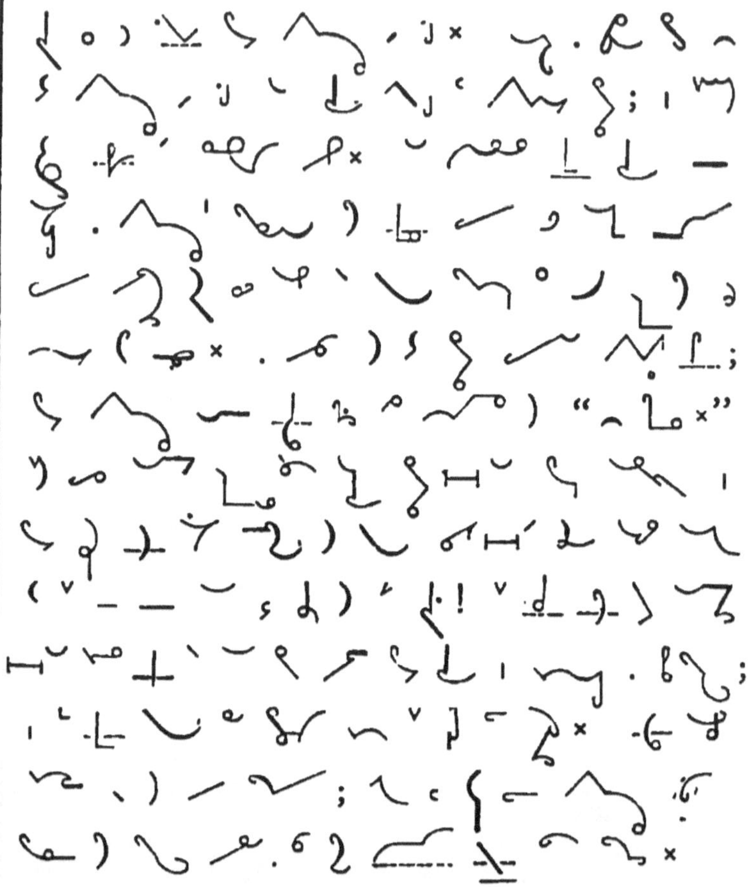

attend. Now and then the suggestion has been made that the reporters should attend after dinner, and be content with reporting the speeches; but I need not say that this has been stoutly and successfully resisted. Not long since, at a dinner given in London, the reporters on presenting their tickets were ushered into a gallery where refreshment was to be served, instead of being permitted as usual to take their seats among the other guests. The result was that the speeches were not reported at all; for the reporters, indignant at this treatment, as the Americans say, "made tracks." I was once engaged to take notes of some after-dinner speeches —not for a newspaper, but for the Society whose annual gathering was being held—and was soon afterwards informed that I could come in when the dessert was on the table! I at once threw up the engagement—not, of course, out of any special regard for the dinner, but to maintain the *status* of the profession; but on a ticket being sent subsequently to me, I attended according to arrangement. These incidents I am glad to say are very rare; and if, when they occur, reporters will for the sake of their profession resent the slight, they are not likely to become more frequent.

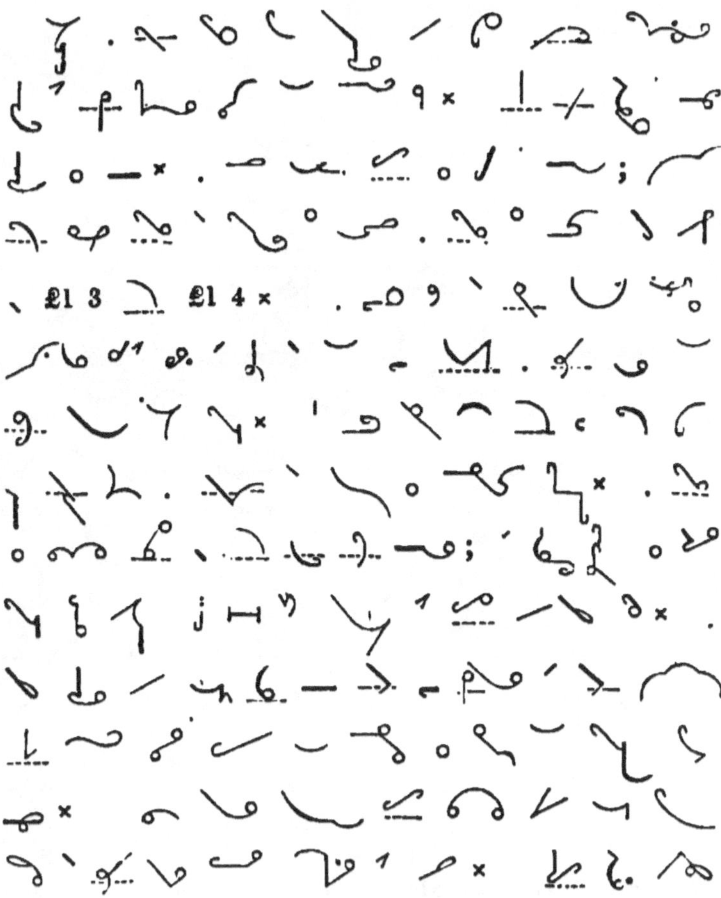

In London the principal places for public dinners are Willis's Rooms, Freemasons' Tavern, and the City Terminus Hotel, in Cannon street. At each of these places an excellent dinner is given. The cost, including wine, is generally £1 1*s.*; latterly, however, since the price of provisions has increased, the price has occasionally been raised to £1 3*s.* or £1 4*s.* The courses consist of soup, fish, entrées, relevés, joints, sweets and dessert, all in great variety, the choicest things in season being commonly provided. On occasions of special importance, or when very-well-to-do people assemble, the bill of fare is exceptionally attractive. The price is sometimes as much as two or even three guineas; and on these occasions turtle-soup is always provided, with its orthodox concomitant—iced punch, and the wines are of the best brands. The best dinners are no doubt those given by the great City Companies and by the Lord Mayor at the Mansion House, where no expense is spared in providing for the guests. Some Companies have their own wine cellars, which are noted for their stores of choicest ports, clarets, Madeiras, and the rest. At one

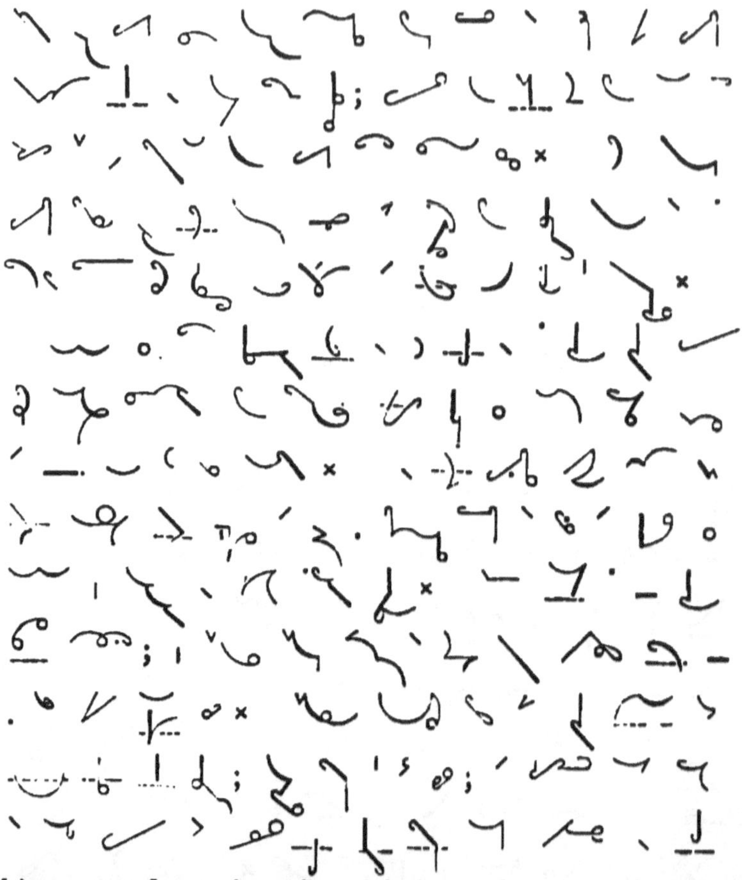

of these repasts I remember to have waited some five minutes for a glass of water, which the waiter apparently had to fetch from a distance; whereas, if I had asked for any kind of wine I should probably not have waited more than as many seconds. There being a waiter present to every three or four guests, and the arrangements for distribution being of a very complete character, there is on these occasions none of the bustle and confusion usually attendant on public dinners.

Nothing is more disagreeable than to sit down to a dinner table where there is a universal scramble for provisions, each one devoting his entire energies to himself and giving no thought to his neighbor. To see the waiters rushing madly about, pulled incessantly by the coat-tails, and to hear the tremendous clatter of plates and dishes, is anything but favorable to healthy, comfortable digestion. I can enjoy a good dinner as well as most men; but I confess I have a horror of so-called public repasts, however good the viands, which are indifferently served. I have seen fish sauce placed on the table long after the fish itself had disappeared; vegetables brought on with the sweets; and on one occasion in the north of England, where all the resources of the town had been brought into

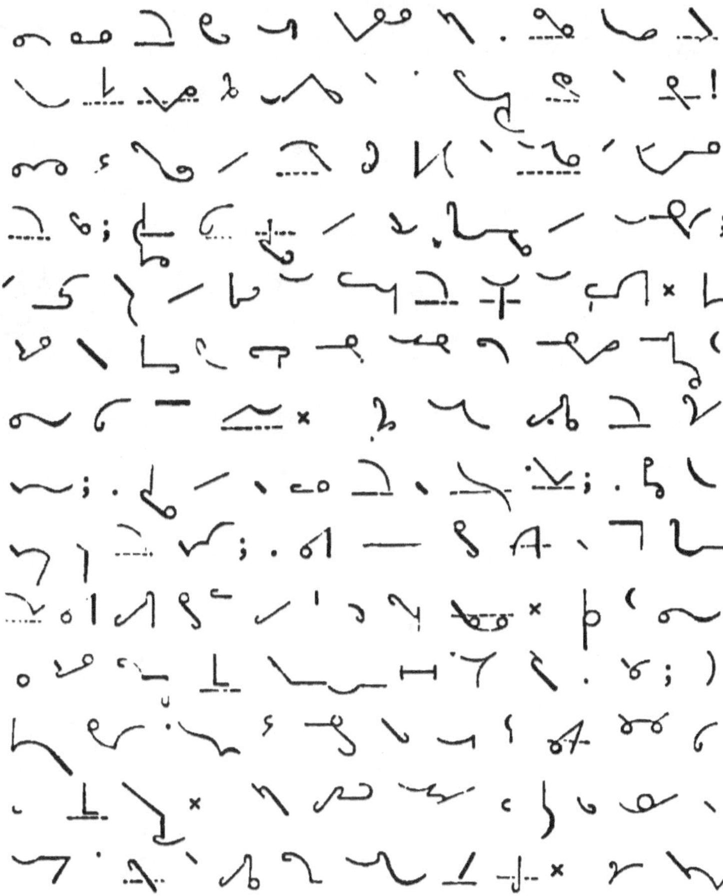

requisition to dine some six or seven hundred persons, I remember the surprise evinced by the company at the appearance towards the end of the repast of a plentiful supply of soup! Sometimes when the provisions are ample there is dearth of knives and forks or plates; at other times while eatables are abundant, drinkables are inaccessible; and occasionally both are deficient in quantity, or indifferent in quality. It may always be taken for granted, except in the case of very experienced caterers, that something will go wrong. There are not enough waiters, or there are too many; the tables are too close or too far apart; the stewards have too much to do, or too little; the head cook has been allowed to get drunk, or the head waiter has been called away on urgent private business. It is said that something is always forgotten at a pic-nic—commonly I believe the salt; so it may be safely affirmed, with the exception above noted, that a hitch of some sort will occur at a public dinner. I remember one occasion in the country when it was found necessary to engage a number of waiters from a neighboring large town. Shortly before the dinner hour they

asked to be paid in advance in order that they might without delay return to their homes by a late train when their services were no longer required. Their request (which seemed not unreasonable) was complied with; but alas! they returned before the dinner instead of afterwards, and the guests had to wait upon themselves.

It was formerly a serious thing to sit down to one of these entertainments, for no one could tell that he might not find himself in front of a huge joint, or a pair of chickens or ducks, and be called upon to carve the same; and if inexperienced in the art, the consciousness of a dozen eyes being fixed upon his frantic efforts to disengage a wing or a merrythought was enough to drive the poor carver to distraction. In my very young days I attended a dinner at the Mansion House, and was horrified to see just opposite my seat an immense cover which might have had under it a baron of beef, or a large turkey, or some other bird or beast of whose anatomical structure I was wholly ignorant. The suspense of those few moments was almost intolerable; but when the cover was removed, and

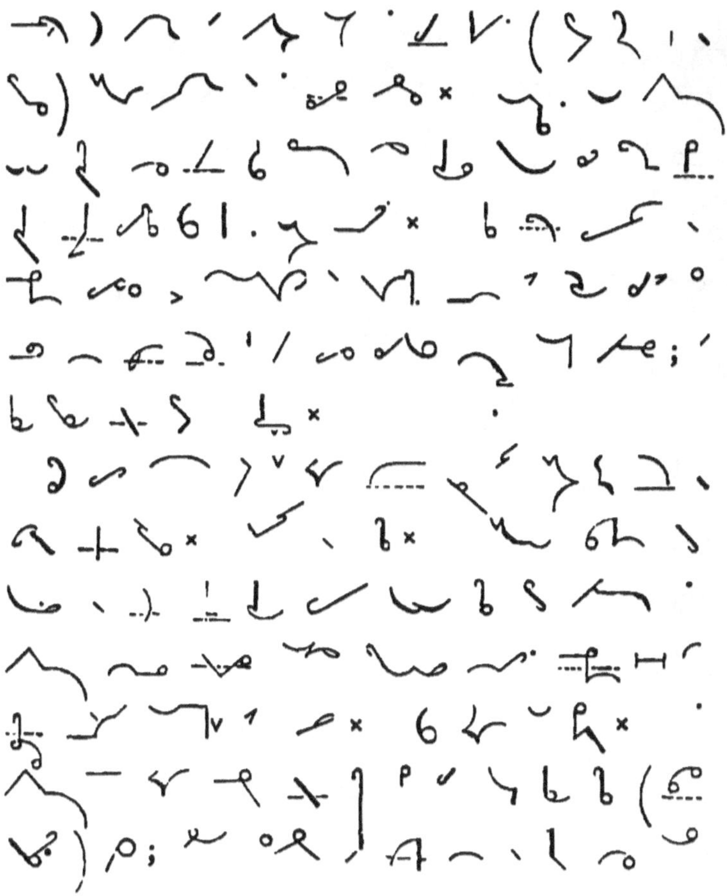

revealed only a John Dorey (for which there were but two applicants), I felt relieved of a serious responsibility. Now-a-days the young reporter need not trouble himself much on this score; most dinners being served from a side table at which the waiters themselves do the needful carving. It is, however, worth while to accustom oneself to the manipulation of poultry, game, and the ordinary joints, as occasions may still arise on which one's services may be called into requisition; and it is not pleasant to be obliged to decline.

There is one matter of which I hardly like to speak, and yet I feel that a word or two will not be out of place. I refer to dress. I have not seldom been vexed to see at a dinner where evening dress has been required, a reporter make his appearance in the most pronounced morning costume—light trousers, colored necktie and the rest. This is assuredly not as it should be. A reporter can hardly expect to be treated as a gentleman if he does not dress (as well as behave) as such; and his own self-respect should lead him to adapt himself in his attire to the company with

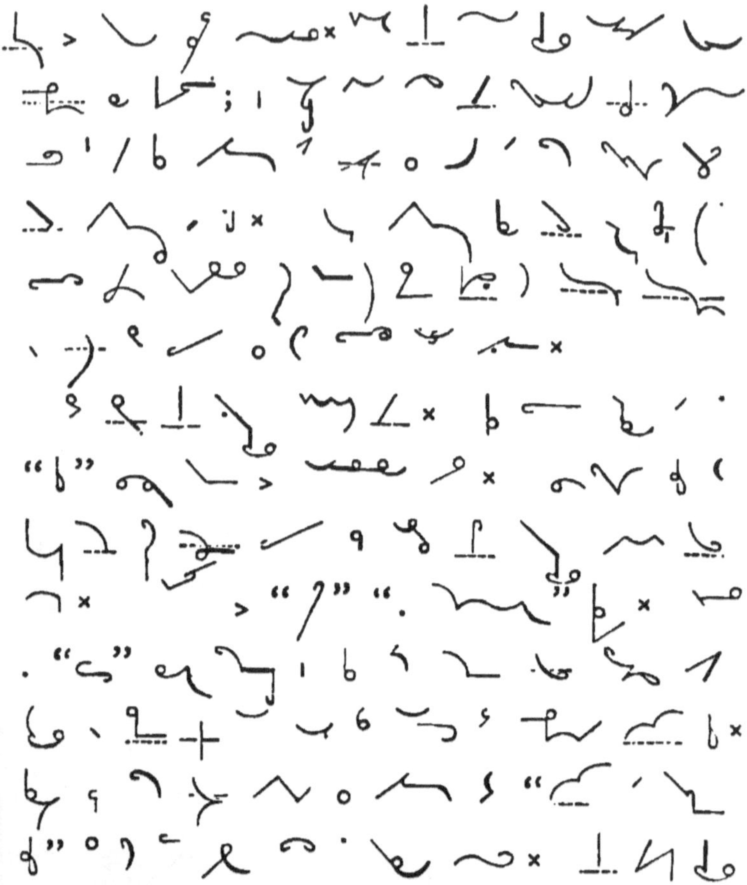

which he mingles. I know that at many dinners in the country, evening costume is not *de rigeur*; but in London and in most large provincial towns, there are many occasions on which it is required, and the rule is usually and very properly observed by the reporters who attend. If a reporter does not happen to have a dress coat (a garment which some persons eschew altogether), he can at least so far conform to usage as to wear his other garments *en règle*.

As to the speaking at public dinners I need not say much. It has a character of its own, and a "toast" seems to be peculiar to the Anglo-Saxon race. Some of the parliamentary toasts that twenty or thirty years ago were considered indispensable at all public dinners, are now often omitted. I refer to the "church," "the army and navy," etc. Of course the "Queen" is never forgotten, but it is hard work even for the most original thinkers to strike out any new thoughts in connection with the customary loyal toast. It is only when a very full report is required that the "loyal and patriotic toasts," as they are called, receive more than a passing mention. At charity dinners the "toast of the evening"—that is, prosperity

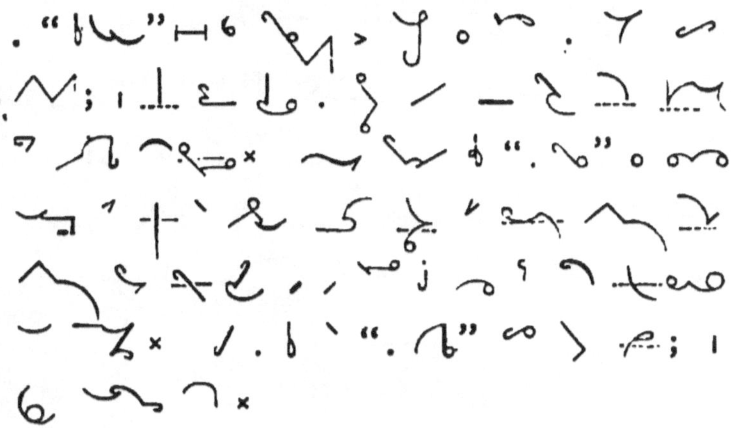

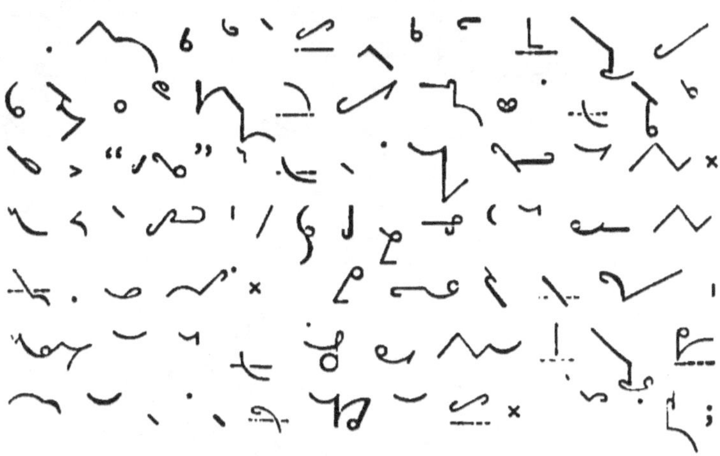

to the institution—is almost the only one reported; but at political dinners the speeches are given briefly, or at length, according to the relative importance of the speakers. Among the complimentary toasts "the Press" is sometimes included, and the duty of responding occasionally falls on the senior reporter, or the reporter for the principal journal, who should of course content himself with a very few sentences in acknowledgment. Generally the toast of "the ladies" winds up the list; but this is not unfrequently omitted.

The reporter who is fond of wine should be on his guard at a public dinner where this beverage is supplied *ad libitum*, or where the caterer sends a few bottles of his best to the "gentlemen of the Press," with a view to a commendatory paragraph in the report. I have heard of one occasion on which this was done to such an extent that not a single report appeared the next morning. Such an occurrence I believe to be very rare; but I have certainly in not a few instances seen the reporting at public dinners sadly marred owing to a too free indulgence in wine. I am not

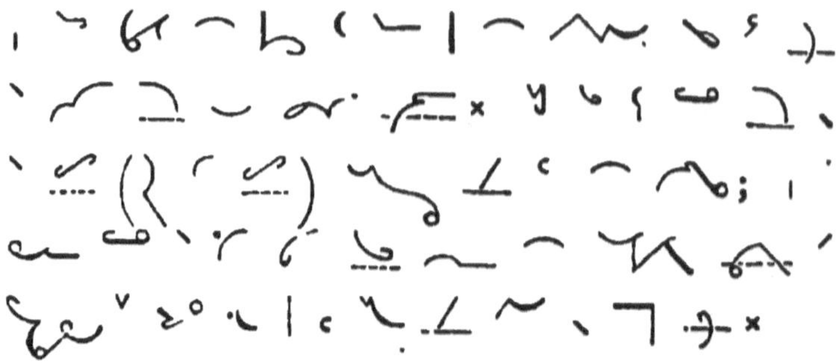

—:o:—

AT CHURCH.

a teetotaler; but I cannot withhold my admission that I can do my reporting best with the use of little or no stimulating beverage. I do not find that a glass or two of wine (especially light wine) interfere much with my labors; but a single glass of ale will often make me intolerably sleepy, and for this reason I always avoid it when I have much writing to get through.

I suppose most young shorthand students have tried their hands at sermon reporting. It was but a few weeks since that, walking through the streets of a town in the west of England, I passed by a small chapel where, as a schoolboy, I ventured to write a few shorthand sentences in my note-book. I did it with fear and trembling, and under the profoundest conviction that everyone was looking at me. It was several years before I knew anything of Phonography. The system I wrote was Lewis's slightly modified. I had only practised it a few weeks, and as may be expected, my report was of a very meagre character, consisting of a number of dis-

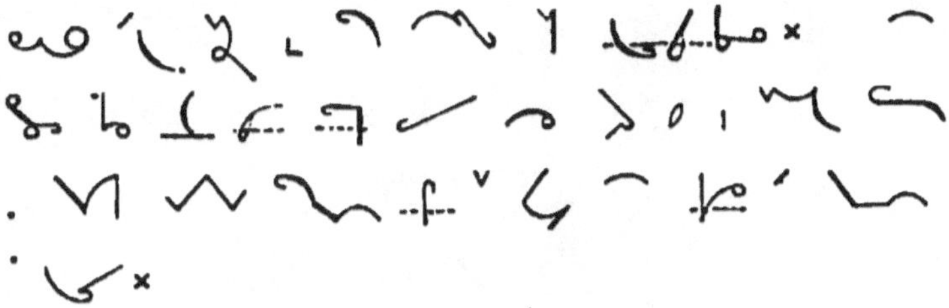

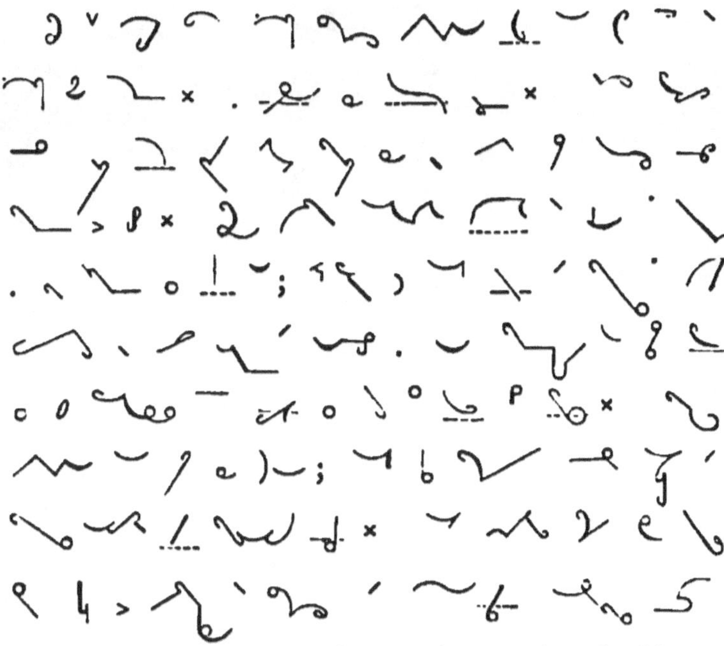

jointed sentences, and conveying, I suspect, but a very imperfect idea even of the gist of the discourse. My subsequent attempts, though still crude, were improvements upon the first, but I never acquired the ability to report verbatim till I changed my tools, and became a phonographer.

There is, I imagine, more amateur sermon reporting than any other kind of amateur shorthand work. The reason is not far to seek. Almost every-one goes to church or chapel, and if the preacher is not too rapid he affords excellent practice to the student. There is no labor involved, like that of attending a public meeting; the opportunity of practice is at hand; and with a comfortable seat in a pew, and perhaps a ledge whereupon to rest note-book and ink-stand, the young practitioner, after he has overcome his first nervousness, can wield his pen as often as he pleases. Professional reporting in church is not so common; indeed, it is very rare except in London and perhaps in one or two large provincial towns. In the metropolis there are several publications specially devoted to the reproducing of sermons, and many of the religious newspapers occasionally report the

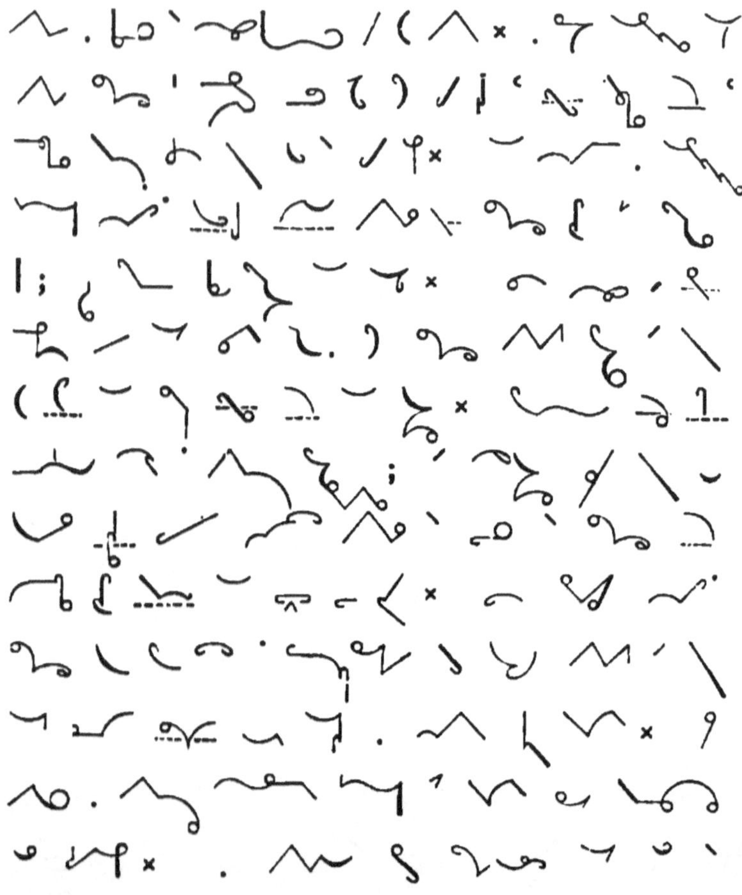

discourses of ministers of the denomination which they represent. The secular newspapers only report sermons on exceptional occasions, and then they are generally contented with brief abstracts, or with extracts bearing on some public event of general interest. In America, the newspapers of Monday morning often contain long reports of the principal sermons delivered on the previous day; but this practice does not prevail in England. Some ministers who speak extemporaneously are in the habit of having their sermons reported for themselves, and publish them either in separate numbers or in volumes. For many years Dr Cumming employed a reporter for this purpose; and most of the volumes which he published under various titles were little more than reports of courses of sermons or lectures delivered by him in Crown Court chapel. Mr Spurgeon's morning sermons have for more than a quarter of a century been officially reported and published in a weekly serial, now entitled the *Metropolitan Tabernacle Pulpit*. He revises the reporter's manuscript on Monday, and the *Pulpit* is in the bookseller's hands on Wednesday. The reporting has been from the commencement in the hands of my own

firm. Dr Parker's sermons are also officially reported, and appear regularly, not in a separate form like Mr Spurgeon's, but in a religious newspaper. The reporter is no other than Mrs Parker; but whether that lady actually takes notes of them as they are delivered and subsequently transcribes them, or simply writes the sermons, before they are delivered, from Dr Parker's dictation, I am not in a position to say. I only know that there is a printed note to each sermon: "Specially reported for the ——— by Mrs Parker." As a general rule ladies do not care to be dictated to by their husbands, but Mrs Parker would seem to be a notable exception to the rule. I may add that Dr Parker writes Phonography, and probably his wife has acquired the same accomplishment.

Sermon reporting ought never to be undertaken for professional purposes by other than very expert shorthand writers. Some sermons are easy enough. When the preacher is deliberate, his style clear, and his delivery distinct, the reporter's work is far from difficult; but even in such cases

great care is requisite. The alteration of a word may seriously misrepresent the speaker's meaning; and as reports of sermons are usually supposed to be verbatim, the reporter cannot omit doubtful passages as readily and unconcernedly as he would in the case of ordinary speeches. When a sermon is read from a manuscript he is especially anxious to be exact, knowing that the *litera scripta* may be produced to confront any errors that he may make. Not that preachers always adhere to their manuscript. I have known them misread, and even skip lines, much to my perplexity when I have come to transcribe my notes and have had to correct an error or supply a hiatus. Texts too are not seldom misquoted, but a Concordance will always enable the reporter to rectify errors of that kind. I remember, however, one case in which an inference was founded on a misquotation, which was absolutely contradicted by the exact words of the text. As it was not an important part of the sermon but only an incidental allusion, I omitted the passage altogether, and thus, I hope, did something to save the preacher's reputation.

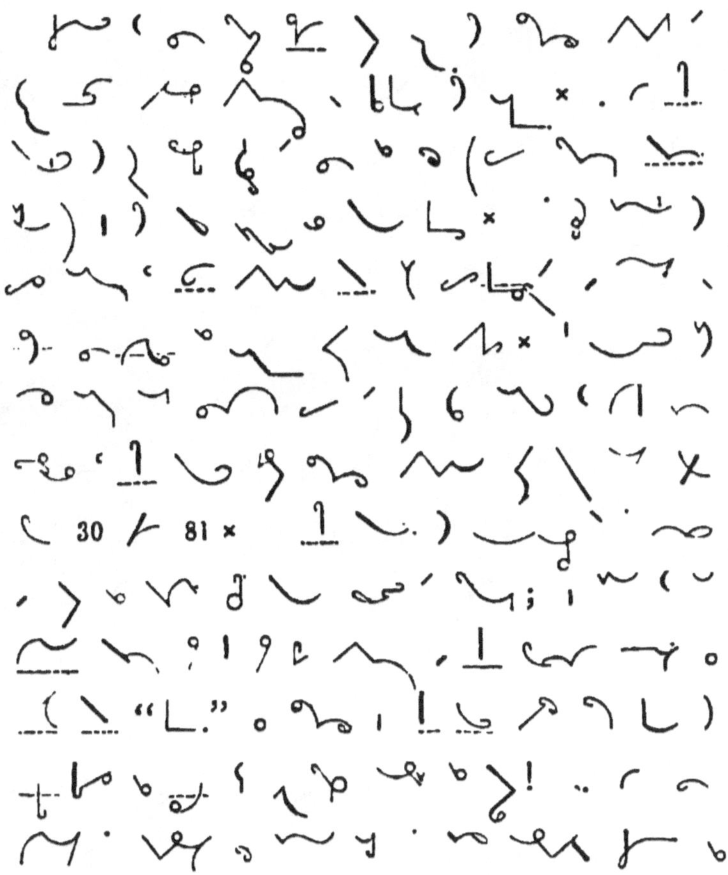

It is well known that some preachers strongly object to having their sermons reported, and they have occasionally requested reporters to discontinue their note-taking. The late Dr Punshon was especially sensitive on this point, and some of his friends (whether prompted by him I do not know) did their best to prevent notes being taken. An assistant of my own was once interfered with, while reporting, by, I think, one of the deacons of the chapel, who managed to seize some of the leaves of his note-book, which were never returned. On another occasion I was myself interrupted in a similar way, and it was this interruption that led to my correspondence with Dr Punshon on the subject of sermon reporting which was published in the *Phonetic Journal* for 30 July, 1881. Dr Binney was another instance of a minister who objected to his pulpit utterances being stenographed and printed; but I know that not long before he died he told the reporter who had formerly kindled his wrath by "taking" his sermons, but had often refrained from doing so out of deference to his wishes, that he should have persisted in spite of his objections! The late Mr Lynch, a personal friend of my own, entertained an almost insuperable dislike to his sermons being

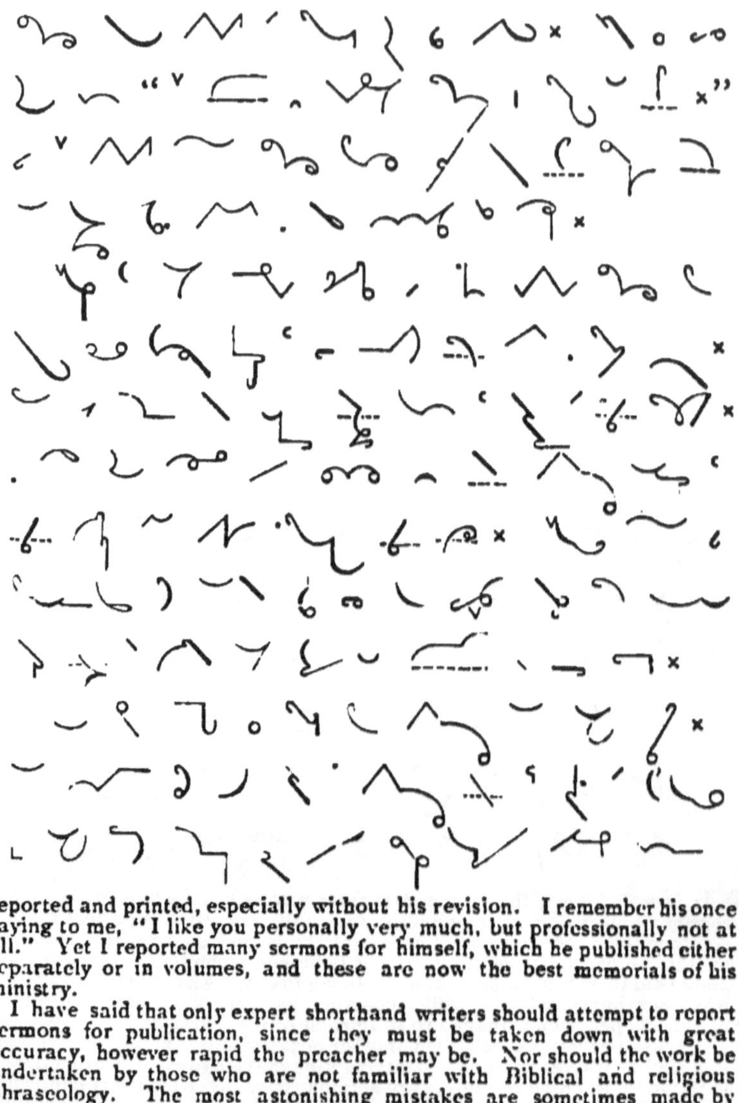

reported and printed, especially without his revision. I remember his once saying to me, "I like you personally very much, but professionally not at all." Yet I reported many sermons for himself, which he published either separately or in volumes, and these are now the best memorials of his ministry.

I have said that only expert shorthand writers should attempt to report sermons for publication, since they must be taken down with great accuracy, however rapid the preacher may be. Nor should the work be undertaken by those who are not familiar with Biblical and religious phraseology. The most astonishing mistakes are sometimes made by reporters unacquainted with religious literature and not readily apprehending religious allusions. I have known many who have frankly confessed their inability on these grounds, and have wisely abstained from entering upon a field of labor in which they were not likely to gain credit.

No special accommodation is provided for reporters in English churches. In America there is usually, I believe, a reporters' pew with a table and other conveniences: but an English ecclesiastical architect would be rather

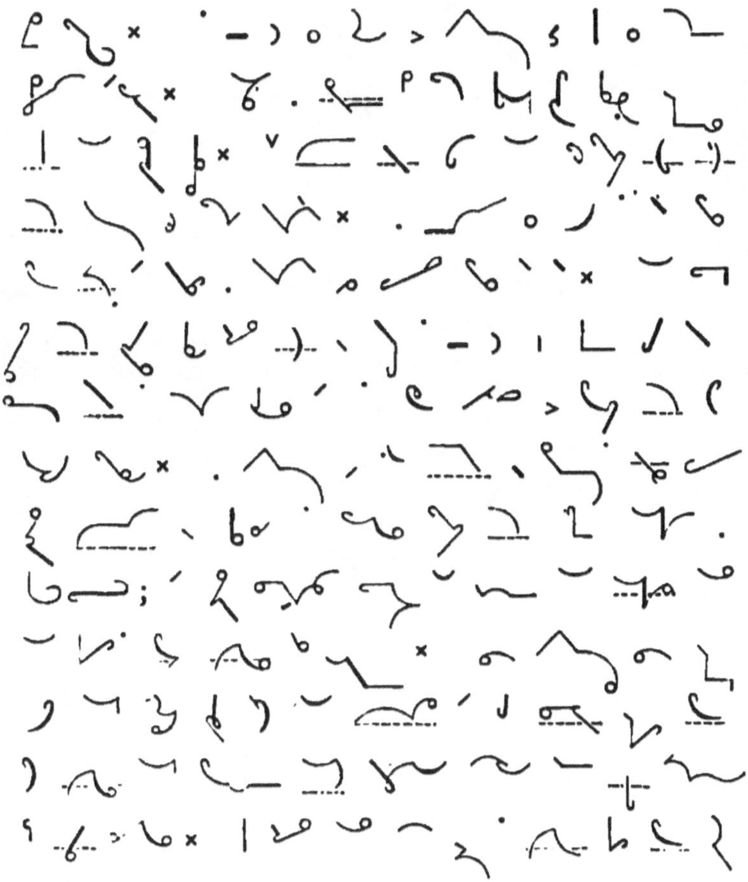

surprised if he were requested to make such a provision. A good seat is essential to the reporter who would do his work satisfactorily and comfortably. Unless the speaker has a very distinct delivery it is not safe to take notes at any considerable distance. I like to be well in front of the preacher, within three or four seats from the pulpit. The gallery is usually a bad place for hearing, and behind the pulpit is the worst place of all. In crowded churches or chapels it is not always easy to obtain a good seat, but it can generally be secured by an early attendance and a civil request to the verger or other official present. The reporter should avoid occupying too conspicuous a position where he would be likely to disconcert a nervous preacher, or attract unduly the attention of the congregation; and he should be scrupuously careful not to make any needless noise in turning over the leaves of his note-book. Some reporters seem to take a pleasure in an ostentatious display of their writing materials, and do not scruple to turn over their leaves in a frantic, noisy, bustling manner, altogether out of harmony with a religious service. It always annoys me to hear a leaf turned over, especially in church, or in a law court. The operation may,

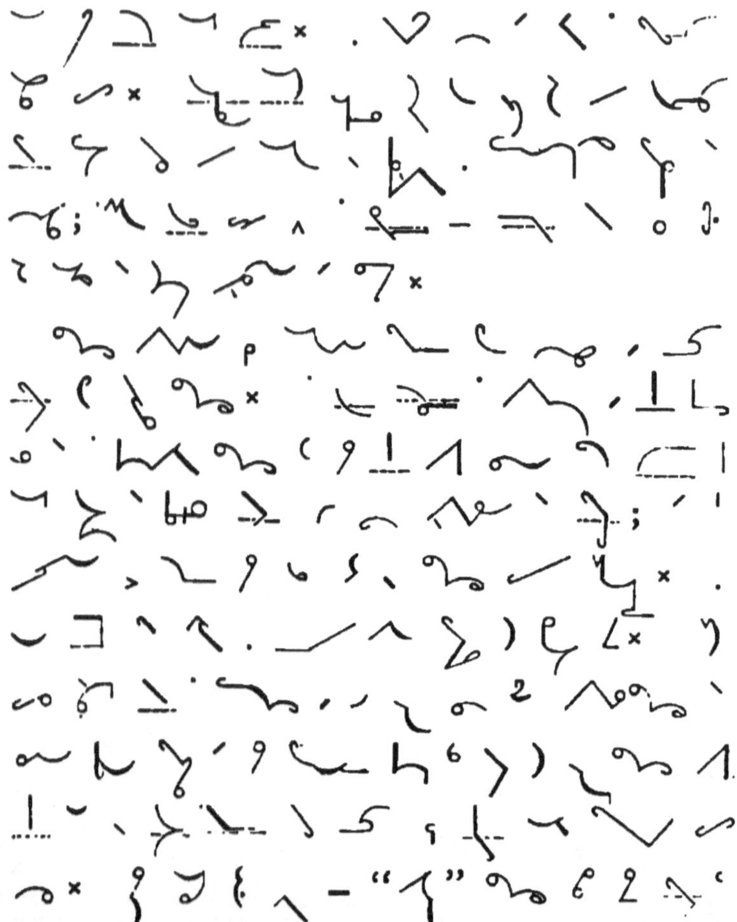

and ought to be a perfectly noiseless one. Half-a-dozen noisy note-takers, especially if two or three of them are vigorously plying quill pens, are enough to disturb the equanimity of the most placid of mortals; and I have often wondered how a speaker could keep up his train of thought in the midst of so much rustling and scratching.

Sermon reporting is an unfortunate practice for ministers who occasionally preach other people's sermons. A few years ago a reporter who had taken notes of an admirable sermon, thought he had read something very like it in a volume of discourses by the late Mr Robertson, of Brighton, and on referring to the work he found that the two sermons were identical. The thing got abroad, and I believe the career of the reverend plagiarist was suddenly checked. I was once consulted by a clergyman who wished to have some shorthand reports of the sermons of certain distinguished preachers, and he frankly admitted that his object was to have a sermon ready at hand to fall back upon occasionally when he had been unable to prepare one himself. He was anxious that they should be good "orthodox"

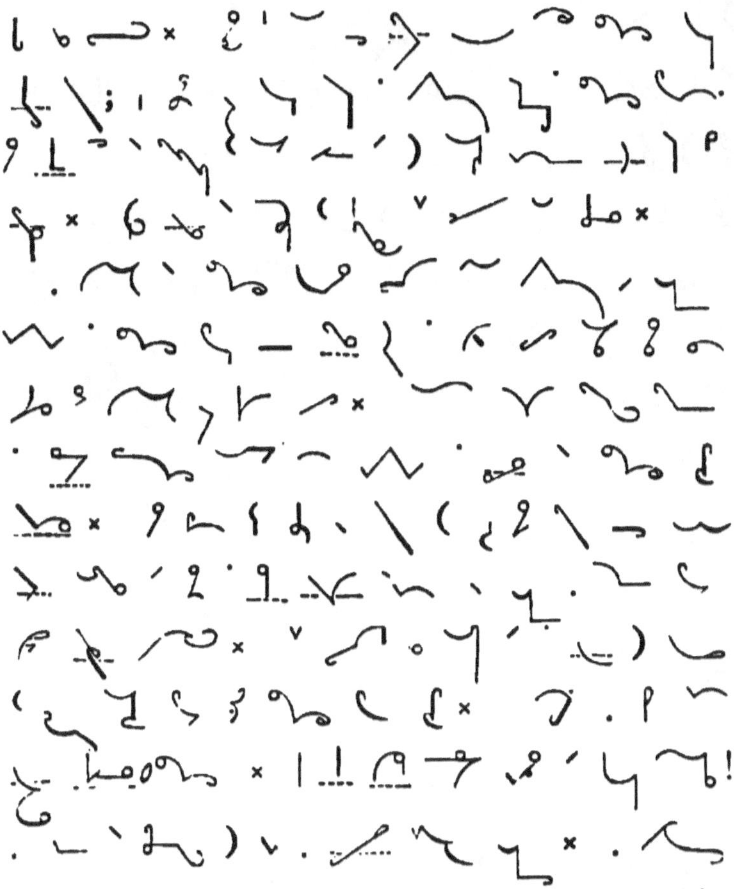

sermons, such as he could preach with advantage to his congregation. He would not on any account preach another man's sermon if it had been published; but he seemed to think that if he paid a reporter to take down a sermon for him he had a kind of proprietorship in the article and was entitled to make use of it as he pleased. This is a piece of casuistry that at present I would rather not discuss.

The length of sermons varies greatly, and no reporter should undertake to report a sermon for a given price, especially a low one, unless he has some assurance as to the length to which it will run. In my early professional practice a Scotch clergyman engaged me to report a series of sermons delivered by himself. He told me that he desired to publish them, but that he should probably gain nothing by the enterprise, and he made a strong appeal to me to undertake the work for the lowest possible remuneration. I yielded to his entreaty, and a fee was fixed that would have been inadequate for the shortest sermons ever delivered. Imagine the state of my feelings at the close of the first sermon, It had lasted exactly two hours and twenty minutes! The work of transcription was about the

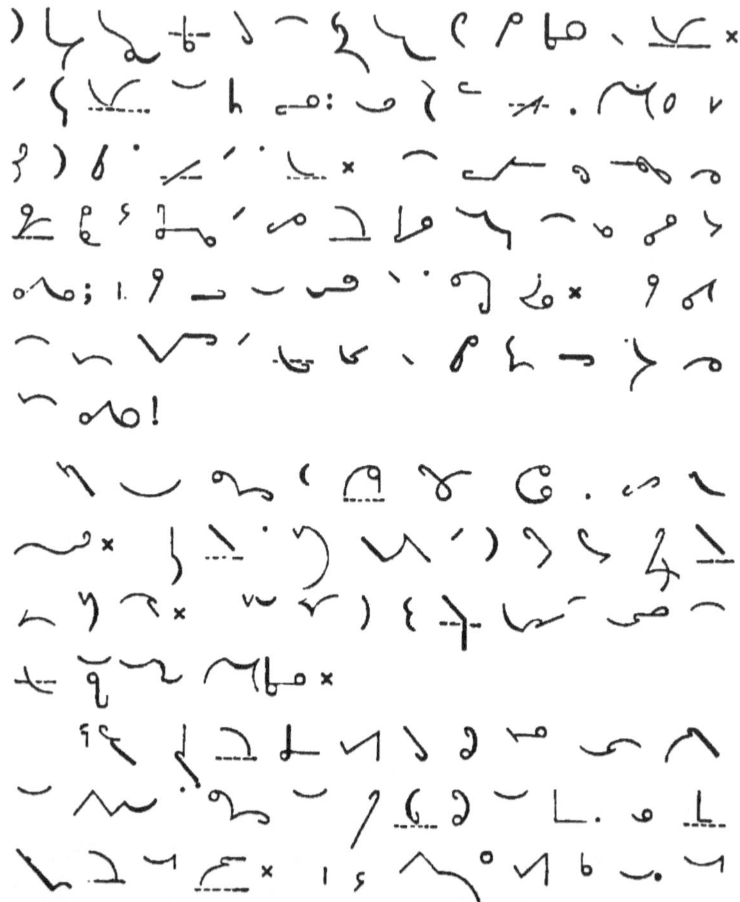

weariest I have ever undertaken. The reflection was continually forcing itself upon me that there were five other such discourses to follow. And they did follow in due course: none of them quite reached the length of the first, but the shortest was just an hour and a half. My clerical friend expressed himself highly satisfied with the transcripts, and once or twice invited me to his house after the service; but he gave no indications of a smitten conscience. He held me to my bargain, and even ventured to suggest that he might again avail himself of my services!

I remember another sermon that lasted precisely as long as the one I have mentioned. It was by an Irish bishop, and was preached for the Church Missionary Society, by whom I was employed. I need hardly say that that body voluntarily increased my fee in consideration of the inordinate length of the discourse.

With a comfortable table or desk to write upon there is, of course, no more labor in reporting a sermon in church than there is in taking notes at a public meeting or in a law court. But when the reporter has to write

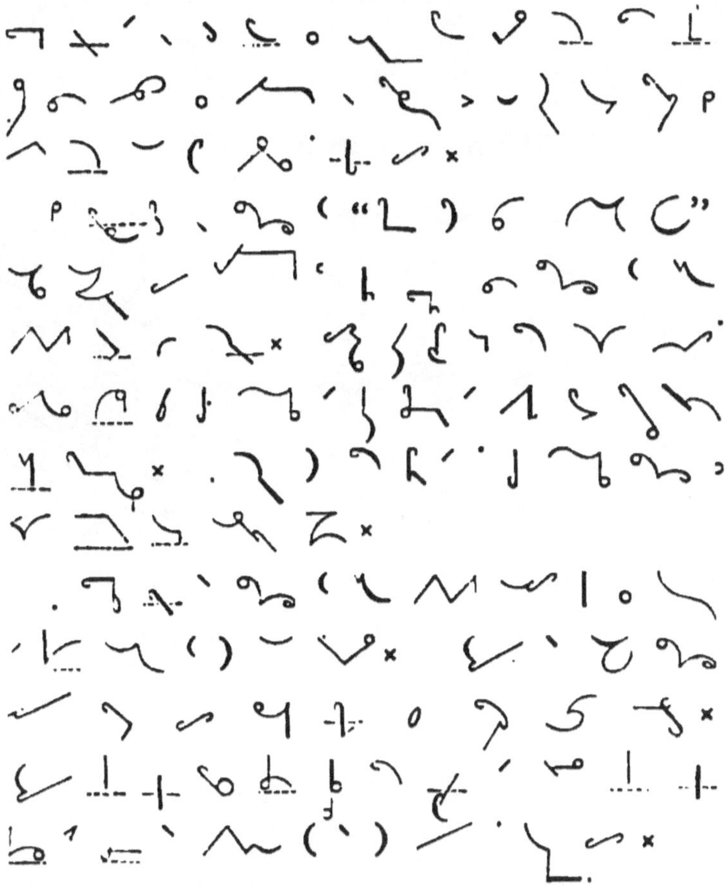

on his knee in a crowded pew and to bend over his note-book for two hours or more at a stretch, some resolution is required to persevere to the end, especially if the preacher is a rapid, or in other respects a difficult one.

As a pleasing contrast to sermons that "drag their slow length along," in this unconscionable way, I recollect with due gratitude some sermons that I have reported by the late Archbishop of Canterbury. One of these, which was delivered after a very early morning service, lasted just ten minutes, and it was transcribed and ready for the printers before I had breakfasted. The Archbishop was very deliberate, and a ten minutes' sermon would hardly occupy half a newspaper column.

The greatest number of sermons that I have reported in one day is four, and, oddly enough, that was in Paris. They were all English sermons, and were preached one Sunday during the first French National Exhibition. They were at different places at some distance from each other, and of course at different times, and the task of reporting them all was rather a fatiguing one.

REPORTING IN FRANCE.

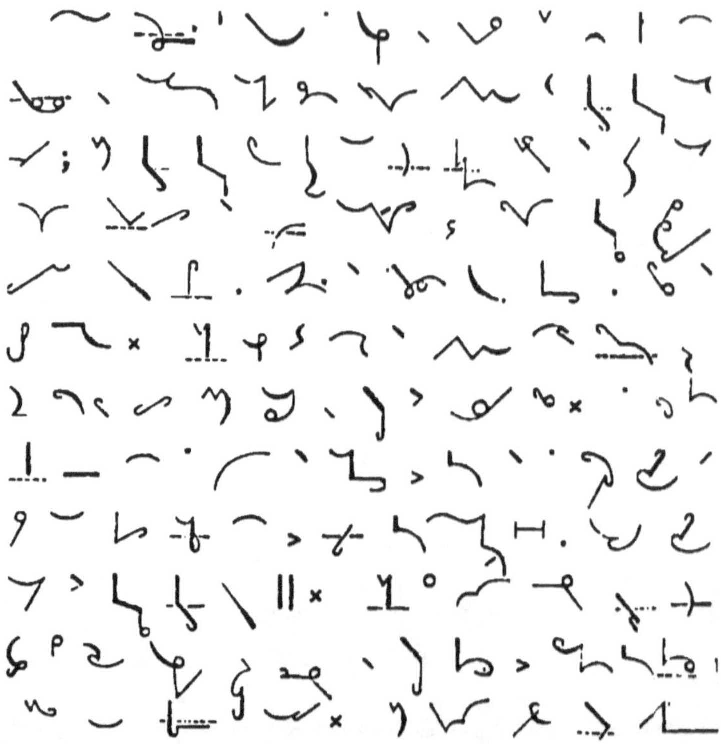

Many years ago, on paying a visit to Paris, I made it my business to inquire into the system of parliamentary reporting that had been adopted in that country: I say had been adopted, for it was not in use at the time I speak of, which was in the early part of the reign of Louis Napoleon, when the parliamentary debates, such as they were, were not published at all, the *régime* of absolutism having taken the place of constitutional government. I had understood that the method of reporting employed prior to that time was a very complete one, and I was anxious to obtain all the necessary particulars. A friend had given me a letter of introduction to the editor of a French journal, and he, in turn, introduced me to the chief editor of the *Moniteur*—the official journal in which all the debates had been published from day to day. I had as little expected to be able to see this gentleman, as an ordinary visitor to London would expect to obtain admission to the sanctum of the editor of *The Times*, but I found no difficulty in the way. I was politely received by the *redacteur*, who,

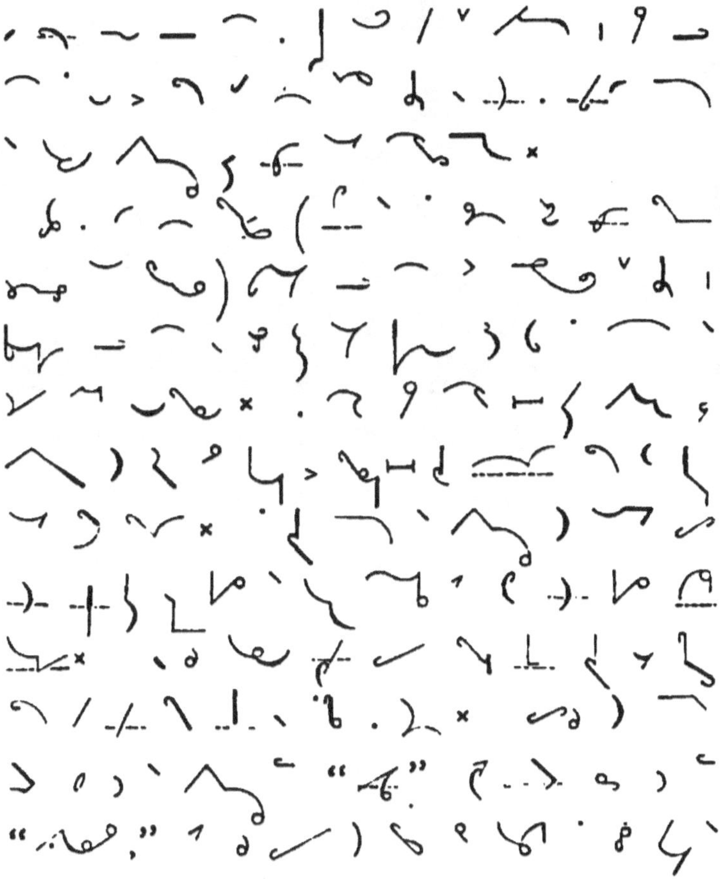

however, could not give me the detailed information which I required, but he gave me a note to the very gentleman whom I most desired to see; the chief of the old corps of official reporters who was still in the employment of the Government.

This gentleman, the late M. Prévost (the author of a system of shorthand still practised to some extent in France), willingly gave me all the explanations I desired, but distinctly gave me to understand that he was only detailing what was then a matter of history, and not a thing of the present. The method he employed—which was revived when the republic was established, and is continued to the present day—differed materially from that adopted in the British Parliament. A double corps of reporters was engaged, one whose duty it was to take turns of five minutes, and the other whose turns lasted half-an-hour. Two seats facing each other were provided at a table under the Tribune, from which each member had to address the assembly. One of the seats was occupied by the first set of reporters, called "rouleurs," and the other by the second set, called "reviseurs;" and the seats were so placed as to facilitate a constant

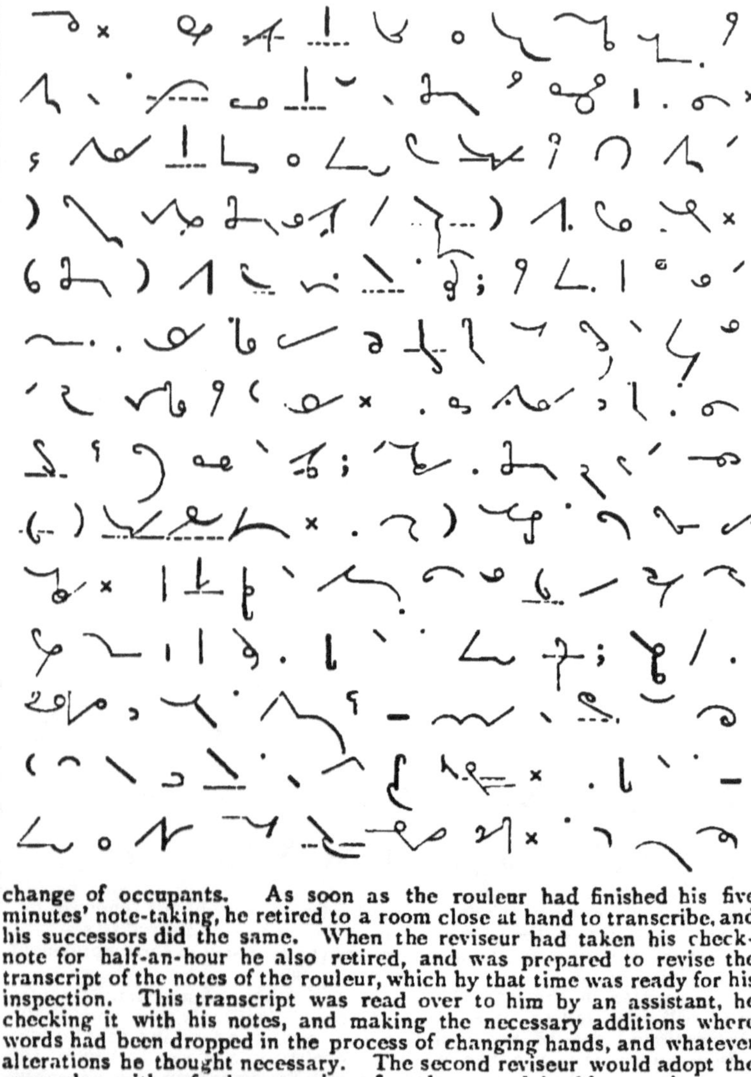

change of occupants. As soon as the rouleur had finished his five minutes' note-taking, he retired to a room close at hand to transcribe, and his successors did the same. When the reviseur had taken his check-note for half-an-hour he also retired, and was prepared to revise the transcript of the notes of the rouleur, which by that time was ready for his inspection. This transcript was read over to him by an assistant, he checking it with his notes, and making the necessary additions where words had been dropped in the process of changing hands, and whatever alterations he thought necessary. The second reviseur would adopt the same plan with a fresh succession of rouleurs, and in this way the transcript would be complete and examined within, say, half-an-hour of the rising of the Chamber. The method was unquestionably a very perfect one in its way. It had the disadvantage of requiring more hands than are ordinarily employed for such work, but it possessed the advantage of a check-note throughout; besides which, the shortness of the turns would enable a reporter with a good memory to supply any omissions that might be occasioned by a too rapid delivery on the part of the speaker. The advantage of a good check note is readily acknowledged by every experi-

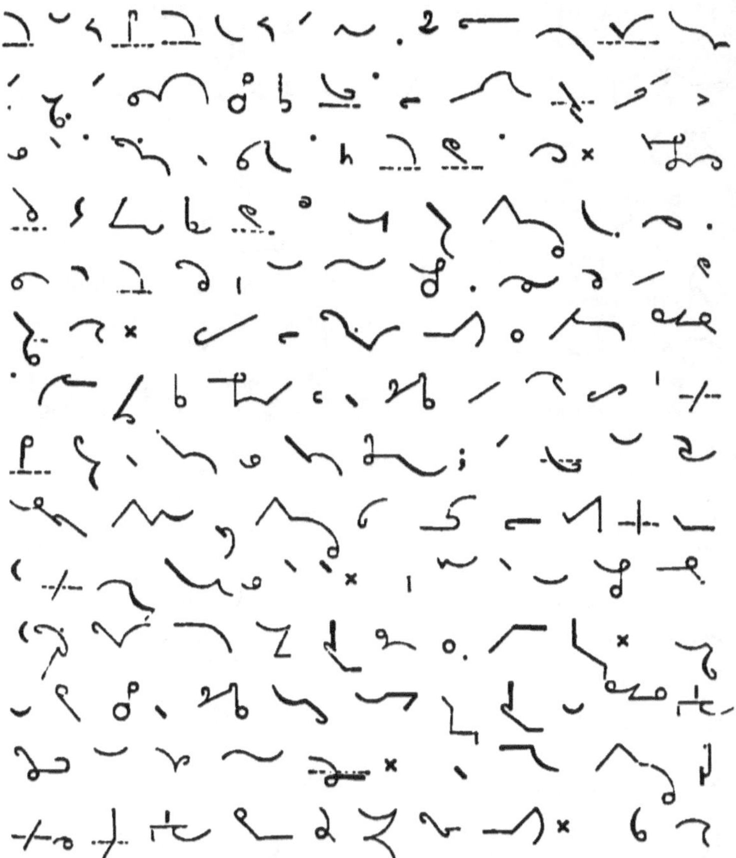

enced shorthand writer. A word may be mis-heard, or not heard at all, or if heard and written, the shorthand character may be badly formed; and under these and similar circumstances, it is often a great relief to be able to refer to the notes of a *confrère* to solve a doubt or supply an omission. Of course it sometimes happens that the check-note does not supply what is needed, both reporters having missed the same word or phrase, but in many instances the missing words are supplied by this method. Where great verbal accuracy is required, as in the case of a legal judgment, it is customary when two shorthand writers are employed, one on each side, for them to compare notes before transcribing; and even in ordinary newspaper reporting, two or three reporters will occasionally agree to write out together, that each may have the benefit of the notes of all. But I know of no instance, except that of the French parliamentary corps, in which a duplicate system is regularly adopted. Now and then, under special circumstances, two shorthand writers have been engaged to take a duplicate note, as in the case of the O'Connell prosecution in Ireland, many years ago. Two Government reporters attended each of the meetings at which O'Connell spoke, so as to ensure perfect accuracy.

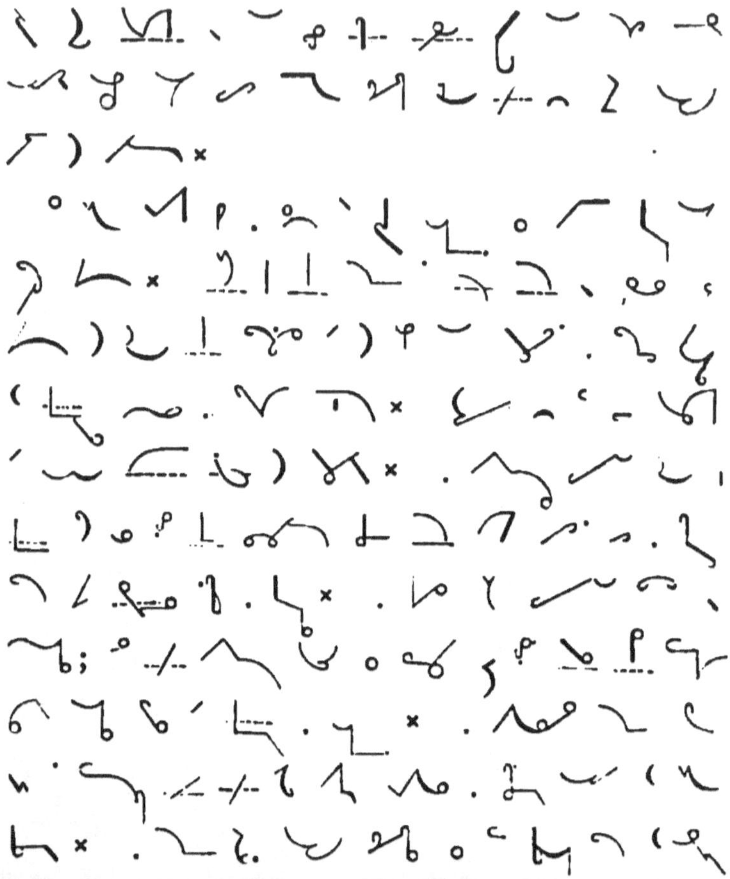

This method, I believe, was not followed to any great extent during the recent agitation in Ireland, except in one or two instances, only one Government shorthand writer attending each meeting of which an official record was required.

As I have already stated, the system of double note-taking is regularly adopted in the French Chamber. I saw it at work a year or two since when the Chamber was sitting at Versailles, and was interested in observing the frequent changes that took place amongst the Parliamentary corps. They were made with great facility, and nothing like confusion was observable. The reporters were not sitting, but took their notes standing at a semi-circular desk or ledge, running round the tribune from which the speakers addressed the deputies. The turns, I think, were not more than two minutes: and as each reporter finished, his successor, who was standing by his side, quietly slipped into his place, and took up the note-taking. The reviseurs worked for about a quarter-of-an-hour each, and then retired to revise the transcript in the way that I have described. The work of these official shorthand writers is quite distinct from that of

the newspaper reporters. The latter have not much to do in the way of note-taking, as they are able to rely on the printed reports supplied to the Press shortly after the sitting is completed. I was myself in the Press Gallery at Versailles, and was amused to see how easily the French reporters were doing their work. As for the few representatives of the foreign Press who were present, they were chiefly occupied during the time I was there (especially the Englishmen) in looking through opera glasses at some pretty girls in the Ladies' Gallery. The foreign reporters have a portion of the Press Gallery specially allotted to them: the Parisian and provincial reporters are also separately accommodated. The Gallery is opposite the president and the speaker's tribune, and as the building is a very large one, it is not easy to hear the members as they are addressing the Chamber. For myself, I could scarcely hear a quarter of what was said; this was partly owing to the general hubbub prevailing, something like that which so often perplexes the reporter in our own House of Commons, and partly to the fact that I was listening to a foreign language. M. Grévy, the then president, was standing ringing his bell to

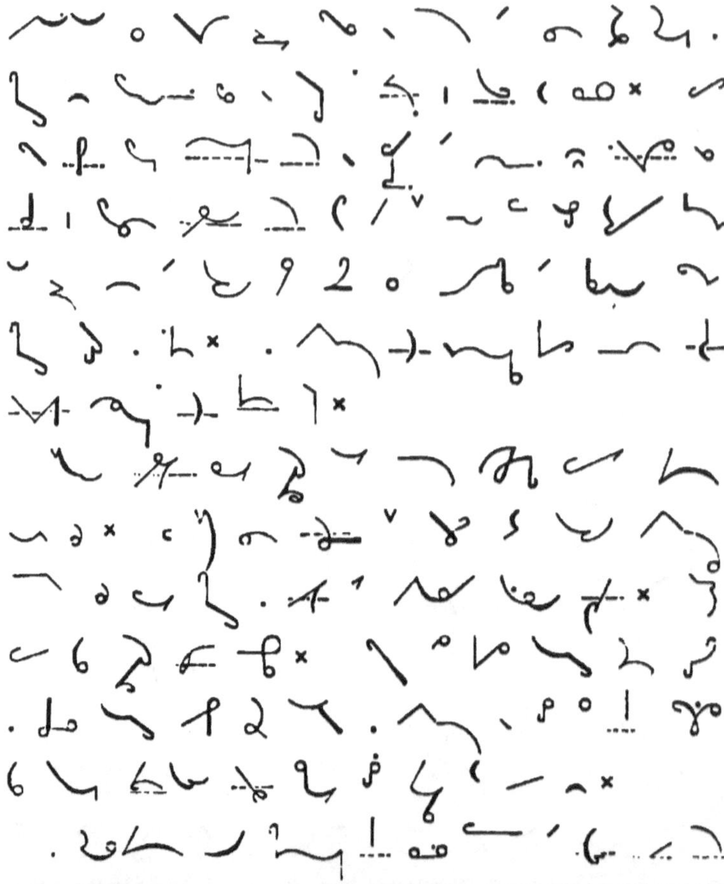

call the members to order, and some of those who ascended the tribune made frantic efforts to obtain a hearing, but often without success. One member stood for a minute or two gesticulating, and making mute appeals to his audience, but for some reasou or other which I could not quite understand, they were determined not to hear him, and finally he shrugged his shoulders, and descending from the tribune, abandoned the attempt. The reporter whose two minutes' turn came at that period must have had an easy time of it!

I have not recently seen the arrangements in the Corps Legislatif where the Chamber now sits. When I was there some years ago I observed that the official reporters occupied seats near the tribune, the rouleur and the reviseur facing each other. I cannot say whether this arrangement still exists. Probably as the turns have been so much shortened, the desks have been raised so as to enable the reporter to stand, as at Versailles, this being a much more convenient position considering the constant changes that are made.

The sittings of the Chamber usually terminate at 6 o'clock, and within

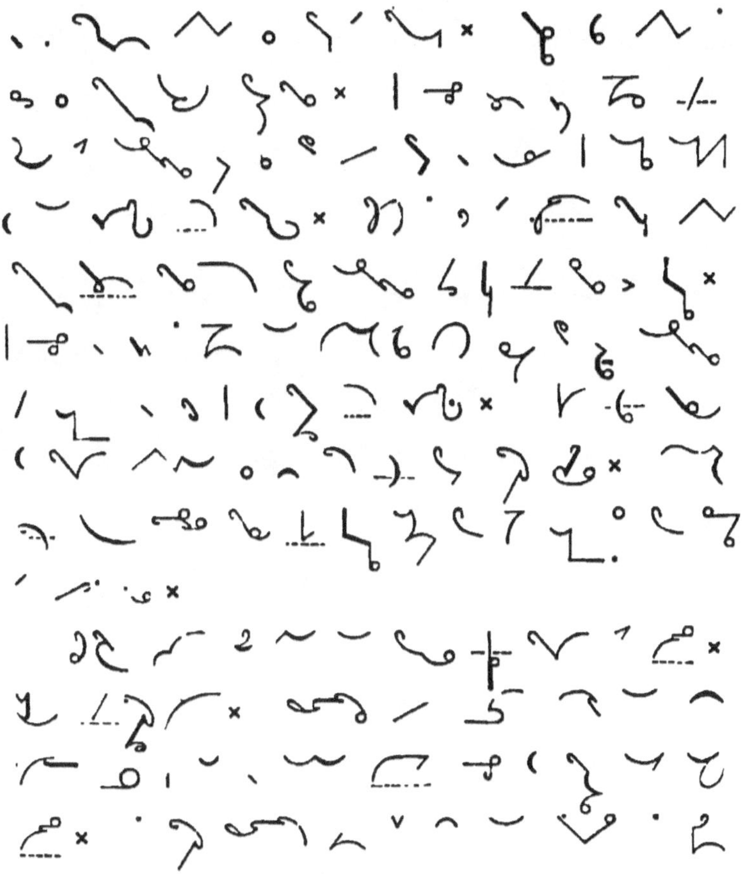

an hour or two the verbatim report is completed and printed. Besides this report, a second is prepared officially for the use of the Press. It extends to some two or three columns each sitting, and the newspapers to which it is supplied are obliged to insert it in its entirety, without any alteration or abbreviation. There is also a third and still more abbreviated report prepared by some members of the corps, for those newspapers which cannot devote much space to the debates. It extends to about a column in length, and this also is only supplied to those newspapers which undertake to print it without abridgement or alteration. It will thus be seen that Parliamentary reporting is made very easy for the French journals. Many of them, however, have their correspondents present at the debates, not so much for actual note-taking as for sketches and running comments.

There is comparatively little shorthand writing in France outside Parliament and the law courts. I do not know much of the arrangements of the latter. Stenographers are occasionally employed in important legal cases, but not to anything like the extent that prevails in the English law courts. A French stenographer, whom I met in Paris a short time since,

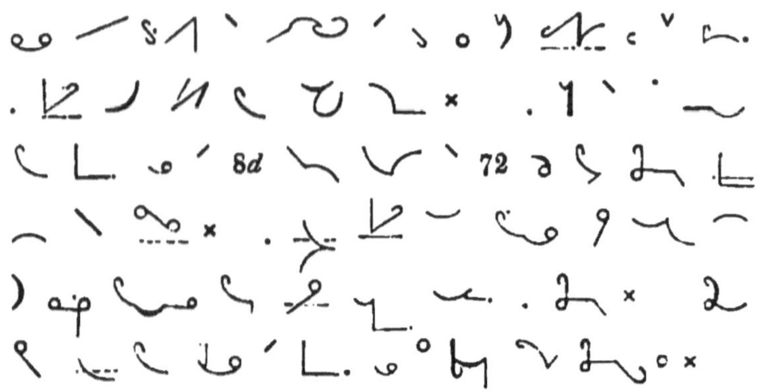

—:o:—

HEARING AND MIS-HEARING.

rather complained of the rate of remuneration, and opened his eyes widely when I told him the tariff usually charged for English work. The idea of a guinea for taking notes, and 8*d.* per folio of 72 words for the transcript, took him by surprise. The full tariff in France, he informed me, was 60 francs for an hour's note-taking, including the transcript. There is no special fee for attendance and taking notes, as distinct from the transcription of the notes.

Hearing is as essential to reporting as sight; and it goes without saying that a deaf reporter is an impossibility: I mean, of course, totally deaf. Partially deaf reporters one does occasionally meet with, but the wonder is how they manage to get through their work. They often receive assistance from their more fortunate brethren, who, of course, are in most cases willing to supply their need. I admit that sometimes, when, for instance, you are pressed for time, it is a little trying to have to turn to half-a-dozen places in your note-book, and find out and dictate the pas-

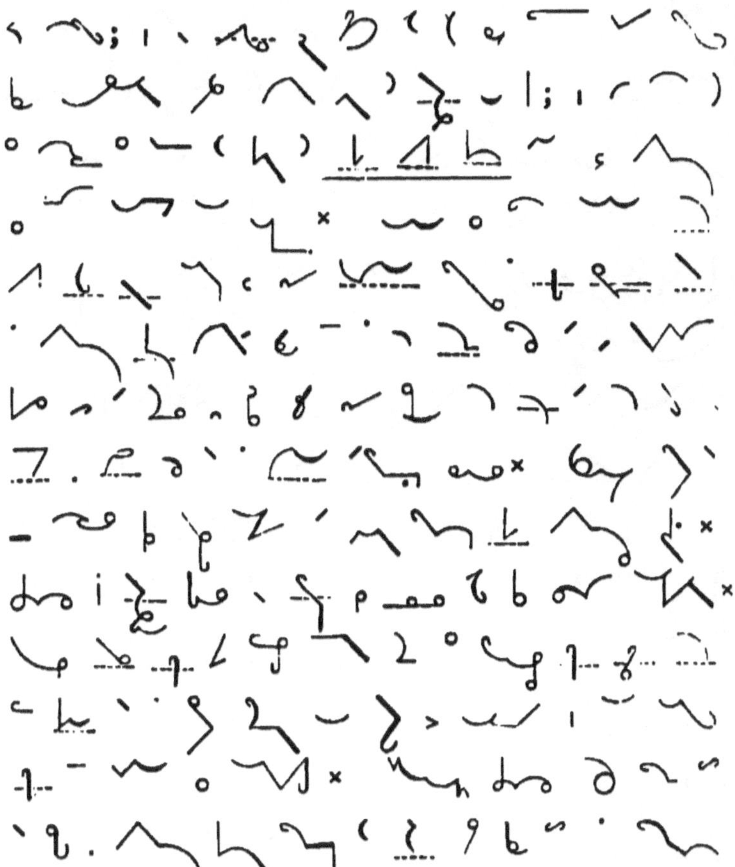

sages which your deaf friend has heard imperfectly; but to refuse would be churlish, and that, I think, is not the character of our profession. It is not unreasonable that such help should be sought by those who need it; but let me say as emphatically as I can that it should be sought *at the right time*, and not when the reporter is actually engaged in note-taking. Nothing is more annoying or irritating than to be interrupted when you are following perhaps a difficult speaker by a reporter at your elbow who has not caught a word or a phrase, and who abruptly turns round and asks you what it is just as you are straining your ear and your pen to catch the last words of a long and complicated sentence. This is not only a breach of good manners, it is a positive injury, and should not be permitted at the reporters' table. It is sometimes committed by those who have no deafness to plead as an excuse, and then it is simply intolerable. If there is a pause during which the question can be asked, as, for instance, during cheers, or quite at the end of a speech, there can be no objection to the inquiry, but any interruption during the act of writing is unpardonable. I have no doubt it sometimes arises from a want of consideration, the re-

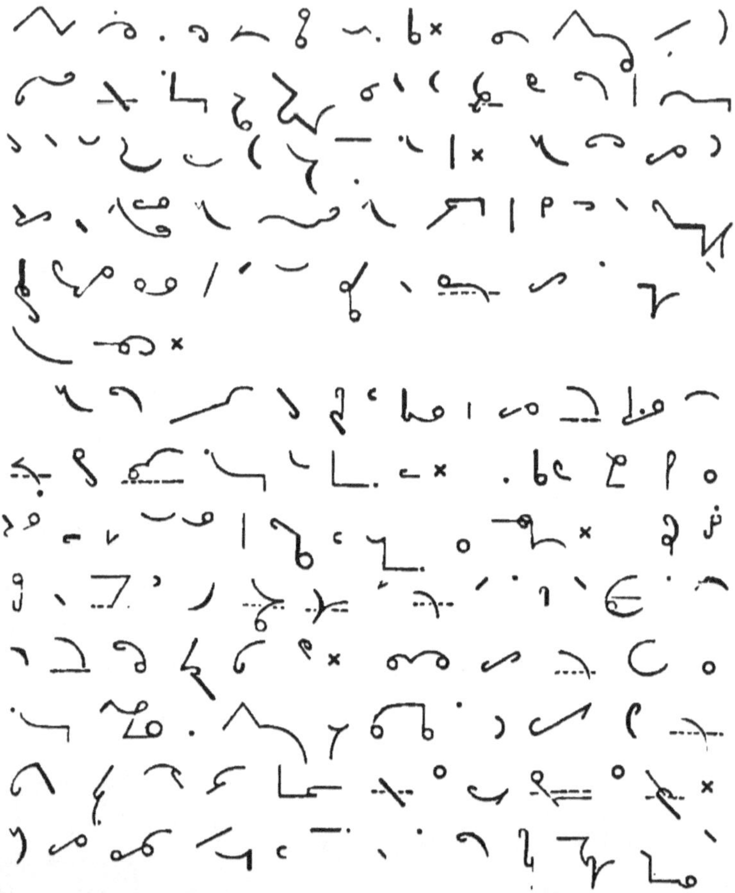

porter, it may be, forgetting that although he does not want a verbatim report himself, the friend whom he is interrupting does. Some reporters are so well known to be addicted to this objectionable habit, that those who have suffered from it make a point of not sitting near them if they can avoid it. I have more than once sat between two offenders of the class I have mentioned, and have regarded it as a kind of purgatorial discipline for one's sins, which ought in justice to secure one a good deal of future exemption.

I have very rarely been troubled with deafness, but once or twice my hearing has been slightly affected after taking cold. The discomfort of such a state is always great, but the annoyance it produces when note-taking is extreme. There is a constant strain to catch what usually falls easily on the ear, and a dread of losing an important word or phrase which cannot be well supplied. Sometimes one ear alone is affected, and in such cases the reporter naturally selects a seat where the other ear will be chiefly employed, and will take care to be as near the speaker as possible. I was once seriously recommended, when going to a very draughty

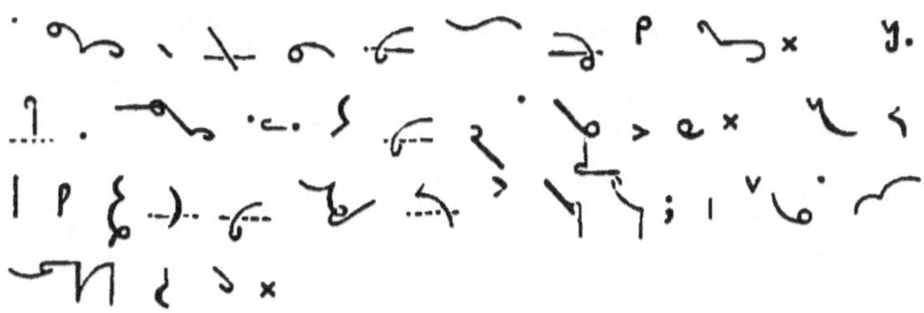

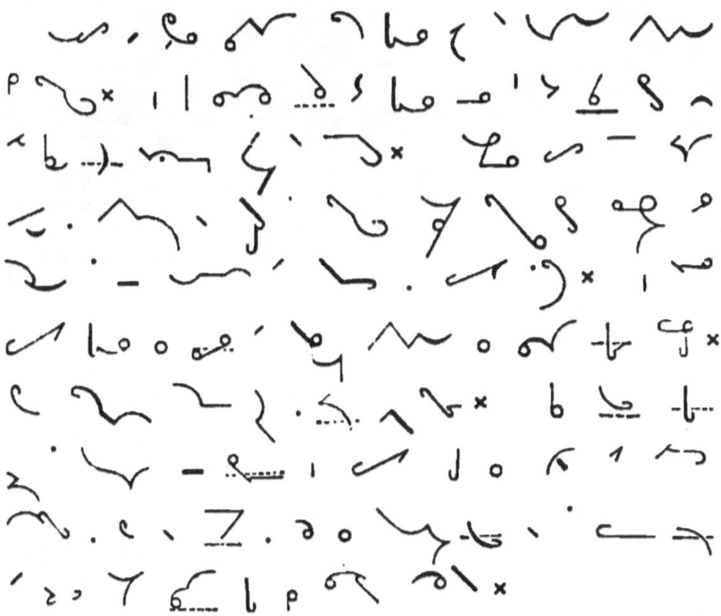

cathedral to take notes of a sermon, to put some wool in my ears as a protection! I did not try the experiment, concluding that the wool would be an obstacle to the sound. I have heard it stated that those who use wool in this way hear all the better for it; but I confess a little incredulity on that point.

No one who suffers habitually from deafness should think of following reporting as a profession. But it sometimes happens that the deafness comes on after the choice has been made, and when it is not easy to make a change of occupation. In such case one can hardly recommend the reporter to abandon a profession in which he perhaps has been successful and is earning a good income, and begin the world afresh. But of course where the deafness is serious and obstinate, reporting is simply out of the question. For verbatim work, especially, the hearing should be perfect. It is often difficult to hear a fairly good speaker, but where the tone is low and the articulation imperfect, the effort to catch the words is painful even to a quick ear, and to one only slightly deaf is a simple impossibility.

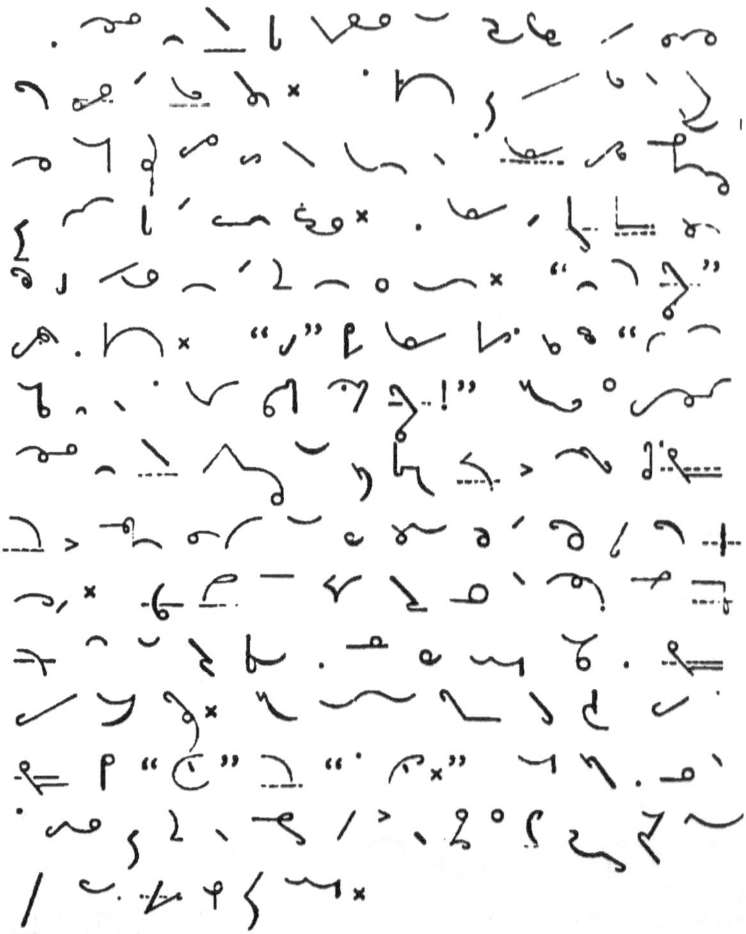

The mistakes made by deaf persons in ordinary conversation are sometimes very serious, and often absurd. A tailor who was rather fond of pushing himself into society once went up familiarly to an officer, one of his customers, who was a little deaf, and claimed acquaintance. The officer, who had been talking to some friends, did not recognize him, and asked him his name. "Made your breeches," whispered the tailor. "Gentlemen," said the officer, turning to his friends, "let me introduce you to a fellow-soldier, Major Breeches!" I have known as whimsical mistakes made by reporters, owing to their defective hearing, to the imperfect utterance of the speaker, or to the extreme similarity in sound of certain words and phrases which have very different meanings. These last can hardly be called cases of mis-hearing, because the acutest ear might not be able to distinguish the exact sound intended unless the speaker were unusually precise. I have, in my own practice, been doubtful whether a speaker said "alone," or "a loan." Indeed, I remember

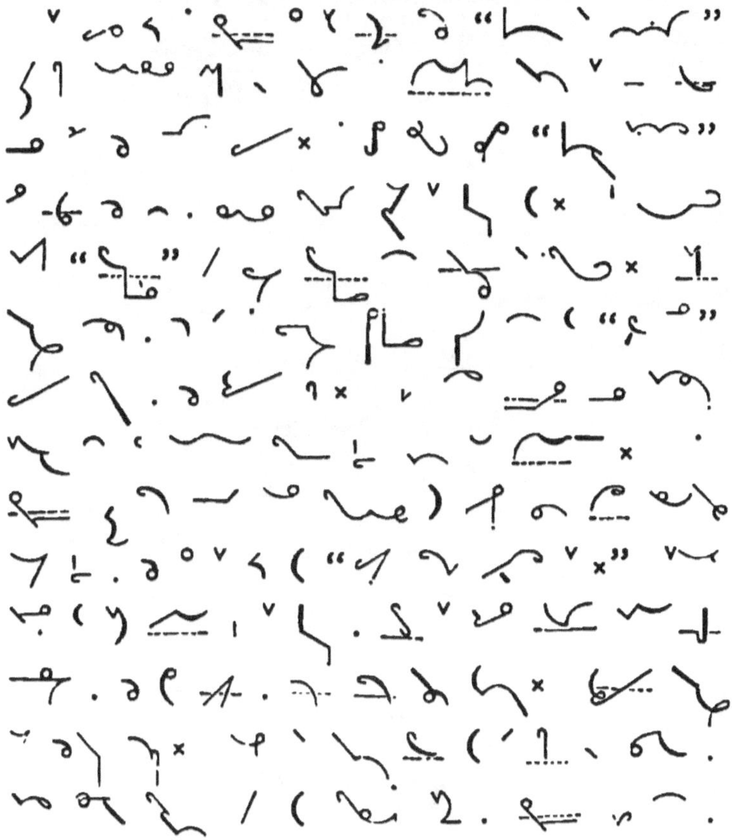

the case of a witness who was asked to explain which of the two he meant, as either would have been intelligible, and neither judge nor jury understood which was intended.

I once heard a speaker, as I thought, use the phrase "timher of Memel," which was utter nonsense, and I had to puzzle a long time before I could even guess what the words actually were. A sudden inspiration suggested "temple of Mammon," and as these words made the sentence perfectly intelligible I adopted them. On another occasion I wrote "overtax," which nearly overtaxed my powers of comprehension. I had obviously mis-heard the word, and a careful study of the context showed me that "overt acts" were probably the words that were uttered. But the most curious case of mis-hearing I have ever met with in my own practice occurred to me not long ago. A speaker, who was not very accurate in his pronunciation, was reciting some lines of his own composition in which occurred the words, as I heard them,

"Watching from the Roman eye."

I knew, of course, that I was wrong, but I adopted the plan I always follow of writing down exactly the words as they reach the ear, however absurd they may be. These were obviously not the words of the poet ora-

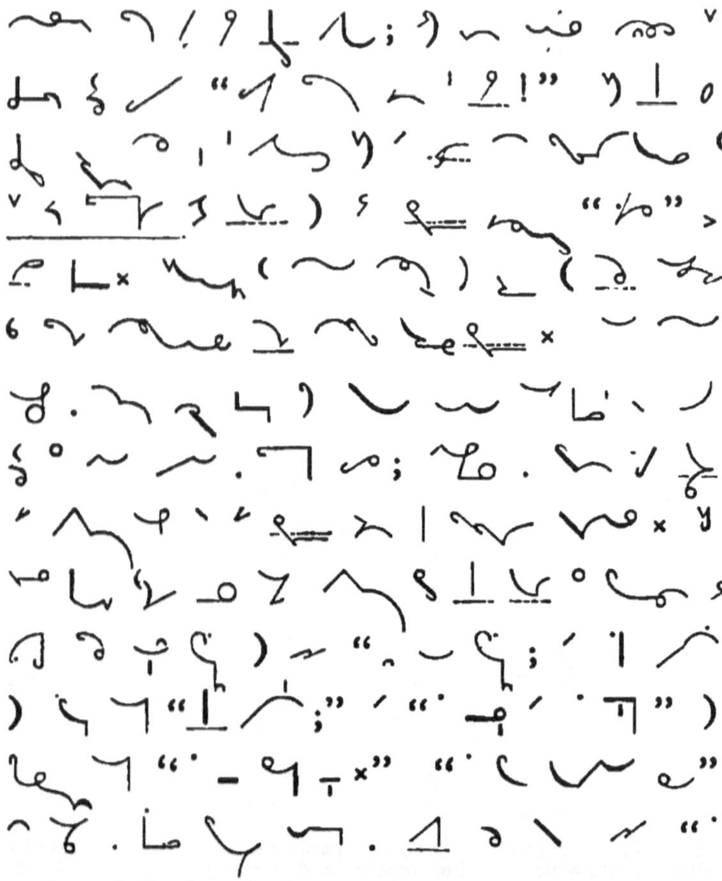

tor. Instead of poring over them and trying to solve the almost inscrutable problem which they presented, I asked the speaker to lend me the manuscript from which he had been reading; and there, to my intense amusement, I discovered that the words were,

"Watching from their home on high!"

I was at first disposed to blame myself, but on reflection I was, and still am, perfectly convinced that *I heard correctly*, and that the fault was with the speaker, who must have been "aitchless" to the last degree. I have no doubt that many mis-hearings, so to call them, arise in the same way, that is, from the mispronunciation, or the imperfect vocalization, of the speaker. In many instances the error may not be detected, there being nothing in the context to show that the words as written are not the correct ones; and in such cases the blame generally falls on the reporter instead of on the speaker, to whom it properly belongs. I do not, of course, deny that there are cases in which the reporter has been at fault, *e.g.*, when the Latin phrase *uno flatu* was rendered "you know flatu;" and *ad rem* was converted into "had rum;" and "a goose and a goat" was transformed into "a good Sunday coat." "An ever-varying scene"

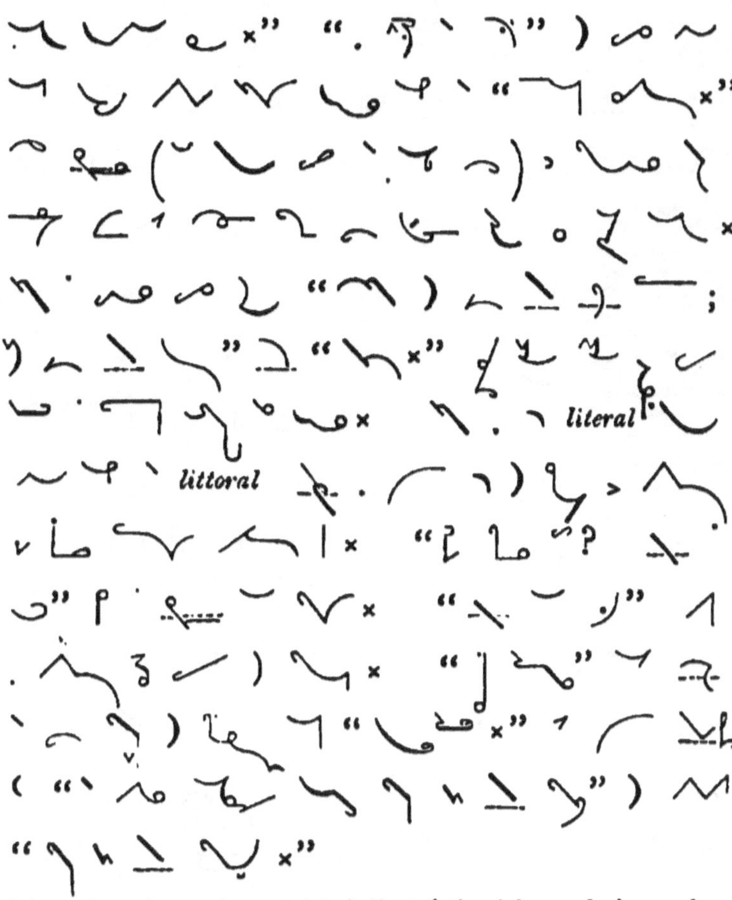

might, unless the context plainly indicated the right words, be rendered "A never varying scene." "The Countess of Ayr" was once written in an official report of parliamentary evidence instead of "County Surveyor." Most speakers (not being West of England men) would pronounce both exactly alike, and the mistake, from a mere phonic point of view, is intelligible enough. I remember a witness once saying, "My brother was home by three o'clock; I was home by four," or "before." Which he meant I did not know, and I do not know to this day whether I gave a correct interpretation of his evidence. I remember the word "literal" being written instead of "littoral." Possibly the latter word was strange to the reporter, bnt the context clearly required it. "What do the Turks want? To be a nation," said a speaker in Parliament. "To be in Asia," wrote the reporter, and the words were so printed. "Attenders of clubs," in the mouth of Mr Bright, was transformed into "vendórs of gloves." And the latter part of the statement that "all reforms in this country have been brought about by pressure" was reported, "brought about by Prussia."

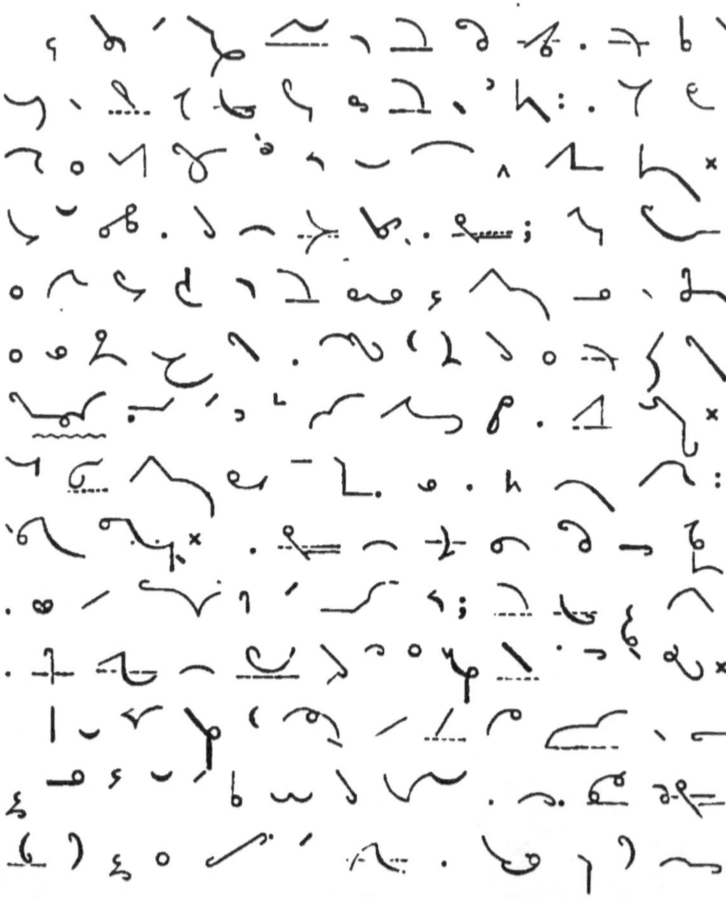

When an absurd and obviously wrong word or phrase reaches the ear it is of no use to stop and think, even for a second or two, what it should be: the only safe method is to write precisely what is heard, no matter how ridiculous it may be. If the hand hesitates, the pen may fall behind the speaker; and if a blank is left for the doubtful word or sentence, when the reporter comes to transcribe his notes, he may no longer remember the impression that was made upon his ear, which was probably *approximately* accurate, and would, on a little reflection, suggest the right interpretation. Indeed, while the reporter is in the act of taking notes, the doubt may be removed: *solvitur scribendo.* The speaker may use the same phrase again, and this time the sounds are clearly uttered and accurately heard; or even without this help the true reading may flash upon the mind, as I have said, by a kind of inspiration.

It need hardly be said that mis-hearings are much less likely to occur when the mind goes with the hand, and it is intent upon following the meaning as well as the words of the speaker, than they are when the mind is wandering, and leaving the fingers to do their mechanical work

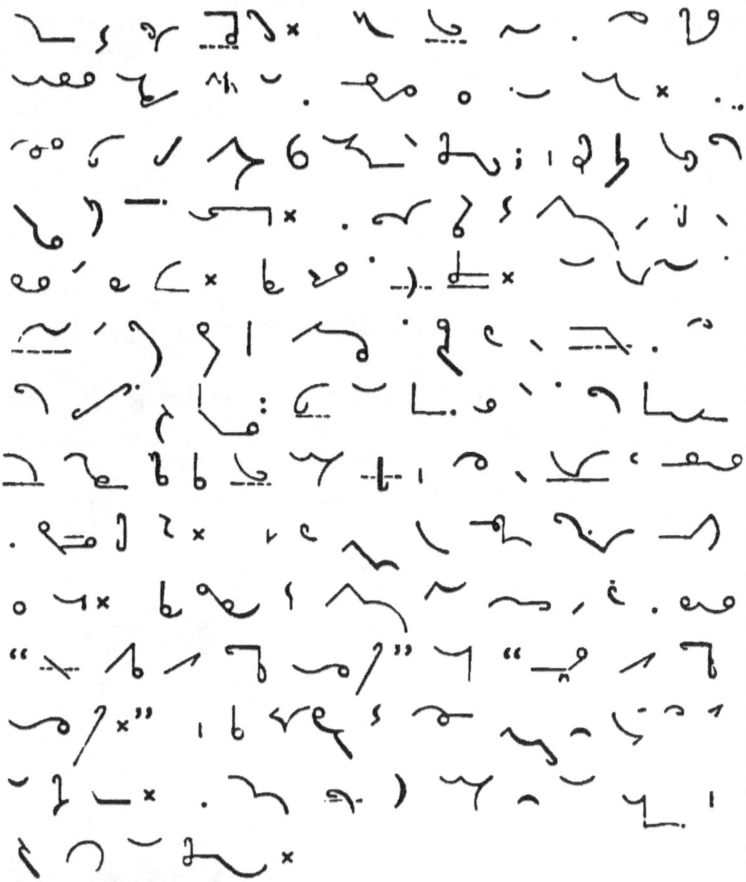

without the friendly guidance of the brain. I have often written the most atrocious nonsense in this way, and I doubt not the experience is common enough. The mistakes will generally reveal themselves in the work of transcription; but there is a danger if they are not very obvious, of their going uncorrected. The moral of which is, that the reporter should attend to sense and sound alike. It is not always an easy task. In following a long and prosy speech it requires a considerable effort to keep the mind from wandering to other topics: while in taking notes of a very technical, or metaphysical address, it is often not only difficult, but impossible, to follow with exactness the speaker's train of thought. But the effort should be made if extreme verbal accuracy is needed. It is not surprising that a reporter, writing mechanically, should convert the sentence, "Pew-rates are the greatest enemies of the Church," into "*Curates* are the greatest enemies of the Church." But it is hardly conceivable that the mistake should have been made if the mind and the hand traveled together. The error, however, was not only made in note-taking, but, I believe, also in transcribing.

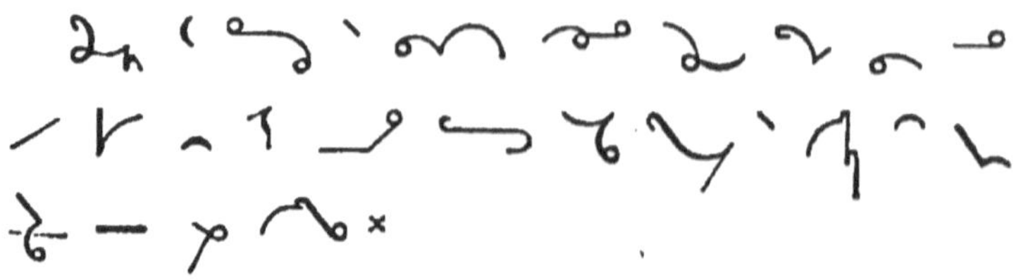

—:o:—

IN COURT.

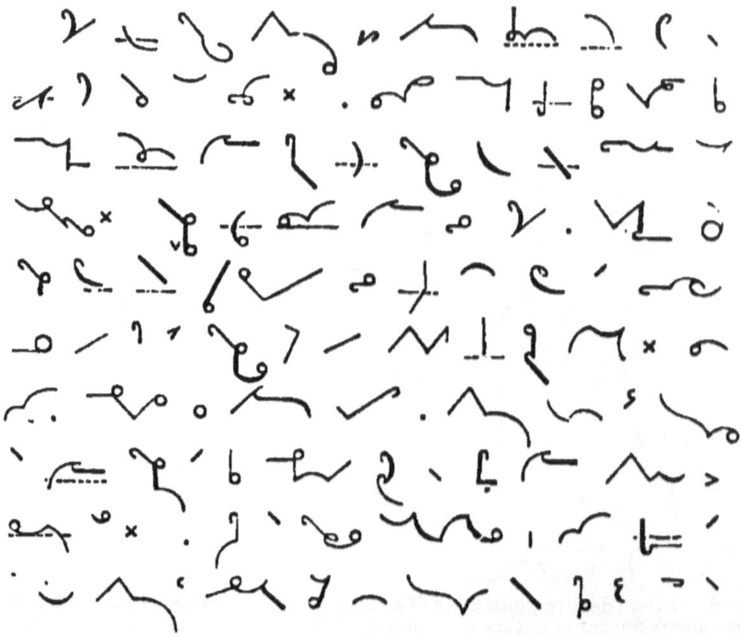

There is no doubt that scores of similar mistakes, arising from the same cause, are daily made, and that a curious collection in this branch of literature might be made by those given to such labors.

There are few professional reporters who are not required at some time or other to wield their pens in courts of law. The smallest county town has its police court, its county court, or some legal tribunal whose proceedings have to be chronicled in the newspapers. Besides these small local courts there are the periodical Assizes presided over by judges of the superior courts, at which important civil and criminal cases are tried, and the proceedings of which are reported at considerable length. Some little experience is required to render the reporter familiar with the forms of legal procedure, and it is customary, therefore, to delegate legal reporting to the senior hands. The trial of prisoners involves but little difficulty, and a young reporter with reasonable intelligence may fairly be trusted

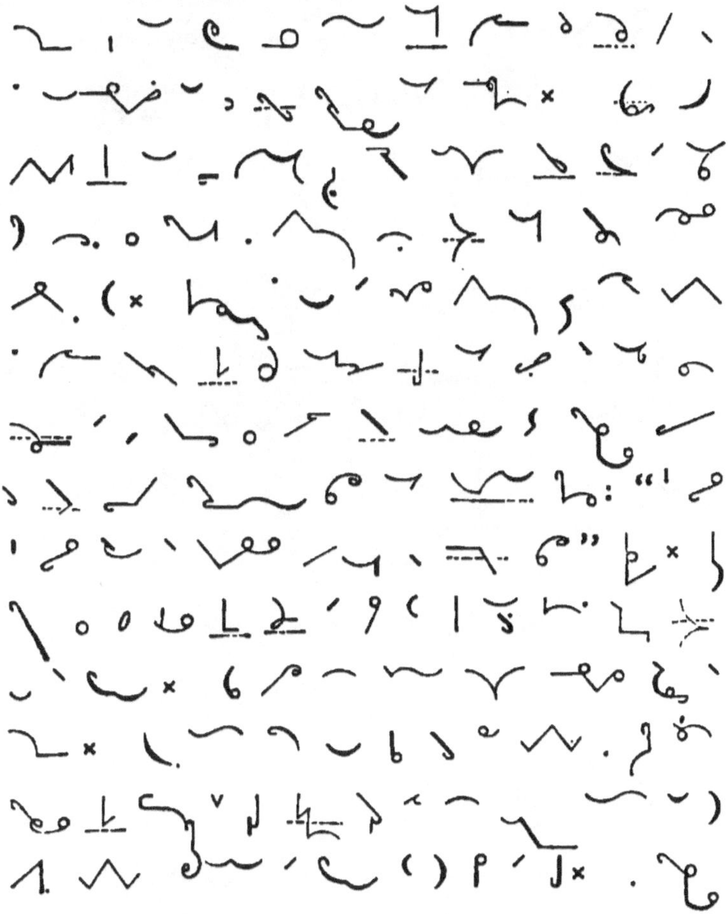

with that kind of work, but in civil cases many knotty legal points arise which to an inexperienced hand would prove perplexing in the extreme. These are not usually reported at any great length, but they cannot be entirely passed over, and unless their meaning is appreciated the reporter may fall into absurd mistakes respecting them. It must have been a young and artless reporter who was employed to represent a local paper at the Assizes in a country town in the west of England some years ago, and who began his record by announcing that the proceedings were opened by the crier proclaiming silence in the following terms: "Oh yes, Oh yes, all manner of persons are commanded to keep silence," etc. It was probably his first attendance at an assize court, and he thought it incumbent on him to take a full note of everything. This reminds me of my own early experience of this kind of work. Having in my very young days been sent to report the trial of some prisoners at the Quarter Sessions, I attended at the time appointed, and with my note-book in my hand was ready to report anything and everything that was said and done. The

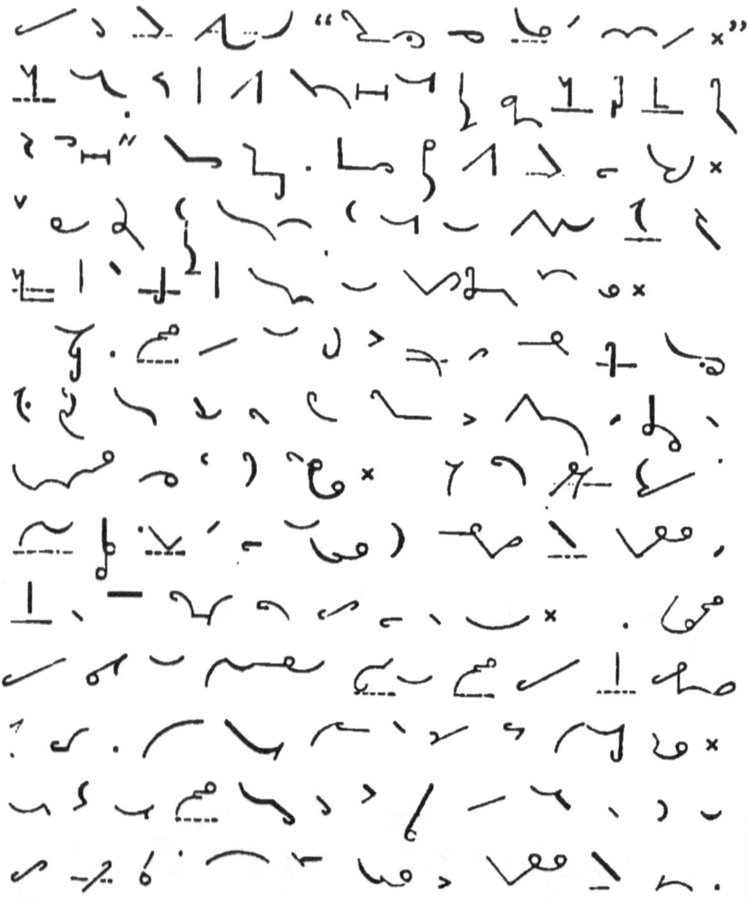

proceedings were opened by the reading of the usual "proclamation against vice and immorality." I had never heard it read before—indeed, it was the first time I had attended at a tribunal of that kind—and I began to take down the document as it was read by the court official. I soon suspected that it was a formality that needed no reporting, and though I believe I took it all down it formed no portion of the transcript of my notes.

In London the law courts are in session all the year round, except during the vacations, and they therefore afford abundant opportunity for practice to the reporter who desires to familiarise himself with their proceedings. Until very recently they were a long distance apart, and great inconvenience was experienced by persons who had to go frequently from one court to another. The Chancery Courts were held in Lincoln's Inn, while the Common Law Courts were at Westminster and the Guildhall, the latter being the *locale* of what are called the London sittings. Now that the New Law Courts have been opened, all the judges are enabled to sit under one roof, which is a matter of great convenience to the persons by whom

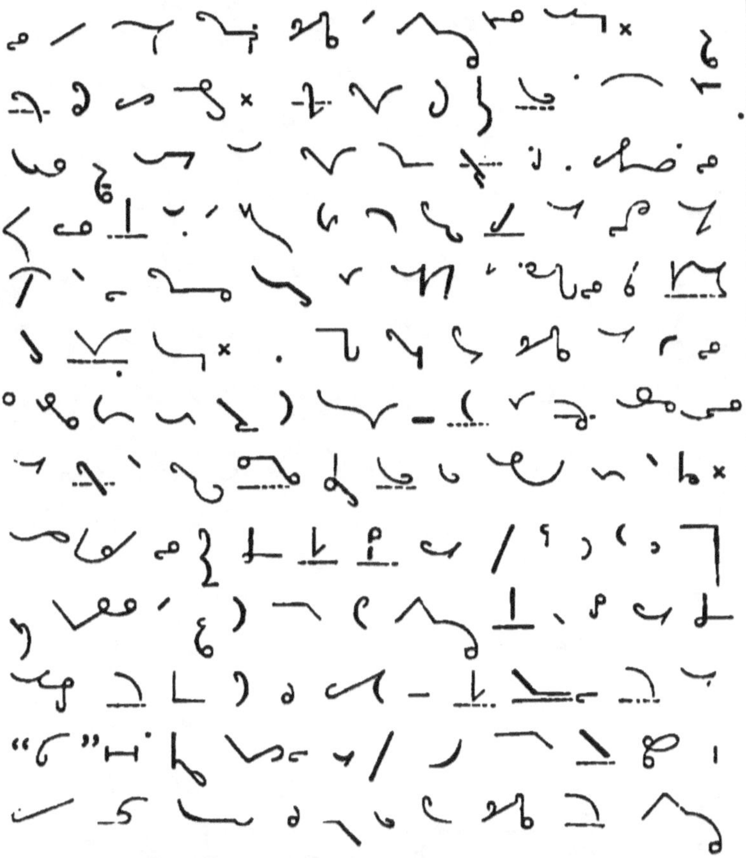

the courts are mainly frequented, shorthand writers and reporters of course included. To this, however, there is one exception. During the Parliamentary session it was often a matter of great convenience to those engaged in Parliamentary work to be ablo to attend the Westminster Courts which were close at hand, and I fear they will not very fervently join in the congratulations in which the majority of court frequenters have heen of late indulging on the concentration of the courts which has at length heen happily effected. The accommodation provided for the shorthand writers in the old courts, as I suppose they may now be called, was fairly good, though of late years in consequence of the increase in the number of professional scribes, it has been often found insufficient to meet all demands. In most of the Chancery courts there was a desk at the side near the judge with a seat that would accommodate two or three persons, and when this was occupied other reporters had to stand near the desk in question or take their seats where they could at the back of the court, or in the "well"—a depressed portion of the court under the judge, usually occupied hy solicitors, hut where occasionally vacant seats could he found for shorthand writers or reporters who could not find suitable accommo-

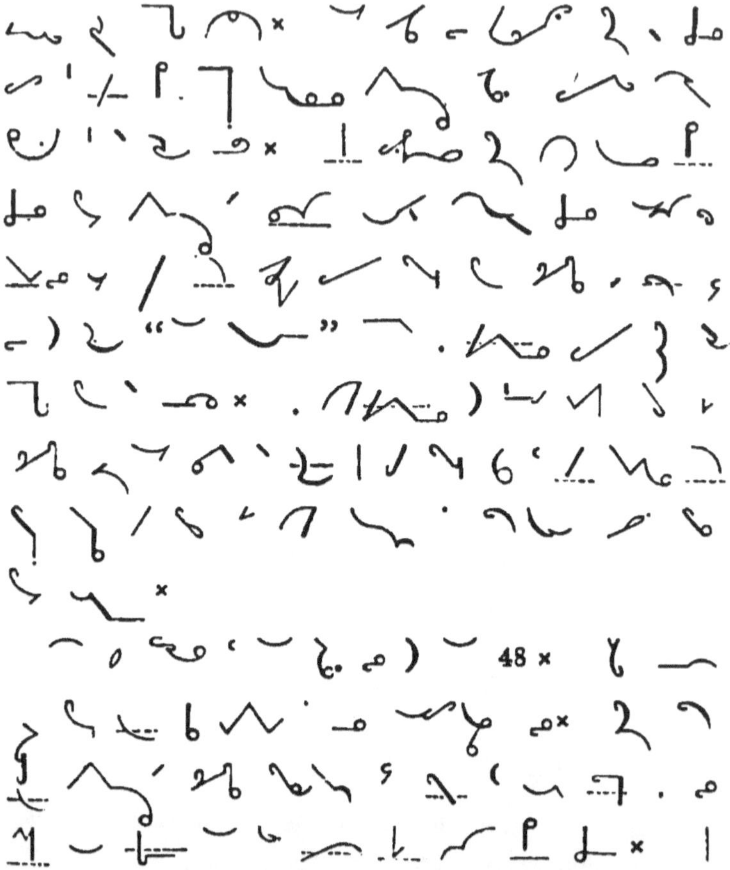

dation elsewhere. In the Rolls Court, Chancery lane, there were two desks, one on each side, accommodating five or six reporters, and these were found amply sufficient on all ordinary occasions. At Westminster there were also fixed side desks for the reporters; and small, narrow, movable desks in the middle of the front part of the Courts under the judge or registrar were provided for shorthand writers, who, however, when the Court was sitting "*in banc*" occupied the jury box, where there was abundant accommodation for all comers. The ledge of the jury box was awkward to write upon, but the shorthand writers who were in the habit of using it generally provided themselves with large portfolios or blotting pads, which, placed on the ledge, formed a very convenient resting place for the note-book.

My first acquaintance with any of these Courts was in 1848. I then came to London for a few days to report a case in one of the Vice-Chancellor's courts. There were very few reporters and shorthand writers present compared with the number that now crowd the Courts, and I had no difficulty in finding room at the little side desk. It took me some little

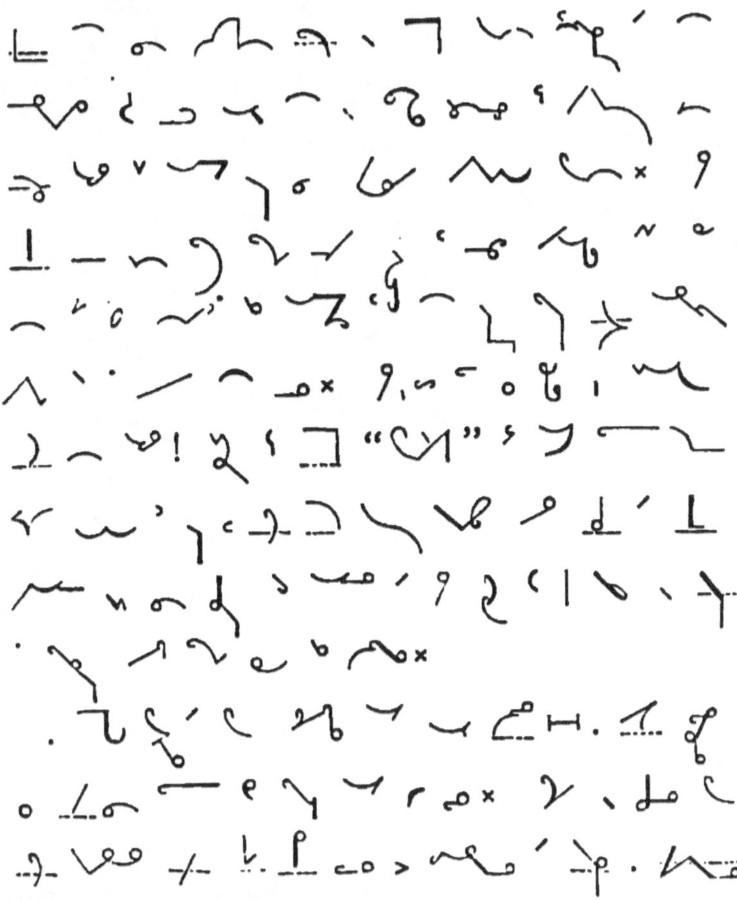

time, however, to get familiar with the mode of procedure, and my experience on that occasion enabled me to sympathise to some extent with a reporter whom years afterwards I engaged to do some Chancery reporting for me. He had come to me fresh from the country to London with excellent recommendations, and I sent him on the first morning of his engagement with me to take a pretty full newspaper report of a rather important case. He went according to his instructions, but I never saw him afterwards! I suspect that he got "flurried" with the unusual character of the work, hardly knowing what to do when three or four barristers rose at once and had a wrangle about some disputed point in the case, and he therefore thought it best to beat a precipitate retreat from the scene of his labors.

The accommodation for the Press and for shorthand writers in the New Law Courts—the Royal Courts of Justice—is much of the same character as that provided in the old Courts. There are two desks for three persons each at the side, close to the witness-box, and opposite the jury box, and

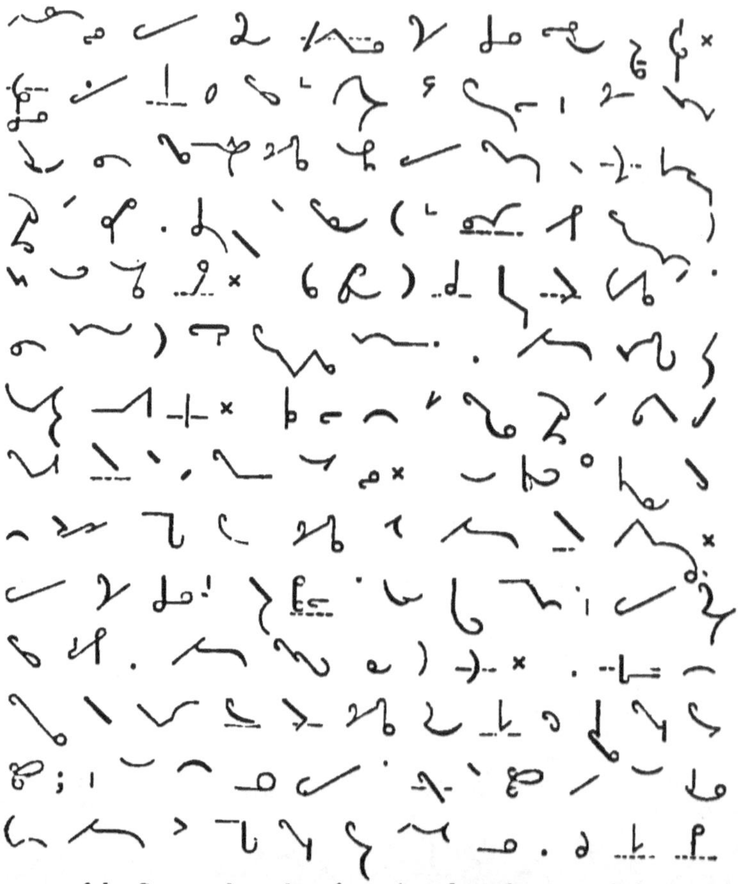

in some of the Courts where there is no jury box there are desks corresponding to those on the other side. These desks were at first placed on a level with the floor of the Court, but shortly before the opening some members of the Council of the Shorthand Writers' Institute were permitted to see the contemplated arrangement, and suggested the desirability of placing them on a small raised platform, say about nine inches high. This suggestion was at once adopted by the authorities, and a sum of money was granted for the purpose of making the required alteration, which was forthwith carried out. It is a great improvement on the previous arrangement, and will be generally appreciated by all who practise in the Courts. No distinction has at present been made between the accommodation for shorthand writers and that required by reporters. Where there are desks on both sides of the court a convenient division can be made, but where they are only placed on one side the required appropriation is not so easy. The difficulty may perhaps be partly overcome by the shorthand writers sitting at the front tables provided for the solicitors; but in important cases where a number of solicitors are in attendance they may require all the accommodation provided for them, and in that case

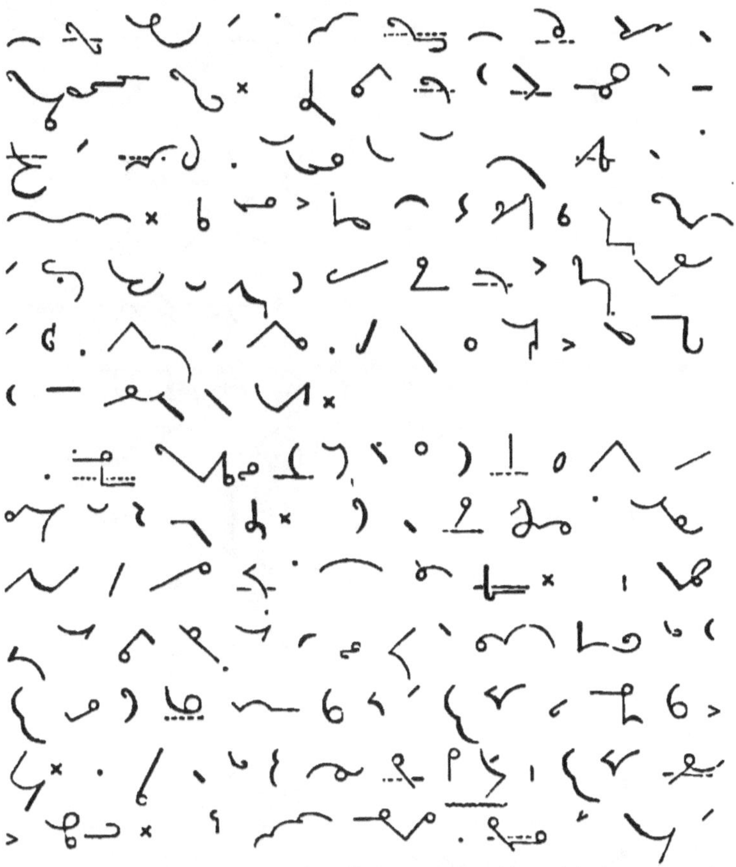

the seats at the side may prove insufficient, and a little friction may arise between the two branches of the stenographic profession. It is to be hoped, however, that by the exercise of good feeling and mutual concession the inconvenience, if any, may be reduced to a minimum. It is, of course, of the utmost importance that the shorthand writer who has to take a verbatim and *quasi* official note should have a seat where he can hear all the *dramatis personæ;* and, on the other hand, the reporter who represents the general public is entitled to the best accommodation that can reasonably be afforded.

The acoustic properties of the Courts, though not so bad as was at first represented, are certainly not all that could be desired. They are too high, and there is sometimes an unpleasant reverberation, which renders hearing a matter of some difficulty. But barristers who were in the habit of speaking in the old Courts, which were of smaller dimensions, find that they have to raise their voices to make themselves heard, and they have hardly yet accustomed themselves to the change. The judges, too, find that they must not speak *sotto voce*, but they have hardly risen to the necessities of the occasion. With a little more experience the speakers

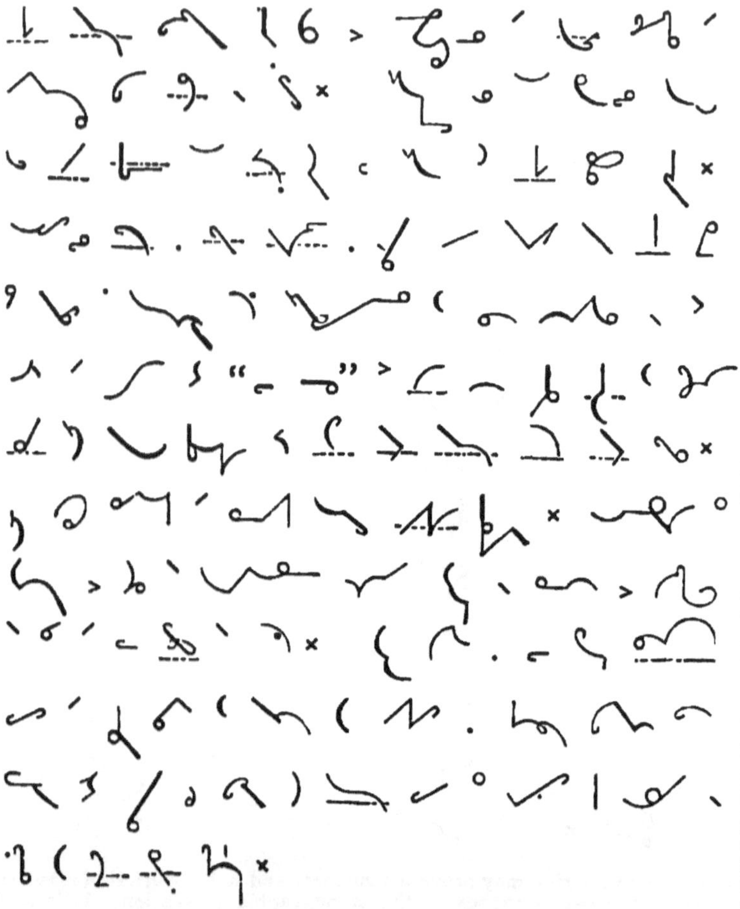

on the bench and at the bar will probably adapt themselves to the exigencies of the case, and even the shorthand writers and reporters will cease to complain. I have taken notes in several of the Courts, and have not found much difficulty in hearing, especially when I have sat at the solicitors' table. In one of the Courts, however, the principal Appeal Court, the judges are perched up at such a height behind a formidable array of breastworks that seem impervious to all the shot and shell that the "great guns" of the law may discharge at them, that there is little chance of their being distinctly heard either by the bar or by the press. But their lordships' serenity and security have been rudely disturbed. Inaccessible as they may be to the assaults of forensic artillery, they have had to succumb to the alternation of hot and cold blasts of air. They have left the Court for a smaller one, and it is to be hoped that before they return the atmosphere will be made more equable, and that the judges' seats will not be so far away as to render it necessary to address them through a speaking trumpet.

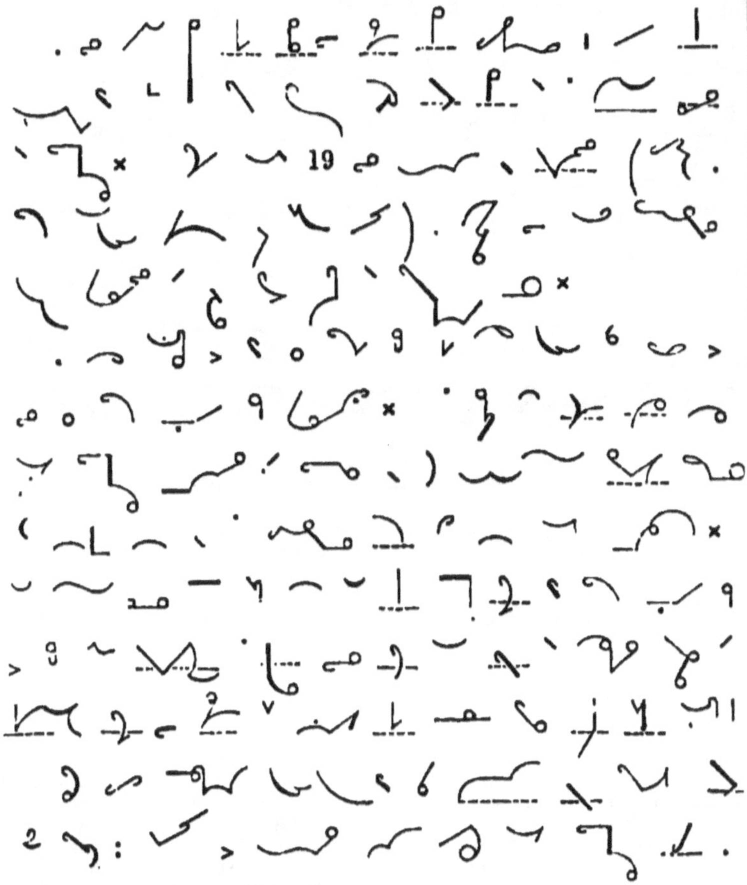

The courts are not situated at the sides of the great hall, as at Westminster, but are at another part of the building, on an upper floor arranged by the side of a long series of corridors. There are in all nineteen courts, namely, two Appeal Courts (one of them the very inconvenient chamber to which I have referred), the Lord Chief Justice's Court, nine Queen's Bench Courts, five Chancery Courts, and two others for the trial of Probate and Admiralty cases.

The main entrance to the building is from the Strand, but the most convenient, that is, nearest to the Courts, is from Carey street, Chancery lane. A stranger might easily lose himself in the corridors, galleries and crypts, to say nothing of the many spiral staircases that may conduct him to a witness-box or land him in a coal-cellar. Not many weeks ago I tried my hand at getting through the building from Carey street to the Strand, and after pursuing a devious course through any number of mysterious passages and at length through the great hall, I emerged at the exact place at which I had entered!

There is one extremely convenient feature of the building which is likely to

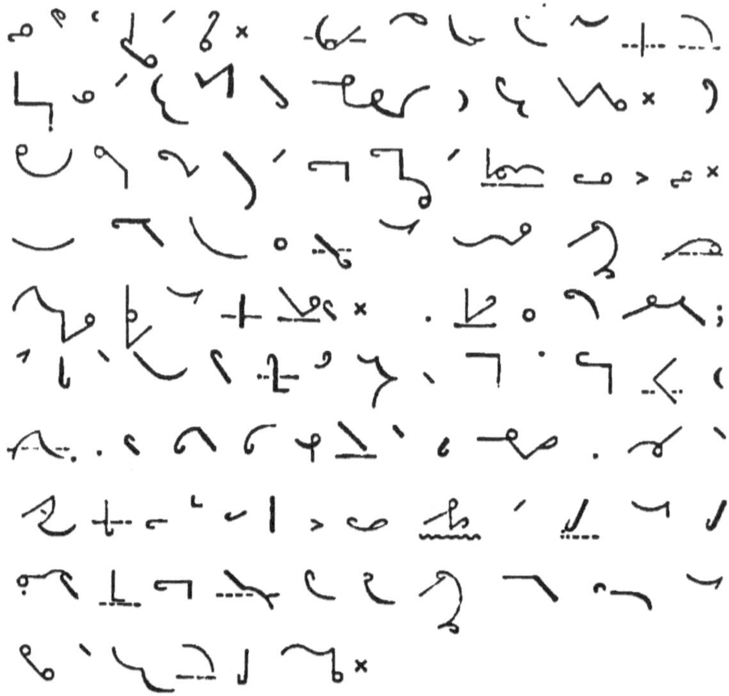

be appreciated by the shorthand brotherhood: I refer to the numerous little recesses in the corridors adjoining the Courts, supplied with tahles and chairs. These are most convenient for writing out or dictating notes, and they have already been extensively used for that purpose. They are sufficiently separated from the busy and crowded corridors, and at the same time close to the Courts. Another agreeable feature is to be found in the numerous refreshment rooms, lavatories, etc., in the different parts of the building. The tariff is very reasonahle; and the advantage of being able during a short interval to get a quiet chop, without leaving the building, will he well understood hy all who have experienced the misery of rushing out of Court on a wet day to the nearest *restaurant*, and joining in a general scramble at a crowded bar for whatever refreshment can be secured in the space of five or ten minutes.

AT THE HOSPITAL.

The experience in the present sketch does not often fall to the lot of members of the reporting craft, but it so happens that I have many a time had a good deal of it. Many years ago I was engaged to report a course of twenty or more lectures at Guy's Hospital, delivered by the late Mr Hilton, one of the professional staff and afterwards President of the College of Surgeons. The course was part of the regular curriculum of the medical school attached to the hospital, and I attended the lectures and reported them for Mr Hilton himself, who subsequently published them in a volume. The subject was the nerves, and each lecture was illustrated by actual dissection. At the first lecture an entire corpse, partially dissected, was brought in for this purpose, and I confess that my own nerves were a little disturbed at its appearance, and at the minute scrutiny which its interior economy underwent. It was my first introduction to this kind of work, and I had a strong inclination to pack up my

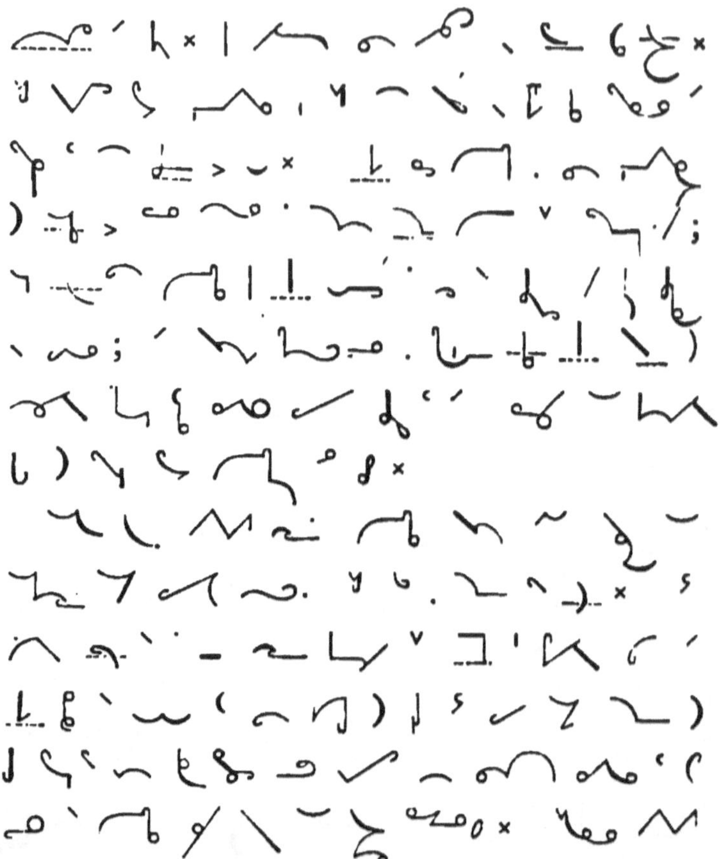

writing materials and depart. It required some resolution to overcome this feeling. I had not bargained for the corpse, but I did my best to tolerate its presence and proceed with my task to the end. At the second lecture the same *corpus vile* was introduced to the class minus an arm or a leg, I forget which; after a few more lectures it had undergone an amount of dismemberment which it was distressing to witness; and before the termination of the course the trunk itself had become so miserably attenuated that its services were dispensed with and a successor in admirable condition was provided for the lecturer and his students.

Never having reported medical lectures before, and not possessing any anatomical knowledge worth mentioning, I did not find the work particularly easy. With the help, however, of a good medical dictionary I got on tolerably well, and had the satisfaction of knowing that Mr Hilton was contented with the way in which the work was done, for he applied to me on several subsequent occasions to render him similar service with other courses of lectures which he published in volumes as in the case of the first. I have since reported many medical lectures at almost all the hos-

pitals in London, either for the medical journals or for the lecturers themselves. Some have been very easy and some very difficult. Some lecturers are distinct and deliberate in delivery, pausing occasionally to give the students an opportunity of making notes, while others rattle on in a rapid and conversational way, which is always more or less trying to the note-taker. But the most difficult lectures of this kind to report are not those delivered to hospital students, which are of course somewhat elementary, but those delivered at Medical Societies or colleges, where the audiences are full-fledged medical men, and the subjects are therefore of a more advanced character. Many of these and of the discussions attending them it has been my lot to report. Such addresses are frequently read, and if (as is sometimes the case) the lecturer's manuscript is not available, the work usually requires a skill that can only be attained by a tolerably long experience. The subjects are often abstruse, and the technical terms employed are numerous and sometimes perplexing, and where, to these sources of difficulty, a rapid delivery is added, the reporter has a hard task

to accomplish. He may be familiar with most of the medical and physiological terms, but if he suddenly finds himself confronted with half-a-dozen names, say of French and German medical writers of whom he may never have heard, the chances are that some of them will be missed. It may be, too, that the lecturer has a number of diagrams and illustrations to which he has frequently to refer, or he may have some experiments to perform, in which case the reporter's work is rendered still more difficult, as he is required, if possible, to make his report intelligible to the readers without the assistance of diagram or experiment. Now and then also it happens that another source of difficulty arises from the fact that the lecturer requires for his experiments that the room be darkened, and the reporter is thus left to grope his way over the pages of his note-book without the slightest assistance from his eyes. This is, to say the least, very inconvenient. Of course a good reporter will not cease writing from the mere circumstance that he has no light. If the subject is not a difficult one and the speaker not too rapid, a good note-taker will be able to preserve the outlines of his words and phrases with sufficient accuracy to enable him to

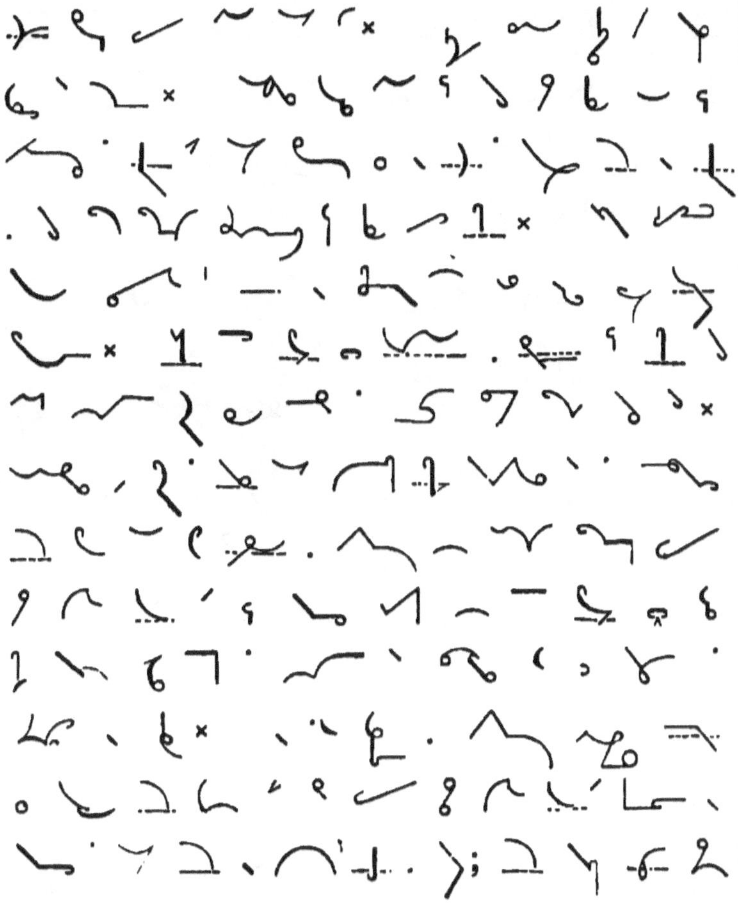

decipher his notes almost as easily as if he were writing in the light. But there are certain dangers which beset this kind of work. In the first place if he is writing with a pen he does not know when he requires a dip, and the only safeguard is to use a pencil or to dip the pen very frequently so as to make sure that it does not run dry. I remember on one occasion being horrified on coming to transcribe my notes to find nearly half a page blank! I had gone over the ground, following the speaker with a dry pen, and not a mark was to be seen except an occasional scratch from the pen's point. In the next place, should there be a pause in the lecture during the performance of an experiment, or for any other reason, the reporter may entirely forget where he left off, and when he begins to write may go over the ground that he has traveled before, and thus get an amalgamation of symbols that would puzzle a Champollion to decipher. To avoid this difficulty the reporter should in such cases keep his finger or thumb on the spot where he has left off, and take care to begin an inch or two lower down the page; or better still he may, *ex abundante cautela*, turn over and begin

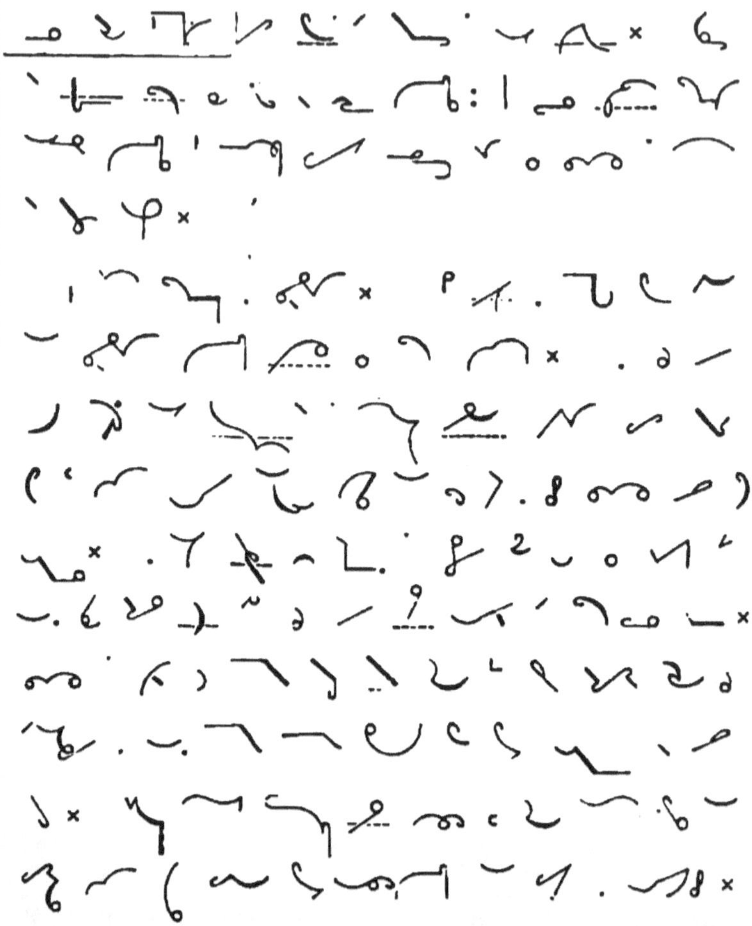

a new leaf. This kind of difficulty, however, is not confined to medical lectures: it occurs still more frequently in the case of lectures on chemistry, where the exclusion of light is sometimes a matter of absolute necessity.

But I am forgetting the hospital. As a rule the accommodation for writing in hospital lecture-rooms is very limited. The seats are usually arranged in the form of an amphitheatre, rising rapidly one above the other with little narrow inconvenient ledges, in front of which the students sometimes rest their note-books. The only possible mode of taking a satisfactory shorthand note is to write on the knee, which is not always easy, as the seats are high, narrow, and very close together. Sometimes a low seat can be obtained by sitting on a step between the ordinary seats, and in this way the knee can be kept sufficiently flat for the note-book to rest upon. I have had many a quarter of an hour's amusement when sitting in my place in one of these little theatres waiting for the commencement of the lecture, in watching the inrush of the students. It is hardly

considered "good form" for a medical student to walk in quietly, and take his seat as in an ordinary lecture-room. To witness a dozen or two young fellows come in together, climb the rails, jump over the seats, and scatter themselves about, might lead one to suppose that they were practising as members of an Alpine club. It is needless to say that there is any amount of banter and chaff going on during the interval preceding the lecture, which is occasionally enlivened by a romp or a scuffle between some of the more muscular and athletic members of the class, to whom I suppose some mode of occasionally letting off the steam is a necessity. I once saw a student, who was carrying in a plate a nice choice anatomical preparation which had just been removed from a corpse, chased about the place by three or four other students and finally captured; but what became of the prize I do not know. To one unaccustomed to hospital sights this sort of behaviour might seem to partake of undue levity, but it would be absurd to expect that young men full of life and spirits can be always moving about with solemn step and serious countenance while in the pur-

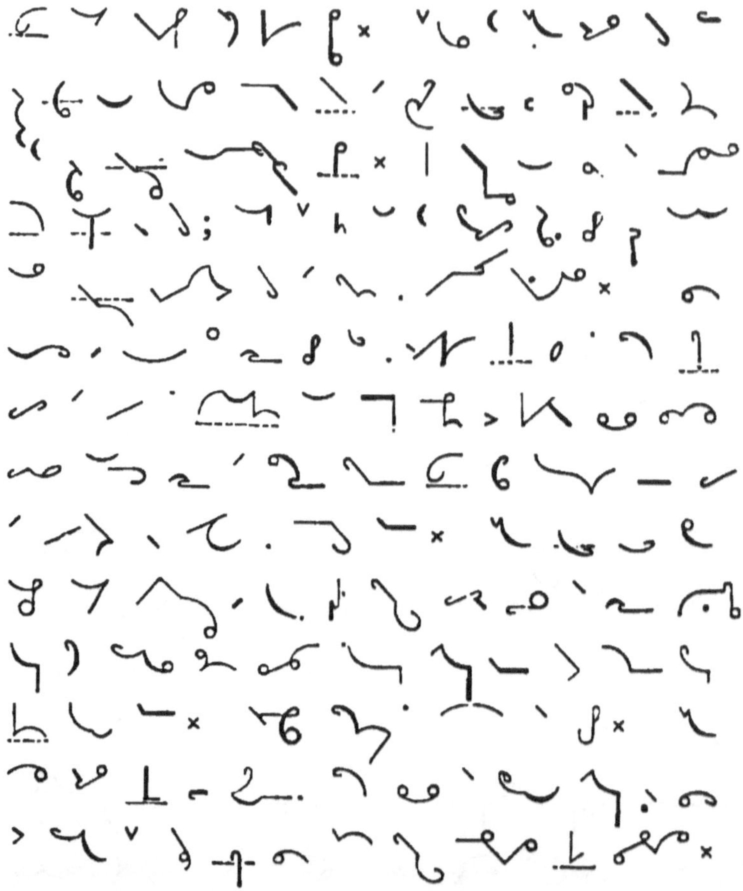

suit of their daily studies. I confess that I have always been glad to think that these young fellows can be happy and cheerful even when surrounded by so much that to others appears inexpressibly sad. It betokens no spirit of callousness or indifference to pain; indeed, I doubt not that everyone of these students would do anything in his power to relieve the pain and promote the recovery of the patients. Some young men who enter as medical students find the ordeal at first a very trying one, and are a long time in getting accustomed to the terrible scenes sometimes witnessed in connection with medical and surgical practice, while others fairly give way and are compelled to relinquish the occupation altogether. I have even known several instances in which reporters who having attended professionally one or two courses of medical lectures have had their nervous system seriously affected, and have had to give up the work for a time, if not altogether. Of course this is very much a matter of constitution. I have myself always had a great shrinking from scenes of suffering, and have had to summon all the nerve I possessed during some of my professional experience at the hospitals. In the course of a clinical lecture it

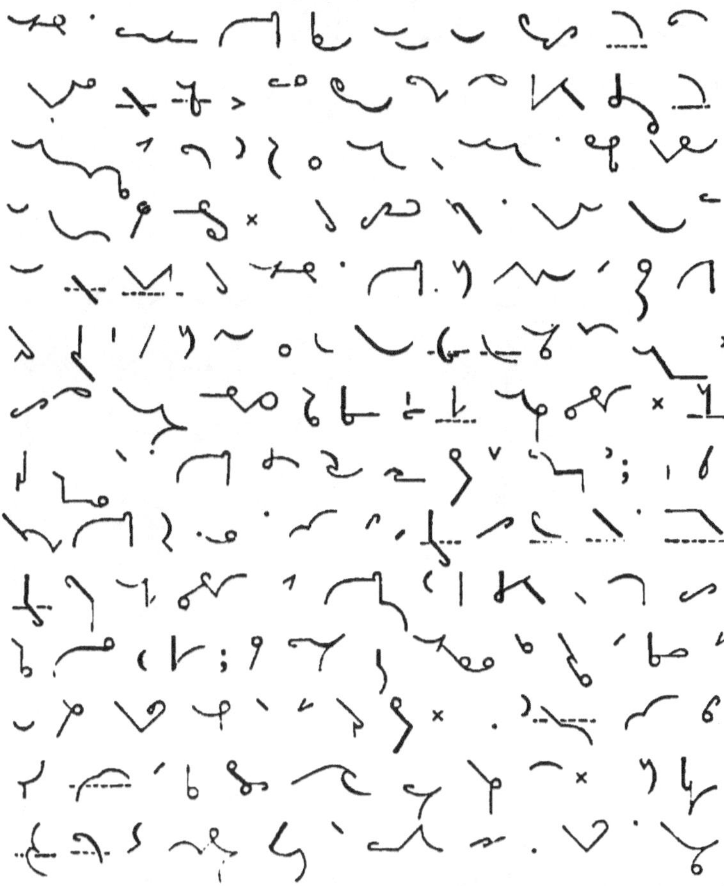

is no uncommon thing for one or more patients to be introduced to the class suffering from the most terrible disorders or infirmities, and the very sight of them is enough to unnerve a sensitive person not familiar with such exhibitions. Upon one occasion I remember a patient being called in to be operated upon in the course of a lecture I was reporting, and he was laid upon the table on which I was writing, his feet being within a few inches of my note-book. One of the most painful experiences of this description occurred at the University Hospital. I had attended to take notes of a lecture on some ordinary medical subject, I forget what; but just before the lecture was to commence a little child who had been run over by a cab, had been brought into the hospital, and the lecturer thought it desirable to amputate one of its legs without delay; he accordingly did so in the presence of his pupils, and discoursed on the nature of such operations instead of on the appointed subject. The sight of the poor little child's shattered limb and its subsequent removal nearly upset me. I was devoutly thankful, however, that the merciful agency of chloroform rendered the operation a painless one. I have seen much more severe opera-

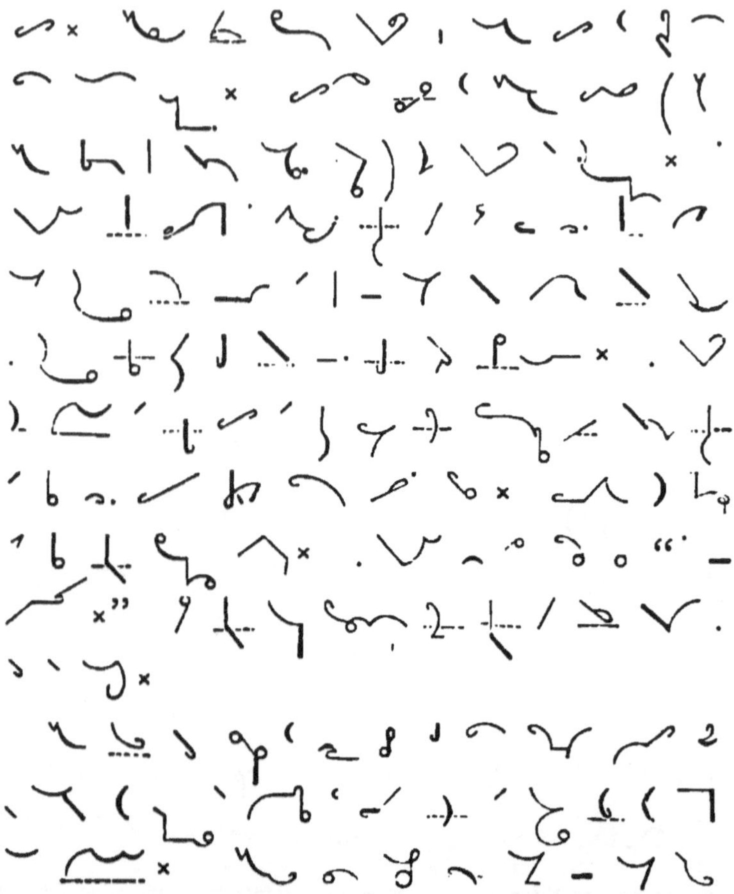

tions, but never one that troubled me more in my note-taking. One of the most serious that I have ever witnessed (I think I have described it before in these pages) was the operation of *æsophogotomy*. A patient had swallowed an artificial tooth, which, with the gold mounting had lodged in the esophagus or gullet, and it could only be removed by opening the esophagus itself, which was done by cutting down upon the side of the neck. The operation was a long and difficult one, and it was nearly three quarters of an hour before the tooth and its mounting were dislodged from their resting place. Chloroform was administered, and the dose had to be several times repeated. The patient made, as the phrase is, "a good recovery." He had to be fed for some time through a tube which passed below the point of incision.

I have often been surprised that medical students do not more frequently learn shorthand to enable them to take notes of lectures with greater ease and fulness than they can do in longhand. I have known some instances, however, in which a good knowledge of Phonography has proved of great

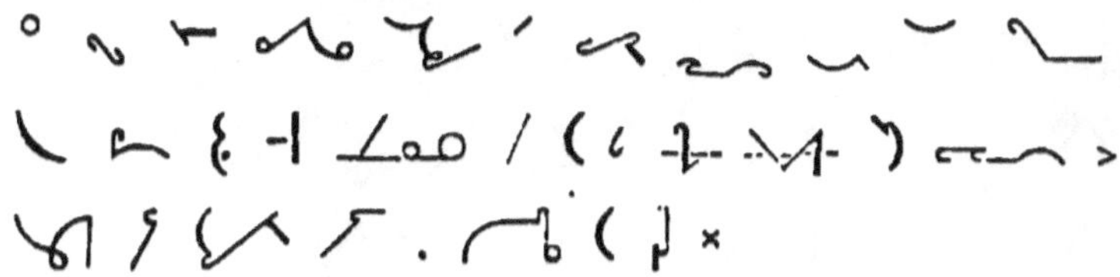

—:o:—

LORD CAMPBELL AS A REPORTER.

service in this way, and one or two medical men now in practice have told me that they owed much of the success which they achieved during the period of their curriculum to the facility with which they were able to record the lectures they attended.

The recently published life of Lord Campbell, edited by his daughter, reveals more of his early reporting experience than was previously known. As the work consists almost entirely of extracts from his own letters there can be no doubt as to the accuracy of the information conveyed. Lord Campbell was born in Cupar, Fife, in 1779, and was educated in the Grammar School of that town, and afterwards in the University of St Andrew's. He was a diligent student and an ardent reader of everything that came in his way. When about nineteen he went to London, and after fulfilling an engagement as a private tutor he became connected with the Press. He began by translating French works and occasionally writing reviews. His first allusion to reporting is in a letter to his father dated

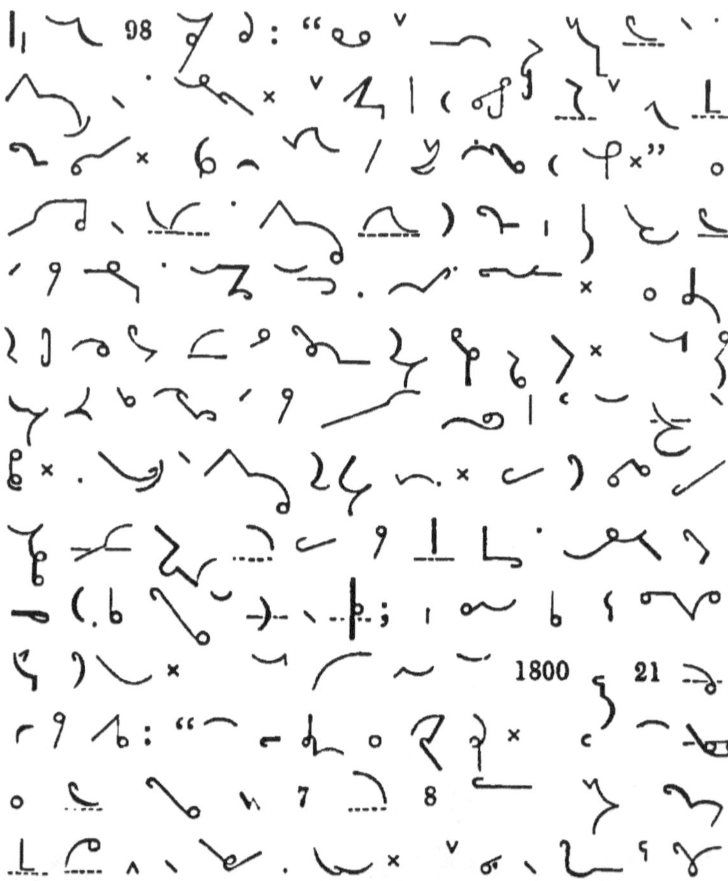

November, 1798, in which he says:—"Since I came to London I have had an offer of a reportership to a newspaper. I rejected it without hesitation, although I should have had a very good salary. This is a mode of life which I shall not embrace without necessity." His reluctance to follow a reporter's life was very great, but it was finally overcome, and he accepted an engagement in connection with the *Morning Chronicle*. His desire was to train himself for the law, and his Press work was only subsidiary to this object. Indeed, he was evidently ashamed of his employment and he rarely mentions it with any feeling of satisfaction. The companionship of reporters was not congenial to him. Whether their habits were in those days really objectionable, or whether he had taken an unreasonable prejudice against them, it is perhaps not easy to decide; but certain it is that he scrupulously avoided their company. In a letter written in 1800, when he was twenty-one years old, he writes:—"My great desideratum is eligible society. When my business is over, perhaps about seven or eight o'clock, I feel very much at a loss how to pass away the evening. I hate to drink with a parcel of dissipated reporters, and I hate to return to my

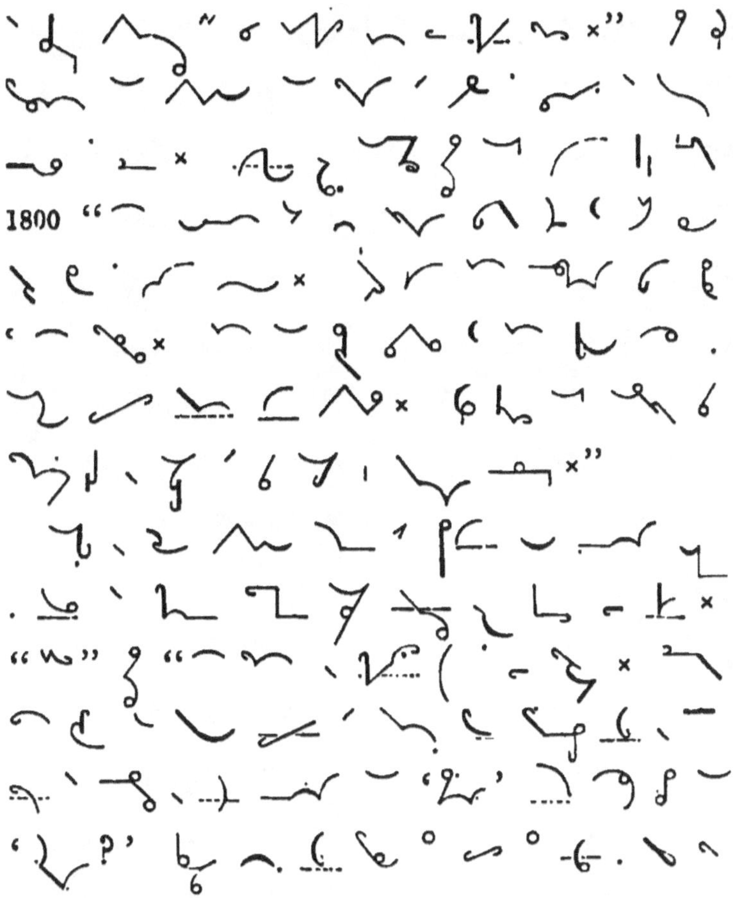

cold, dreary apartment." He assisted for some time in reporting in Parliament, and received a salary of four guineas a week. Alluding to these engagements he says in a letter dated October, 1800, "My income after the meeting of Parliament will be so great that I shall soon be able to save a little money. Upon the whole I am extremely well satisfied with my prospects. I am in considerable hopes that I may distinguish myself the ensuing winter by my law reports. This is a department in a newspaper which is very much attended to in London, and which is in general but poorly executed."

In addition to ordinary reporting work and the study of the law, young Campbell undertook the office of dramatic critic, in which he appears to have taken great delight. "I find," he says, "my freedom to Drury lane theatre a great privilege. What can be more delightful after being weary and poring over Blackstone, than to go free of expense to see Kemble in 'Hamlet' or Mrs Siddons in 'Isabella?' It is no less improving than pleasant, as one has thus the best opportunity of becoming acquainted

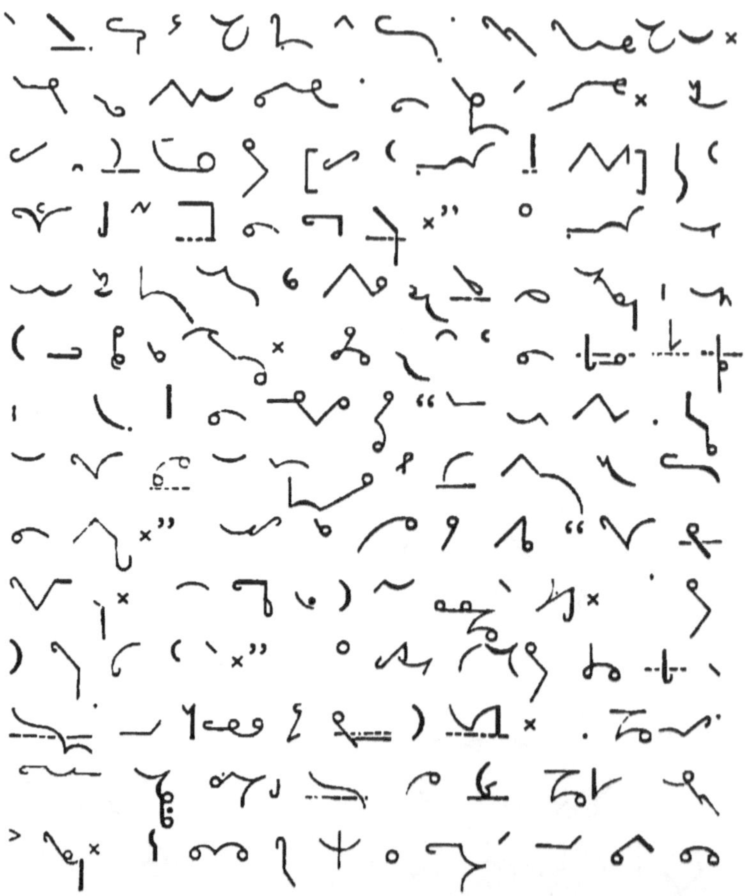

with the English drama, and of acquiring a proper pronunciation of the English language. I expect to find reporting henceforth a mere pastime and relaxation. I do not know whether you saw Fox's speech [one that Campbell had reported], it was thought very well done, and I got some credit by it." As Campbell knew nothing of shorthand it may be inferred that his reports would not have passed muster in the present day, but no doubt they gave satisfaction to his employers. He seems to have met with some difficulties at the outset, but, after having had some experience he says, "I can now report the debates in Parliament as well as any of my contemporaries, and as a law reporter I have acquired some reputation." In one of his letters he writes, "Parliament is to be prorogued to-day. My greatest feat was writing six columns of Sheridan. The speech was pretty well thought of." As we do not know the length of the speech it seems difficult to form an accurate idea of the closeness with which the speaker was followed. The columns of the *Morning Chronicle* in those days certainly contained far less than the columns of the daily newspaper of the present day. That he sometimes tripped, notwithstanding his careful

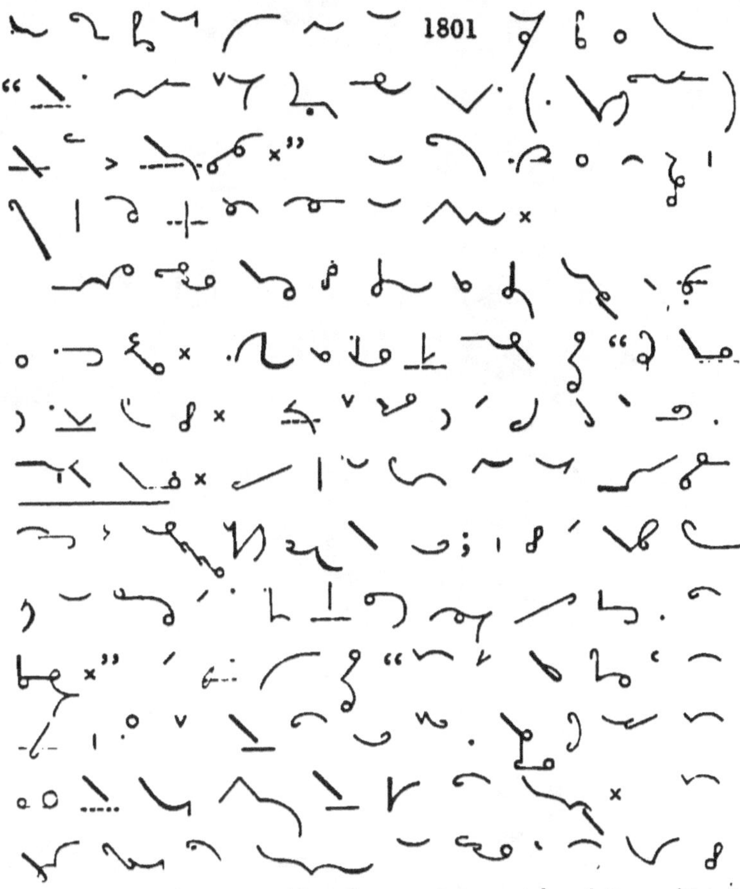

and accurate habit, seems evident from a statement in a letter written in 1801 in which he tells his father, "By a miracle I only escaped causing Perry (the publisher of the *Chronicle*) to be called to the bar of the House of Lords." No further allusion is made to this circumstance, but probably it arose out of some mistake in reporting.

Campbell's correspondence bears constant testimony to his desire if possible to conceal his connection with the Press. Alluding to his attendance at the King's Bench he says, "There is a box set apart for students. Here I always sit and shun upon all occasions the *ignobile pecus*. Were it not for my writing in the gallery of the House of Commons my connection with the newspaper press I daresay would never be known; but students and barristers flock hither in scores, and an attempt at secrecy must only render detection the more disgraceful." And still later he says, "I am on the best terms with my chief, but as I become more known I find the obstacles thrown in the way of my success by being a reporter become daily more formidable. I am absolutely prevented from forming any acquaintance with my fellow students, and I am constantly in a terror

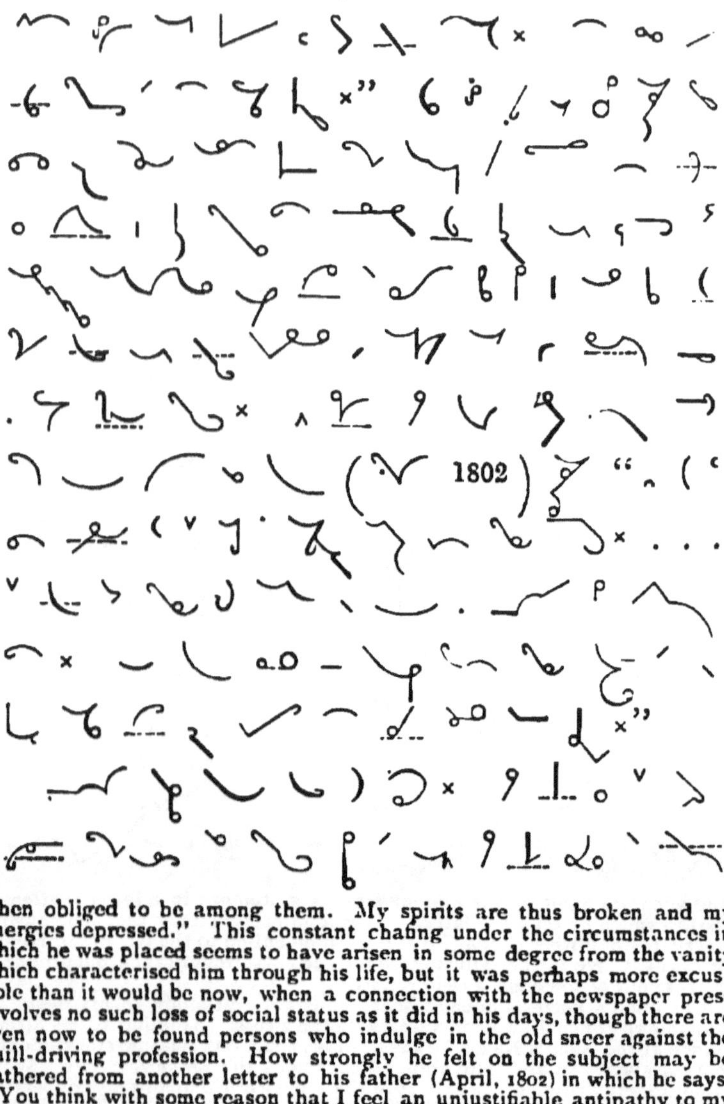

when obliged to be among them. My spirits are thus broken and my energies depressed." This constant chafing under the circumstances in which he was placed seems to have arisen in some degree from the vanity which characterised him through his life, but it was perhaps more excusable than it would be now, when a connection with the newspaper press involves no such loss of social status as it did in his days, though there are even now to be found persons who indulge in the old sneer against the quill-driving profession. How strongly he felt on the subject may be gathered from another letter to his father (April, 1802) in which he says, "You think with some reason that I feel an unjustifiable antipathy to my present occupation. . . . . . . I vow after the present session never to enter the gallery as a reporter more. No future success could compensate for my present feelings, and to continue in this line would be to render my chance of success altogether desperate."

Campbell, besides being vain, was ambitious. He had his eye upon the woolsack from the commencement of his professional studies, and no doubt he had the consciousness of power which belongs to all true genius.

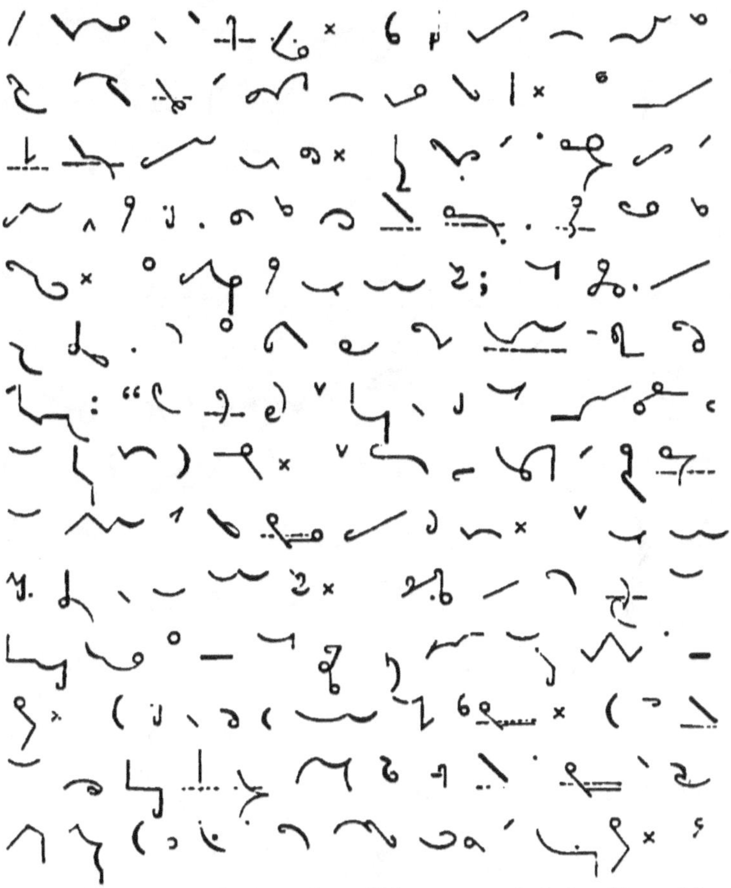

This tended to render him impatient of his comparatively humble position, and stimulated him to rise above it. With his career at the bar we are not now concerned. It was a brilliant and a successful one, and we know how he attained the summit of his ambition by securing the highest honors of his profession. As we have said, he knew nothing of shorthand; indeed he seems rather to have despised the art as will be seen from the following extract from his autobiography:—"For three sessions I continued to attend in the gallery of the House of Commons when any debate of importance was expected. I acquired great facility and considerable skill in reporting, and the best speakers were assigned to me. I knew nothing, and I did not desire to know anything, of shorthand. Shorthand writers are very useful in taking down evidence as given in a court of justice, but they are wholly incompetent to report a good speech. They attend to words without entering into the thoughts of the speaker. They cannot by any means take down at full length all that is uttered by a speaker of ordinary rapidity, and if they did, they would convey a very imperfect notion of the spirit and effect of the speech. With the exception of Pitt

the younger, there probably never was a parliamentary debater in whose language there was not some inaccuracy, and who did not fall into occasional repetitioms. These are hardly perceived in the rapid stream of extemporaneous eloquence, and are corrected and remedied by the voice, the eye, the action of him to whom we listen; but blazoned on a printed page which we are deliberately to peruse, they would offend and perplex us. If Pitt could have been taken down *verbatim*, all his sentences, however long and involved, would have been found complete and grammatical, and the whole oration methodical and finished, but it would have been sometimes stiff and cumbrous and vapid, although, animated by his delivery, it has electrified the House. Nay, if he himself had written it for publication, it would probably have been much altered. No man knew better the difference between what is permitted in speaking and in writing. . . . . To have a good report of a speech, the reporter must thoroughly understand the subject discussed, and be qualified to follow the reasoning, to feel the pathos, and relish the wit, and to be warmed by the eloquence of the speaker. He must apprehend the whole scope of the

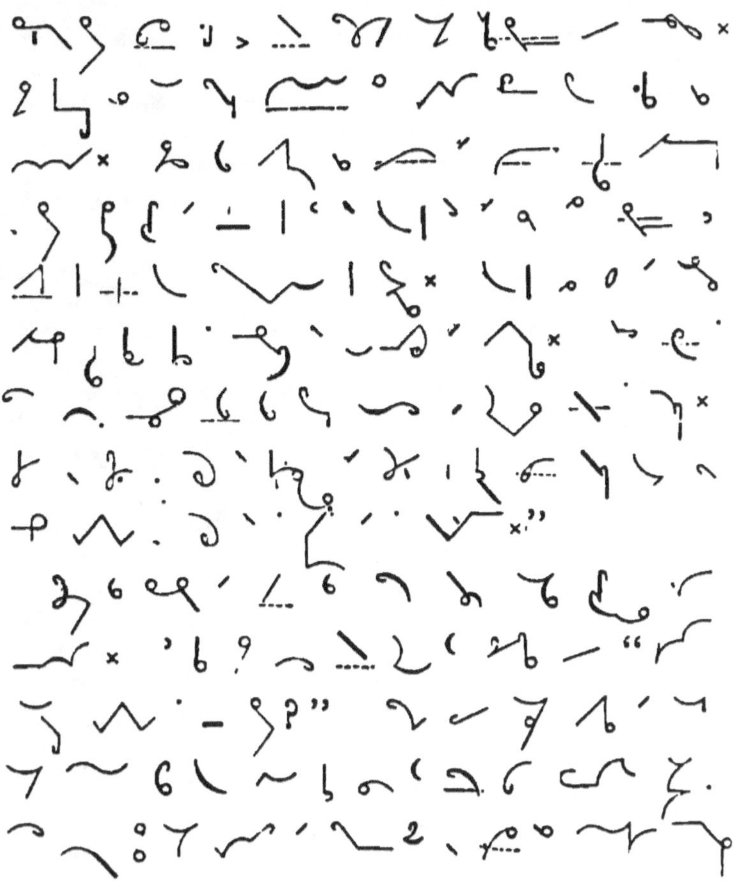

speech, as well as attend to the happy phraseology in which the ideas of the speaker are expressed. He should take down notes in abbreviated longhand as rapidly as he can for aids to his memory. He must then retire to his room, and, looking at these, recollect the speech as it was delivered, and give it with all fidelity, point and spirit, as the speaker would write it out if preparing it for the press. Fidelity is the first and indispensable requisite, but this does not demand an exposure of inaccuracies and repetitions. I cannot conceive a more improving exercise than this for a young man who aspires to be an orator. It is well to translate the orations of Demosthenes and Cicero; but it would be still better, if the opportunity existed, to report the orations of a Chatham and a Burke."

There is much that is sensible and much that is very absurd in this deliverance of Lord Campbell. What does he mean by saying that shorthand writers are "wholly incompetent to report a good speech?" From the way in which he writes, and indeed in which many others have written, it would seem that however well qualified, intellectually, a man may be, he has only to learn and practise shorthand to lose all his mental capacity

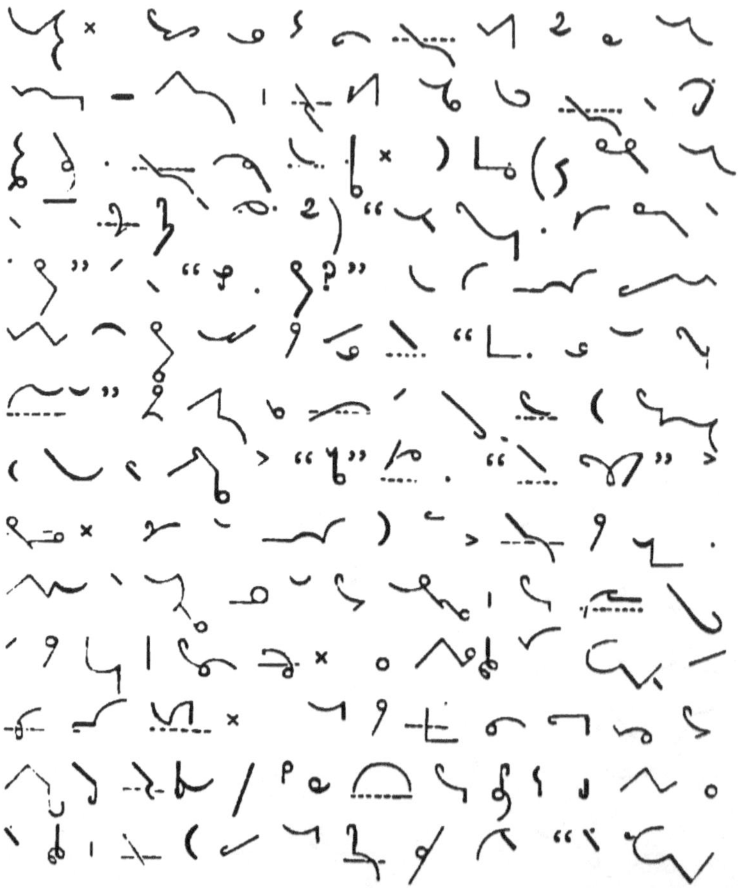

forthwith. Everyone knows that the mere power to write shorthand is not enough to make a good reporter, but people who write in this fashion appear to imagine that those who possess the power must be half idiots. Was Dickens (who was sensible enough to go through the drudgery of mastering shorthand) "unable to apprehend the whole scope of a speech," and to "understand the subject?" If Lord Camphell were now to report important speeches in the way he recommends, by "taking notes in abbreviated longhand," he might retire to his room and ponder over them for a month without being able to reproduce all the "ideas" much less the "happy phraseology" of the speakers. Shortly after Campbell was called to the Bar he undertook the reporting of *nisi prius* cases, not for the newspapers, but for a legal publication, and he continued it for some years. His reports of the decisions of Lord Ellenborough are still greatly valued. Indeed he took some credit to himself for the reputation obtained by that distinguished judge as a sound lawyer, for he tells us that he did not report his bad decisions, but put them away in a drawer which he labelled "Bad Ellenborough Law." We imagine, however, that few reporters

—:o:—

SPEAKING AND SPEAKERS.

FROM A SHORTHAND WRITER'S POINT OF VIEW.

The sign for *he* having been changed from  to (as a single word) while this book was in the printers' hands (see *Phonetic Journal*, page 430), the latter and briefer sign will in future be used.

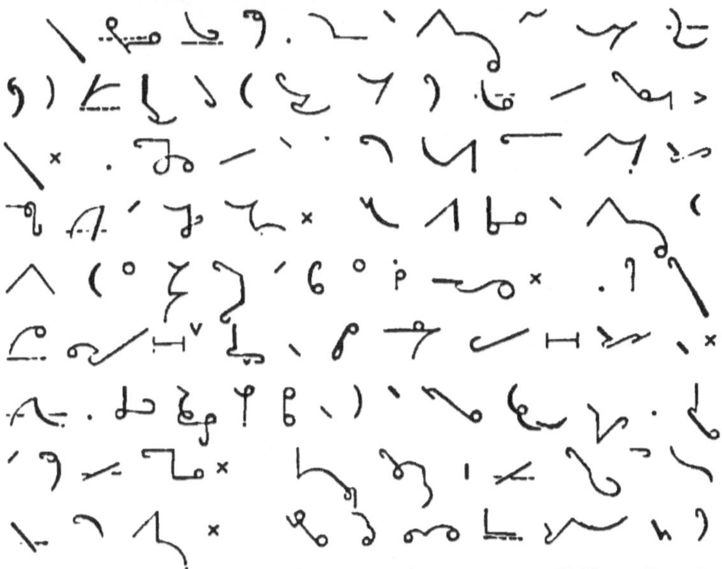

would now take upon themselves so serious a responsibility. But then Campbell was not an ordinary reporter.

Public speakers often criticise the work of reporters, and not unnaturally, seeing that they are so largely dependent upon them for the manner in which their views are presented to the public. The criticisms are of a very varied character, ranging between extravagant eulogy and undeserved anathema. I have read descriptions of reporters that represented them as intellectual prodigies, and others as conceited ignoramuses. The truth probably lies somewhere—I decline to suggest exactly where—between the two. Leaving the discussion of this question, interesting as it is to us all, I propose this evening to turn the tables, and criticise our critics. It may be considered presumptuous, but our profession cannot afford to be very retiring. I suppose artists sometimes talk to one another about their

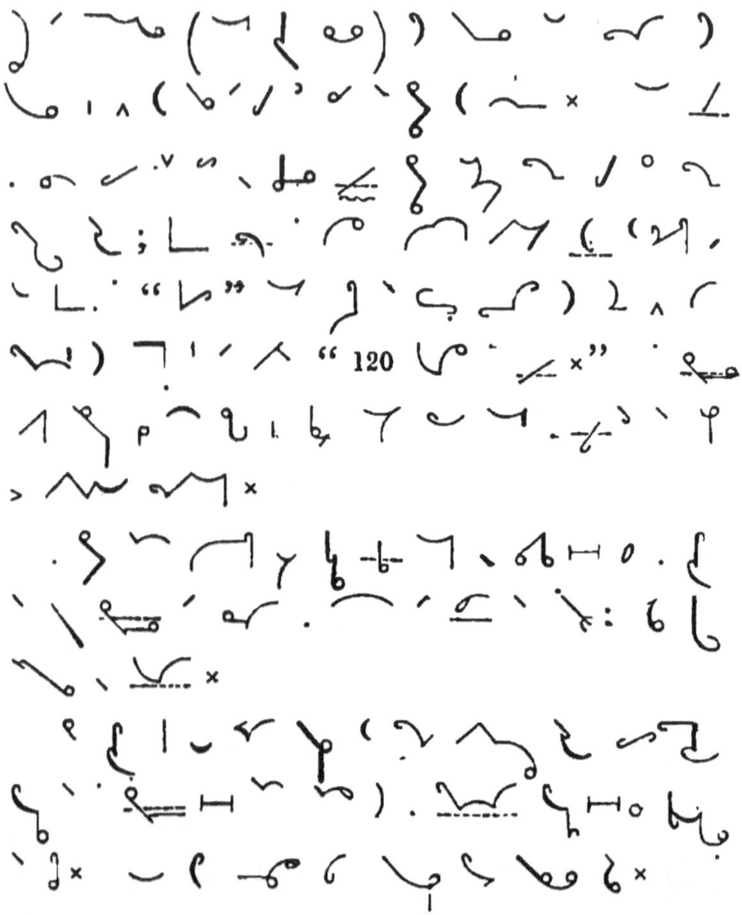

sitters, and canvass (in a double sense) their peculiarities, not merely their features, but how they pose, and generally what sort of subjects they make. In much the same way, I want to discuss *our* subjects, not so much from a general as from a professional point of view; taking, however, a less limited range than that of the shorthand writer who, after taking a "turn" in the trial of Queen Caroline, was asked how Lord Brougham was getting on, and replied, "A hundred and twenty folios an hour." A speaker's rate of speed is an important consideration, but it is not the only nor indeed the chief point of interest to the reporting fraternity.

The subject of my lecture naturally divides itself into two heads—first, the delivery of public speakers; and secondly, the matter and style of composition: and this division I propose to follow.

As to delivery, it need hardly be said that, from the reporter's point of view, one of the cardinal virtues of a speaker—I might almost say the primal virtue—is distinctness of utterance. No other excellence will compensate for the absence of this. A speaker may be slow and deliber-

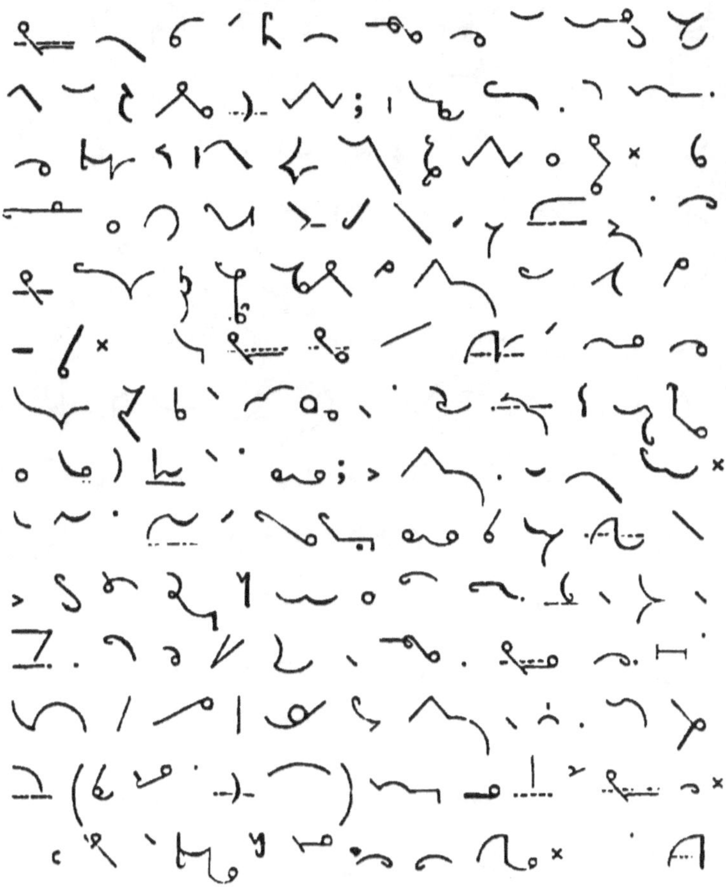

ate, may express himself in unexceptional English, and be in all other respects easy to report; but if he has not acquired the art of making himself distinctly heard, he will be assuredly unpopular with those who have to report his speeches. This characteristic is also appreciated by the general public, who naturally like to hear a man speak clearly, but they are not so fastidious in this respect as the reporter, nor are they such good judges. If a speaker speaks rather loudly, and makes himself fairly intelligible, it is of little consequence to an ordinary hearer that he now and then drops his voice, say at the end of a sentence; to the reporter the end may be everything. After writing a long and perhaps complicated sentence, which is evidently leading up to the completion of some suspended idea, nothing is more aggravating than to fail to catch the very words which are essential to express the speaker's meaning—a failure which renders it necessary for the reporter to omit the entire passage, or (which is not always an easy matter) to make a guess at what the speaker meant.

When I speak of distinctness I do not, of course, mean mere loudness.

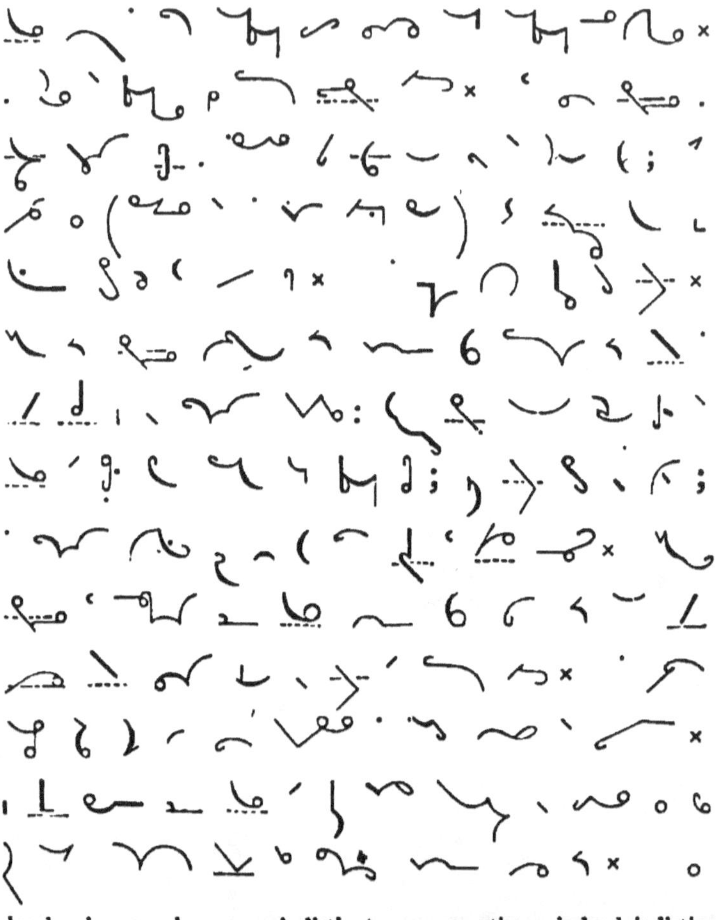

A loud voice may be a very indistinct one, sometimes indeed indistinct because of the loudness. The essence of distinctness is a clear, crisp articulation. With some speakers the vowels absolutely drown the consonants, which have thus no opportunity of asserting themselves; and the result is (as in the case of a badly articulated song) that the hearers have but a vague conception of the words that are uttered. A good deal also depends upon pitch. I have heard speakers laboring hard to make themselves clearly heard by a large audience, but to very little purpose: they have been speaking in their ordinary tone of voice, and straining every nerve after a distinct utterance; but their pitch has been too low; a very little elevation would have made them more audible with much less exertion. I have known speakers with extremely weak voices make themselves well heard in large rooms by simply attending to pitch and clear articulation. A remarkable instance of this was the late Mr Parsons, an Independent minister of York. He had a singularly weak voice, and it was almost painful to witness his efforts, especially in the earlier part of

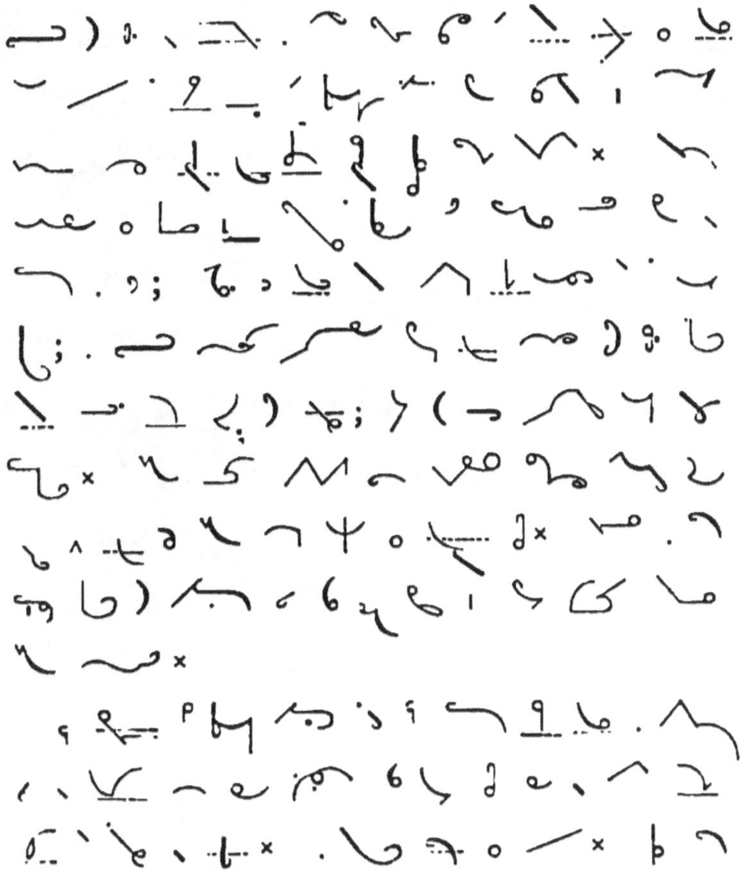

his sermon, to make himself heard. His congregation was trained to keep the most perfect silence, and by pitching his voice in rather a high key, and distinctly articulating every syllable, he managed to make himself audible even at some considerable distance from the pulpit. Before announcing his text, he would give perhaps a dozen short nervous coughs, as if to clear the throat; and these would often be repeated at the commencement of a new division; the congregation, meanwhile, relaxing for a few moments their own strained attention by coughing or shifting their position; after which they again relapsed into absolute quietness. I have occasionally reported Mr Parsons's sermons, and have been astonished to find how few words I have omitted, notwithstanding his feeble utterance. Of course the very closest attention was required, yet this would not have sufficed but for the elocutionary peculiarities I have mentioned.

When a speaker has a distinct articulation combined with a clear strong voice, the reporter who has to follow him is in Elysium, that is, if the utterance is not too rapid, or the style of composition too difficult. The combination, however, is rare. It has a very striking example in Mr

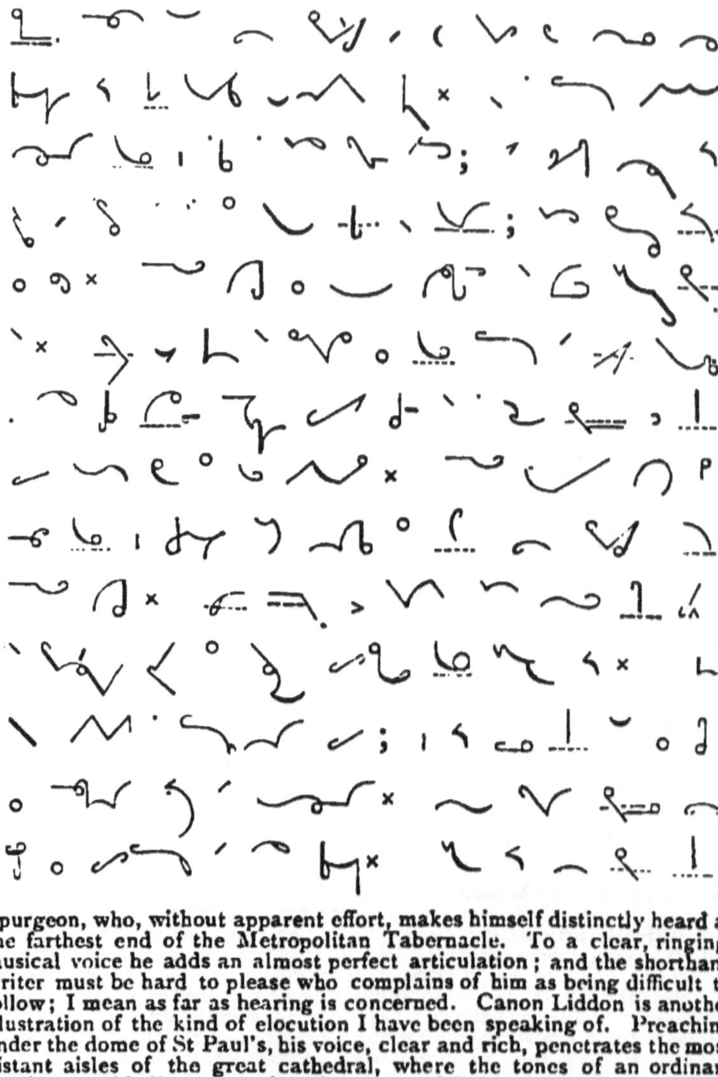

Spurgeon, who, without apparent effort, makes himself distinctly heard at the farthest end of the Metropolitan Tabernacle. To a clear, ringing, musical voice he adds an almost perfect articulation; and the shorthand writer must be hard to please who complains of him as being difficult to follow; I mean as far as hearing is concerned. Canon Liddon is another illustration of the kind of elocution I have been speaking of. Preaching under the dome of St Paul's, his voice, clear and rich, penetrates the most distant aisles of the great cathedral, where the tones of an ordinary speaker would die away unheard, save as faint reverberations. Canon Farrar also has an excellent voice, but it is certainly not so melodious as either Mr Spurgeon's or Canon Liddon's. Still keeping to the pulpit, I may mention Dr Chown, of Bloomsbury Chapel, as possessing one of the strongest voices I have ever heard. He might be reported a quarter of a mile away; but heard close at hand his utterance is extremely harsh and unmusical. Among parliamentary speakers Mr Gladstone is one of the clearest and most distinct. I have heard him speak at open-air meetings

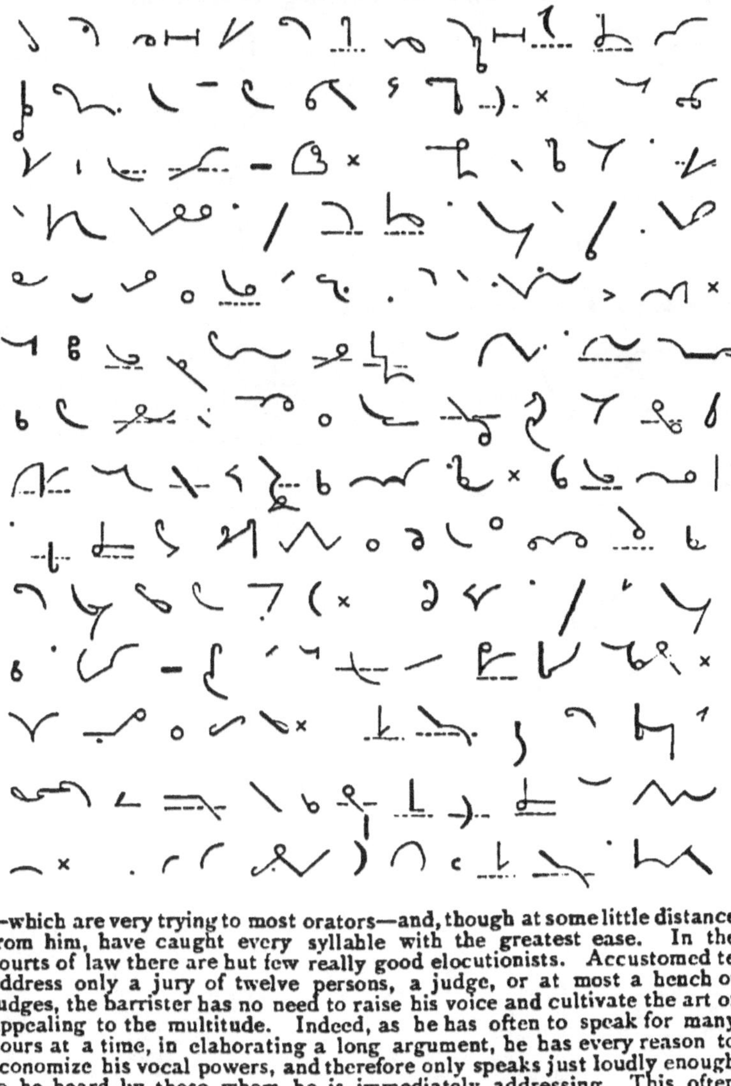

—which are very trying to most orators—and, though at some little distance from him, have caught every syllable with the greatest ease. In the courts of law there are but few really good elocutionists. Accustomed to address only a jury of twelve persons, a judge, or at most a bench of judges, the barrister has no need to raise his voice and cultivate the art of appealing to the multitude. Indeed, as he has often to speak for many hours at a time, in elaborating a long argument, he has every reason to economize his vocal powers, and therefore only speaks just loudly enough to be heard by those whom he is immediately addressing. This often makes it a difficult task for the shorthand writer to report his words, if, as sometimes happens, he is not very conveniently placed for catching them. There is hardly a judge on the bench who has a thoroughly good delivery, and not a few are sadly deficient in this respect. Earl Cairns is one of the best. At the bar he was very distinct, and the stenographer who could keep up to his speed had an easy task in reporting him. The late Lord Westbury was also, when at the bar, an admirably clear and precise

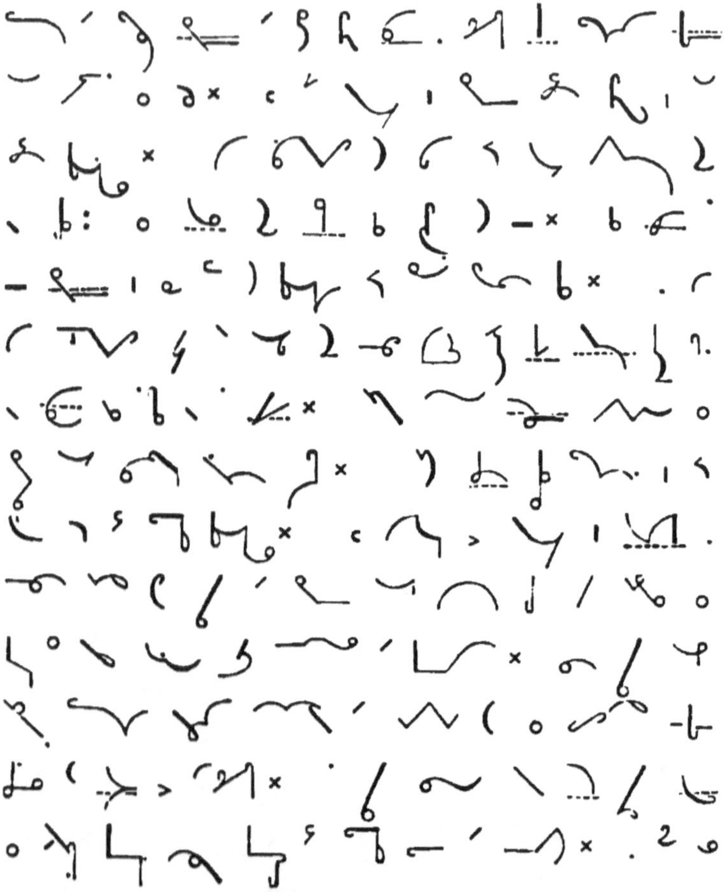

speaker, and as he was deliberate as well, the shorthand writer had very little difficulty in recording his words. When on the bench he spoke with the same deliberation, but not with the same distinctness. Lord Selborne was well heard if the reporter was not too distant; his voice was not strong, but his delivery was good. He is still a good speaker, but is not quite so distinctly heard as in former days. The late Lord Cockburn, Chief Justice of England, was an excellent elocutionist, and when he was at the bar it was a treat to listen to his address to a jury. I remember, many years ago, reporting his speeches in the celebrated Palmer trial. I was at some distance from him, but heard every word with the greatest distinctness. When elevated to the bench he followed the example of most other judges, and spoke in a lower tone, which I suppose is adopted as best fitting judicial calmness and decorum. Some judges, instead of speaking clearly, absolutely mumble, and to report them is one of the most difficult tasks that fall to the lot of the shorthand writer. A judge's summing-up or judgment, even his *obiter dicta*, must be taken down with the greatest care and accuracy. The shorthand notes are often

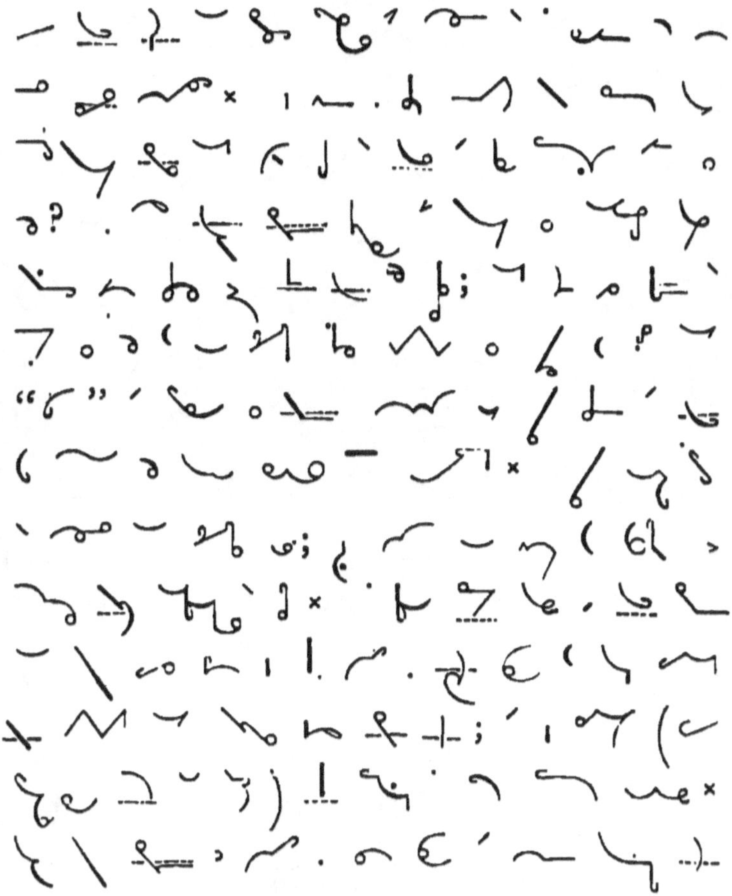

cited in subsequent proceedings, and the mistake of a single word may cause serious embarassment. But how can the desired accuracy be secured if the occupant of the bench speaks in a low tone of voice, and does not clearly articulate his words? The most feeble speaker at present on the Bench is unquestionably Vice-Chancellor Bacon, whom it is impossible to hear at a few yards' distance; indeed, so great is the difficulty of catching his words that no shorthand writer attempts to report his judgments without standing in the "well," and placing his book immediately under the judge's desk, and even then many words, if not sentences, go unrecorded. Judges now and then complain of mistakes in shorthand writers' notes; but they little know how much they themselves contribute to the errors by their indistinctness of utterance. A distinguished Scotch physician, who often spoke in public, once told me he had learned the useful lesson that if he wanted to be reported in the papers he must speak out; and he certainly (whether for this reason or not I cannot say) had cultivated a very clear enunciation. If every public speaker would learn

the same lesson, and make effective use of his vocal organs, our labors would be materially lightened, and our tempers less sorely tried.

I have at times been astonished to observe how far a good voice will travel, and how well it may be heard at a great distance. I was once walking, on a calm summer's evening, between some pleasant hedgerows in Norfolk, and was surprised to hear the tones of a human voice, but could not tell whence they came. I listened attentively, and caught distinctly some words of a sermon, which was evidently being preached, I knew not where, in the open air. I took out a note-book, and wrote several complete sentences; and I question whether (the telephone apart) a speaker had ever before been reported at the distance. I learned on the following morning that the sermon had been preached by one of Mr Spurgeon's students, at a village nearly a mile, in a straight line, from the point at which I stood. Not far from the same spot, standing outside a country church, I once reported part of a sermon on a stone in the porch wall; and for ought I know my notes are there still; I certainly saw them there a

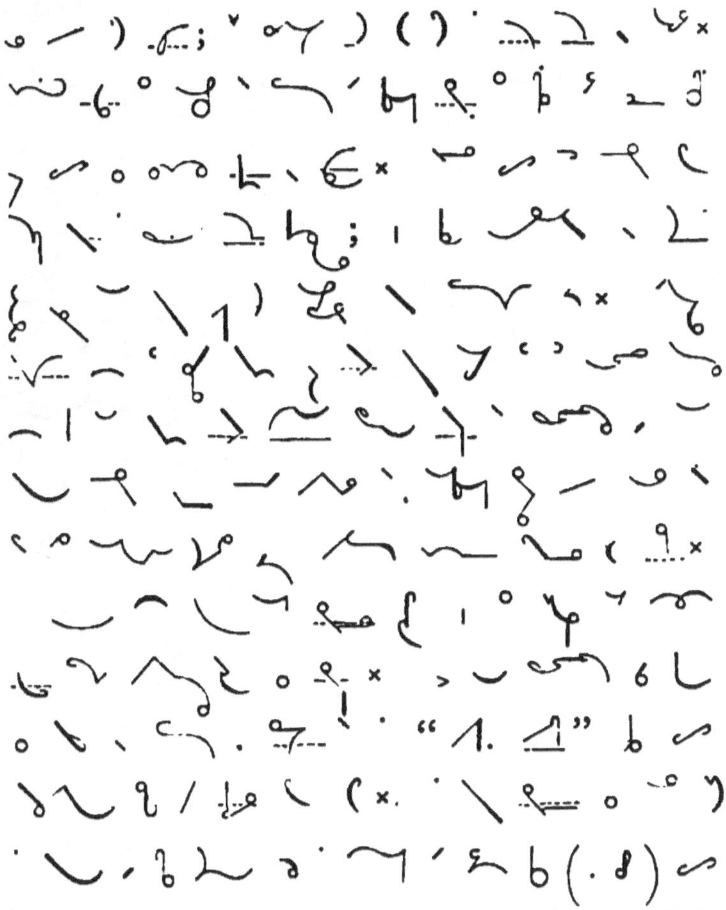

year or two afterwards. I mention these as instances of clear and distinct speaking as contrasted with the weak utterances to which one is sometimes doomed to listen. Of course one cannot expect every orator to be a Stentor or a Demosthenes; but it is not unreasonable to ask that those who have to speak in public should do so in such a manner as to be clearly heard. And if this appeal may with justice be made to them by the public in general, with what increased force may it not be made by the long-suffering body of stenographers who, in being expected to give accurate reports of indistinct speeches, are in as bad plight as the unfortunate Israelites who were required to make bricks without straw?

Another important feature in a speaker's delivery, but, as I have said, not the most important, even from the reporter's point of view, is speed. To the young stenographer, who is doing his best to acquire the skill of a "ready writer," it is the one absorbing consideration which outweighs every other. A public speaker is, in his eyes, a being who utters so many words a minute, and with whom it is his (the student's) one ambition to

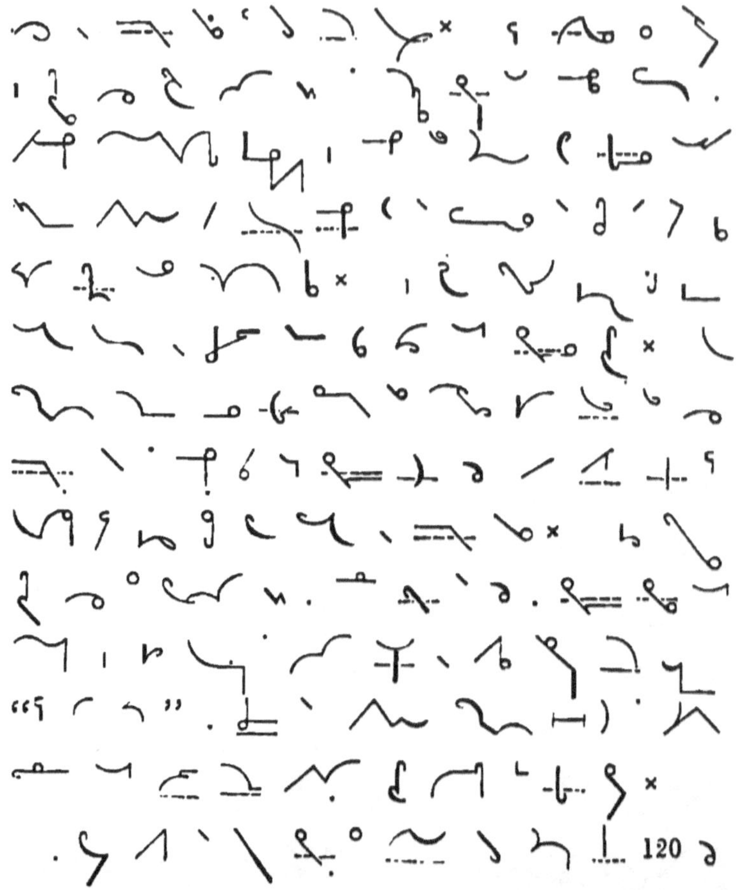

keep pace with pen or pencil. When he leaves his pupilage, he troubles himself comparatively little about an orator's speed, not because he has acquired the requisite manipulative dexterity, but because he finds so many other difficulties in the way of practical reporting which far exceed that of quickness of utterance, and of which he has hardly dreamed in his earlier days. But whatever proficiency he may have attained he can never afford to disregard altogether this element in a speaker's delivery. If verbatim work comes within the scope of his employment he will often find himself keeping up an exciting chase after a speaker whose words are rattled out with a velocity with which he must strain every nerve to keep pace. He may not perhaps trouble himself, as formerly, about the exact number of words the speaker speaks in a minute, but he will not affect a lordly indifference to rates of speed, or undertake "with a light heart" the task of reporting verbatim—say a sharp cross-examination in a law-court, or a rapidly delivered lecture on a difficult subject.

The average rate of public speaking has long been estimated at 120 words

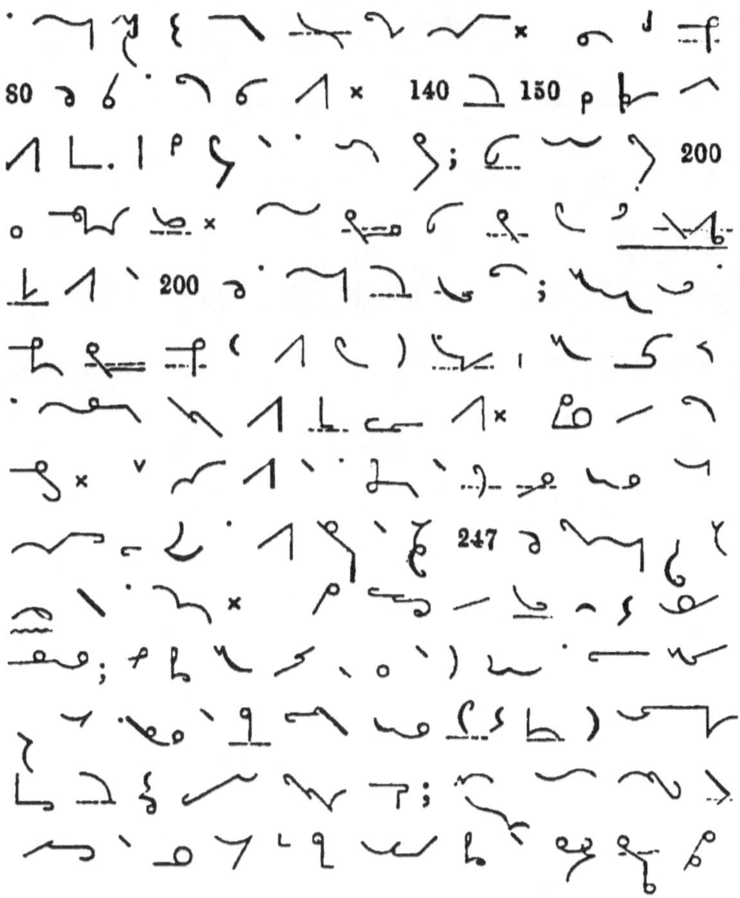

a minute, and I do not think that that can be far from the mark. Some do not exceed 80 words, which is a very slow rate. 140 or 150 is a decidedly rapid rate, taking it as an average of an entire speech; while anything approaching 200 is extremely fast. Many speakers will speak for *short periods* at the rate of 200 words a minute, or even more; I have never known an extempore speaker exceed that rate for say half an hour, but I have occasionally heard a manuscript paper read at a quicker rate. Such cases are very exceptional. I lately read of a transcript of three hours' evidence in an American court showing a rate of speed of not less than 247 words per minute, but this, I think, *must* be an error. Such calculations are often made without the necessary exactness; and, as the statement I have referred to is of so astounding a character, I venture to think, in the absence of strong corroborative evidence, either that the time was incorrectly taken, or that the words were not properly counted; and I am confirmed in my impression by the recollection of cases in which, on a strict inquiry, statements of sensational speeds, such as the one I have

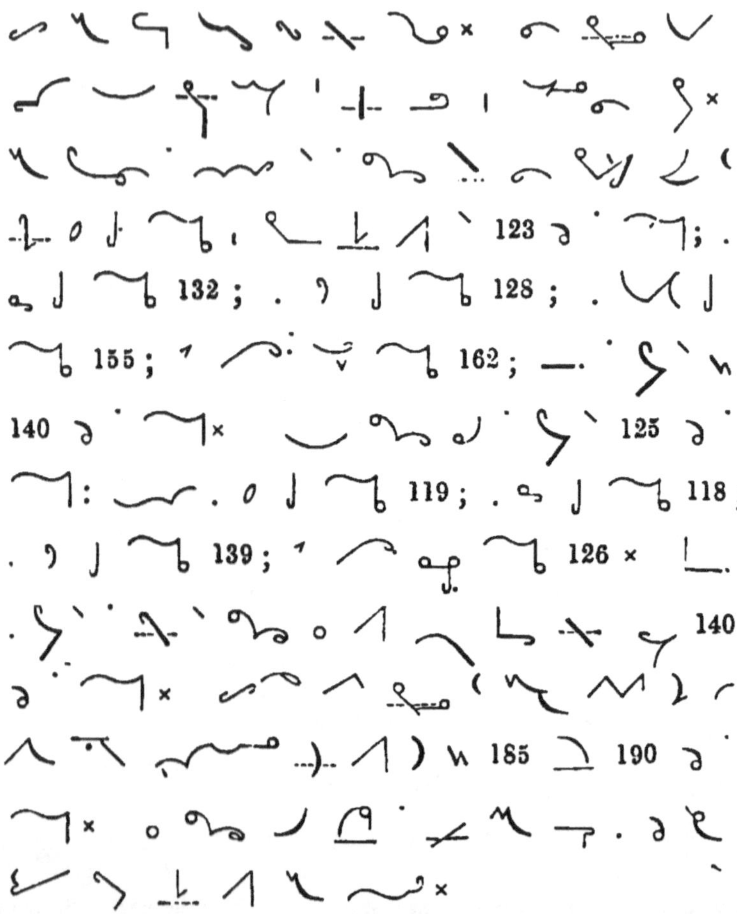

quoted, have been proved to be erroneous. Some speakers vary greatly in their speed, not only on different occasions, but in the course of the same speech. I have, for example, a memorandum of a sermon by Mr Spurgeon, showing that during the first ten minutes he spoke at the rate of 123 words a minute; the second ten minutes, 132; the third ten minutes, 128; the fourth ten minutes, 155; and the remaining nine minutes, 162; giving an average of about 140 words a minute. Another sermon shows an average of 125 words a minute: namely, the first ten minutes, 119; the second ten minutes, 118; the third ten minutes, 139; and the remaining sixteen minutes, 126. Taking the average of a number of sermons his rate may be taken to be nearly 140 words a minute. One of the most rapid speakers that I have ever reported was the late Rev. Capel Molyneux, whose rate was about 185 or 190 words a minute. His sermons usually lasted an hour, and I have counted the words of several that were preached at the rate I have mentioned.

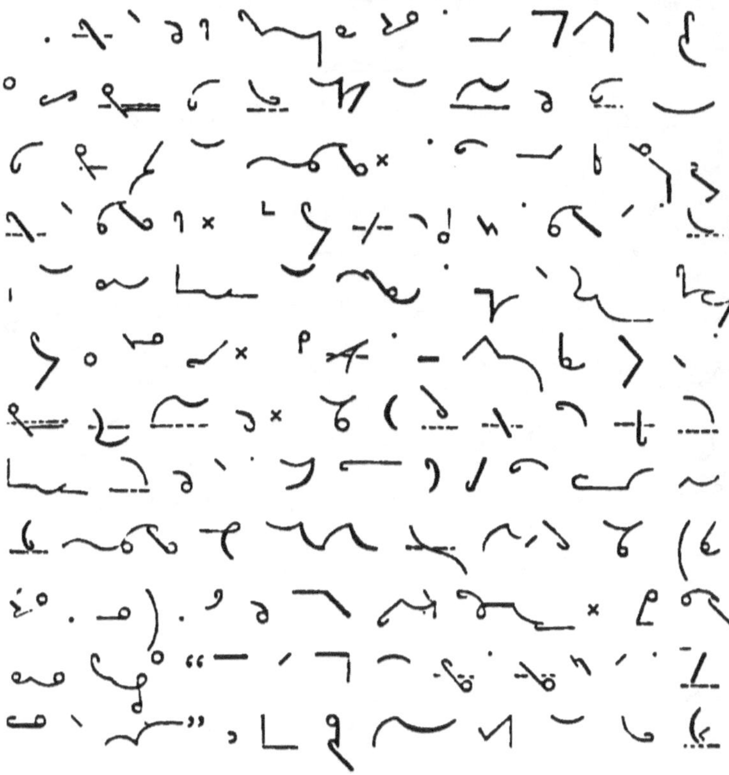

The number of words uttered per minute is not always an accurate gauge of the rapidity of delivery, as one speaker will often indulge in long words while another will speak chiefly in monosyllables. A more accurate test of speed would be the number of syllables uttered. On an average, each word contains about a syllable and a half; but in certain technical language, embracing a good deal of scientific terminology, the average is of course greater. As a rule a good reporter does not object to a speaker using long words. Unless they happen to be very difficult or technical, or words of an unusual character, they are generally more quickly written than monosyllables, because they involve fewer liftings of the pen, unless (which is not always the case) the short words can be united phraseographically. Such a simple sentence, for example, as "Go and get me, please, a piece of bread and a large glass of milk," would take considerably longer to write in Phonography than the words, "Extraordinary manifestation of enthusiasm." Each sentence contains the same number of syllables, but in the first sentence the monosyllabic words do not admit of being

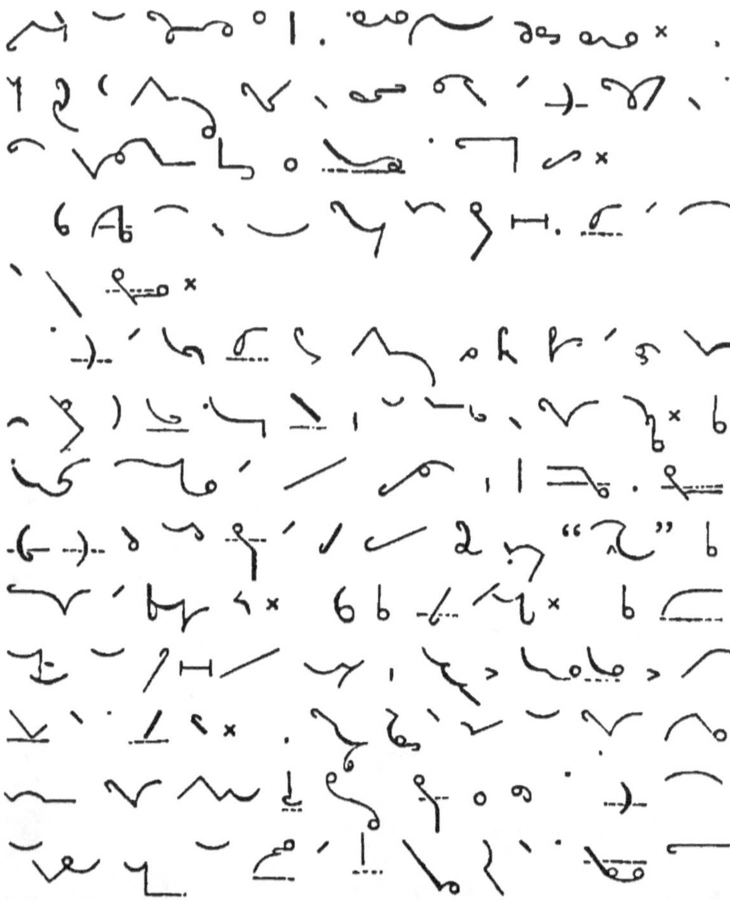

united in phraseograms as do the consonants of the longer words of the second sentence. The idea, therefore, that reporters prefer to stenograph simple and easy phraseology to a more polysyllabic diction is by no means a correct one.

This leads me to another branch of my subject—the style and matter of public speakers.

An easy and favorite style for the reporter is the deliberate, stately, and somewhat pompous mode of speech so often affected by, but not altogether confined to, parliamentary orators. It is conventional, monotonous, and rather wearisome, but it keeps the speaker within easy bounds in point of speed, and generally, where there is not too much "mouthing," it is clearly and distinctly heard. This is its chief recommendation. It is like intoning in church—rather unnatural, but favorable to the conveyance of the voice to the remotest part of a large building. The prevalence of this kind of oratory in Parliament helps to make parliamentary reporting, at any rate as far as speed is concerned, an easy matter in comparison with note-taking in law-courts and at public meetings, especially of a business character,

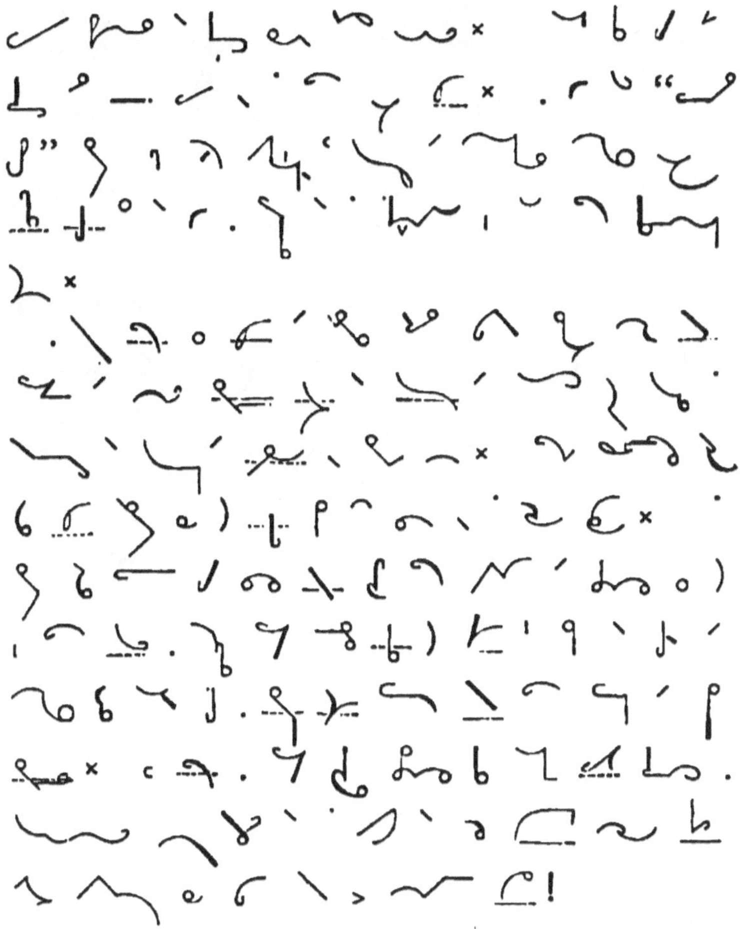

where stateliness of diction is now almost unknown. Indeed it is generally on the decline, and is giving way to a more natural style. The old fashioned "glorious constitution" speech, uttered *ore rotundo*, with forced and monotonous emphasis, no longer draws down, as of old, the plaudits of an admiring but not very discriminating assembly.

The public, however, is still, and I suppose always will be, strongly moved by the energetic and impassioned speaker, full of fire and animation, especially if he has a backbone of fact and reason to support him. From the stenographer's point of view this style of speech is not so difficult as it might seem to an ordinary listener. A speech of this character generally seems to be delivered very rapidly, and it sometimes is so, but more often the orator's energy expends itself so largely on strength of tone and emphasis that he is unable to attain the speed easily acquired by more quiet and steady speakers. When, however, the energy develops, as it sometimes does, into a wild declamation, the phenomenon may be observed

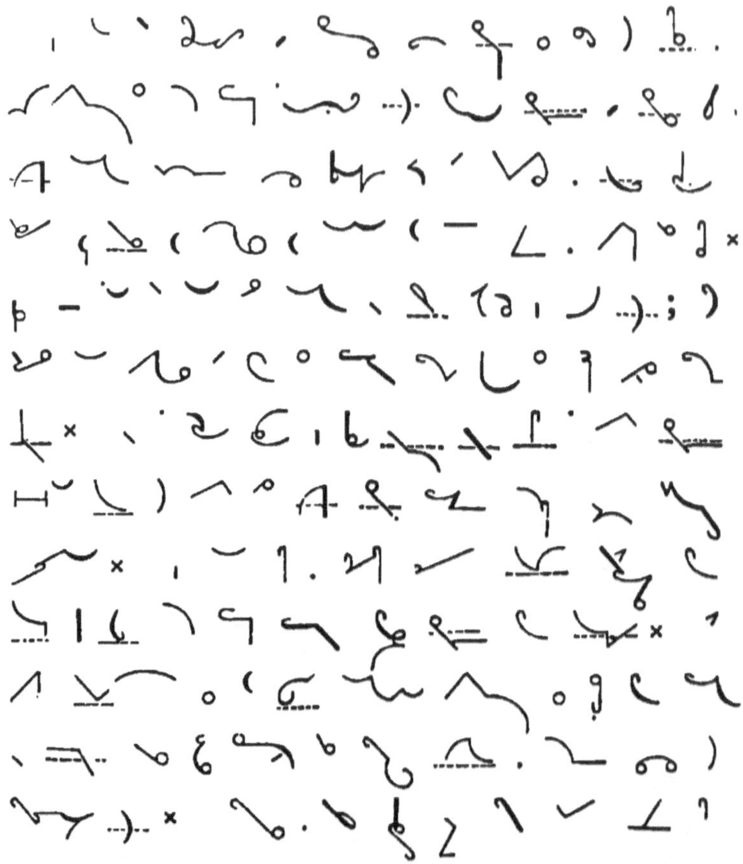

of a rush of words like a mountain torrent, and if the reporter is not well up to the mark, alas!

But after all, there is no one who, as far as mere speed is concerned, so tries the mettle of the reporter as your quiet, unimpassioned, easy, flowing speaker, who speaks just loudly enough to make himself distinctly heard, and pursues the even tenor of his way without a pause, without emphasis, without anything that can check the rapidity of his utterance. He has a good command of language, and has never to stop and think of the words he shall use; they are always in readiness, and flow as glibly from the tongue as water runs from a tap. To an ordinary listener he does not appear to be at all a rapid speaker,—not half so rapid as the loud-speaking energetic orator to whom I have been referring. But in truth the shorthand writer would rather follow Boanerges for half a day than your quiet, glib, conversational speaker for half an hour. And the irritating part of the matter is that while the unfortunate reporter is straining every nerve to keep pace with this scourge of his professional life, the work seems so provokingly easy. Perhaps the best discipline to which a member of our much tried profession can be subjected (I am still limiting my observations to the question

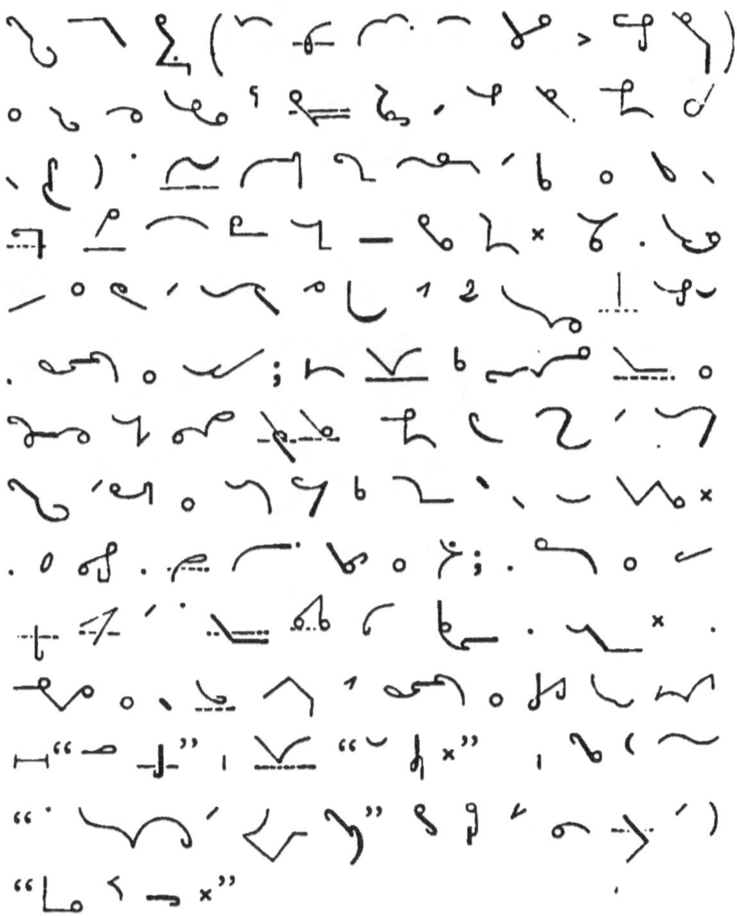

of speed) is to find himself face to face with a speaker of this kind who, instead of speaking extemporaneously, chances to deliver say a long lecture from a manuscript, and does his best to crowd as much matter as he can into a given space of time. Unless the fingers are as supple and nimble as the tongue, and the shorthand forms at instant command, the stenographer is nowhere: he may pile on his grammalogues, pack his phraseograms into the smallest possible compass, extemporise every imaginable and unimaginable abbreviation, and concentrate his entire energy on his work, all to no purpose. The first hesitation, the least lagging behind, is fatal; the scourge is away out of reach, and a big hiatus will disfigure the note-book. The experience is too often repeated, and the stenographer is disheartened if not humiliated—"cast down, but," happily, "not destroyed." He remembers that many "a forlorn and shipwrecked brother" has been stranded on the same beach, and so "takes heart again."

It has been said over and over again that American speakers speak

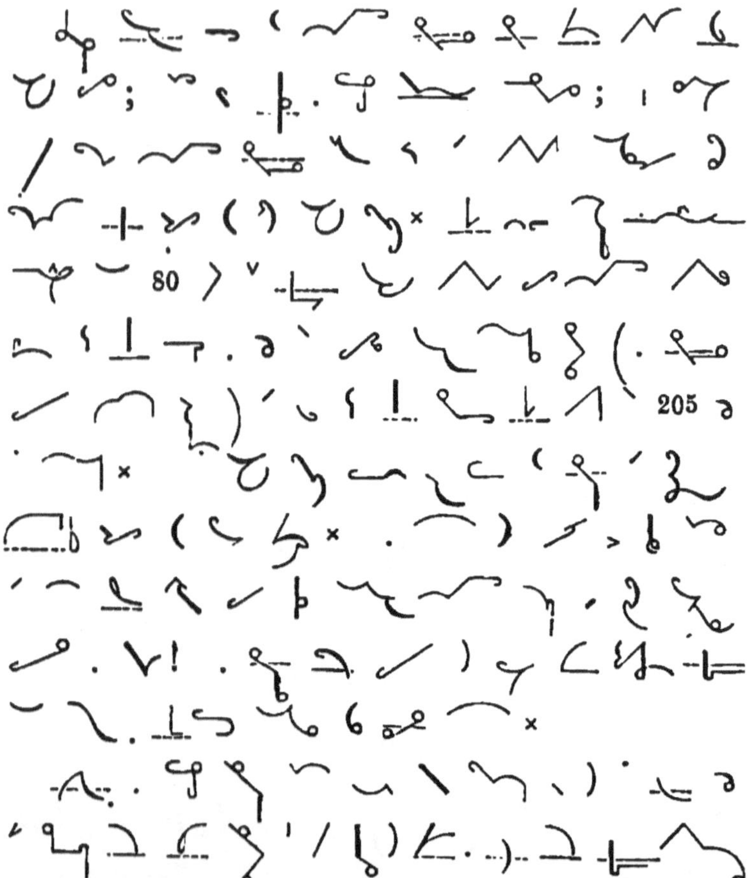

much more rapidly than English ones; I am not able to decide the question by my own experience; but certainly, judging from the American speakers I have heard and reported in this country, there is very little difference between them and their English brethren. At the meeting of the great Methodist Œcumenical Council in 1880, of which I took the official report, one of the American representatives told me that he had counted the words of one of his five-minute speeches (the speakers were limited to that time) and found that he had spoken at the rate of 205 words a minute. An English brother claimed to have equalled that speed, and there was something like a contest between them for the championship. The matter was referred to the decision of myself and my staff, and I believe we decided in favor of the American orator, who, therefore, for the present wears the belt! The speeds, however, were so nearly alike that we had some difficulty in arriving at a conclusion in reference to this serious matter.

Leaving the question of speed, I may now be permitted to say a few words on the structure or style of speeches, on which depends so largely the ease or difficulty of the reporter's task. Some speakers speak with the

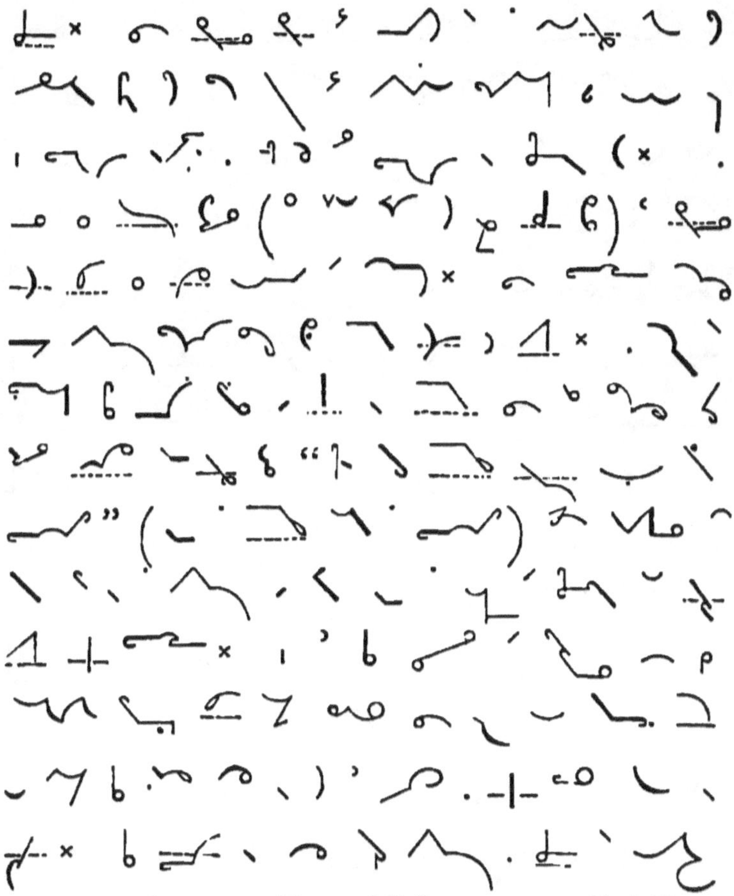

accuracy of a written composition, and if they are reasonably deliberate, they are very popular with the reporting fraternity, who have nothing to do but carefully to record the uttered words and as carefully to transcribe them. The case is far otherwise (as I need hardly say to such an audience as this) with speakers whose style is loose, inaccurate, and ambiguous. Mere grammatical errors give the reporter very little concern, as they can be easily set right. The Archbishop of Granada tells Gil Blas, who had to copy some of his sermons, which were not always models of good composition, that he is "*trop bon copiste pour n'être pas grammarien*" (too good a copyist not to be a grammarian) and the same paradox might be applied to a reporter, who ought to be too good a note-taker and transcriber not to be able to write out grammatically. But what does harass and perplex him is an involved, complicated style in which the sentences seem to have no beginning or end, and in which it is almost impossible to say what relation the different clauses have to each other. It is cruel to impose upon a reporter the task of unravelling such a tangled skein of

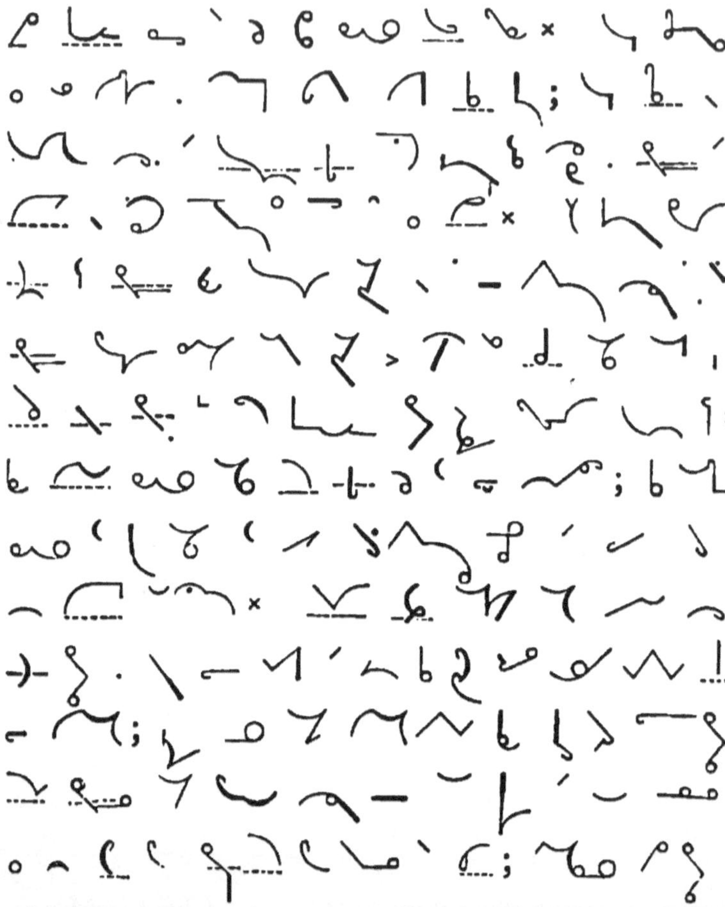

words as these sentence. often present. If he transcribes his notes literally, the ambiguity will be laid at his door; if he tries to evolve meaning and form out of chaos, he may be told that he has misconceived the speaker, and, like the too ambitious cobbler, has gone beyond his last. I think it may be safely assumed that a speaker who is not fairly intelligible to a good reporter must be a bad speaker, for he will certainly not be intelligible to the majority of his audience, unless indeed he happens to be speaking on a very technical subject to those who are perfectly familiar with it. It is not long sentences in themselves, or difficult words, that create embarrassment; it is intricate sentences that defy analysis that are the bane of the reporter's existence, and weigh upon him like a nightmare. Happily those who indulge in them are not men whose speeches the public care to read, and whom it is therefore always necessary to report at great length; but there are cases in which the length of the report does not depend upon the character of the speeches, or the speakers, in which everything must be given in detail, and no excuse is made either for speed or for peculiari-

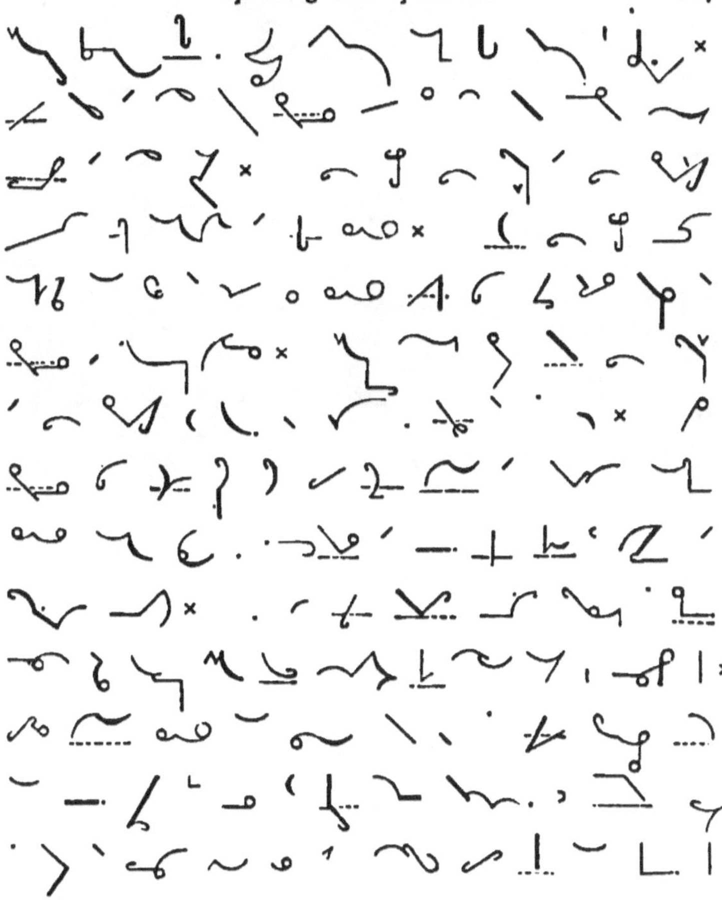

ties of style: and in these cases such speeches I have been describing drive the conscientious reporter into a condition bordering on despair. Our best and most popular speakers are, as might be expected, among the clearest and most intelligible. Mr Gladstone, Mr Bright and Mr Spurgeon, rarely utter involved and difficult sentences. Though Mr Gladstone occasionally indulges in flights of oratory, his sentences read well, which cannot always be said of speakers who affect eloquence. I have taken many a speech by Mr Bright and Mr Spurgeon without having to alter the position of a word. Such speakers will easily thread their way through a long and apparently intricate sentence, never losing the connection of the parts, and coming out at the end with logical and verbal accuracy. The late Chief Baron Kelly presented a striking example of this faculty, and I have often marveled at the manner in which he exercised it. One of his long sentences, in summing up to a jury for instance, or in giving judgment on a case that had been argued before him, would occupy nearly a page of closely written notes, and the impression one had in taking it down was

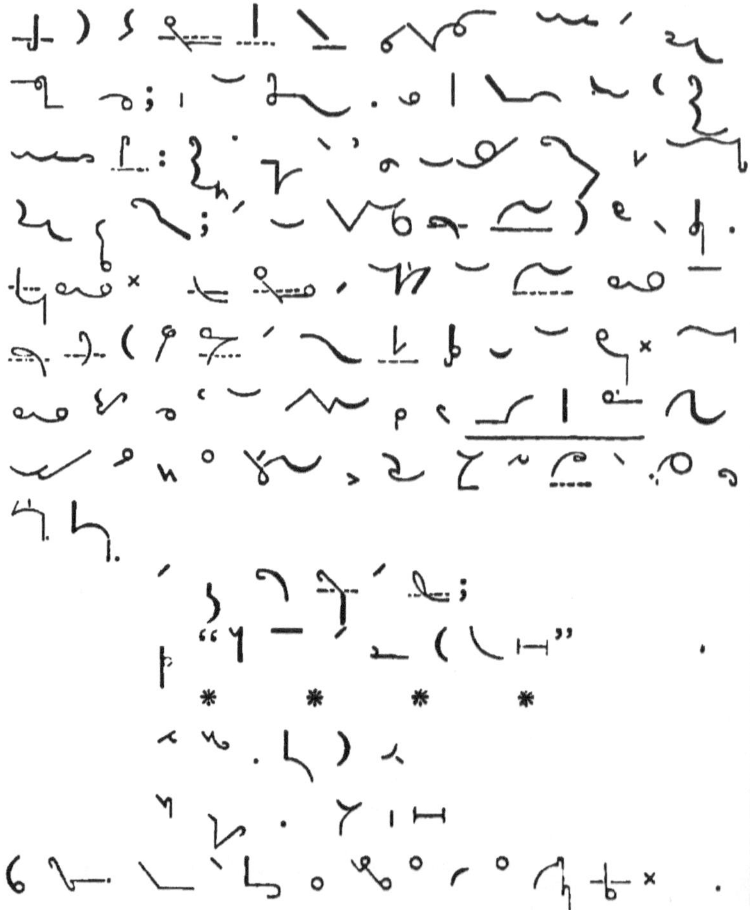

that the speaker had become hopelessly entangled, and would never extricate himself; but in transcribing the notes it became evident that there was no entanglement at all: there was no doubt a good deal of what seemed unnecessary verbiage, but the nominative was never without its verb; and no parenthesis, however long, was suffered to destroy the continuity of the sentence. Few speakers who indulge in long sentences can steer through them with such skill, and arrive at the destined end in safety. Many a sentence that one meets with in reporting is a complete *cul de sac*, leading nowhere, and is about as puzzling to the ordinary intellect as the lines of Alice's friend Humpty Dumpty,

And he was very proud and stiff;
He said, "I'd go and wake them if—"

* * * *

And when I found the door was shut,
I tried to turn the handle, but—

This provoking peculiarity of diction is, I suppose, as old as literature

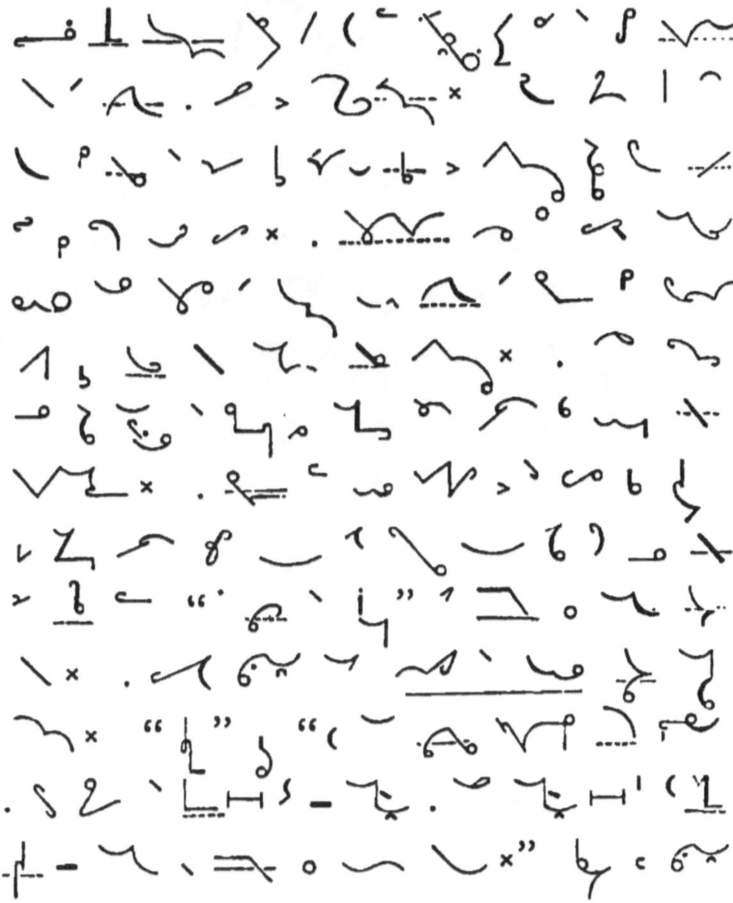

itself. The Greeks had a form of speech which they called *aposiopêsis*, which was a sort of sudden pulling up and leaving the rest to the imagination of the hearer. Whatever charm it might have as a piece of oratory, it would hardly commend itself to the reporters of those days, for our craft is a very ancient one. The Apostle Paul himself has one or two unfinished sentences in his Epistles, and if he were now alive, and spoke as he formerly wrote, he would often be anathematized by his reporters. The most frequent cause of this incompleteness of structure is the introduction of some remark that is intended to be parenthetical. The speaker quite intends to return to the point whence he has diverged, but the interjected remark suggests another, and that perhaps another, and thus there comes to be what the doctors call "a solution of continuity," and the gap is never filled up. The wordy Salanio in the *Merchant of Venice* falls into this error. "It is true," he says, "without any slips of prolixity, or crossing the plain highway of talk,—that the good Antonio, the honest Antonio,—O that I had a title good enough to keep his name company." It is only

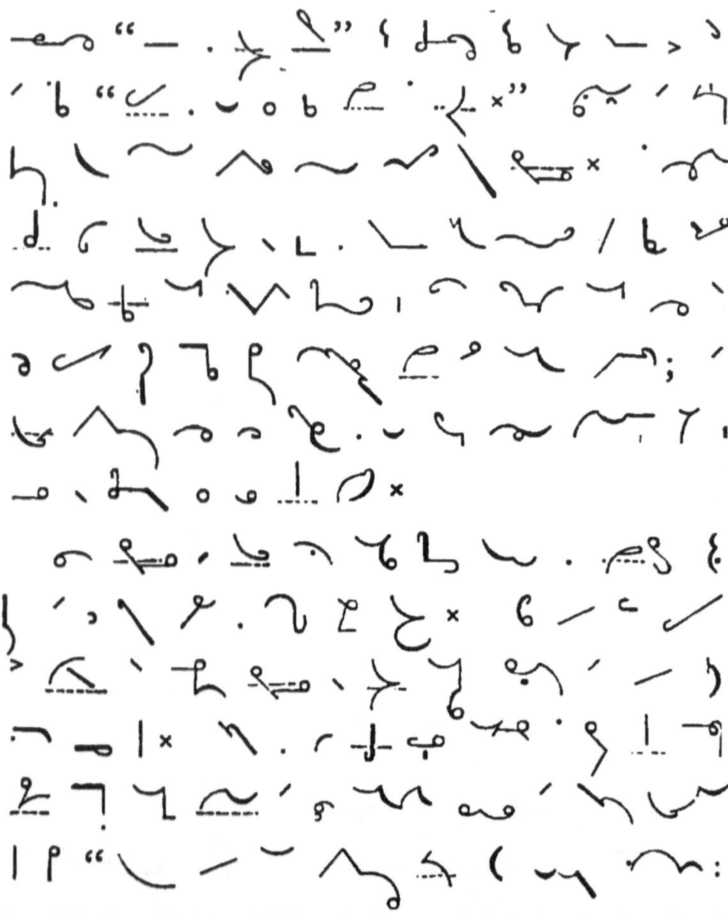

when Salanio exclaims, "Come, the full stop," that he discovers that he has failed to come to the point, and adds, "Why the end is, he has lost a ship." Salanio and Humpty Dumpty have many representatives among modern public speakers. A miscellaneous audience will often fail to detect the peculiarity I have mentioned, which does not always manifest itself in an abrupt termination, but more frequently in a maze of words, where the thread gets, as it were, imperceptibly lost, and is never recovered; and even the reporter himself may not perceive the need for a missing link until he comes to transcribe his notes at leisure.

Some speakers, who often err in this direction, have not the least conception that they do so, and would probably resent the imputation of such a failing. Others are quite aware of the liability of extempore speakers to fall into this snare, and are on their guard against it. I remember the late Dean Close, in the course of a speech at Exeter Hall, getting into a long and somewhat involved sentence, and before finishing it, said, "If there are any reporters here they need not be alarmed: I shall finish in due

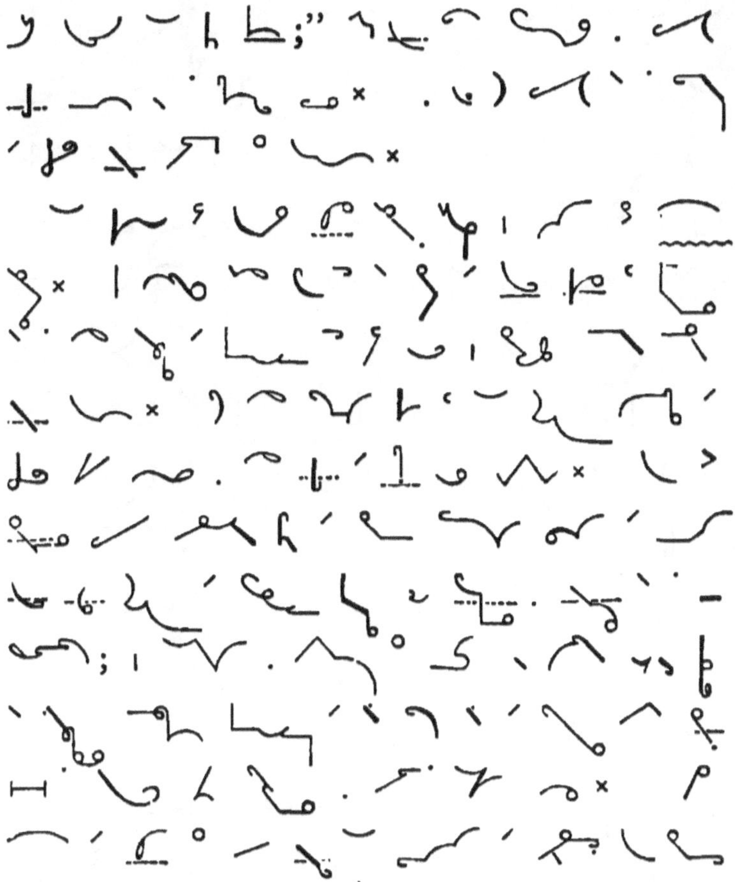

time;" and after a few more flourishes, the worthy Dean came to a triumphant close. The feat was worthy of an acrobat, and deserves to be recorded as phenomenal.

In dealing with the various styles of speaking, I have said but little as to the *matter* of speeches. It embraces almost every kind of subject, and often deals with topics of a most abstruse and technical kind, with which none but specialists can be expected to be familiar. They are most frequently dealt with in scientific lectures and discussions, which are amongst the most difficult and trying things to report. If all the speakers were reasonably deliberate, and spoke clearly, simply and accurately, even these scientific and philosophical debates would not overtax the powers of a good stenographer; but unhappily, the reporter has occasionally to labor under the combined disadvantages of abstruseness, extreme technicality, and bad, very bad, and perhaps rapid, speaking—a combination which might perplex the Recording Angel himself. Such matter and style as are to be found in Carlyle and Ruskin, if spoken in anything but the best elo-

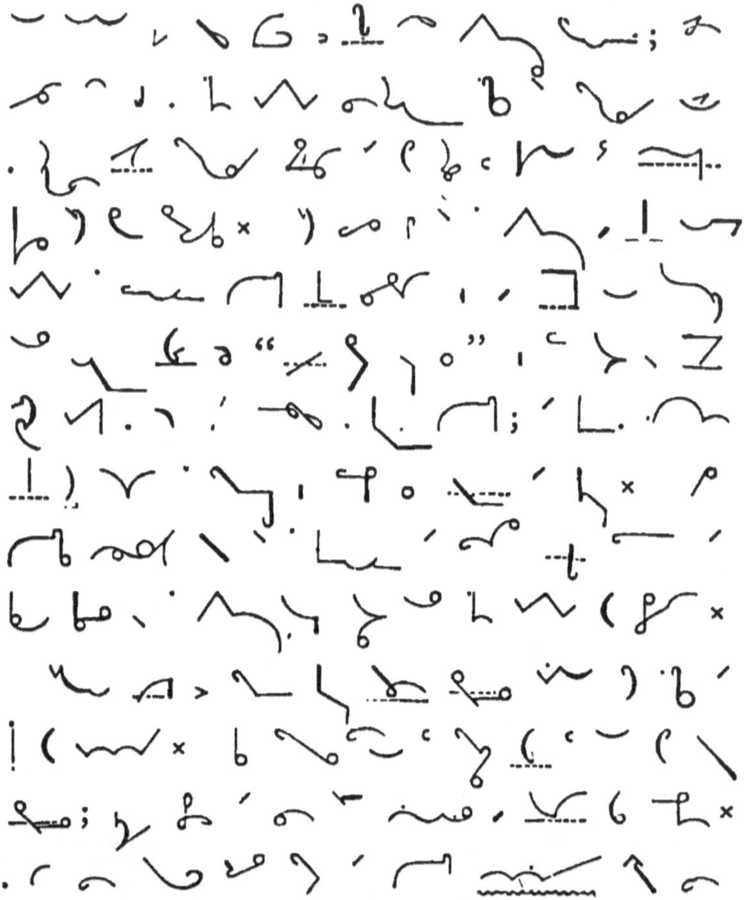

cution, would drive most reporters frantic; and the same result might attend the attempt to report some of the scientific addresses of Prof. Owen, the Astronomer Royal, Prof. Huxley, and other scientists when dealing with the minute details of their several specialities. I was once told of a reporter who had engaged to report a clinical lecture at a hospital, but who got no farther in his note-book than the words, "Our subject to-day is." He quite failed to catch, and therefore to write, the word which expressed the topic of the lecture; and taking alarm at so early a break-down, he closed his book and departed. Such lectures must necessarily be of a technical and more or less difficult character, and it is no disgrace to a reporter if he fails in his attempt to report them satisfactorily.

I have not alluded to the practice adopted by some speakers of writing their addresses and committing them to memory. It is perhaps more common with preachers than with any other public speakers: but there are statesmen, and some of great eminence, who follow this custom. The late Mr Punshon always preached and lectured *memoriter*, and I believe

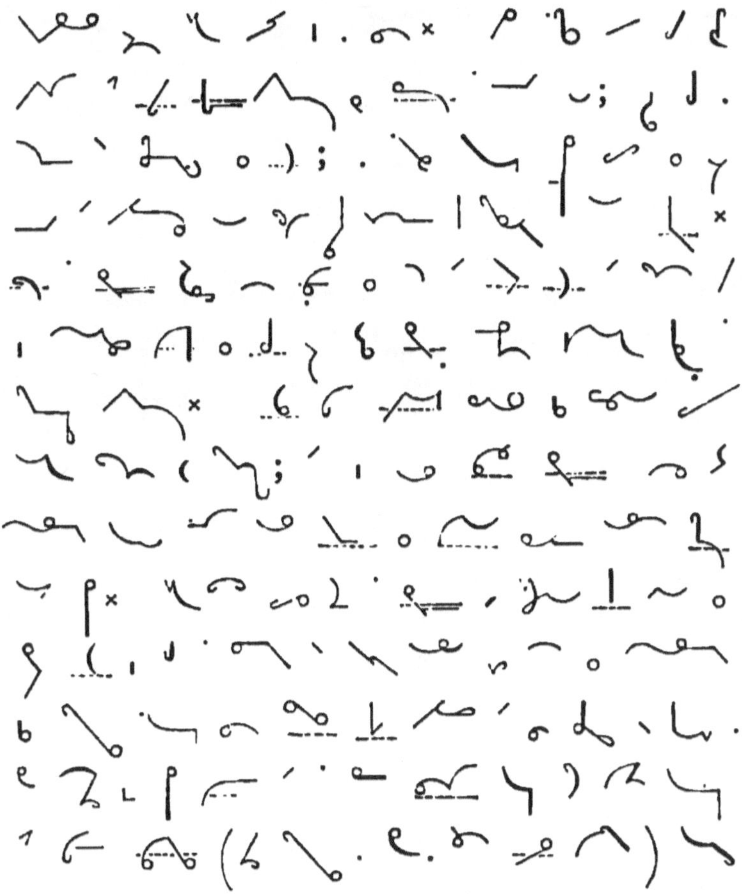

Mr Parsons, to whom I have referred, did the same. Such addresses are generally delivered rapidly, and the chief difficulty of the reporter is to secure an accurate note: but this done, the work of transcription is easy; the composition, being a studied one, is naturally accurate, and requires no friendly touches to make it presentable in type. However a speaker of this kind may conceal his art, and, by the ease and freedom which he manifests, lead his audience to think that he is speaking extemporaneously, he will never deceive a practised reporter. Those well-rounded sentences, he is quite certain, were never framed without premeditation; and he knows as well as the speaker himself that the manuscript, if not actually in his pocket, is lying snugly in some drawer in the study. I have more than once asked a speaker who I was certain had written his speech, though he had not a scrap of paper in his hand, to lend me his manuscript; he has perhaps affected some surprise at the request, and seemed disposed to deny the soft impeachment, but a steady look and a significant smile have had their legitimate effect, and the welcome slips (which meant perhaps

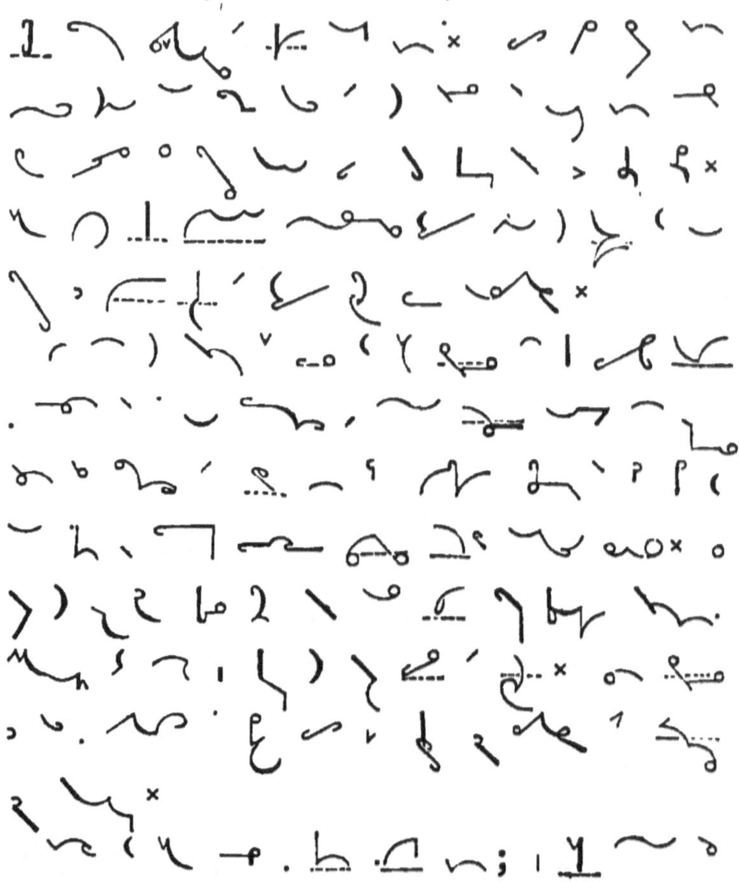

the saving of some hours' labor) have been drawn from their hiding-place, and duly handed to me. One such speech, I may mention, was written in very good Phonography, and was, of course, of no use to me except for reference, as printers have not yet been educated up to the desired standard. I have also had longhand manuscripts that were written so vilely that no printer would look at them, and they were therefore equally unserviceable.

Let me say, before I close, that I think speakers might do worse than follow the example of a young clergyman who, many years ago, engaged me to take notes of some of his sermons and supply him with a literal transcript of what he said, without any attempt to correct grammatical slips or complete unfinished sentences. His object was to have whatever defects there might be in his style brought distinctly before him, and I have no doubt that the method he adopted was both wise and useful. Some speakers would find the revelation a startling one, but the discipline would be serviceable, and the hearers would be benefited.

I am afraid that I have exceeded the time allotted to me; but I had many points to touch upon, and there are yet others to which I cannot

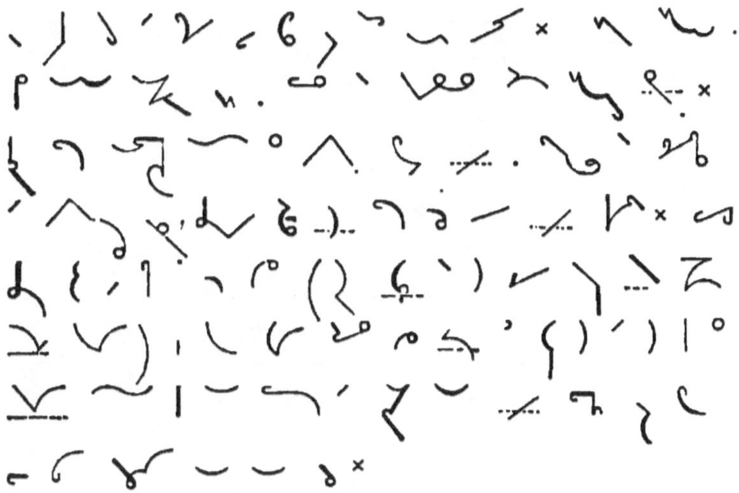

——:o:——

PHRASEOGRAPHY.

A Lecture delivered before the Phonetic Shorthand Writers' Association, London.

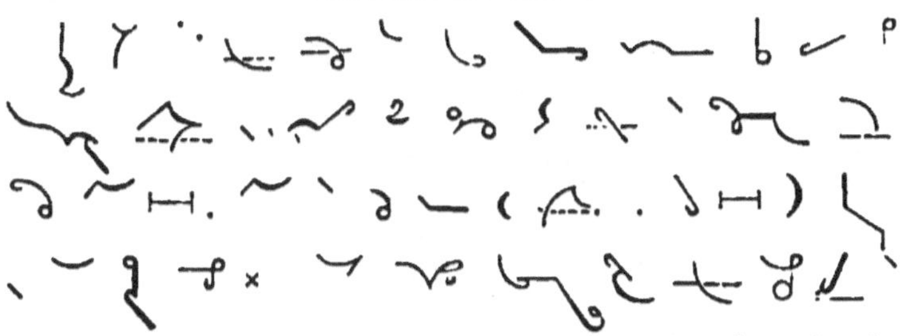

now refer. I hope I have not said anything uncharitable about the class of persons of whom I have been speaking. It would be very ungrateful in me, as representing, for the hour, the professions of shorthand writers and reporters, to speak disparagingly of those whose very words are our daily bread. We do not desire that they should utter a word less (especially those of us who are paid by column or the folio), but if they will always let us hear what they do say, and say it, as happily many do, in clear and intelligible language, our gratitude to them ever great, will absolutely know no bounds.

It was not until a few years after Phonography began to make its way as a formidable rival to modern shorthand systems that the principle of Phraseography, or phrase-writing,—the writing of words together without lifting the pen,—was adopted to any considerable extent. In the earliest phonographic publications comparatively few instances of the joining of

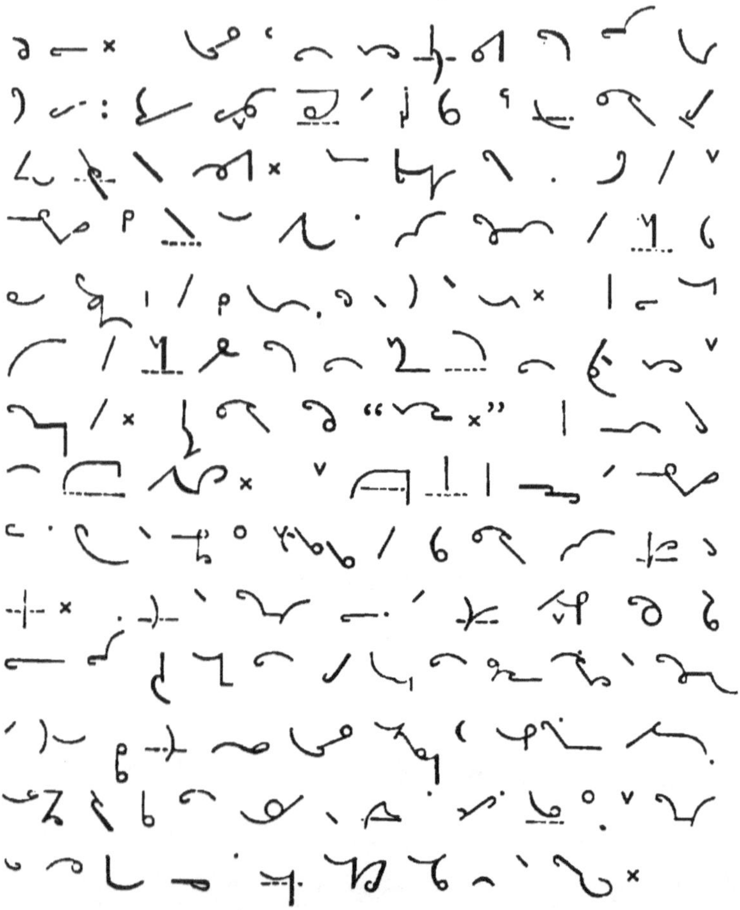

words occur. Phonographers, with Mr Pitman at their head, very gradually felt their way: they were wisely cautious, and contented themselves with a few simple junctions which could not possibly be misread. I can distinctly remember the pleasure which I experienced as a boy in reading a little phraseogram which I had then seen for the first time, but which is a familiar friend to us all now. It occurred in a letter which I had received from Mr Isaac or Mr Joseph Pitman, I forget which. It was the simple phrase ... *I am glad.* It came upon me like a revelation. I looked at it again and again, and experienced quite a flutter of excitement as I thought of the possibilities which this simple little outline opened out. The use of frequently occurring and easily recognised phrases of this character gradually developed into a more general, if not a more systematical, employment of phraseography, and so common is its use in the present day amongst phonographers that, instead of the practice requiring encouragement, I believe it is more necessary to lift a warning voice, as I frequently find myself doing, against an undue indulgence in this mode of abbreviation.

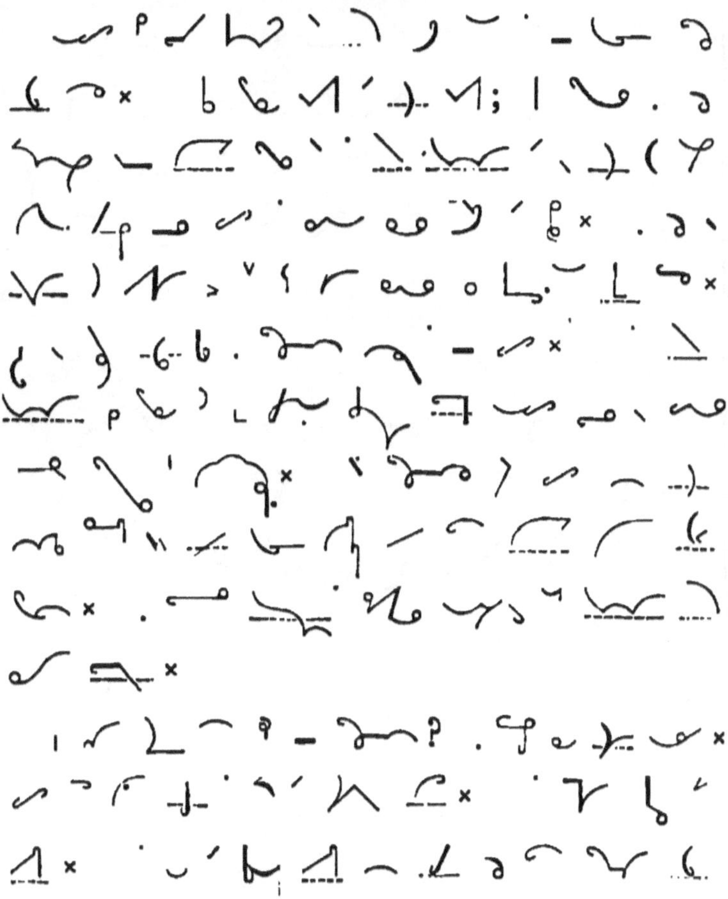

No one has a greater admiration of, or pleasure in, a good phonographic phrase than myself. It is pleasant to read and easy to write; it brings the words harmoniously together like the members of a happy family, and to see them in such loving juxtaposition gives one a certain sense of pleasure and satisfaction. The words, too, appeal so readily to the eye that a whole sentence is taken in at a glance. But then to possess these advantages the phraseogram must be a good one. A happy family is a pleasant sight, but a jostling disorderly crowd no one cares to witness except perhaps on Lord Mayor's Day. Bad phraseograms, of which one may see multitudes scattered about our phonographic literature, are more like the latter than the former. The characters form a heterogeneous unnatural compound, not a family or social group.

But you will ask me, What is a good phraseogram? The question is not easily answered. One cannot lay down a hard and sharp line. A good deal depends on the writer. A neat and distinct writer may join words more frequently than one who is clumsy, careless and inaccurate; in fact

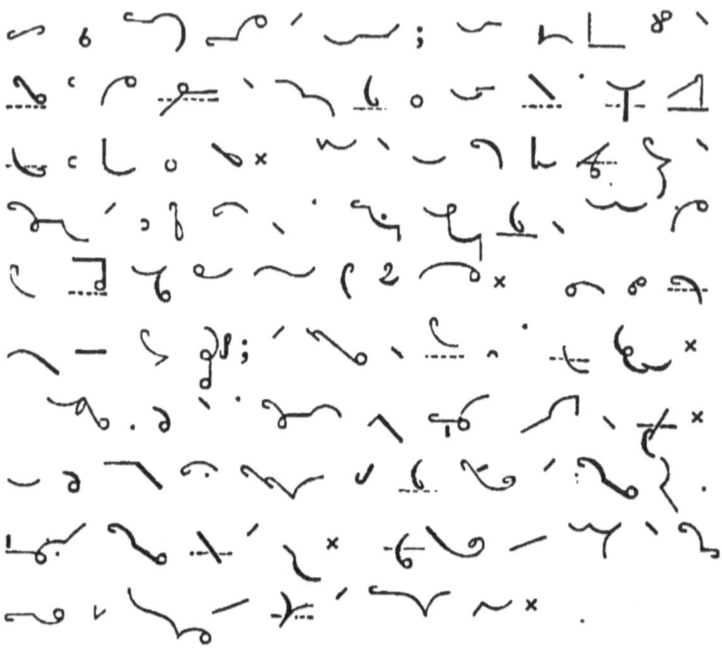

I

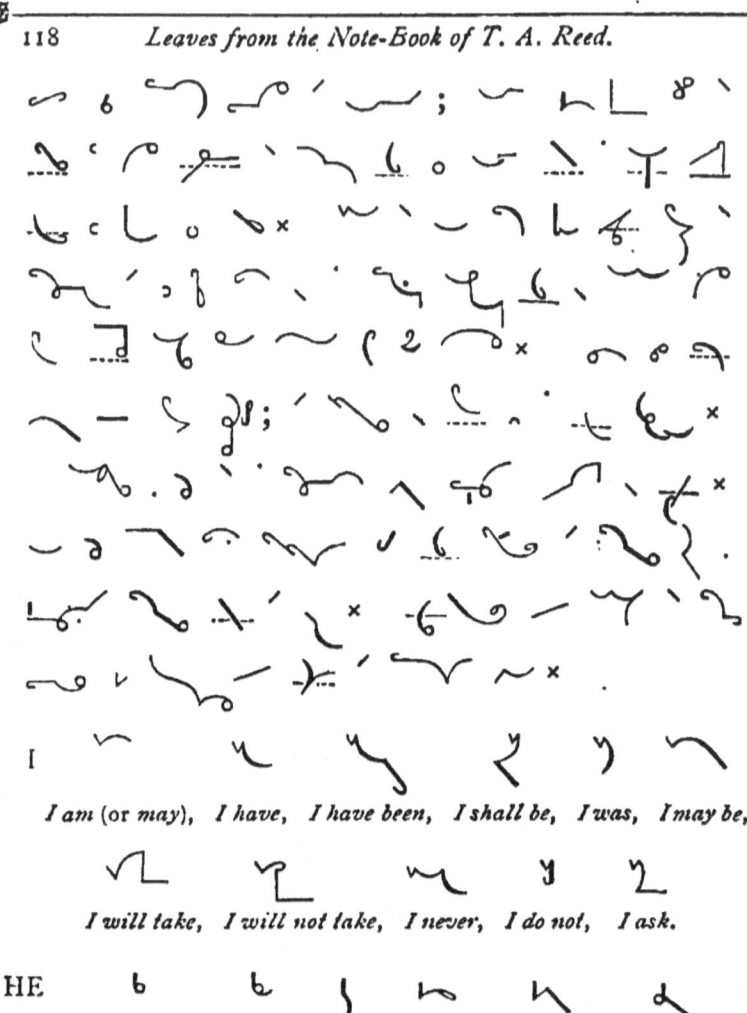

I am (or *may*), *I have*, *I have been*, *I shall be*, *I was*, *I may be*,

I will take, *I will not take*, *I never*, *I do not*, *I ask.*

HE

he is (or *he has*), *he is not*, *he was*, *he must*, *he should be*, *he has been*,

he may take all sorts of liberties with less risk of error than is incurred by an indifferent writer even when doing his best. I know of no very definite rules for the use of phraseography; and would trust more to a cultivated instinct than to anything else for guidance in this as in many other shorthand matters. Some hints, however, may be given for the assistance of the student; and I propose to offer you a few this evening.

In the first place the words of a phraseogram should be closely related to each other. No words can be more properly joined than pronouns and verbs, especially the auxiliary verbs *to be* and *to have*. These combinations are not only of frequent occurrence, but the forms are easily and clearly written.

he would, he will have, he may be, he could not.

WE 

we have, we have this, we are, we were, we shall not, we shall have.

YOU 

you are, you may, you may be, you will find, you should.

THEY 

they have, they may, they may be, they are, they have been, they will be.

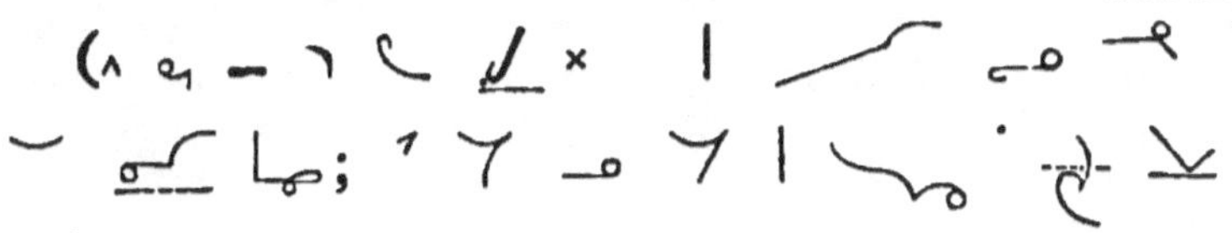

 *thou hast.*

I do, I think, I think it, I think there, I fear, I suppose,

I deny, I desire, I wish, I suspect.

 *in, for, with, by, to,* 

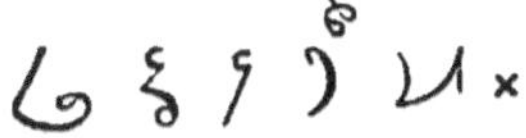 *In* 

Thou is not a good word for joining. It rarely occurs except in Scriptural texts; and the only case in which it forms a useful part of a phraseogram is in the common *thou hast.*

Other verbs of common occurrence may also be joined to pronouns with great advantage, as—

The common propositions *in, for, with, by, to,* etc., form convenient phonographic junctions with the words with which they are associated. "*In*" is perhaps the most commonly joined, as—

IN

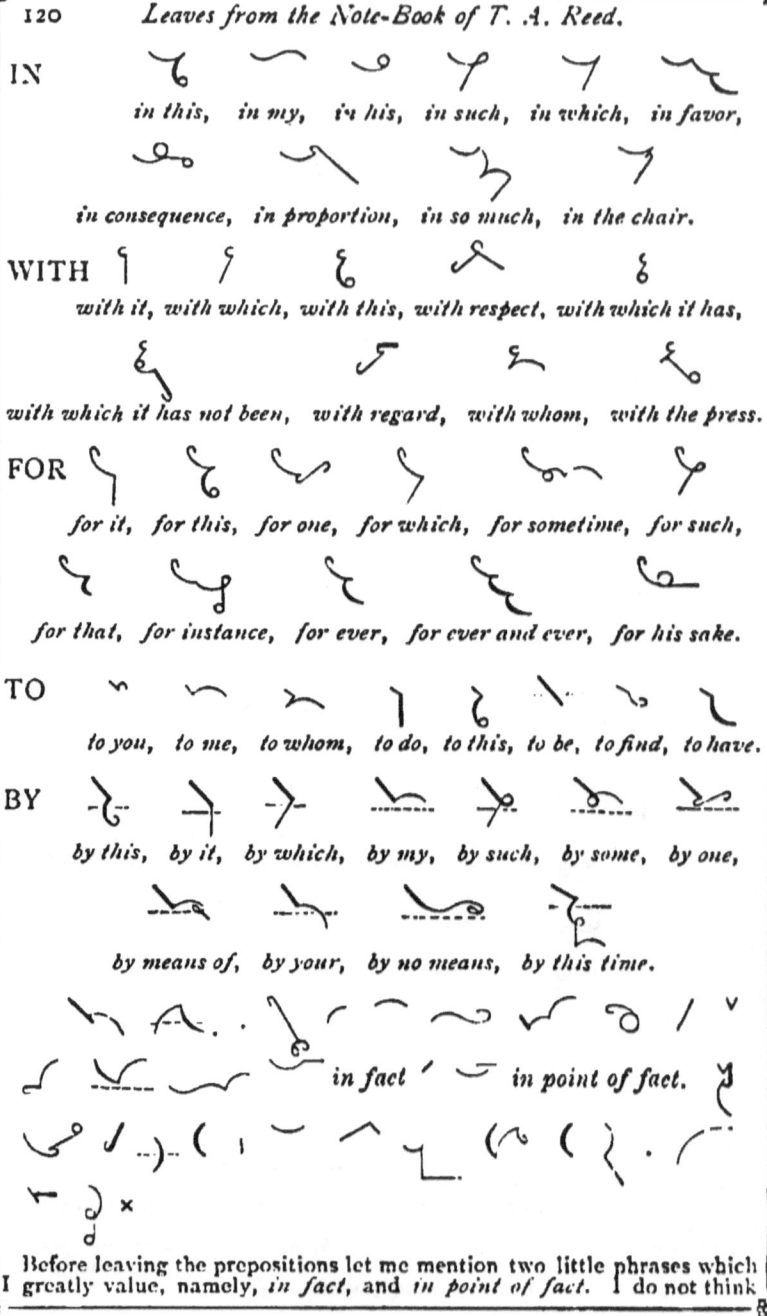

in this, in my, in his, in such, in which, in favor,

in consequence, in proportion, in so much, in the chair.

WITH

with it, with which, with this, with respect, with which it has,

with which it has not been, with regard, with whom, with the press.

FOR

for it, for this, for one, for which, for sometime, for such,

for that, for instance, for ever, for ever and ever, for his sake.

TO

to you, to me, to whom, to do, to this, to be, to find, to have.

BY

by this, by it, by which, by my, by such, by some, by one,

by means of, by your, by no means, by this time.

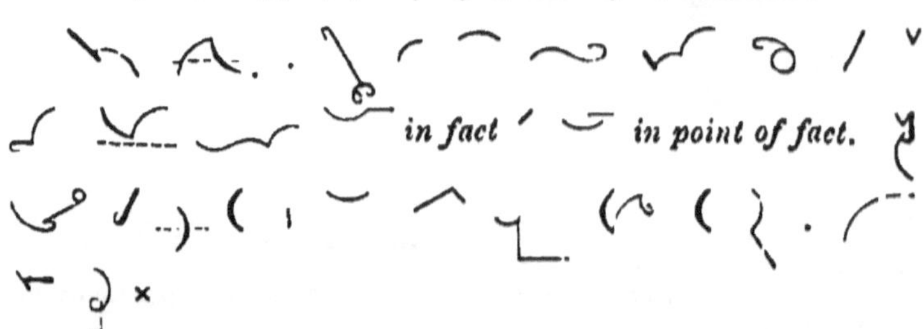

Before leaving the prepositions let me mention two little phrases which I greatly value, namely, *in fact*, and *in point of fact*. I do not think

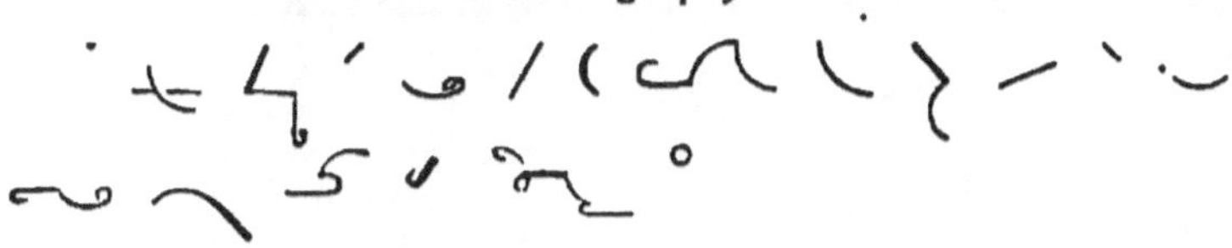

good men, good deal, great deal, great men, great judge, great pleasure.

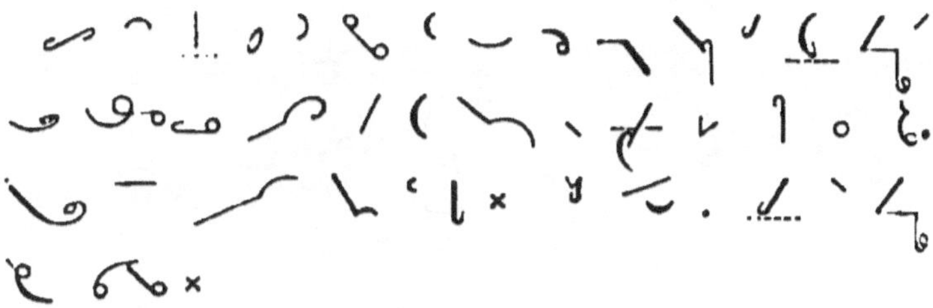

 *infinite satisfaction,*  *beautiful scenery,*  *excellent material,*

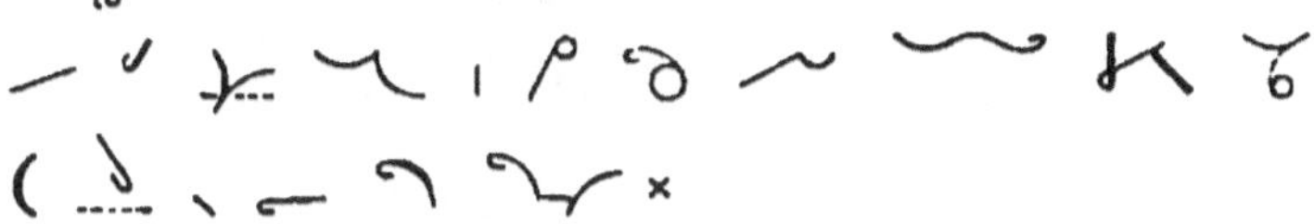

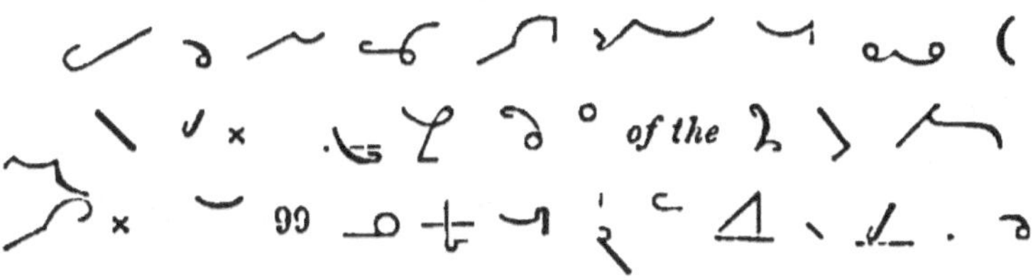

phonographers generally use them, but in rapid note-taking they will find them, especially the latter, of great assistance.

A few adjectives and nouns which they qualify, if both are of common occurrence, may be occasionally joined phraseographically, as—

One might at first sight suppose that no words could be better joined than adjectives and nouns, in consequence of the close relation which they bear to each other, but the truth is that these combinations can rarely be made with advantage. I do not recommend the joining of adjectives of several syllables.

are joined easily enough, but such phrases are not in my opinion desirable unless they happen to occur very frequently.

Where words are not closely related to one another in a sentence they should never be joined. Even in such a phrase as *of the* there may not be the required relation. In ninety-nine cases out of a hundred it would be quite right to join the words (where they are not expressed by bringing the preceding and following words close together), but in such a phrase as

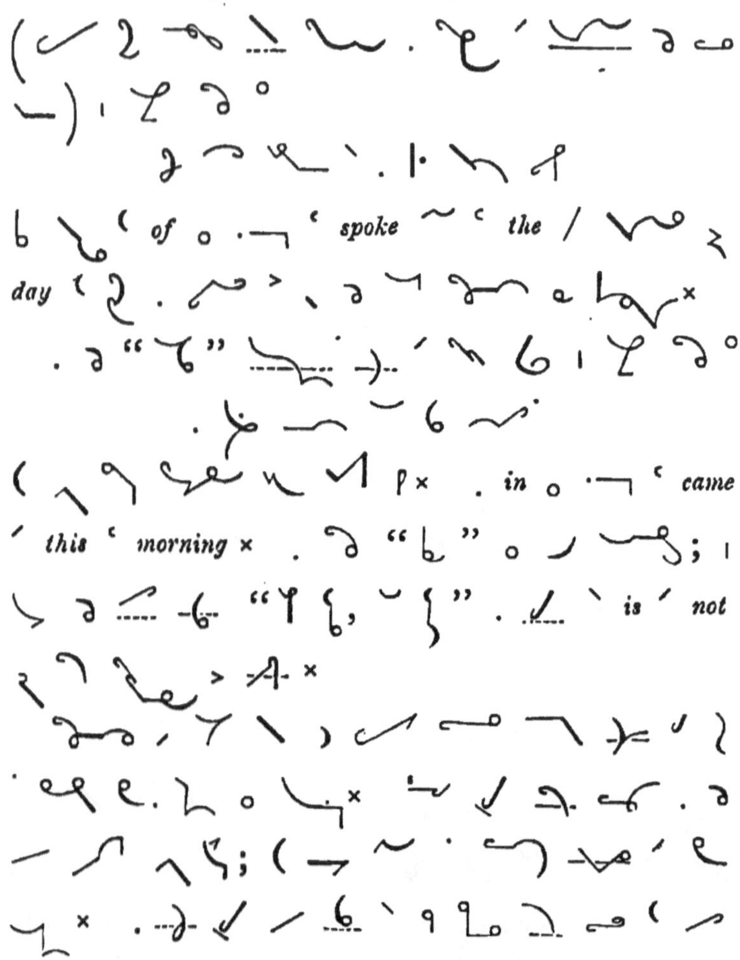

"There is the man I spoke of the day before yesterday," it is obvious that *of* is connected with *spoke*, and not with *the*, which belongs to the word *day*, and that therefore the union of the two words in a phraseogram is not admissible.

The words *in this* form an easy and appropriate junction, but in such a phrase as "The vessel came in this morning," they should be separated for the reason I have already stated. The *in* is connected with *came*, and *this* with *morning*. The phrase *it is not* is usually unexceptionable; but if the words ran thus, "I said that it is, not that it was," the joining of *is* and *not* would be very perplexing to the reader.

Phraseograms should only be used where the characters can be easily joined, so that a sensible saving of time is effected. Awkward joinings, however closely the words are related, should be avoided: they give the

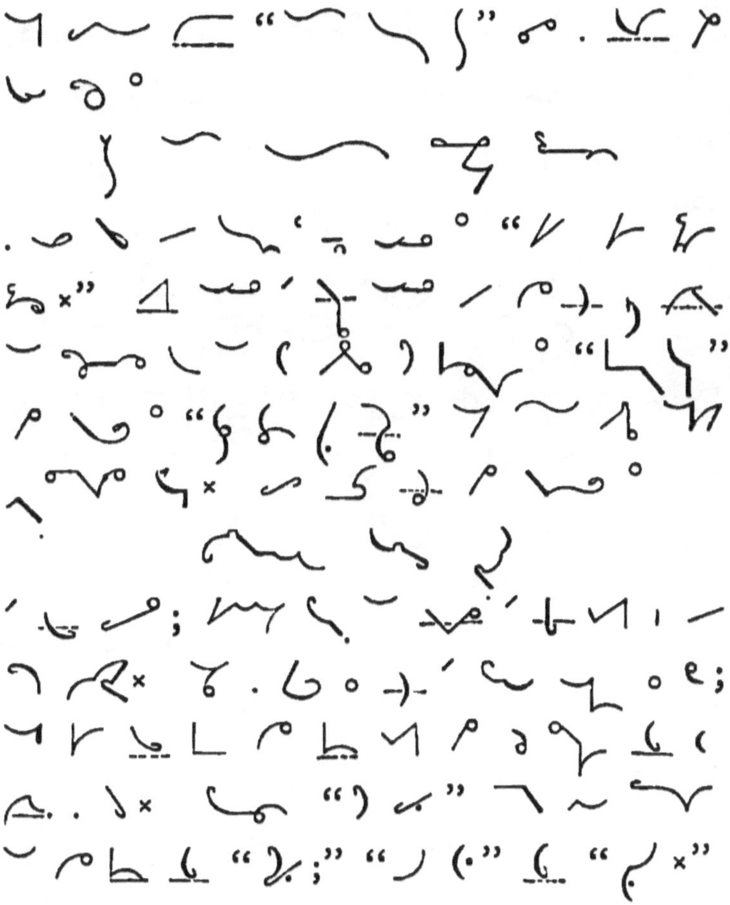

writing a clumsy appearance and save no time. The easiest joinings are those of straight strokes or curves that run into one another like ...... hence the value of such convenient phrases as, "I tbink so, in my, another matter, stock exchange, political economy." The next best are formed with acute angles, as, "Which are, whicb will, witb which you will, witb the means." Right angles and obtuse angles are less easy, but they are allowable in phraseograms if in other respects they are admissible, as, "It can be, have had." Such combinations as "This was, this may, whicb they, or this," in which many writers indulge, should be scrupulously avoided. One occasionally sees such abominations as "Will you be good enough, have you been, was she able," and even worse; whicb are not only forbidding in appearance and difficult to write, but are very illegible. Unless the junction is easy and flowing no time is saved; indeed, it will often take less time to write sucb words separately than without lifting the pen. For example, ... *their way* can be written clearly in less time than ......; ...... than ....

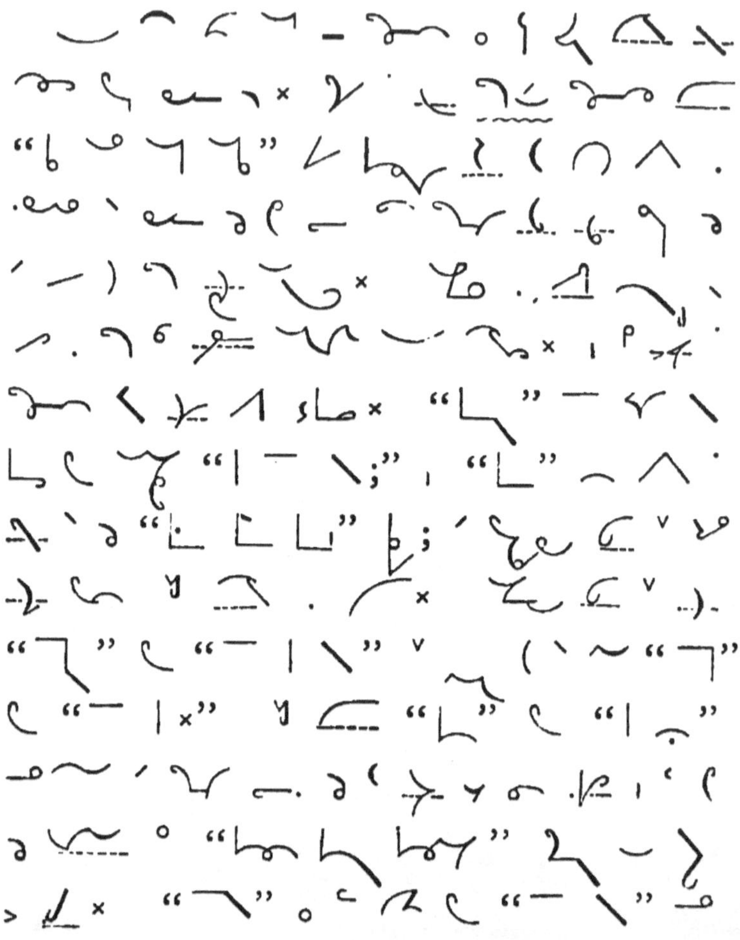

Another important element in a good phraseogram is, that it shall not be liable to be mistaken for a single word. There are a few *very common* phraseograms like "It is, in his, in it, in its," which are admissible, although they also represent the consonants of single words, as they occur more frequently than these separate words, and are so very useful in combination. In such cases the writer may be content to run the very slight risk involved in their employment. But as a rule a phraseogram ought to be easily read without the context. ...... can hardly be taken for anything else than *it can be;* but ...... may represent a number of words, *take, talk, took*, etc.; and for this reason, while I always use the former, I do not employ the latter. In like manner, while I use ...... for *can it be*, I should never think of writing ...... for *can it*. I do not like ...... for *it may*, because of the many and frequently occurring words that fall under the same outline, but with other words following, as ...... *it may seem*, ... *it may be*, ... *it may certainly*, there can be no objection to the joining.

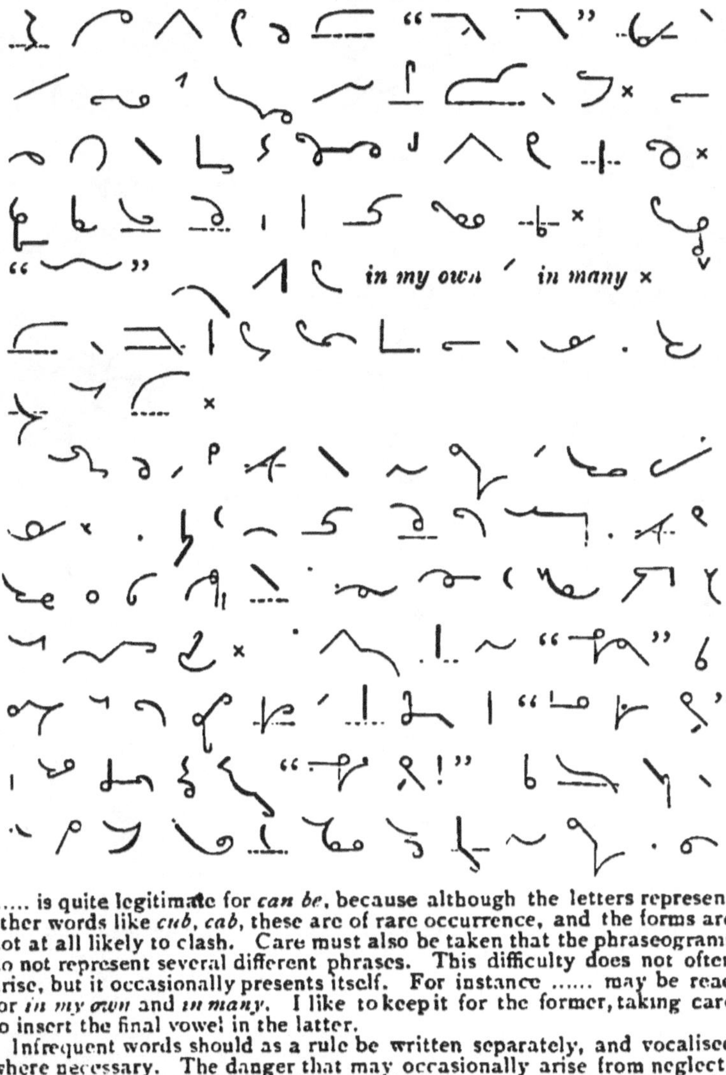

...... is quite legitimate for *can be*, because although the letters represent other words like *cub*, *cab*, these are of rare occurrence, and the forms are not at all likely to clash. Care must also be taken that the phraseograms do not represent several different phrases. This difficulty does not often arise, but it occasionally presents itself. For instance ...... may be read for *in my own* and *in many*. I like to keep it for the former, taking care to insert the final vowel in the latter.

Infrequent words should as a rule be written separately, and vocalised where necessary. The danger that may occasionally arise from neglecting the rule as to vocalisation is well illustrated by an amusing mistake that I have seen recorded, I think in an American journal. A reporter had written ...... which is certainly not a very suggestive outline, and had transcribed it *Ox-tail soup*, but afterwards discovered that the words ought to have been *Castile soap!* It is far better to avoid such unusual combinations, though in this case if the words had been written separately the same mistake might have been made unless a vowel had been thrown in, as it certainly should have been.

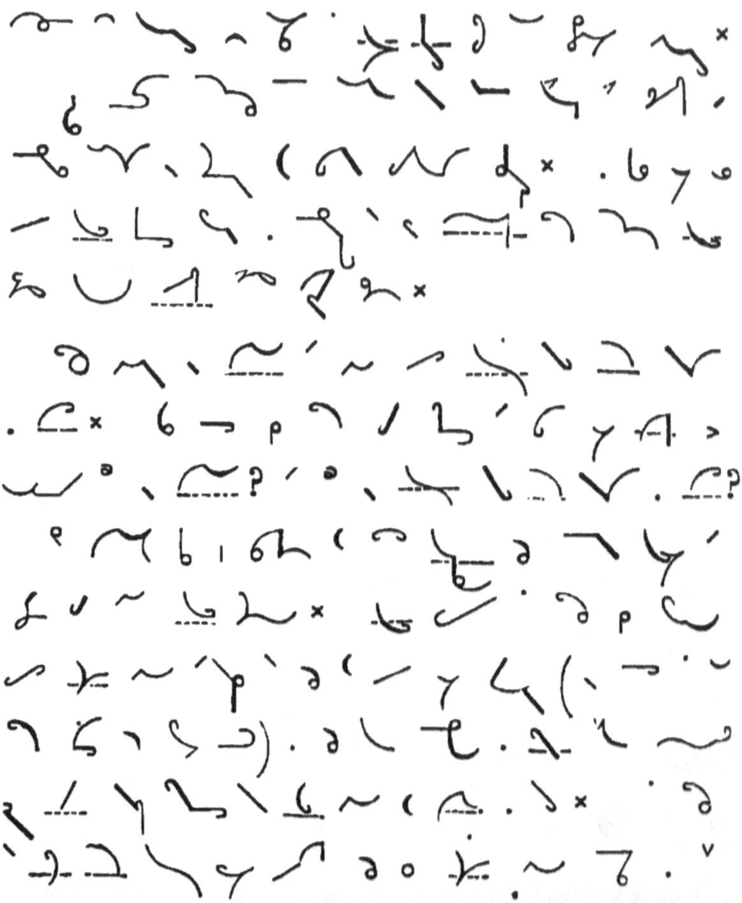

But these occasional errors can never be altogether avoided, and the shorthand writer who expects entirely to escape them will be wofully disappointed. The conditions under which notes are often taken forbid the expectation of complete immunity from error even with the most efficient writer and the most legible system.

Phrases should not be too long, and should not run far above or below the line. This again, is a very general direction, and will naturally lead to the inquiry, What is too long? and What is too far above or below the line?

As to length it is but seldom that more than half-a-dozen words can be conveniently and judiciously joined, and not often so many. Even where a phrase is a flowing one, easily written, and composed of words that are naturally joinable (to coin a not very elegant word for the occasion), the words, if exceeding the number I have mentioned, would be much better broken up than written without lifting the pen. A phrase of three or four nearly related words is easily written, catches the eye readily, and is

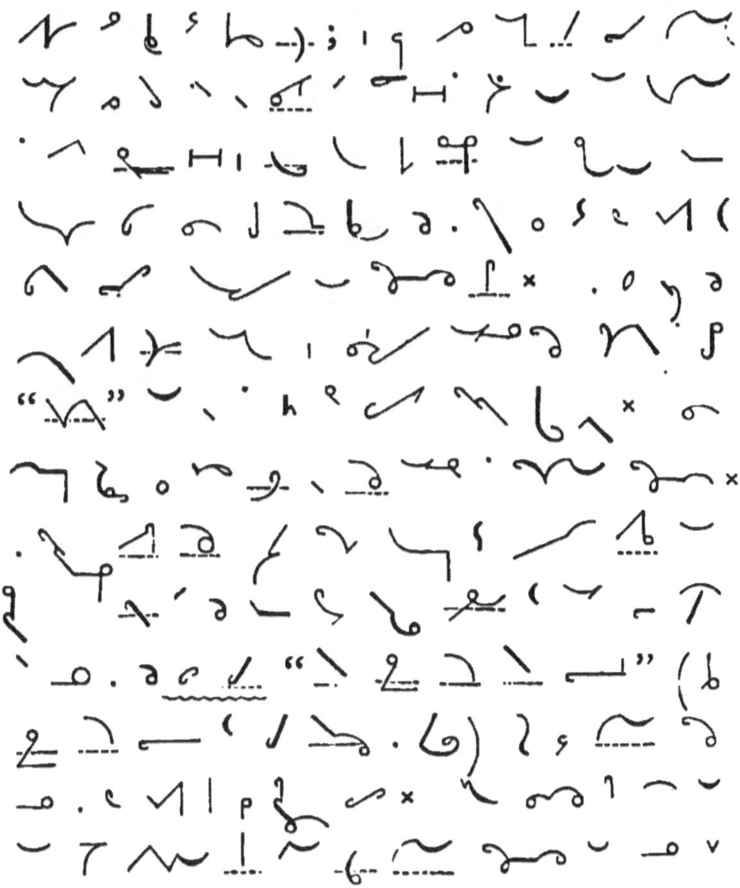

deciphered with the utmost ease; but when it runs into a much greater length, not only is the pen apt to halt and stagger—a fatal thing in following a rapid speaker—but even if it should succeed in stringing together fairly well some ten or a dozen words, the probability is that the effort to read them will be greater than if there were no phraseograms at all. The first two or three words may be read easily enough, but somewhere in the course of the phrase there will be a sudden "pull up" owing to a doubt as to where the proper division should be. Some ambiguity of this kind is almost sure to arise in the case of a very long phraseogram. The perplexity of the writer arises chiefly from the fact that he rarely writes any considerable number of words together, for the obvious reason that in the great majority of cases the words *will not join*, "by hook or by crook" (it is the hook or crook that generally bars the junctions), so that when the long phrase comes the effort to write it is a troublesome one. I have sometimes tried my hand in actual reporting at writing these long phraseograms, not because I approve of the practice, but simply for amusement;

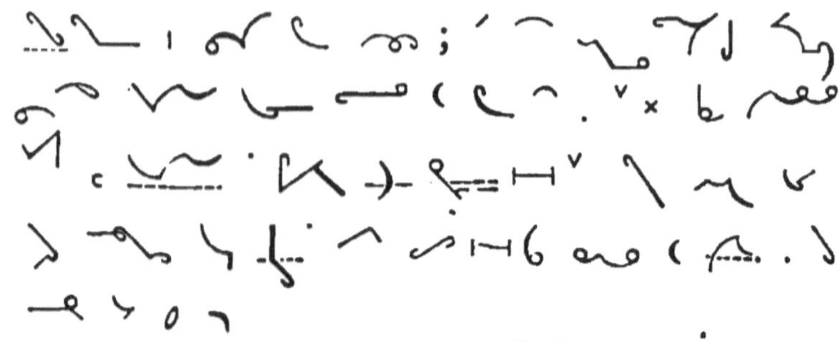

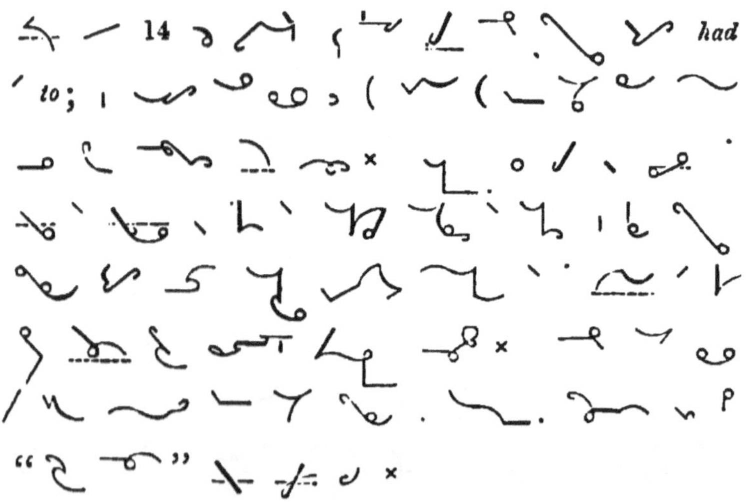

and my note-books, accordingly, contain here and there some of the most appalling phonographic characters that ever met the eye. It is not long since I wrote, when following a tolerably easy speaker—I probably should not have ventured upon the experiment if he had been a rapid one—this sentence, without lifting the pen, except after the first word—"The longer they were under examination the more reason they had to regret it."

Here are fourteen words united without an awkward joining, except, perhaps, between *had* and *to;* but no one in his senses would think of writing them together, unless, as in my own case, for experiment or amusement. Note-taking is generally too serious a piece of business to admit of indulgence in this kind of entertainment, but it is not perhaps surprising that one occasionally endeavors to relieve the monotony of a long and dull speech by some playful stenographico-gymnastic exercises. Except in the sense which I have mentioned, I can only present the foregoing phraseogram to you as a "frightful example," to be religiously shunned.

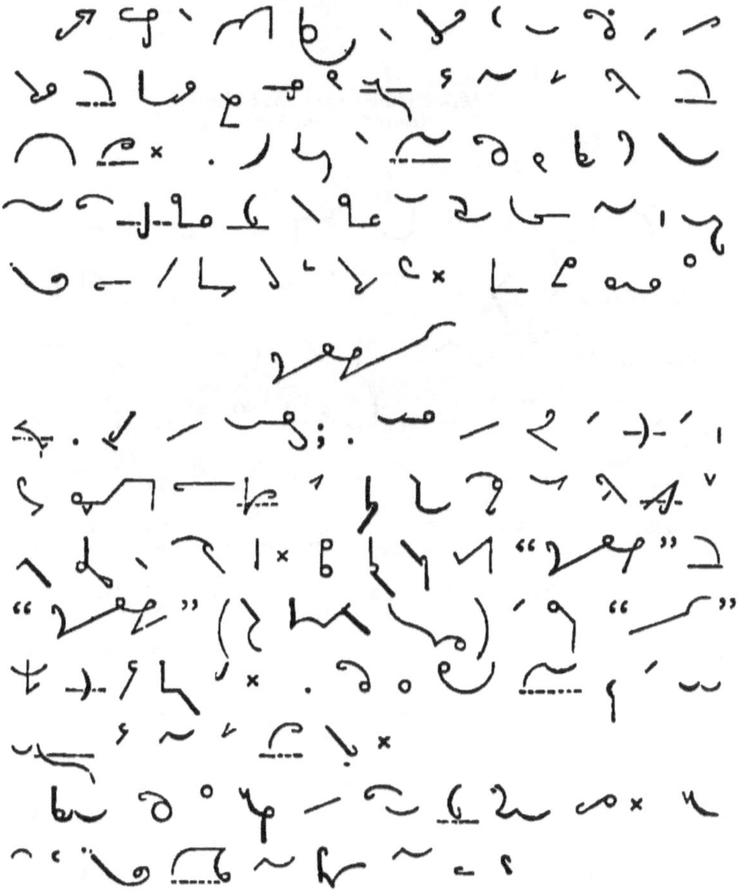

With regard to the question of lineality, it is sufficient to observe that no phrase should run upwards or downwards to such an extent as to interfere with the writing on the upper or lower lines. The usual tendency of long phrases is to descend, there being many more down strokes than up strokes in ordinary phonographic writing, but now and then combinations occur which take the pen on an upward flight. Take such a sentence as "There are reasons which are rarely." Here the joinings are unexceptionable: the angles are sharp and easy, and but for the sky-rockety character of the outline, and the danger of doing mischief in the upper region, I should be disposed to employ it. As it is, it would be better to write ...... or ...... (both admirable forms) and separate ...... notwithstanding the ease with which it could be joined. The phrase is sufficiently long without it, and need not interfere with the writing on the line above.

Descending phrases, as I have said, are more common than ascending ones. I have met with combinations like this, written deliberately and in cold blood. "I think it was said that there would be such."

I think it was said that there would be such.

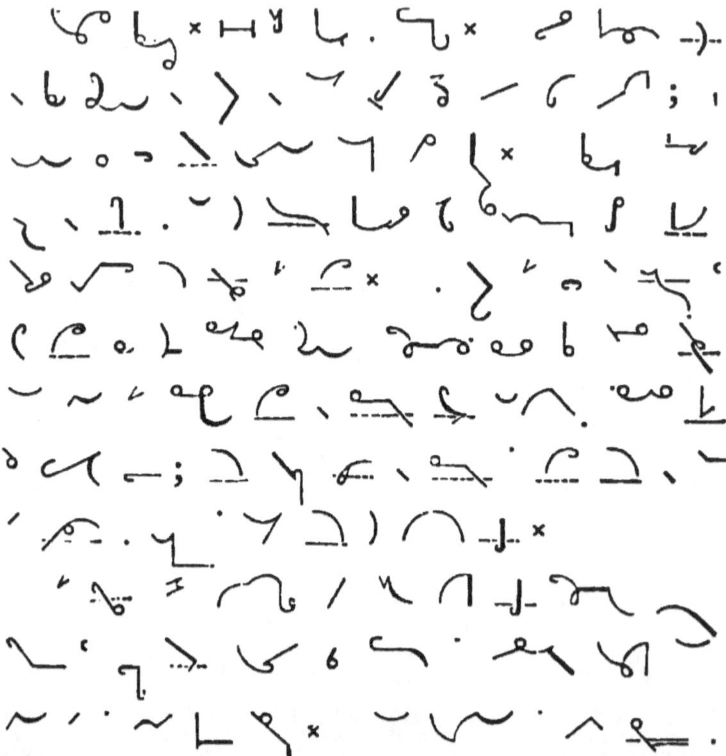

Fasilis descensus.—I do not continue the quotation. Yes, it may seem easy to descend, there is nothing to object to in the joinings, and the words are well related; but nothing is gained by venturing into such depths. It is, indeed, awkward to have to draw the hand so far downwards, and then to make a sudden dash upwards to regain your position on the line. The objection on the ground of interfering with other lines is not so great as in the case of ascending phraseograms since it is, of course, possible in writing on the succeeding lines to skip over the interloping consonants at the points where they occur; or, better still, to skip a line or two altogether and resume the note-taking an inch or so lower down.

On the principles, and with the limitations, which I have laid down, Phraseography may be practised with great advantage by the phonographer who has acquired a reasonable facility in writing and a moderate

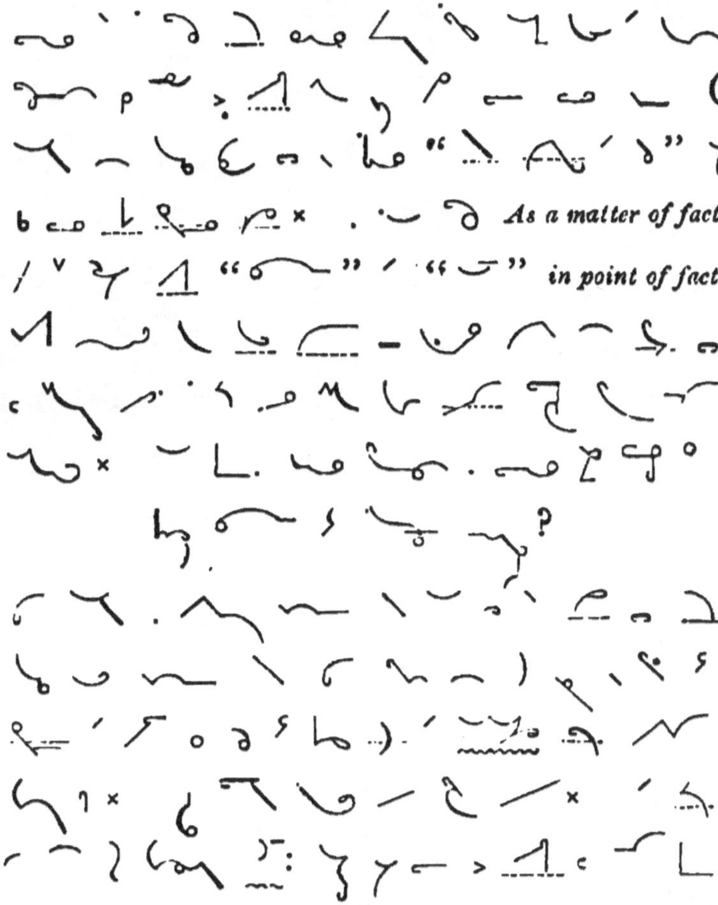

degree of speed. In following a rapid speaker the occurrence of a phrase or sentence which can be compressed into a convenient and familiar phraseogram is a godsend to the writer, and if two or three such occur close together they enable him, if he is losing ground, to advance "by leaps and bounds" until he is close at the speaker's heels. The common phrases, "As a matter of fact," which I ordinarily write ...... and ...... "In point of fact," already mentioned, have often, like good fairies, helped me over the ground when I have been running a hard race, and I have felt really grateful for their kindly intervention. In taking evidence, for example, the occurrence of such a question as, "Do you mean to say as a matter of fact that the affairs of the Company could not be settled?" will enable the reporter to make up any amount of lost ground, or, if he has none to make up, will permit him, so to speak, to play with the speaker and record his words with the utmost ease and *nonchalance*, however rapidly they may be uttered. But these agreeable combinations are comparatively rare. And here let me say that they must not be *sought:* if

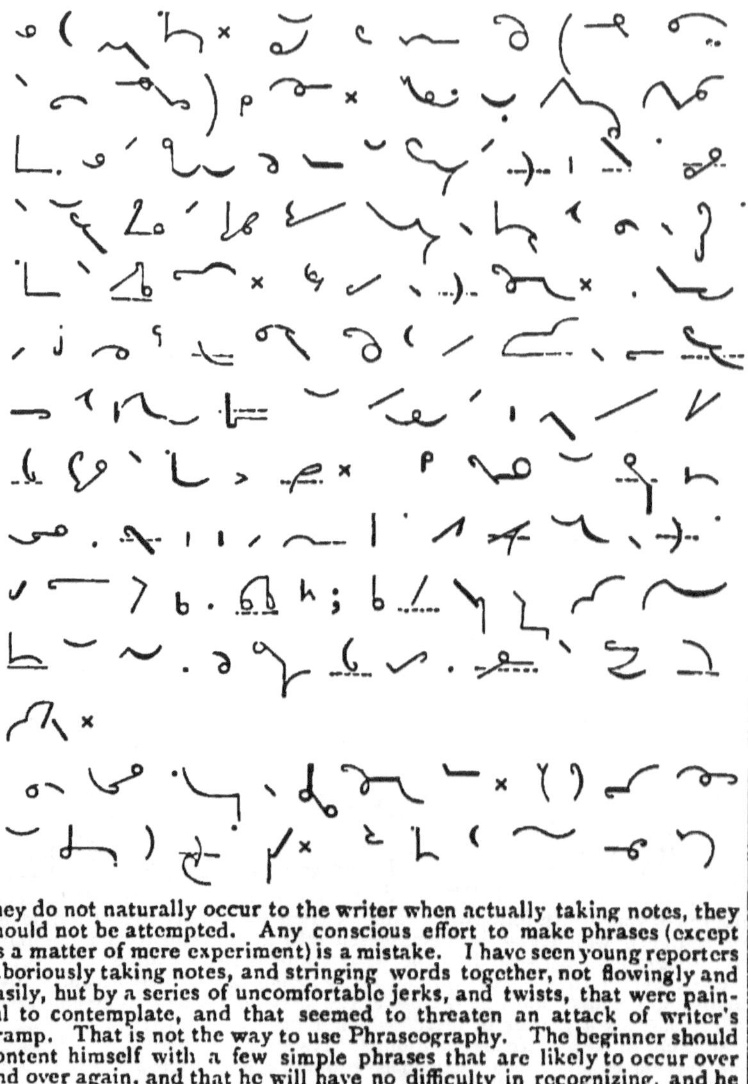

they do not naturally occur to the writer when actually taking notes, they should not be attempted. Any conscious effort to make phrases (except as a matter of mere experiment) is a mistake. I have seen young reporters laboriously taking notes, and stringing words together, not flowingly and easily, but by a series of uncomfortable jerks, and twists, that were painful to contemplate, and that seemed to threaten an attack of writer's cramp. That is not the way to use Phraseography. The beginner should content himself with a few simple phrases that are likely to occur over and over again, and that he will have no difficulty in recognizing, and he should be rather chary than otherwise of adding to the list. As he progresses in speed he may increase the number, but he should make it a rigid rule never to use a joined character of which he has the slightest doubt; it is much better to take a little longer time in writing the words separately than to run the risk of clashing or illegibility.

Some phonographers affect to despise Phraseography altogether. I think they are greatly mistaken in discarding so useful an agent. I quite admit that many excellent, I may say some of the best, reporters, write

almost all their words separately; but, on the other hand, I think that the most skilled writers I have met with are glad to avail themselves of phraseograms to a moderate extent. I do not know a single thoroughly expert phonographer who indulges in their use beyond the limits which I have endeavored to prescribe.

Whenever I see a phonographer perpetrating those inconvenient, puzzling, ill-assorted combinations, of which I have given you a few and not exaggerated examples, I am disposed to say of him, though of course in a different sense, what Shakspere says of another kind of objectionable person,—"Let no such man be trusted." As to all such unnatural alliances I can only, in a concluding word, repeat my emphatic warning against them, and declare solemnly that I forbid the banns!

PENS, INK, AND PAPER.

A Lecture delivered before the Phonetic Shorthand Writers' Association, London.

When I was asked to give a short address on the occasion on which we are now met it occurred to me that I could not select a more appropriate subject than that of our familiar writing materials, pens, ink and paper, which form so conspicuous an element in civilised life, and especially in the daily life of the shorthand writer. Let me say at the outset of my remarks that I have no desire to encourage any of my hearers to be fastidious, not to say "faddy" in regard to the writing materials they employ. The old saying that it is the bad workman who complains of his tools is as applicable to our craft as to any other, I confess that I like to see a reporter who can take notes with a worn-out nib or quill, or with the stump of a pencil half-an-inch long; and, if need be, on a sheet of brown paper. The exigencies of a reporter's calling do not always permit him the luxury of a neatly-pointed pencil, or a well-tested gold pen, or a note-book well

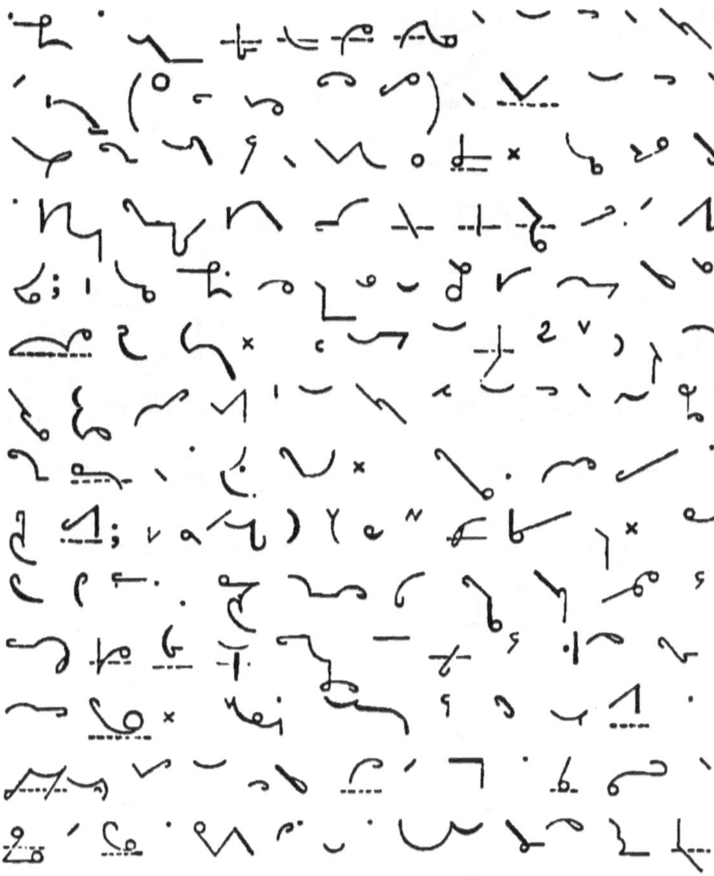

filled with the best paper. He may now and then be called upon to extemporise a note-book out of a few loose leaves of any kind of paper, and he may be glad (as has occurred to myself more than once) to borrow any kind of pencil from a neighbor with which to perform his task. If he has always been a dilettante practitioner he will be greatly put out by these rough-and-ready shifts; but if he has accustomed himself to take notes under all circumstances he will make the best of his materials, whatever they may be. When engaged in teaching shorthand I used to tell my pupils that they must learn to write on any paper and with any kind of writing instrument from a skewer to a shaving brush. Perhaps the limits were a trifle wide; but the spirit of the recommendation was, I think, sound, and I still adhere to it. As in every other calling, the skilful workman will produce better results with the clumsiest tools than an indifferent craftsman can achieve with the aid of the most perfect mechanical appliances. I have seen an angler with a brand new rod, a winch of the newest pattern, any amount of the best line and gut, a choice selection of hooks and flies, a superb landing net, a fishing basket of the most artistic type,

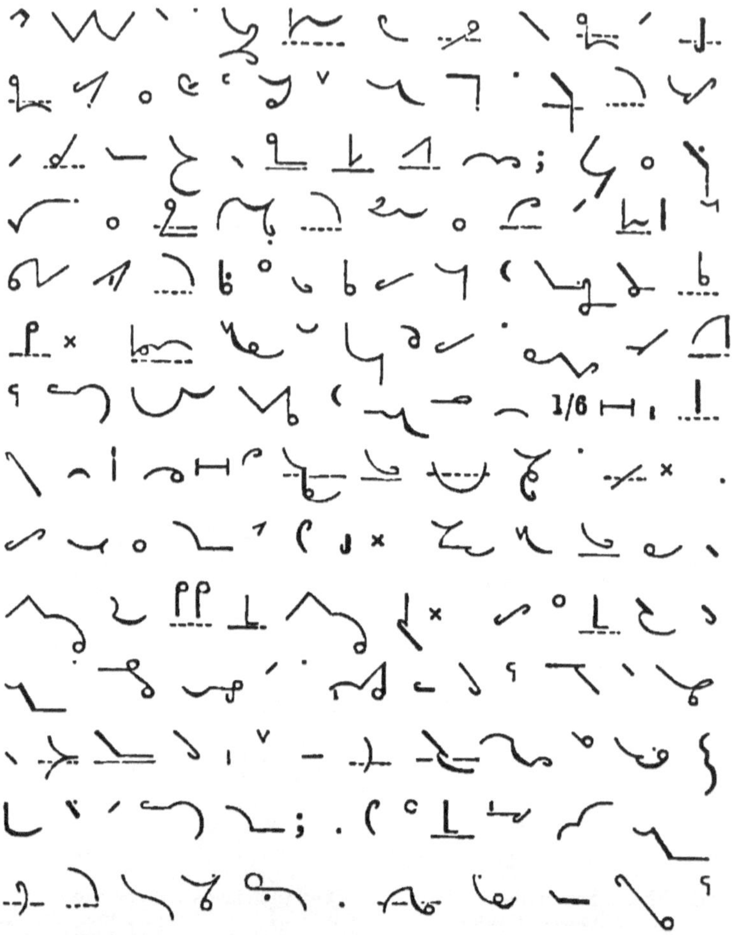

and all the paraphernalia of a fisherman, toiling for hours up-stream and down-stream, watching his float with anxious eye, never getting a bite, or if one should chance to come, failing to strike at the right moment; changing his bait, altering his hook, lengthening or shortening his line, and at the end of the day not a solitary roach or dace has found its way into that picturesque basket at his side. At the same time I have seen, not twenty yards away, a sun-burnt country lad, with a clumsy fishing apparatus that could not have cost him eighteenpence—he had probably made it himself—land half-a-dozen fine fish in less than an hour. The one knew his work and the other did not. In like manner I have often seen two reporters sitting side by side at a reporters' table. One has had a beautifully bound note-book, an expensive inkstand, and a Mordan's gold pen, with a couple of pencils to fall back upon, but I could see by every movement of his fingers that he was doing bad and clumsy work; the other has had an awkward little note-book three or four inches square, the leaves fastened

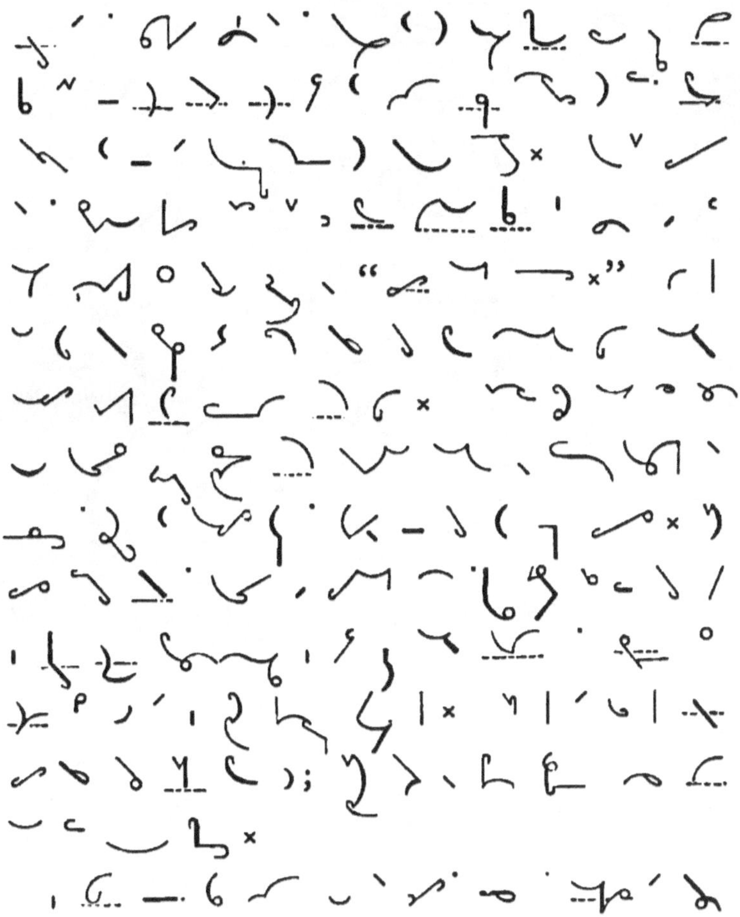

together perhaps with a pin, and a solitary stump of a pencil that was evidently drawing near to its last days, and I could see by the ease with which that little cedar implement was gliding over the paper that good and effective work was being accomplished. If I were of a sporting turn of mind I would offer long odds on Stump, who, with only Mordan as his opponent, would be sure to "win in a canter." Let it not then be supposed that the very best pen ever manufactured will enable anyone to write either quickly or well. I am afraid there is in the minds of some young phonographers who have not been skilful or patient enough to acquire facility of execution a suspicion that if they once had a thorough good pen they could do wonders. I was once called upon by a phonographer who wanted my advice on the subject of his gold pen which he had been using for some months, but with which he was unable to follow a speaker as easily as he wished, and he therefore contemplated changing it. I tried it and found it to be one of the best pens I had ever used; I was therefore compelled to tell him that his difficulty must lie in quite another direction.

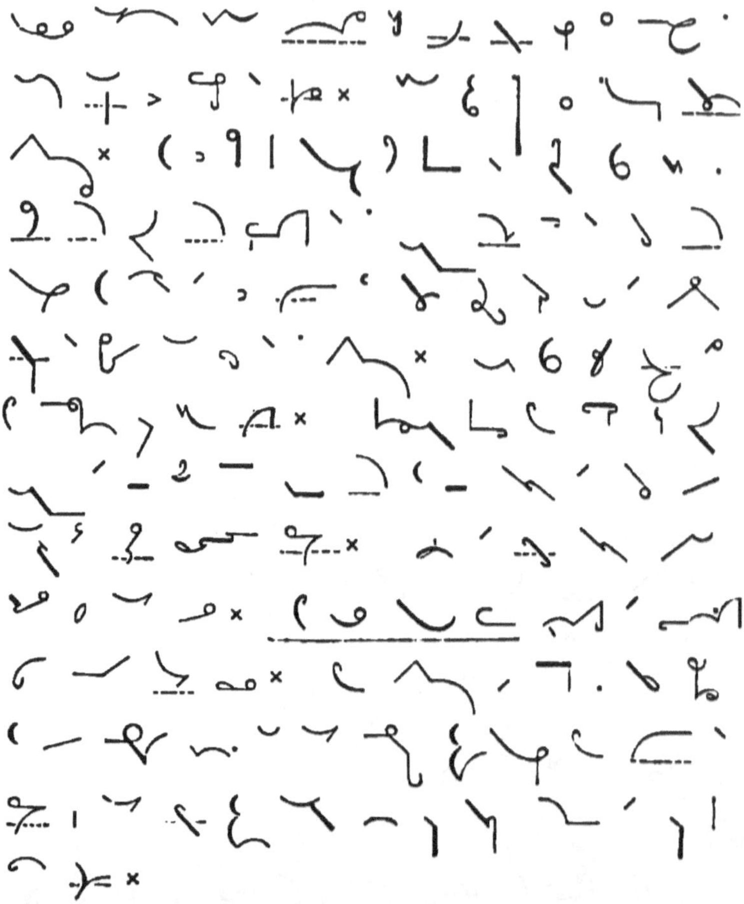

But while giving this little note of warning against a needless and absurd fussiness in the matter of writing materials, I do not wish to be understood as counseling an entire indifference to the question of tools. I know that this attitude is affected by some reporters. They would consider it beneath their dignity to trouble themselves about the size or shape or quality of a note-book, or the kind of pen or pencil they employed, and would look with absolute suspicion upon a neat and respectable bit of stationery in front of a reporter. Now this is just as foolish as the other extreme to which I have alluded. It must not be taken for granted that a shabby note-book and good shorthand go together, or that good paper and pens are incompatible with the highest stenographic skill. Stump and brown paper are not always first in the race. *Other things being equal*, Mordan and creamlaid will carry off the stakes. Every reporter should get the best instruments that are accessible to him, not in the expectation that they will compensate for lack of skill, but in the belief that they may enable him to do better work and to do it more easily.

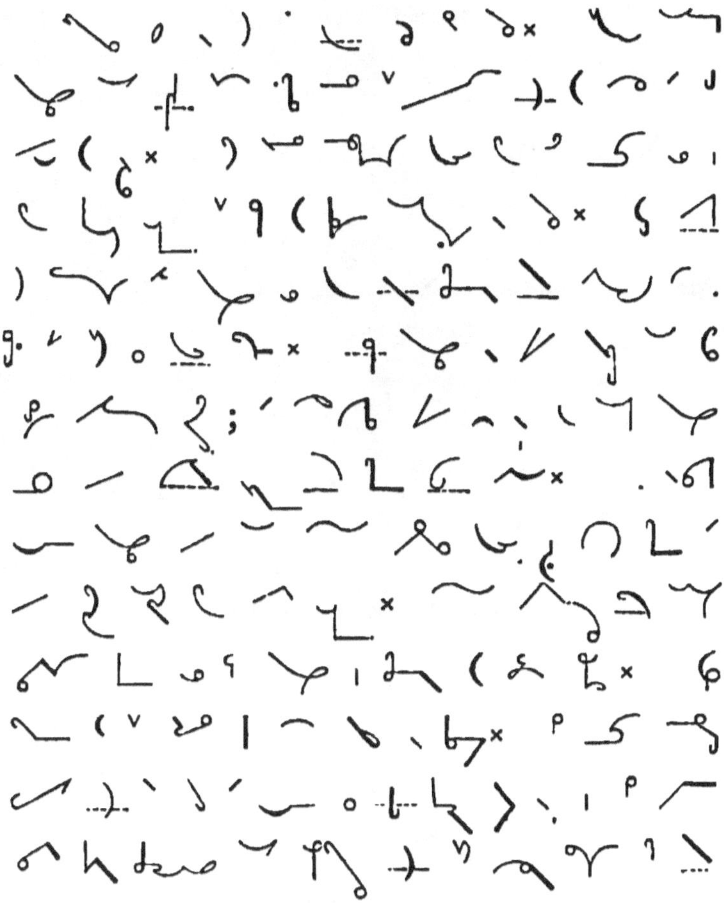

I propose first to say a few words as to pens. I have not included pencils in the title of my address, because I rarely use them myself, and do not recommend them to others. They are of course extremely convenient for short occasional notes, but for continuous note-taking I consider them decidedly inferior to pens. They do not write so clearly, and when pencil notes have to be transcribed by artificial light the strain on the eyes is often very great. Cedar pencils too, which are better than any others, constantly require sharpening; and most of the leads which are made to fit into pencil cases are liable to break or drag while writing. The solid ink pencils are in many respects convenient, but they also drag, and are therefore unsuitable for rapid note-taking. Many reporters, however, not only habitually take notes with a pencil, but transcribe them with the same instrument. This is a practice that I always do my best to discourage. As an occasional expedient where the use of pen and ink is difficult, it cannot be objected to, but as a regular habit it should be discountenanced in the interest of the printers, whose eyesight must be sorely tried

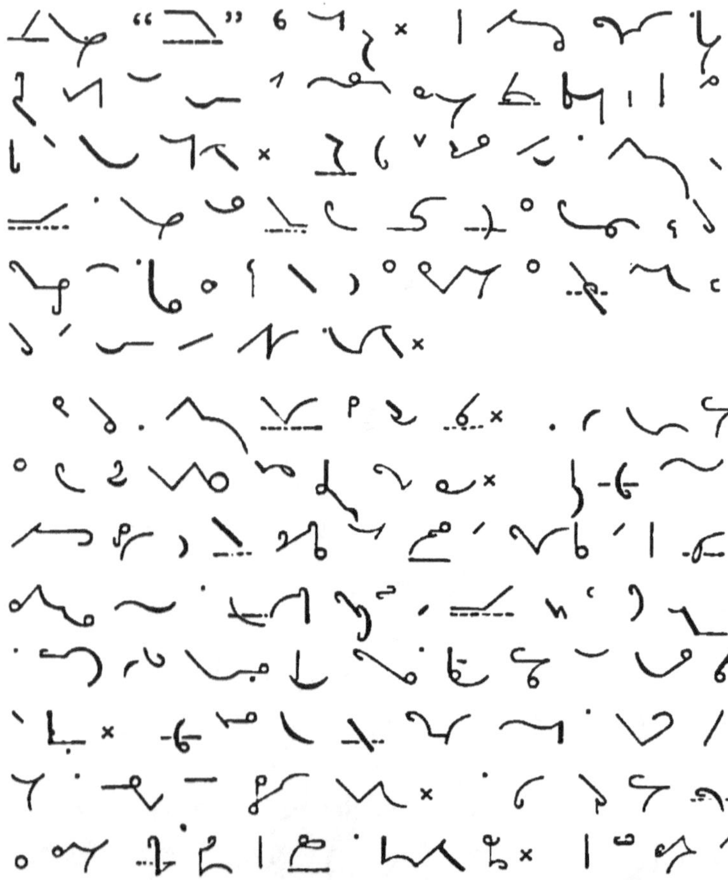

by much of the pencil "copy" that is handed to them. It requires very little additional trouble to write in ink, and the manuscript is not only much more distinct but it has the advantage of being indelible. Although, then, I always recommend a reporter to carry a pencil in his pocket for occasional use, as for example when a pen breaks down, my advice is that it be used as sparingly as possible, and never when pen and ink are readily available.

As to pens the reporter happily has an abundant choice. The old familiar quill has, for shorthand purposes, almost disappeared from the scene. It was, within my own recollection, constantly used by shorthand writers in the law courts and parliamentary committees, and it still survives among a few of the elder brethren of the craft who carry about with their note-book a clumsy old-fashioned pen-case containing perhaps a dozen quills in various stages of decay. These, of course, have to be frequently mended, an operation which only an expert can satisfactorily perform. A well-pointed quill, however, is certainly, during the short time it lasts, an admirable instrument. It glides swiftly and easily over the paper, but, unless

the touch is very light, its movement is accompanied by a scratching or scraping noise which is anything but agreeable, and which, when three or four pens are tearing along at the same time is positively offensive. The quill is better adapted to the old systems of shorthand than to Phonography. The latter requires a distinction in the thickness of its letters, and with a quill pen, except when just made or mended, this distinction cannot be easily preserved.

Of steel pens there are many hundreds of kinds from which to make a selection, and each writer should choose that which is best adapted to his own style of caligraphy. A heavy hand will naturally shrink from a light and finely pointed pen; while a light hand will, at least for shorthand purposes, avoid a blunt and heavy instrument. My advice in this respect must be very general. Anything like a scratchy nib is objectionable. The point should, as a rule, be rather fine, should run smoothly, and be sufficiently flexible to make a good distinction between thick and thin strokes. Any pen which answers this description will serve the purpose of a short-

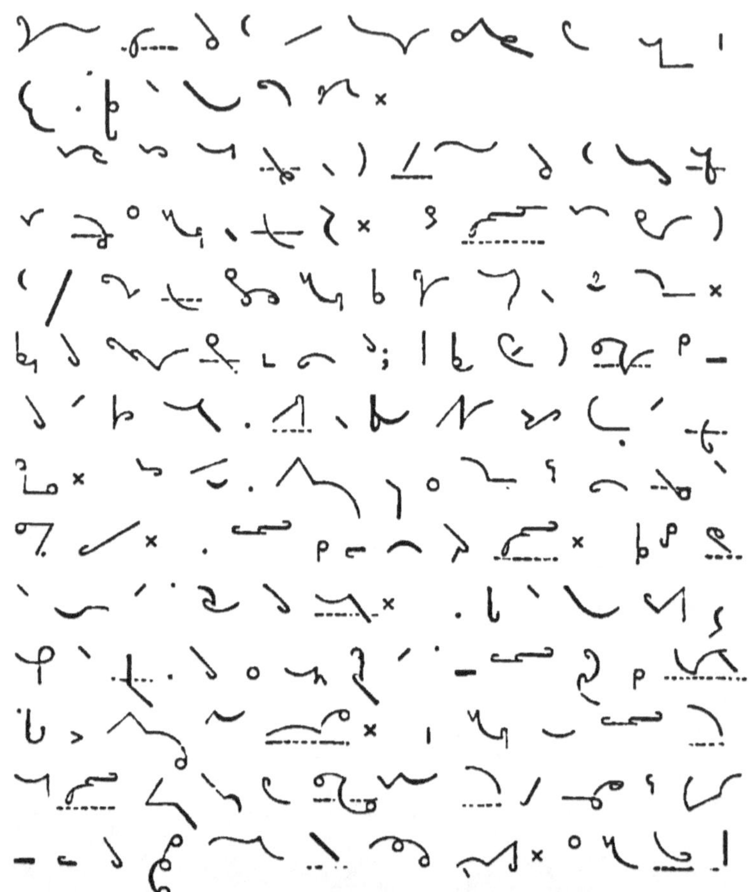

hand writer. There are many steel pens that are fairly serviceable for note-taking, but they have the disadvantage of being very short-lived.

I am afraid I am not in a position to say much of the many pens that have been introduced of late years, as I have tried too few of them. As to the stylographic I may safely say that judging from the few specimens I have tried, it is utterly unsuited to shorthand work. It is not a pen, properly speaking, but a mere point; it does not flow so smoothly as a good pen, and it will not enable the writer to distinguish readily between thick and thin strokes. I cannot recommend the reporter to do his work with a mere piece of scratchy wire. The caligraph is a great improvement upon the stylograph. It has a constant supply of ink and an ordinary pen nib. The advantage of being able to write without the necessity of dipping the pen is no doubt considerable, and a good caligraph, therefore, is a valuable addition to the reporter's writing materials. But I have tried no caligraph or Anti-stylograph which can be compared for smoothness of writing or general excellence with a thoroughly good gold pen, such as those manufactured by Messrs Mordan. As I have often had occasion to say, I think

there is no better instrument for shorthand purposes than one of these pens. I can speak from long experience. I had one of them in 1847, nearly at the commencement of my professional practice, and it lasted me for more than 30 years. I hold the pen in my hand, and I naturally regard it with a certain amount of affection as an old friend, and a faithful servant. I regret to state that it is now *hors de combat*, not from any fault or inherent weakness of its own, but from the results of an accident. It fell to the ground one day when I was sitting in an Assize Court, and the point was injured, I fear irreparably. Messrs Mordan have done their best to put it right for me, but though it will still write it has not the old certainty and smoothness of stroke. I have not yet written its epitaph, but when I do it must be one something like that of the lady of whom it is recorded:—

She lived to the age of four score and ten,
And died of a fall from a cherry tree then.

With regard to ink. it is only necessary to say that it should be flowing

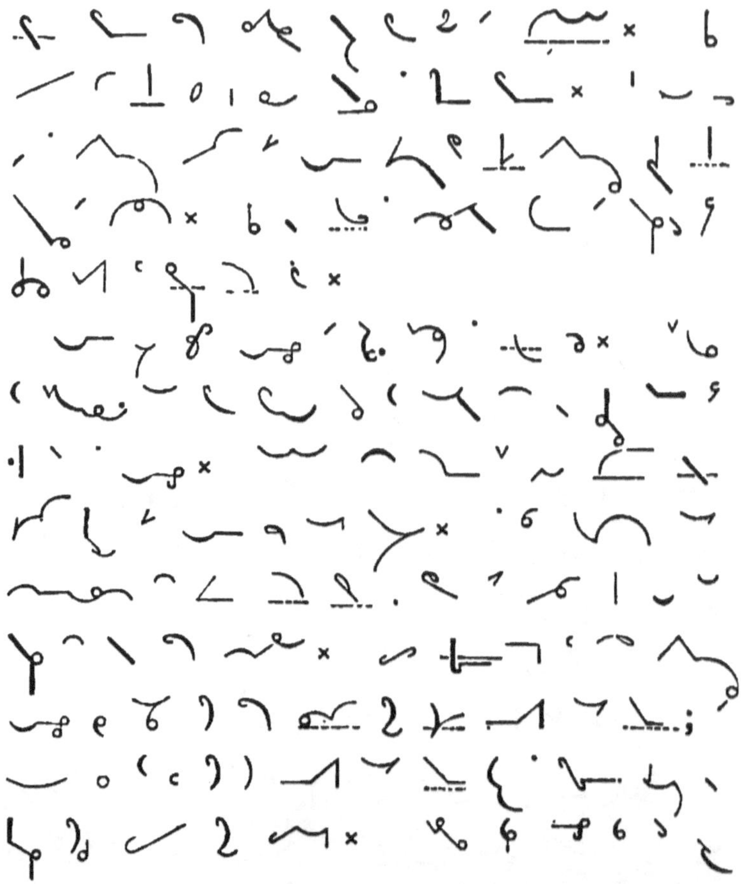

and not too light. The best pen in the world will not work well with bad ink. I find Stevens's blue black very serviceable both for shorthand and longhand. It is rather light at first, but soon becomes a dark black. On no account should a reporter rely on the ink which may be supplied at the reporters' table at public meetings and elsewhere. It is too often a miserably thick and pasty compound with which it is impossible to write with speed or comfort

Ink naturally suggests inkstands, and of these I must say a few words. I confess that I have not seen any ever-flowing pens that enable me to dispense altogether with the aid of an inkstand. In any important work I should not like to be wholly dependent on the ink stored in a pen-holder. A slight failure in the mechanism might check or stop the supply, and the result, it need not be said, might be very embarrassing One difficulty connected with most reporters' inkstands is that, unless they are very small, they are not easily carried in the pocket; and another is that when they *are* so carried in the pocket they have a provoking tendency to deposit their contents where they are not wanted. I suppose that is an accident

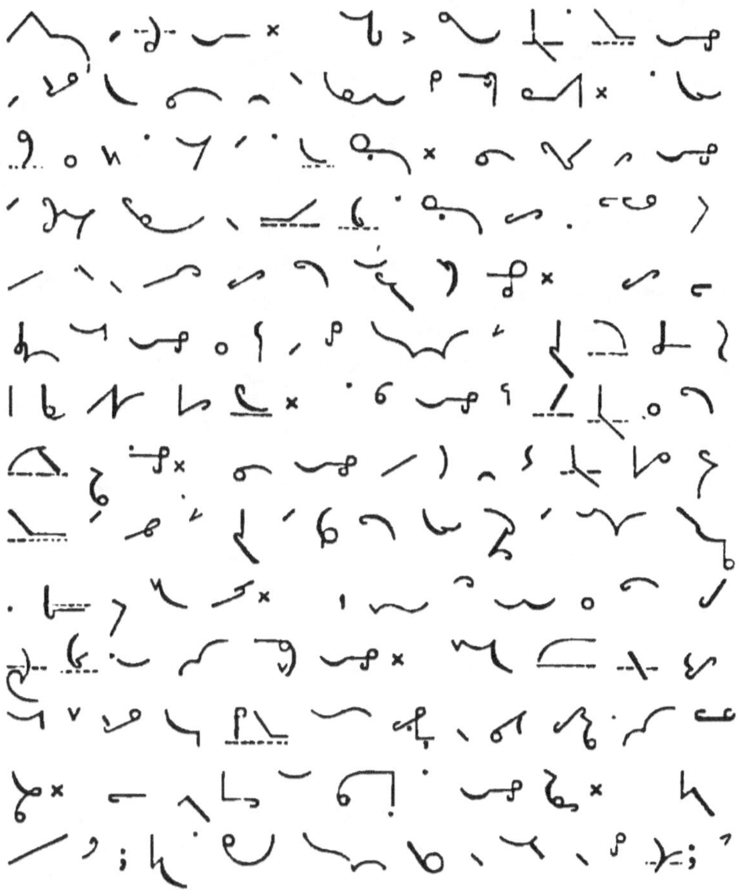

that has happened to every reporter who uses ink. In addition to the spring top, a pocket inkstand should always have some other mode of fastening as an extra security. A convenient size is about an inch and a half square. Some prefer round inkstands, and they are certainly pleasanter to carry than a square one, the corners of which are apt to remind one very uncomfortably of their existence. One great desideratum in an inkstand is that it should stand firmly on the table or desk, so that it does not readily turn over. A slight inkstand with a large top is very liable to this accident. Some inkstands are so made that the top turns completely back and rests on the table, and this is a very convenient arrangement, and entirely obviates the difficulty to which I have referred. But to my own mind nothing is more generally useful than the common little excise inkstand. I never like to be without one; indeed I always have a side-pocket in my waistcoat to hold one of these little glass vessels. Care should be taken in selecting an inkstand of this kind. It should be rather short; it should have a sufficiently firm basis to enable it to stand easily; and the neck

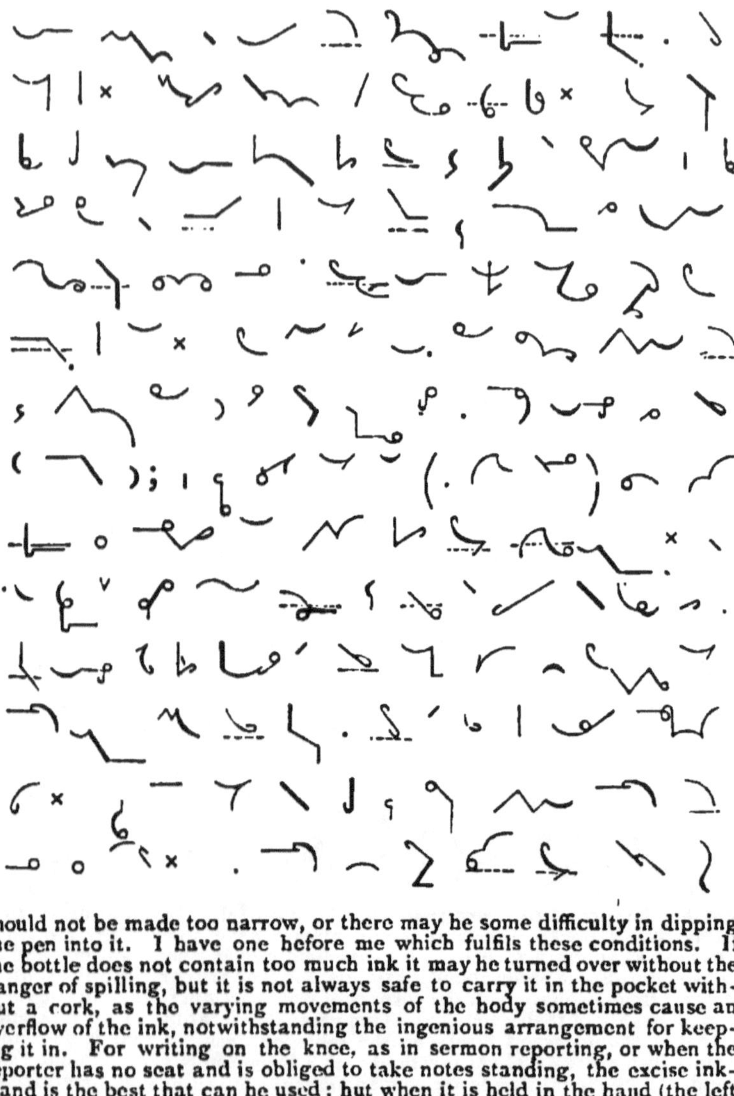

should not be made too narrow, or there may be some difficulty in dipping the pen into it. I have one before me which fulfils these conditions. If the bottle does not contain too much ink it may be turned over without the danger of spilling, but it is not always safe to carry it in the pocket without a cork, as the varying movements of the body sometimes cause an overflow of the ink, notwithstanding the ingenious arrangement for keeping it in. For writing on the knee, as in sermon reporting, or when the reporter has no seat and is obliged to take notes standing, the excise inkstand is the best that can be used; but when it is held in the hand (the left of course) some little difficulty is experienced in rapidly turning over the leaves of the note-book. To avoid this difficulty I suggested many years ago that a piece of wire be fastened round the top of the inkstand and then turned downwards and passed into a hole made for the purpose in the cover of the note-book, and I have often adopted the plan and found it answer extremely well. But this can only be done when a separate reporting cover or case is employed. The cover may project slightly over

the paper so that a hole can be easily made in it, but with ordinary note-books in which the cover is bound up with the paper no such holes could well be made. I have lately thought of a very simple way of getting over the slight difficulty in the manipulation of the leaves, arising from the necessity of holding the inkstand in the hand. Tie a piece of string or tape or an india-rubber band round the neck of the inkstand, and make a loop two or three inches long; let this loop go over the thumb, and the inkstand can then fall over the back of the hand quite out of the way of the note-book, being sufficiently near for the purpose of dipping, and at the same time leaving the fingers perfectly free to manipulate the leaves. I assure you that for writing on the knee or standing this is a very convenient arrangement, and the only wonder is that nobody seems to have thought of it before. I can hardly forgive myself for having been in full practice so many years without adopting some contrivance of this nature. I have here an inkstand showing the arrangement I have described, and you will see how easily it works. Instead of putting the loop over the

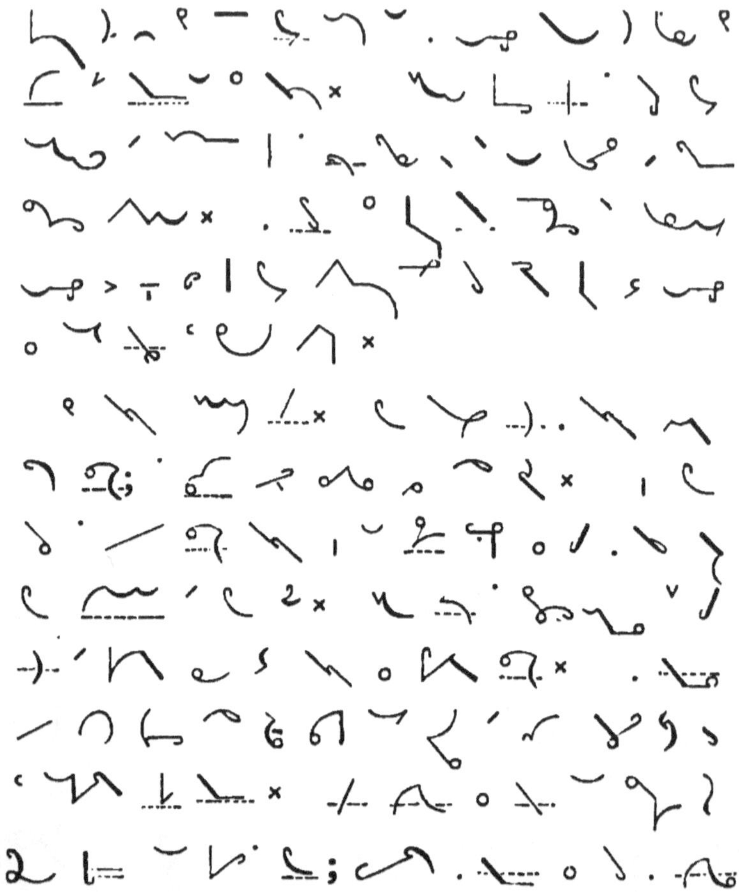

thumb, as I have suggested, it may be so made as to go over the entire hand, the inkstand being so fastened as to lie on the back of the hand as before. I have not taken out a patent for the invention, and I make it a free present to all young phonographers who practise sermon reporting. The plan as adopted by excisemen of fastening the inkstand to the coat will not do for the reporter, because the pen cannot be dipped when the inkstand is in that position with sufficient rapidity.

As to paper I need not say much. For pencil use the paper should not be very smooth; a slightly rough surface is the most suitable. But for pens a rather smooth paper, but not highly glazed, is generally the best both for longhand and for shorthand. I have here a specimen of the note-books I generally use, and it will be seen that the paper is tolerably smooth. The books are also thicker than most of those sold in the shops, and you will observe that they are bound with india-rubber at the back. Each leaf is put in separately, so that there is no difficulty in turning over; wherever the book is open the leaves lie flat, and there is none of that

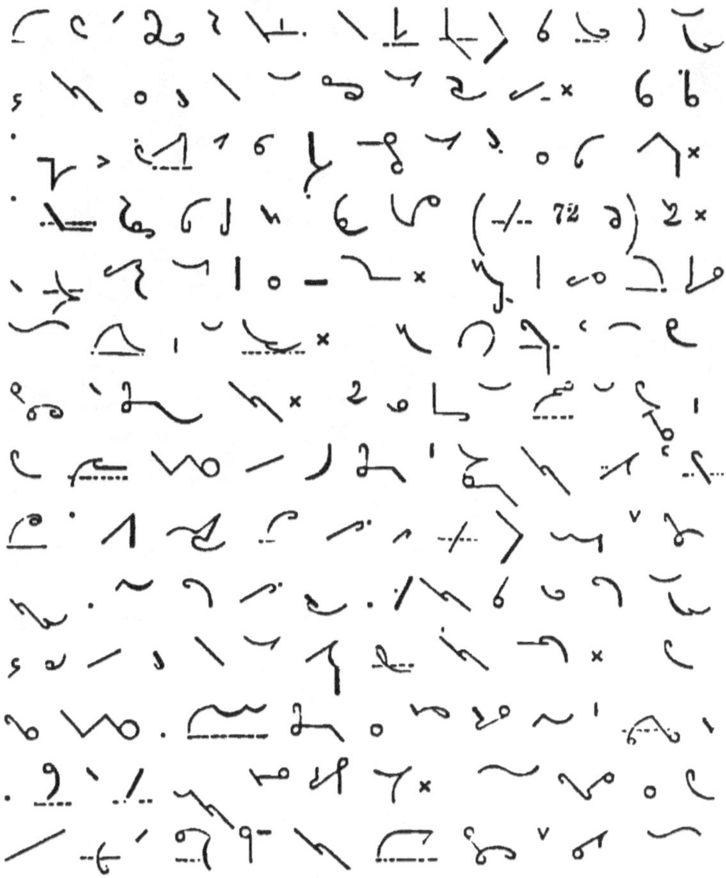

puckering up at the top of the page which is often so inconvenient when the paper is bound up in sections in the ordinary way. This adds a good deal to the comfort of the writer, and the slight additional expense in the binding is well repaid. A book of this kind will contain about a thousand folios (each 72 words) of shorthand. To fill one of them in a day is good work. I have done it once or twice in my life, but not oftener. I have also brought with me several specimens of transcribing paper. Shorthand notes taken in law courts, not for the press but for legal purposes, are usually transcribed on foolscap paper ruled with blue lines, a red marginal line running round each page, intended, I presume, to prevent the writing from running too near the edge of the paper, which is found very inconvenient when the sheets are bound up in the orthodox stiff paper cover. For press purposes the longhand transcript is almost always written on slips about the size of large note-paper, of course on one side only. My own preference is for rather thin and smooth straw paper, like the specimen I hold in my hand, over which the pen glides very

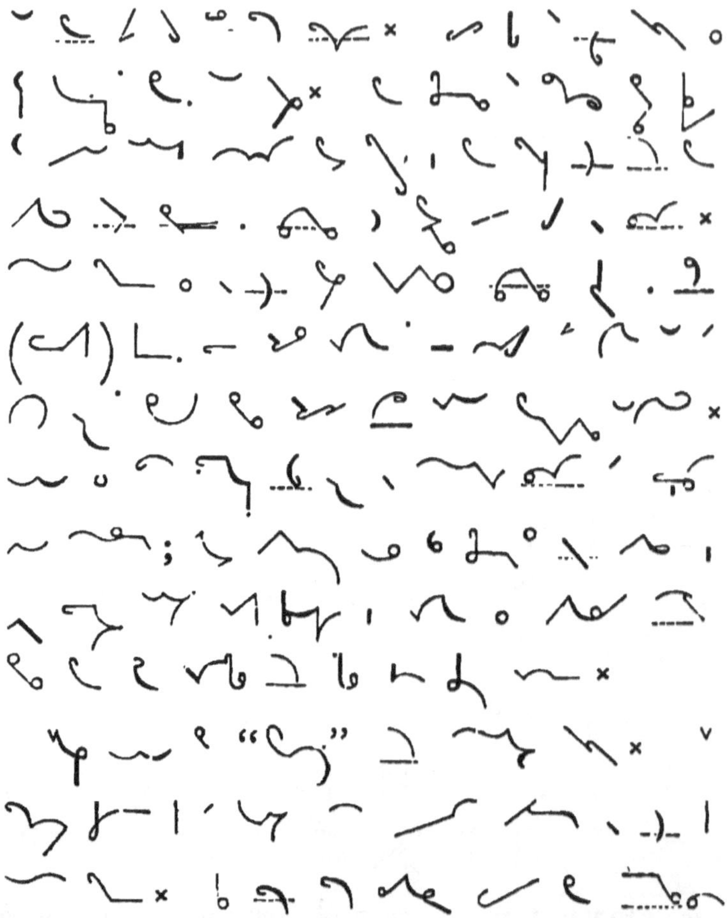

freely. One advantage of thin paper is that it effects a saving in postage. For transcripts of sermons, speeches, etc., that are not intended immediately for the printer, but for private use, or for revision by the speaker, the slips used for the press are generally too small. My own practice is to use for such purposes slips double the size (quarto), taking care always to leave a good margin on the left hand, and also to have a sufficient space between the lines of writing for the purpose of interlineation. Nothing is more aggravating than to have to manipulate small and closely written manuscript; and if the reporter knows that his transcript has to be revised, he should be careful not only to write distinctly, but to leave his reviser ample space for whatever alterations or additions he may desire to make.

I have said nothing as to "flimsy" or manifold paper. I very much dislike it, and fortunately am rarely required to use it in my practice. It is, however, very serviceable where several copies of the same report are

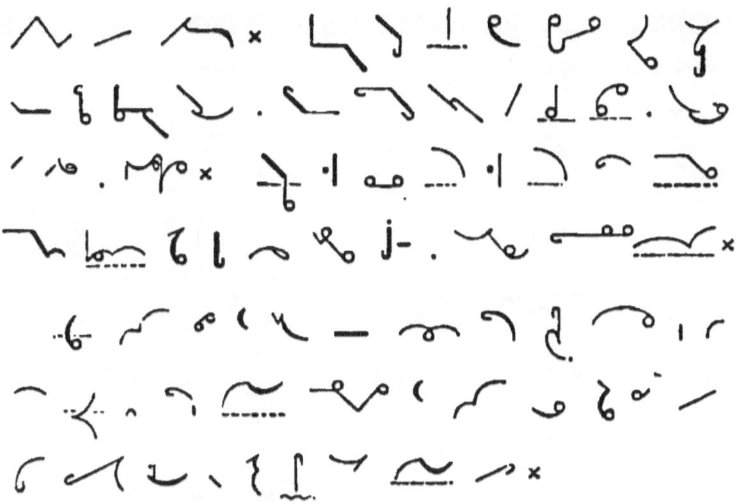

required. It can be obtained at several stationers' shops in London, together with its disagreeable companion, the black carbon paper, which at once soils the fingers and offends the nostrils. By its aid, six or eight or more copies can be made at the same time, and this advantage must, I suppose, condone the unpleasant characteristics of the material.

These little hints that I have given may seem very trifling matters, but let me assure you from long experience that little things of this sort are well worth attending to, and that they *tell* in the long run.

SHORTHAND AS A MEANS OF MENTAL DISCIPLINE

An Address read by Thomas Allen Reed before the Shorthand Society.

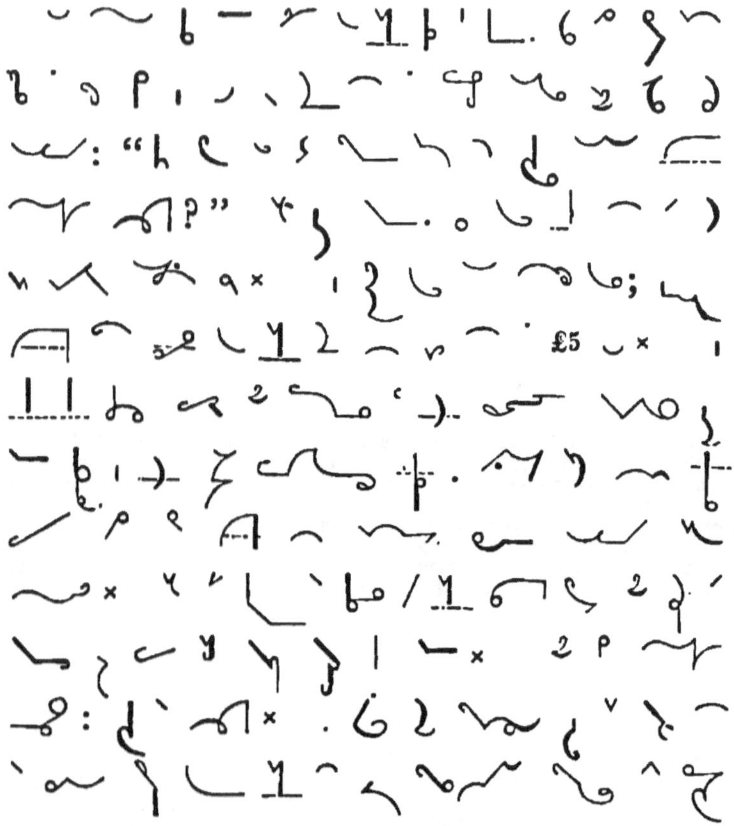

Not many days ago, shortly after I had decided on taking this as the subject of my address, a friend said he wished to ask me a question in reference to shorthand, and this was his inquiry: "Do you ever find that the practice of your art develops anything like mental imbecility?" I thought he was poking his fun at me, and was about to reply in the same spirit. But there was no fun in my friend's face; he could not have looked more serious if I had asked him to lend me a five-pound note. He had had, it seems, one or two shorthand clerks with whose stenographic performances he was not altogether dissatisfied, but whose intellectual qualifications outside the range of their immediate duties were such as to lead him to make the singular inquiry I have mentioned. I thought on the topic of discourse which I had selected for the Shorthand Society, and began to think whether I had not better abandon it altogether. Shorthand as a mental exercise: development of imbecility. The conjunction was not promising, but then I bethought me of certain stupid folk I had met

who were members of the learned professions, and of skilful artists and mechanics I had known whose mental endowments were not of a high degree. I told my friend that I believed I could answer his question in the negative, but I was forced to admit that the practice of shorthand and stupidity (I would not go so far as imbecility) did sometimes go together. And I suppose I must make tbe same admission now and here. But I take it that the same thing may he said with regard to every art and every calling. However calculated may be the art or tbe profession to develop the mental faculties it must never be forgotten that there will be persons who will embrace it without the necessary qualifications in tbe shape of average ability and a reasonahly good education.

That this has been the case with shorthand some of us know only too well. I do not forget that my predecessor in this chair, in the abundance of his good nature, has told us that he thinks every reporter must he a clever fellow. Happily for the craft it is not every student of shorthand who becomes a reporter or a shorthand-writer, but even among those who attain to that dignity there are to he found persons of the slenderest ac-

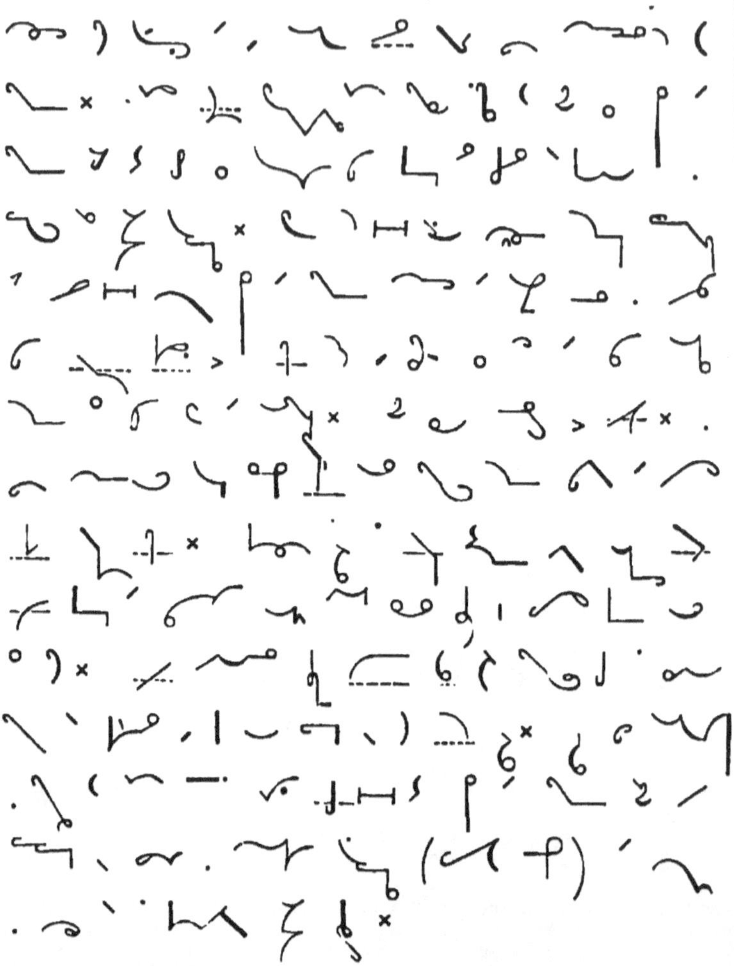

quirements—persons who have mistaken their vocation, and who never rise above the mere mechanics of the art they practise. I must assume for the purpose of my present address that shorthand is studied and practised intelligently, that the student is fairly well educated, and is desirous of continuing the cultivation of his intellectual faculties. Every art—painting, music, architecture, sculpture, and the rest—may be studied and practised mechanically, and in such a case the result will appear, at least to the true artist who throws his mind and soul into his work, as stale, flat, and unprofitable. Shorthand is no exception to the rule. The mere mechanician, if he succeed at all in his professional work, will be and remain at the bottom of the tree. It may seem to others a pity that the work should be undertaken by the ill-educated and slenderly-endowed, and in a sense it is so, but we must take things as they are. Our ranks, it is true, like those of other professions, contain a certain proportion of

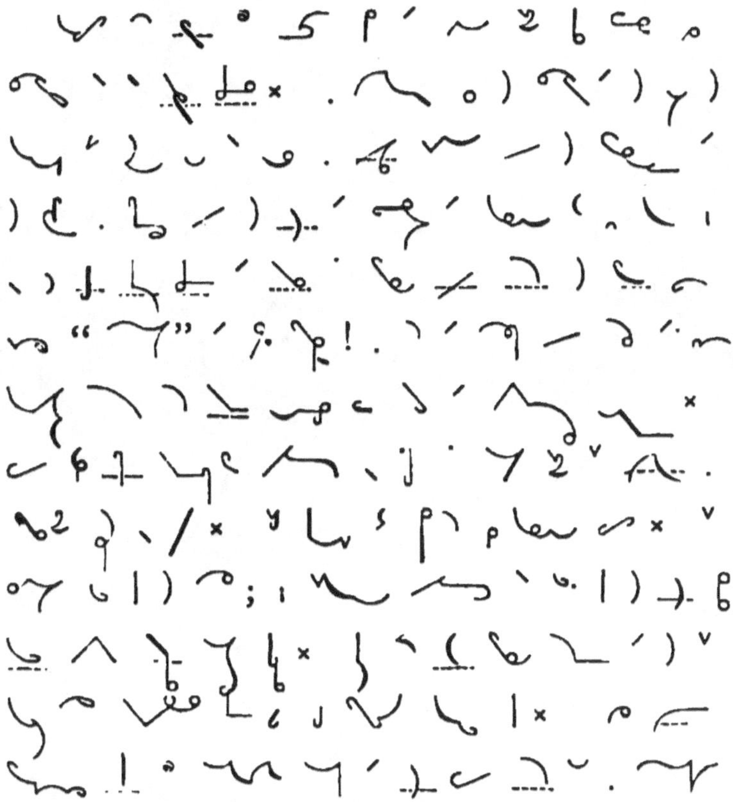

dullards who do no credit to us or to themselves. But this will not invalidate the proposition that I am going to lay down—that the study and practice of shorthand are calculated to stimulate the mental faculties (where they exist), and may be made the means of an admirable intellectual discipline.

If one might believe what is occasionally said and written of shorthand, its acquisition is the simplest of all possible tasks. The alphabet is so simple and so natural, so founded on the essential nature of things, the rules of writing are so philosophical and so delightful, the contractions are so easy and graceful and fascinating, that you have but to sit down at your task and pass a pleasant hour or so over Mr Pitman's "Manual," and heigh! presto! the art and mystery are yours, and you may forthwith order your pocket inkstand, gold pen, and reporter's note-book. Whether that is a true picture of the effort required to attain a knowledge of shorthand I leave the members of the Shorthand Society to judge. I do not deny that the study of the art is a fascinating one. I certainly found it so myself; but I have no recollection of finding it so easy as it is often represented by its enthusiastic devotees. It was hard though pleasant work, and so I fancy most persons who have attained proficiency have found it. Let us look for a moment at what is involved in it and see whether or not

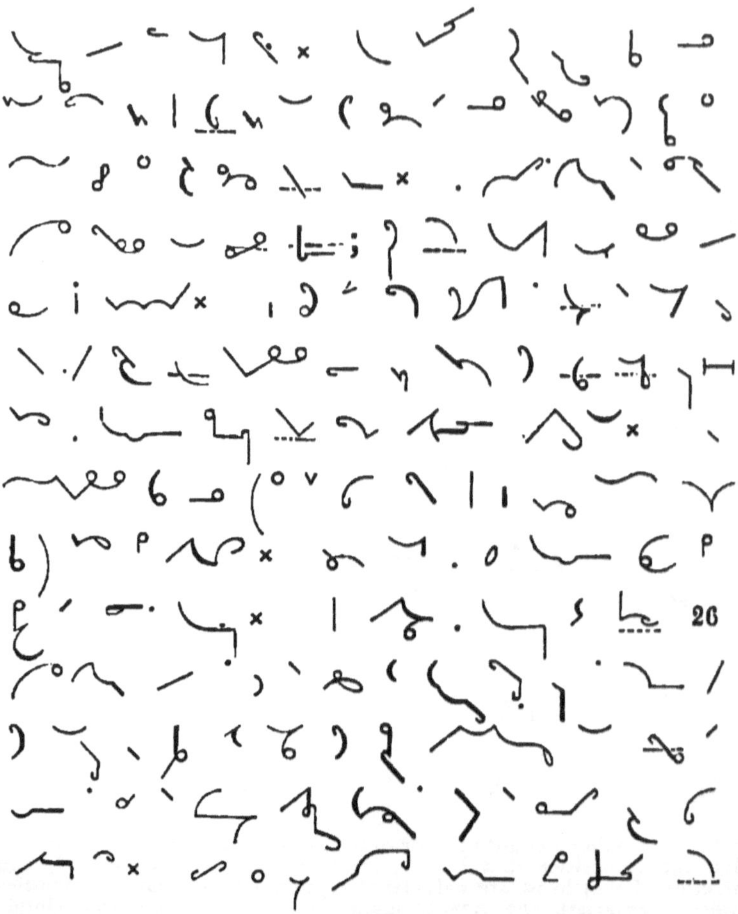

the mental faculties are called into play. If I refer especially to Phonography it is because I know more about it than about any other system, and because I suppose I may say that it has as many students as all other systems put together. The learning of the alphabet of simple letters presents no serious difficulty; thirty or forty new signs are soon committed to memory. But there is on the very threshold a field of knowledge opened up which comparatively few persons care to tread before they are thus introduced to it—I mean the phonetic structure apart from the orthographic representation of the language. To many persons this comes (as I well remember it did to myself in my early days) almost as a revelation. To some, indeed, the first phonetic lesson has a startling and staggering effect. It reveals the fact that the time-honored twenty-six letters of the alphabet are a set of imposters, that they have been pretending to do a work which they are incompetent to discharge, and that unless they are considerably reinforced in numbers and undergo a sort of electoral redistribution they must be an object of scorn to every well-regulated mind. One is naturally reluctant to make such a discovery or accept such a con-

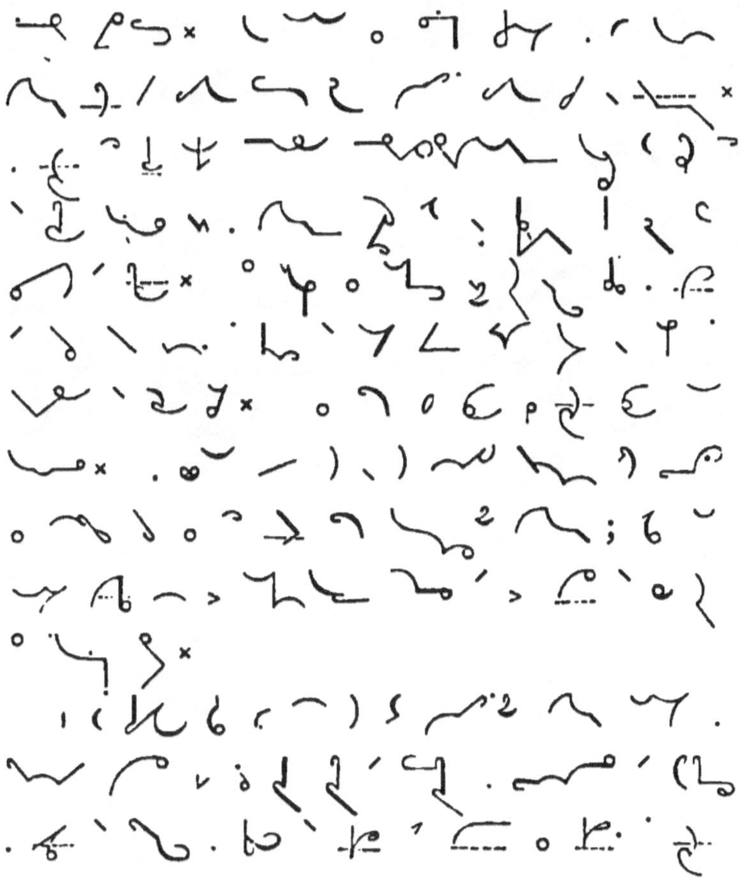

clusion. If anything is sacred it is certainly the old familiar alphabet through which we have acquired whatever learning we have chanced to pick up. The youthful mind, at any rate, notwithstanding the agonising experiences of the spelling-book, fancies that there is a kind of eternal fitness about the alphabetic arrangement, and that to disturb it would be flat heresy and treason. As I have said, his introduction to shorthand, especially to Phonography, dissipates the illusion and opens up to him a department of knowledge which can hardly fail to interest a person of ordinary intelligence. His very first lesson is a useful lesson in phonetics. The sounds of the language are, so to say, marshalled before him, and their correlation is impressed upon his mind by the very forms of the short-hand alphabet; and this not unnaturally leads him to the anatomy of the vocal organs and to the laws of sound, especially as affecting speech.

But without dwelling on this let me say that the learning of the short-hand alphabet, not only the primary letters but the compounds, double, treble, and quadruple, the grammalogues and other contractions, the rules of abbreviation, the distinction of outlines, and the like, is at least a useful

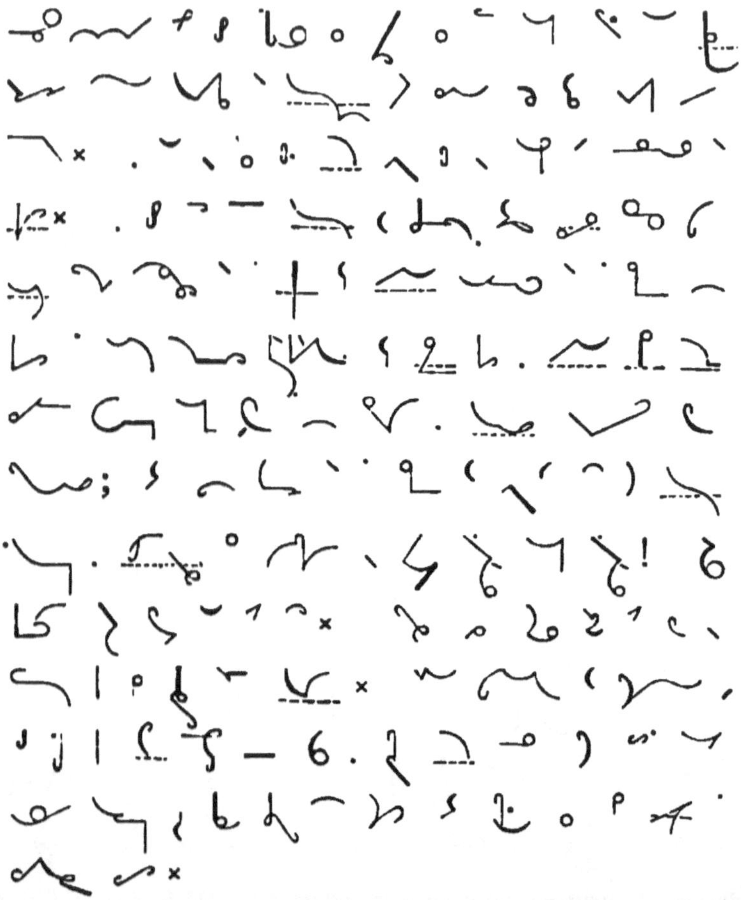

exercise of the memory, and as the student advances, his judgment is called into play in deciding between the many varieties of form of which certain words that he has to write are capable. The hand too is trained, or should be trained, to nicety and exactness of outline. The student cannot go far without discovering that the most serious consequences will ensue from the misplacement of a dot, that a wrong inclination of a stroke may turn an entire argument topsy-turvy, that a hook turned the wrong side or a circle elongated into an oval may spoil the finest peroration ever pronounced; that the mere thickening of a stroke that should be light might so far affect the style of the composition as literally to change *pathos* into *bathos!* All this is educational, both for the hand and the mind. Precision is the essence of shorthand, and the effort to acquire it is a discipline of great value. I know well enough that there are many who do not attain it, either because they do not give themselves the trouble or because they are wanting in the necessary faculty, but that does not disprove my assertion that the training is, as a rule, a serviceable one.

I have hitherto referred chiefly to the early efforts made to acquire a knowledge of the elements of shorthand. Let me now refer to what is involved in the practice required to attain even a moderate proficiency in the art. To this end the student needs a good deal of reading and writing, and he ought to benefit mentally by both. I am obliged to admit that much of the shorthand literature at his disposal is not of the highest class. Our best historians, poets, scientists, novelists, unfortunately do not contribute to our shorthand magazines; but happily there are not wanting shorthand reprints of some of our choicest literary gems, which can be read for practice; and in writing from dictation (a necessary task for every shorthand student) the whole field of English literature lies before him, and it must certainly be his own fault if he does not select something which will contribute to his intellectual improvement. A good historical book is a capital exercise for the student. If he reads what he has written, as of course he ought to do, he goes through the same pages a second time, and thus gets them impressed upon his memory. The effort required to decipher indifferently-written characters, to supply the necessary vowels and other

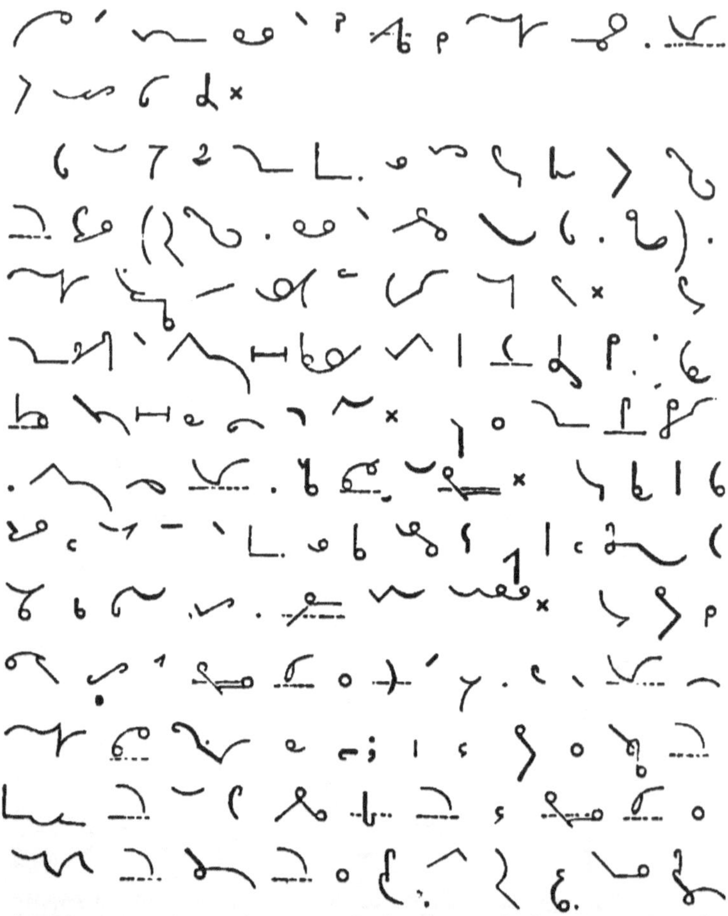

omitted letters, and to make sense of what he reads, is a mental exercise the value of which no one will dispute.

Then in actual shorthand work, taking notes, I mean, for a definite object, professional or otherwise (especially professional, the sense of responsibility being then the strongest), the mental faculties are necessarily called thoroughly into play. For the work of the shorthand-writer and reporter—it is necessary to repeat it, though it has been said a thousand times before—is not mere word-writing. To do his work at all satisfactorily the reporter must follow the ideas, as well as the language, of the speaker. If he does not do this always when in the act of taking notes it is indispensable that he should do it when transcribing them, unless he is willing to run the risk of writing nonsense. If the subject is a simple one, and the speaker's style is easy and natural, the effort to follow him mentally as well as verbally is not great; but when the subject is abstruse or technichal, or in other respects difficult, or when the speaker's style is involved or obscure, or his delivery rapid, especially when these peculiarities,

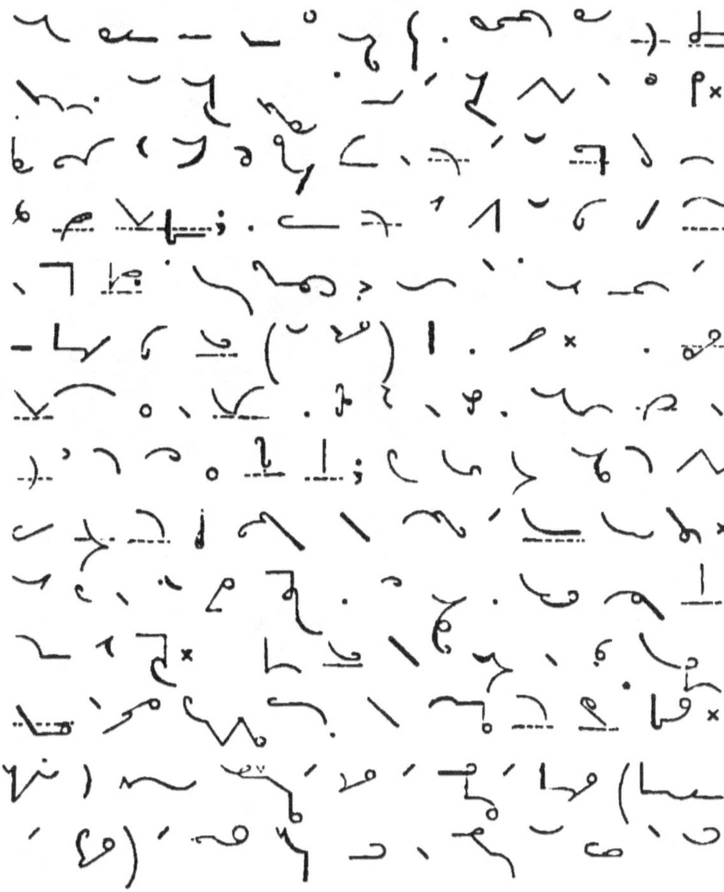

troublesome enough singly, come together, as now and then they do, the stenographer has no easy task before him in endeavoring to present an accurate and intelligible report of what is said. It is not merely that unusual words, strange alike to ear and hand, crowd upon him; that is the least part of the difficulty: the quick ear and the ready hand will generally manage to get at least a fair approximation to the name of a new-comer, and a good dictionary will often (not always) do the rest. The serious part of the matter is to follow the train of thought, to understand the unfamiliar allusion, to see what your man is driving at; for if you fail in this, your report, whether full or condensed, will probably be imperfect and foggy, if not absurd. In the effort to avoid such a catastrophe the mind no less than the fingers must be at work, and that actively. It may often be needful to consult, if there is time, books of reference for the purpose of clearing up ambiguities or supplying deficiences. I dare not say how many encyclopædias, and histories, and gazetteers, and dictionaries (technical and otherwise), and concordances I have had occasion to explore in

quest of information that I had not possessed to enable me to transcribe accurately some shorthand notes that from the speaker's fault or mine were hazy and unintelligible, or perhaps in search of the name of a person or a city that had entirely escaped my memory, if it ever had a place there. No reporter, however well informed, can be independent of such aid, and in seeking it he is adding to his knowledge and cultivating his intellectual powers.

Let me here interject a parenthetical remark. It is to recommend any of my young hearers who may find themselves in the difficult position I have described, and who may be tempted to shirk the labor of appealing to books of reference, never to begrudge any reasonable amount of time thus employed. It may seem tiresome to have to hunt up an unknown name or a technical expression when you can guess at the spelling, or give it the go-by altogether; but believe me, the satisfaction of securing your doubtful word, or phrase, or quotation, will amply repay your couple of hours' research. No doubt a great deal will depend upon the importance of the

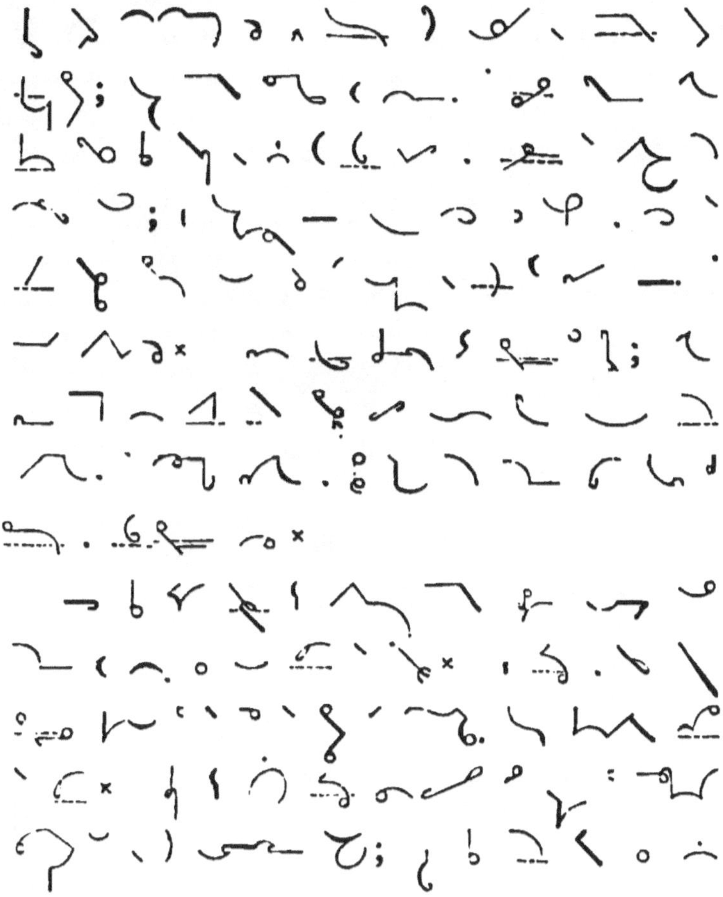

ambiguous words, how far they are necessary to keep up the continuity of the speech; if they can be sacrificed without making a serious break, and if time presses, it is better to omit them than to run the risk of revealing your imperfect information; but if they must be given, if their omission would necessitate the omission of much besides, spare no pains and no time to see that you are giving an accurate report of the words. You may even discover that the speaker has tripped; and if you can get him right by substituting one name for another, or rectifying a misquotation, you will have the satisfaction of doing your work well, if you do not secure the thanks of the speaker himself.

Again, it is hardly possible that a reporter can be constantly engaged in his work without improving his own style of composition. He hears the best public speakers dealing with all kinds of subjects, and many of these afford admirable models of style. It is true that he also hears some of the worst, and has to deal with extremely slipshod, not to say ungrammatical, English; but then it is, or ought to be, his aim to give such utterances a

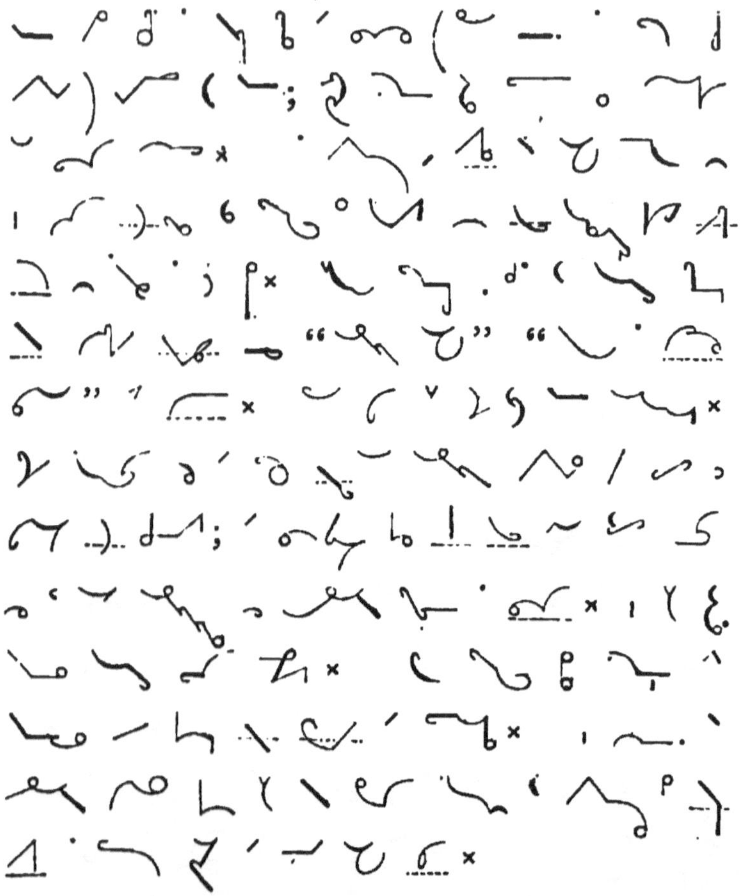

better dress, and sometimes (as in giving a very condensed report) to re-cast them altogether; and therefore work of this character is mental, not merely mechanical. A reporter who writes bad English can have made but little use of the opportunities that his profession has afforded him, even if he has not been a diligent reader, or made composition a set study. I have not forgotten the taunts that have been directed by literary purists against "newspaper English," "penny-a-liners' slang," and the like. Nor will I assert that they are altogether unfounded. There are conventional words and phrases to be found in newspaper reports which one would willingly see discarded; and some of the juvenile attempts at fine writing that one occasionally meets with in the newspaper press may not unreasonably provoke a smile. But I think that these peculiarities have been greatly exaggerated. Every profession has its *argot*, and all beginners are tempted to be flowery and grandiose. But, making all reasonable allowances, it may, I think, be safely affirmed that reporters, as a body, write a clear, intelligible, and accurate English style.

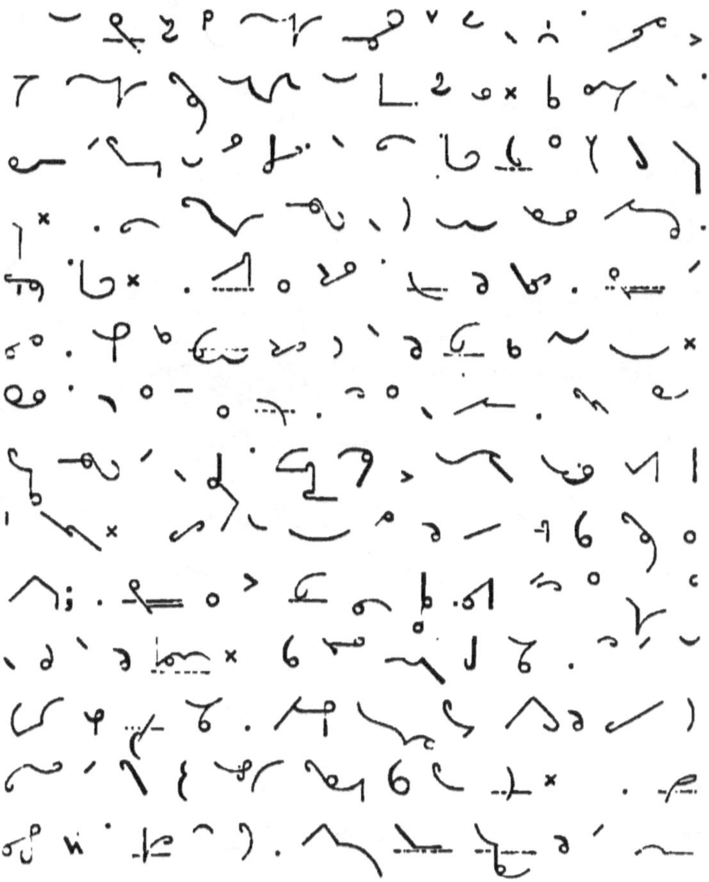

In speaking of shorthand as a mental exercise I ought not to omit a reference to the actual mental process involved in taking shorthand notes. It is certainly of a singular and complicated nature, and is deserving of more attention than has, I think, been paid to it. The mere verbal expression, to say nothing of sense, requires the closest attention. The writer is always a few words behind the speaker, and hence the necessity of his listening to one set of words while he is writing another. As soon as a word has caught his ear the mind has to recall the appropriate sign for its expression and to despatch an electrical message to the nimble fingers to write it on paper. One after another, as the words are uttered, this process is repeated; the speaker is all the while some distance ahead, and the mind has to deal with two sets of words at the same time. This, of course, could not be done unless the mind and hand thoroughly understood each other, unless the requisite forms for the representation of the words were so well known and remembered that they instantly presented themselves for use. The least hesitation about an outline might throw the reporter back half-a-dozen words, and make him lose the thread of a

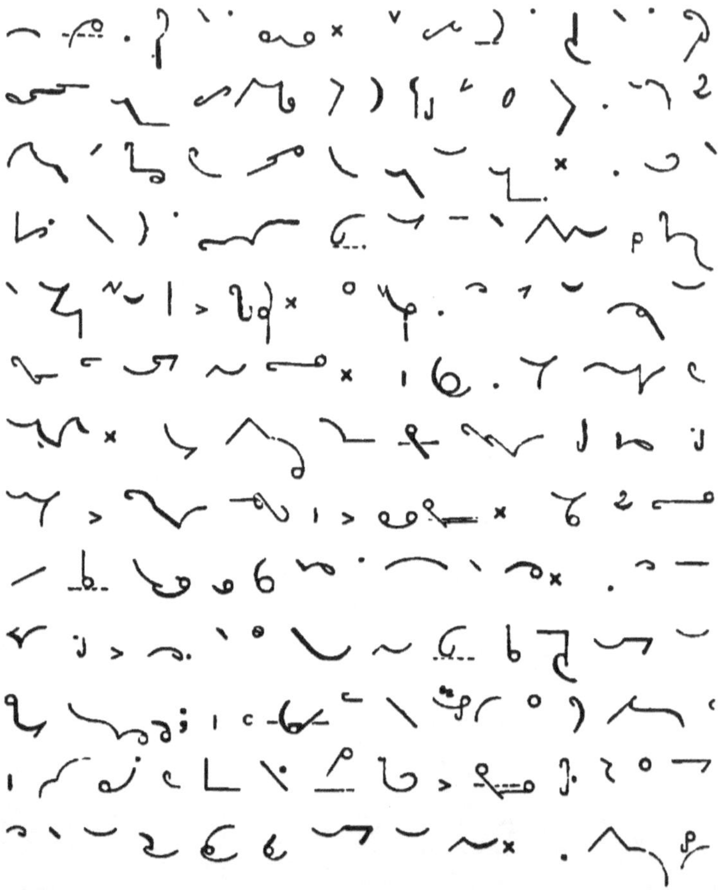

sentence. I once saw an advertisement of a French Stenographic note-book, one of the recommendations of which was that it contained on the first page the entire shorthand alphabet and contractions for reference, if need be, in note-taking. The notion of turning up, say a grammalogue, while in the act of reporting, is a triumph of ingenuity, and I commend it to the consideration of the Society. As I have said, the mind and the hand must be in perfect accord in regard to the written characters. But this is not the only mental effort involved. If the reporter's work is to be properly done he must attend not only to the verbal expression but to the sense of the speaker. Unless shorthand characters are at his fingers' ends this is almost a matter of impossibility. The mind can hardly attend to the meaning of what is being written while it is actively engaged in considering the forms of the words; but when these are called up instantly, as they are required, with but little conscious effort, it can pay as much attention to the speaker's train of thought as can the mind of any ordinary listener who is not engaged in writing. The reporter constantly hears the

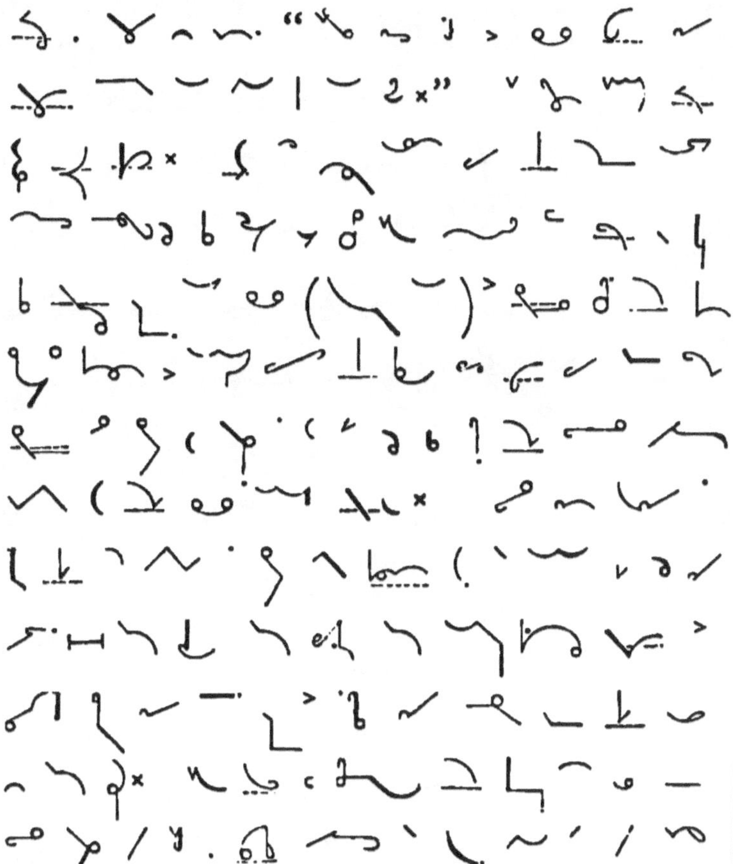

observation made to him, "I suppose you cannot attend to the sense while you are busily occupied in writing it in shorthand." I presume I need not say here that that is a sheer delusion. Though the mind must be in some way at work in regard to the mechanical expression of the words, it is ordinarily, under the circumstances I have mentioned, quite free to devote its powers to taking in the sense (if there be any) of the speaker's utterances, or it may, strange as it may seem to the uninitiated, wander at its own sweet will away altogether from the speaker and his speech, without bestowing a thought on the words he is uttering or the characters required to represent them or the sense intended to be conveyed. Yes, you may, if you are an adept at the art, report a speech and be at the same time thinking of anything but the words you are recording—of your dinner, of your sweetheart, of your unpaid tailor's bill, of the holiday trip you are going to take, of the address you are expected to give at the next meeting of your society. I have often, when transcribing or dictating my notes, come across passages which I had not the slightest recollection of having written,

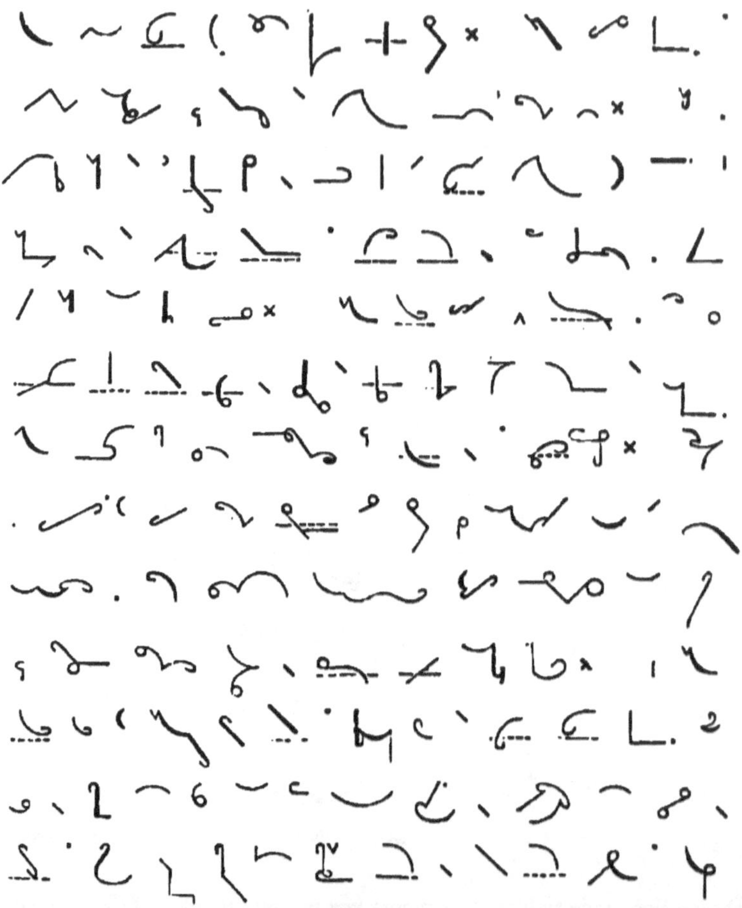

and which I must have written while thinking of some totally different subject. I remember once taking a report in this way when a burst of laughter came from the meeting. I had not the remotest idea of what had been said to occasion it, and while the laughter was going on I took the opportunity of reading back a line or two in order to discover the joke, which I did in due course. I have often wondered how far the mind is really at liberty thus to dispose of itself during the actual work of note-taking, and have occasionally tried some experiments with a view to a solution of the question. Ordinarily the wandering of the thought away from the speaker and his speech is an involuntary thing, and may be nothing more than the very similar phenomenon that one experiences in church when a prosaic sermon fails to secure our undivided attention. But I have often found that I have been able, by a distinct effort of will, while taking shorthand notes, to direct my thought in quite another channel, to refurnish my house, to plan a journey, to take a trip on my tricycle, or to pay or receive a visit, and the like, paying no attention whatever to

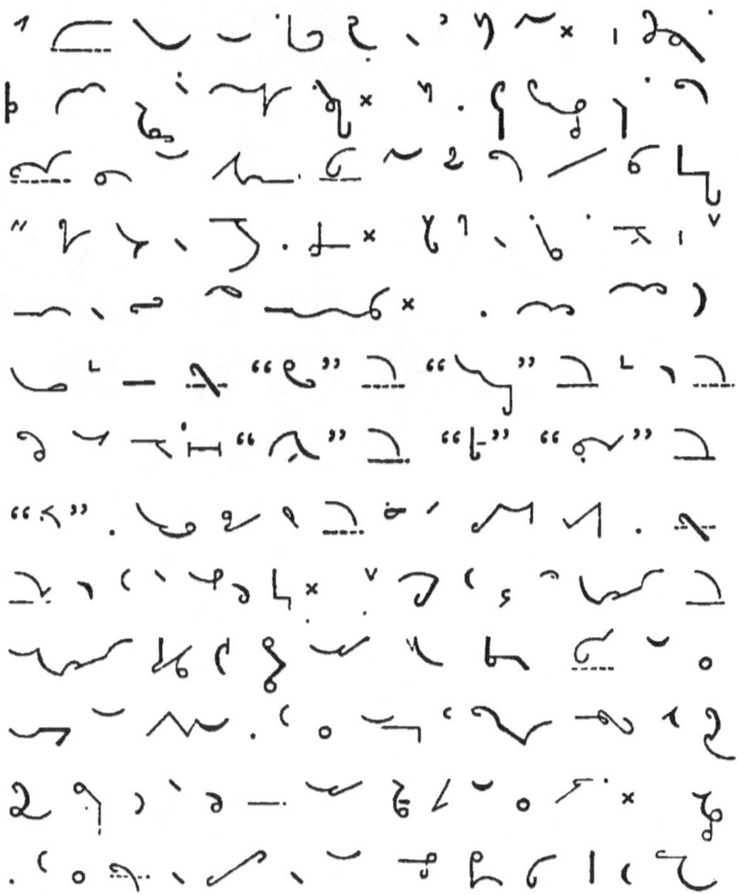

what I was writing. But there seems to be a decided limit to this kind of mental abstraction. I tried the other day, for instance, to do a very small sum in arithmetic while writing shorthand from rather slow dictation, and I utterly failed to accomplish the task. I then tried to compose a couplet, but I came to grief most ignominiously. The moment my mind was fixed on a given number, "seven," or "fifteen," or on a word or phrase in the couplet—"love" or "dove," "smart" or "heart"—the fingers straightway stopped or staggered, and wanted to write the number or the word thought of instead of the words dictated. I imagine that when the mind voluntarily or involuntarily dwells on other subjects in the way I have described, while the hand is engaged in reporting, the thought is unconnected with verbal expression, and that therefore there is no separate set of words coming in the way of those which the hand is recording. Under these circumstances the thought is free to wander to any extent, as it may well do, without clothing itself in language. But when definite words are

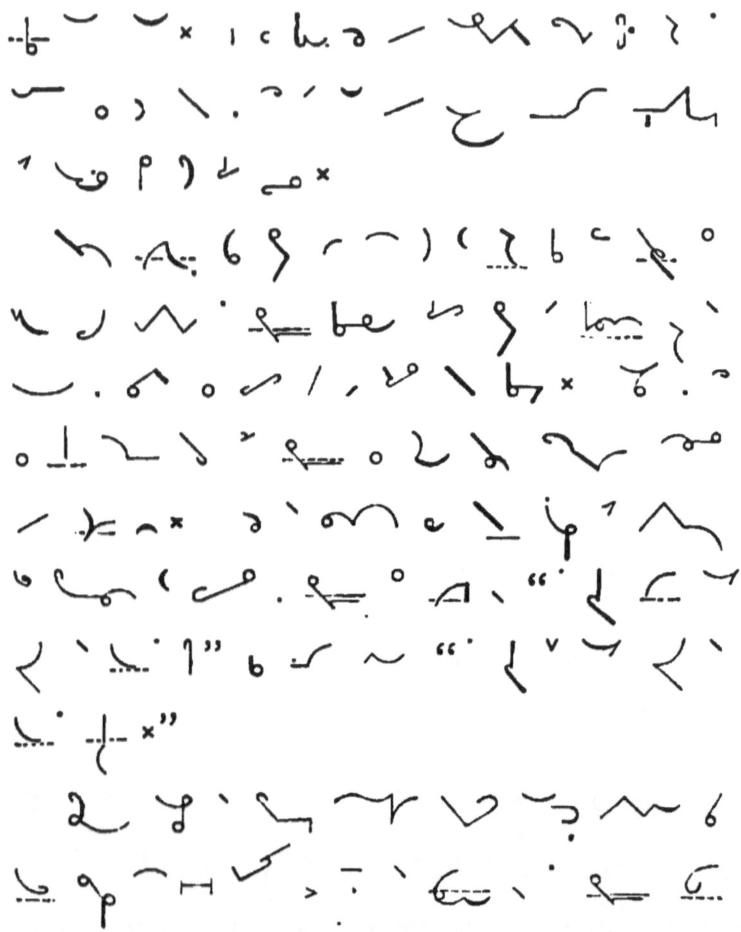

inseparable from the train of thought an antagonism is set up, the mind and hand are no longer accurately co-ordinated, and the fingers stay their onward course.

Before leaving this subject let me say that although it is quite possible, as I have shown, to report a speaker discoursing on one subject and at the same time to think of another, the habit is one which should always be discouraged. Unless the mind is at work upon what the speaker is saying, absurd verbal mistakes are easily made. Words of similar sound become confused, and the reporter finds, for example, that whereas the speaker has alluded to "a double lie in the shape of half a truth," he has actually written "a double eye in the shape of half a tooth."

There is another instance of complicated mental operation in connection with reporting which has often surprised me—I refer to the act of listening to a speaker while transcribing the notes of another part of his speech, or

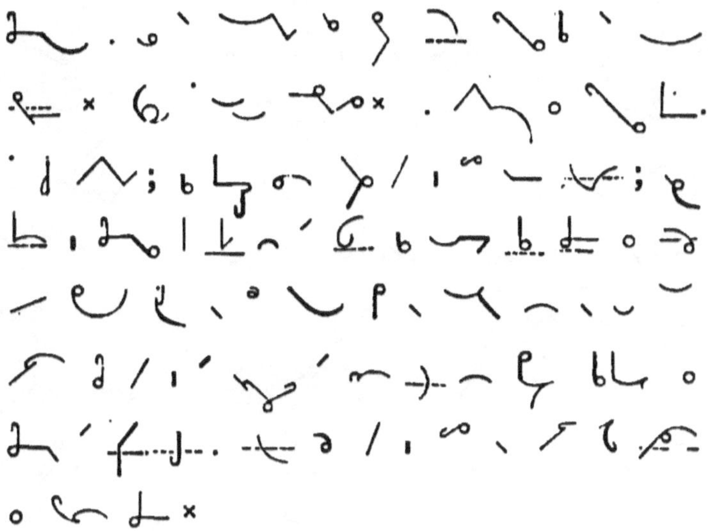

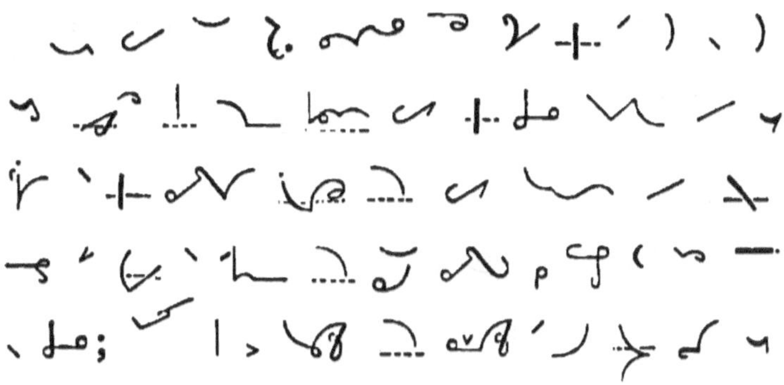

perhaps of the address of another speaker. This is not an uncommon experience. The reporter is, perhaps, taking a condensed report; he has taken down some passage which he wants to give fully; to save time he transcribes it at the meeting, and while he is engaged at his task his ears are sufficiently attentive to what is being said to enable him to note any remarkable utterance which he ought to preserve, and you may see him suddenly discontinue his transcript and jot down the few words which he wants to record, and then resume his former task.

Now, whether in all these simultaneous actions there are different, and, so to say, independent regions of the mind at work at the same time, whether the different tasks performed are under the control of different cerebral convolutions, or whether the phenomena are to be explained on the theory of automatic or unconscious cerebration, is a question that I am not going to discuss; I refer it to the physiologists or psychologists, and

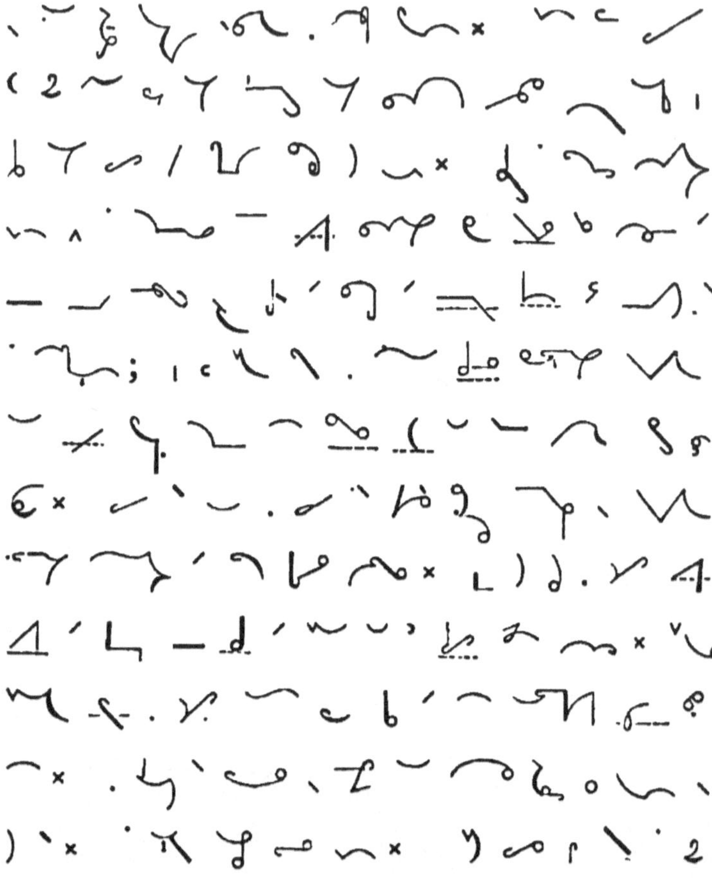

shall feel greatly indebted to any of those gentlemen if they will solve the mystery for me. I am quite aware that shorthand-writing is not the only occupation in which similar results may be noticed, but it is the only one which directly concerns us now. It has been a frequent marvel to me how an organist can read simultaneously several parts of his music and give accurate expression to every tone and semi-tone, and keep time with the accuracy of a metronome; but when I have remembered the many tasks synchronously performed in our everyday work, my surprise, though not altogether removed, has been somewhat lessened. We all know the story of Julius Cæsar's capacity to perform concurrently manifold and very diverse labors. He could, so says the historian, read, write, and dictate, give audience, and I know not what, at one and the same moment I confess I never believed the historian in my younger days, and my incredulity still haunts me. The tendency of narrators to exaggerate in matters of this kind is familiar to us all. A notable instance occurs to me. I was

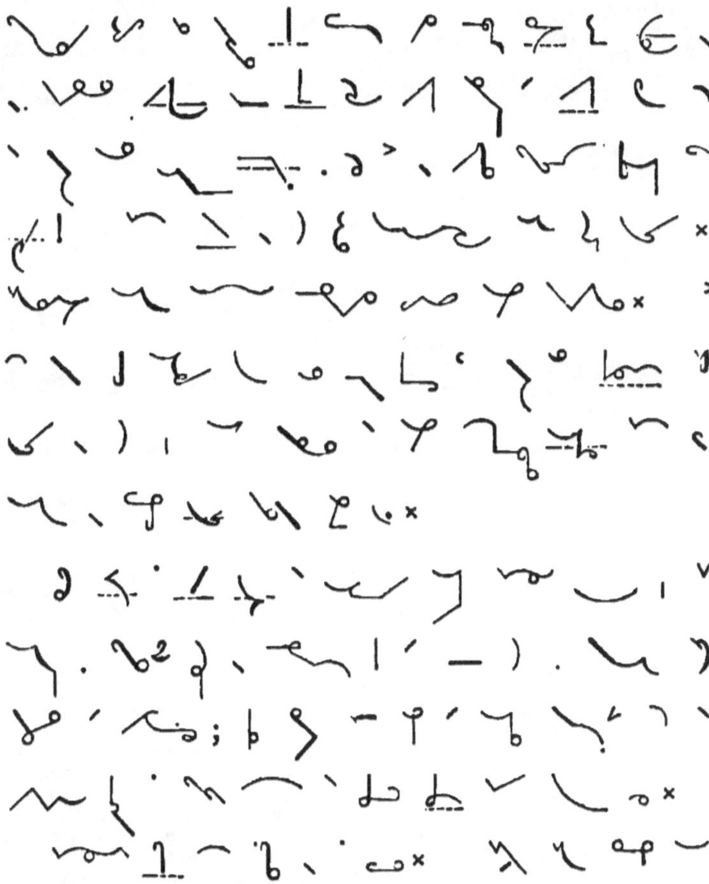

once told by a shorthand professor that one of his pupils had acquired such extraordinary skill that he could listen to two persons reading together at an ordinary rate of speed and write every word of both in his note-book, keeping the words of the two readers perfectly distinct from each other! I am happy to say that this phenomenal individual was not a phonographer. I have certainly never in my own experience witnessed any such performance. What might be done in this way if notes could be taken with both hands at the same time I do not venture to say, but in the absence of any such ambidextrous endowment I am bold enough to question even the possibility of such a feat.

There is here a large field of inquiry into which I must not enter, but I invite the members of the Shorthand Society to explore it and give us the benefit of their observations and reflections; it is a subject of great interest, and in its bearing on the art of reporting it would be an appropriate matter of discussion at some of our future meetings.

I must now draw my address to a close. I hope I have succeeded in

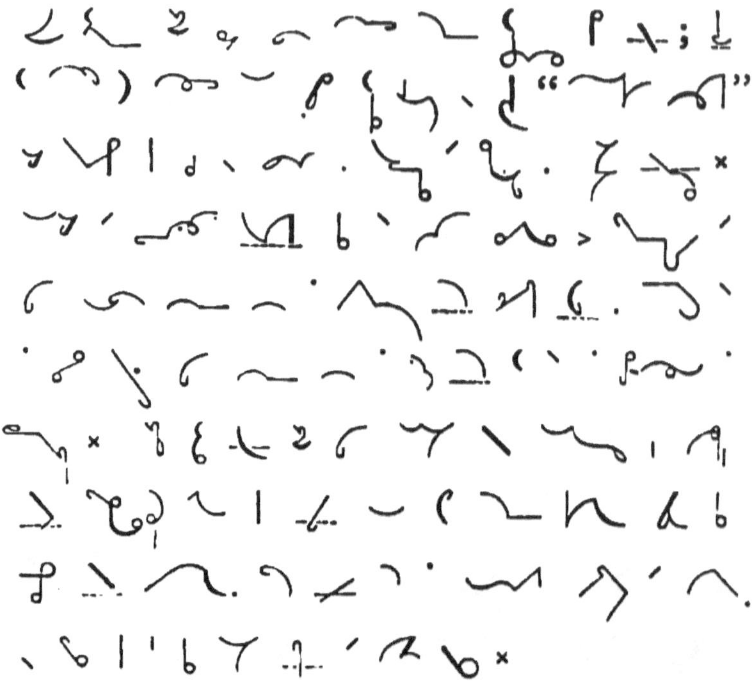

showing that the practice of shorthand is not the mere mechanical work that it is sometimes said to be; at any rate that my friend was mistaken in suggesting that it has a tendency to develop "mental imbecility." Intelligently pursued it tends to stimulate the faculties and strengthen the intellectual powers. Unintelligently and carelessly followed it is of little service to the practitioner, and will no more make him a reporter or shorthand-writer than the occupation of a house-painter will make him an artist, or that of a stonemason a sculptor. I trust that this view of shorthand will not only be enforced but illustrated by the proceedings of the Society, and if it achieve no other work it will have justified its existence by removing from our art an unmerited reproach, and helping to place it on its only true and legitimate basis.

SOUND AND SENSE.

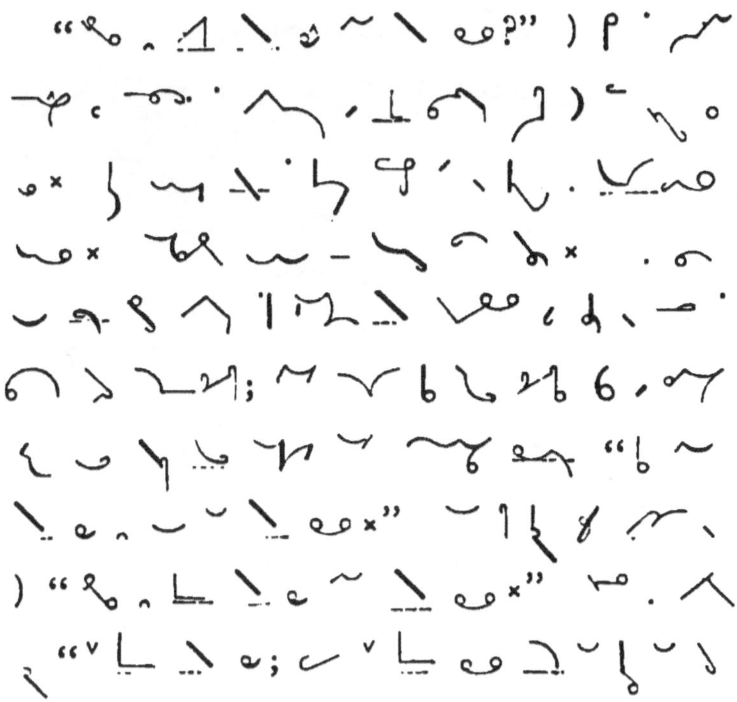

"I suppose you write by sound, and not by sense?" So said a learned counsel when examining a reporter, who, at a celebrated trial, was called to prove his notes. It was intended to be a damaging question, and to depreciate the value of the witness's evidence. In this respect nothing could have been more absurd. The same thing, however, has been repeated *ad nauseam* by persons who have desired to cast a slur upon the work of the shorthand writer; and in the early days of Phonography shorthand writers themselves, who certainly ought to have known better, often indulged in the meaningless sneer, "It is writing by sound, you know, not by sense." In truth, it would be just as rational to say, "I suppose you talk by sound, and not by sense." Of course (the reply would be), I talk by sound; whether I talk sense or not depends not upon my vocal

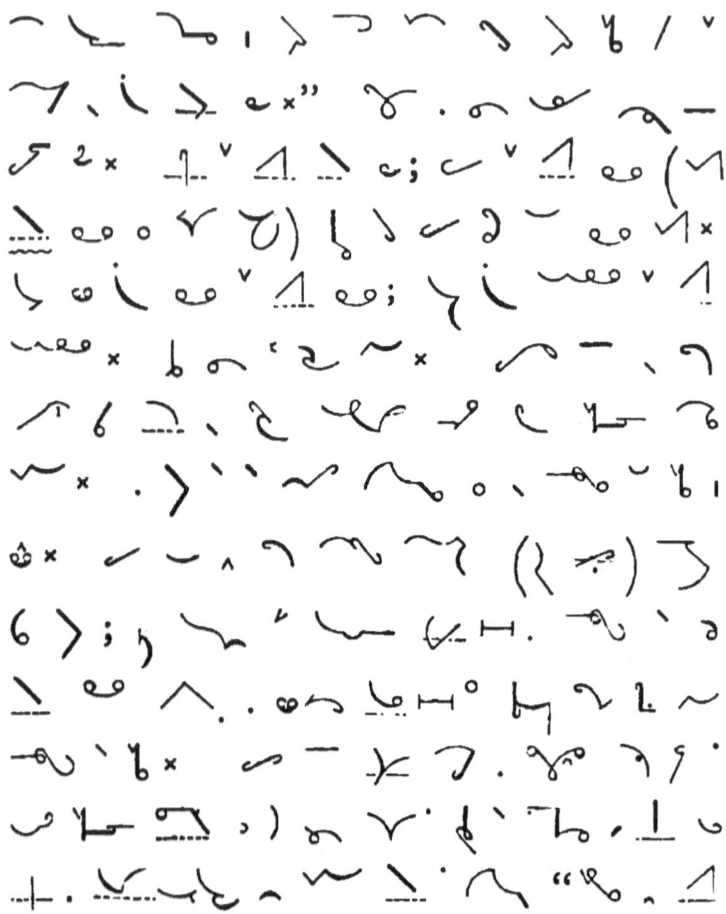

organs, but upon the action of my brain, upon the ideas which I manage to convey by the sound. Precisely the same answer must be given with regard to shorthand. True, I write by sound; whether I write sense (to "write *by* sense" is hardly English) depends upon whether there is any sense to write. If the sounds convey sense, I write sense; if they convey nonsense, I write nonsense. It is the same with ordinary writing. We must go to very remote ages, or to comparatively uncivilized countries for ideographic methods of writing. The object of all modern alphabets is to express, not ideas, but sounds. We know how very imperfectly many of them (especially our own) accomplish this object; but they are formed on the phonetic theory—the expression of words by signs representing the sounds of the human voice—as distinct from the direct written expression of ideas. One can easily imagine the supercilious air with which an ancient ideographic scribe would say to some early disciple of Cadmus, who had found out the value of the new-fangled mode of writing by an alphabet,

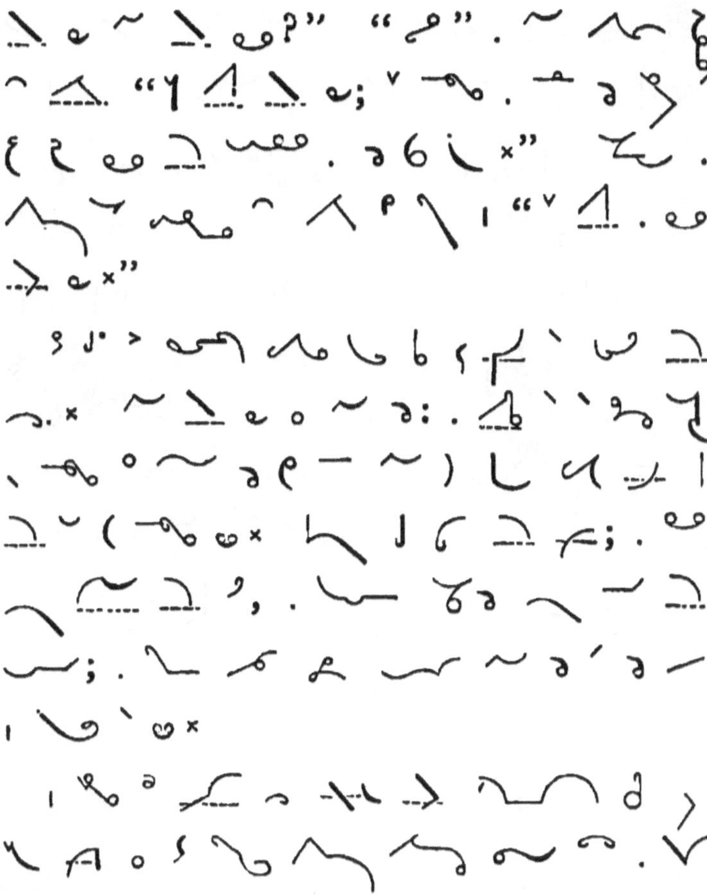

"I suppose you write by sound, and not by sense?" "Yes," the writing reformer of those days might reply, "I do write by sound; I express the exact words of speech, and with them whatever sense or nonsense the words themselves convey." In like manner the reporter in the witness-box might reply, as he probably did, "I write the sense by the sound."

As to the taunt of the stenographer with reference to Phonography, it is without a shadow of foundation or meaning. Writing by sound is writing *words:* the writers of all systems endeavor to express as many *words* as they can, and in so doing, whether they wish it or not, they express sounds. It may be done well or ill; the signs may be long or short, the phonetic analysis of the words may be accurate or inaccurate; the practical result is the same, namely, written words, and words are but combinations of sounds.

But I suppose what is really meant to be conveyed by the oracular utterances to which I have alluded is, that the professional reporter requires something more than the ability to write the sounds that he hears. That

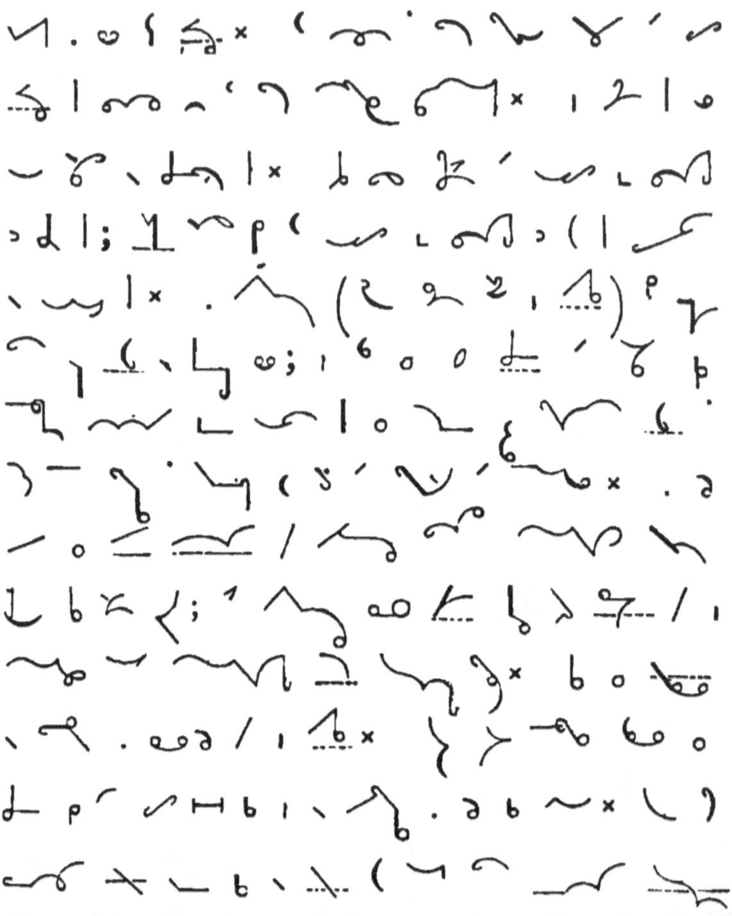

may seem a very profound observation, and one hears it sometimes made with very impressive solemnity. But surely it needs no Solon to discover it. It is the merest truism, and no one but a simpleton would dispute it; I had almost said that no one but a simpleton would think it worth while to enunciate it. The reporter (whatever system of shorthand he writes) has a good deal more to do than to take down sounds; but that is his first task, and, unless he has an extraordinary memory, he can no more do his work without this preliminary than an artist can produce a picture without paint and brush and canvas. The words are his raw material, which requires more or less manipulation before attaining its ultimate shape; and the reporter's success largely depends upon the skill which he manifests in the manipulative or formative process. It is his business to grasp the sense of the words which he writes. If they fitly express that sense his task is a light one—he has but to reproduce the words he has written. If they are clumsily put together, he has to put them in a more comely form,

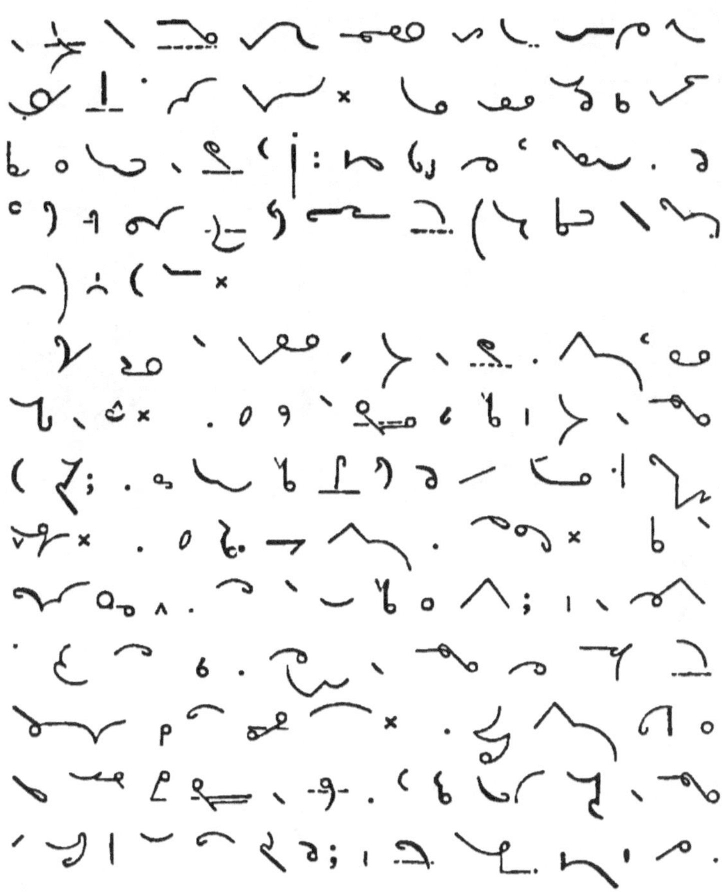

to fill up gaps, to remove excrescences, to round off angularities, and if necessary add a little polish. If there is no sense in the words he has to record, it is not his function to supply that commodity: he must then content himself with presenting the words as they are uttered, simply seeing that they are grammatical, or (if that discretion be permitted him) omit them altogether.

There are two classes of persons who fail to supply the reporter with sense in addition to sound. The first consist of speakers who have ideas, but fail to express them intelligibly; the second have no ideas at all, and their words are *Vox et præterea nihil.* The first of these give the reporter the most concern. It is of very little consequence how the man of no ideas is represented; but to misrepresent a thoughtful man, who has the misfortune to express himself awkwardly or obscurely, is a more serious matter. The conscientious reporter will do his best, in the case of such a speaker, to seize the thought that he has vainly endeavored to express, and enshrine it in more suitable words; but, however painstaking he may be, he runs

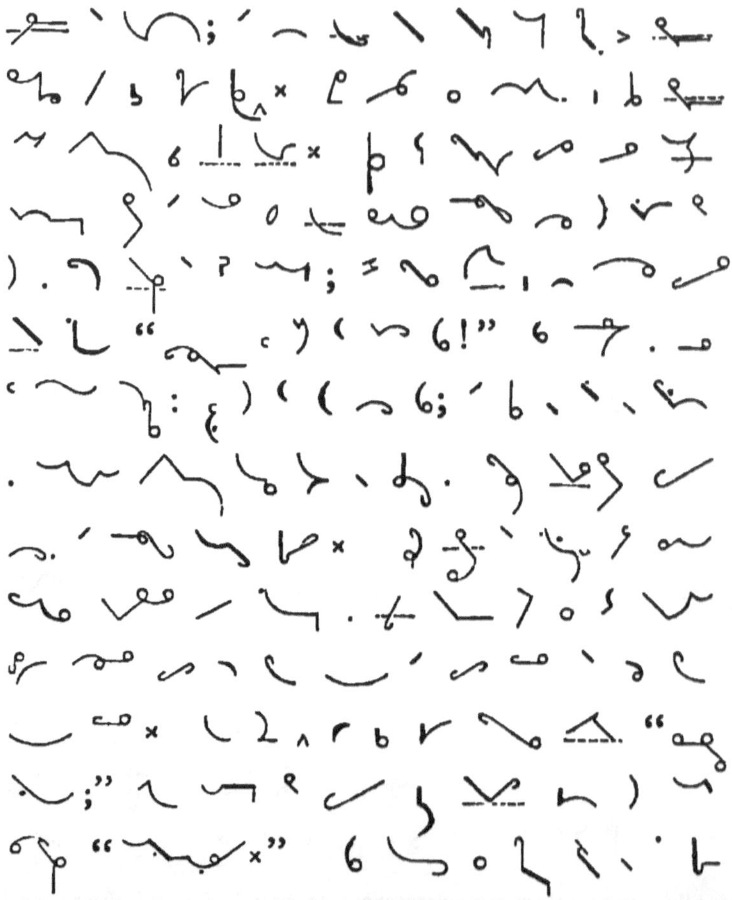

the risk of failure, and may even be betrayed into attributing to the speaker sentiments which he would utterly disavow. Such a result is mortifying, but it is the speaker and not the reporter who is at fault. It is said that a Member of Parliament once rose in the House of Commons to make a speech, and in his first few sentences expressed himself so badly as to say the very opposite of what he intended; and when the members laughed he made matters worse by adding, "Mr Speaker, when I say that, I mean this!" That is exactly the case with many orators: when they say that, they mean this; and it is too bad to blame the unfortunate reporter if he has failed to discern the precise parts of the speech where meaning and expression have been divorced. There is a species of *aphasia* with which certain nervous persons are affected, the chief peculiarity of which is that the patient constantly mistakes one word for another, and one class of words for another class. If asked how old he is, he will perhaps reply, "Sixpence halfpenny;" and if interrogated as to where he was born, he may say in all simplicity, "Nebuchadnezzar." This affection is attributed,

I believe, to a defect in certain of the convolutions of the brain; and I have sometimes thought that some such cerebral mischief might explain the singular misuse of words on the part of speakers whom now and then it is one's misfortune to report. Whatever the explanation, it is certain that sense and sound are not duly co-ordinated, and what Madam Malaprop calls "a sad derangement of epitaphs" is the result, bewildering the auditors, and driving the reporter to the verge of despair. How many of the complaints of inaccuracy that one reads in the newspapers from irate orators are due to this cause I do not pretend to say, but there can be very little doubt that it is the origin of not a few of them. Like most other reporters, I have often pored over sentences (which I have been certain I have written correctly) until my head ached in the vain endeavor to extract the speaker's meaning; and have ended by omitting the passage entirely, or letting it pass in the hope, not perhaps a very sanguine one, that others might solve a mystery which had been impenetrable to myself. The speaker may or may not have had a clear perception of his meaning; at any rate, he has failed to convey it in language adapted to ordinary

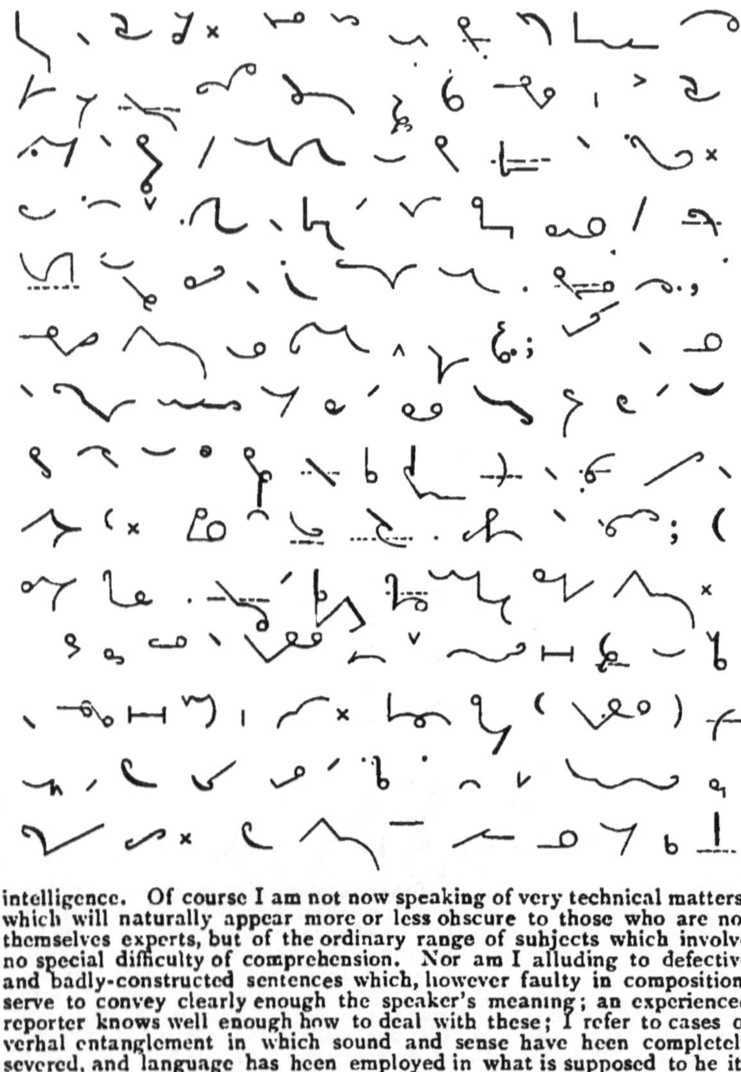

intelligence. Of course I am not now speaking of very technical matters, which will naturally appear more or less obscure to those who are not themselves experts, but of the ordinary range of subjects which involve no special difficulty of comprehension. Nor am I alluding to defective and badly-constructed sentences which, however faulty in composition, serve to convey clearly enough the speaker's meaning; an experienced reporter knows well enough how to deal with these; I refer to cases of verbal entanglement in which sound and sense have been completely severed, and language has been employed in what is supposed to be its diplomatic use, to conceal rather than to reveal thought. Such cases might often baffle the wisdom of Solomon; they certainly transcend the powers and disturb the dreams of the nineteenth century reporter.

As to the second class of persons whom I mentioned—those who have no ideas to express—I need say but little. It may seem strange that persons so ill-endowed should ever venture to rise and address a meeting, but the phenomenon is not a very rare one. Every reporter can recall cases in which he has had to read through whole pages of shorthand notes,

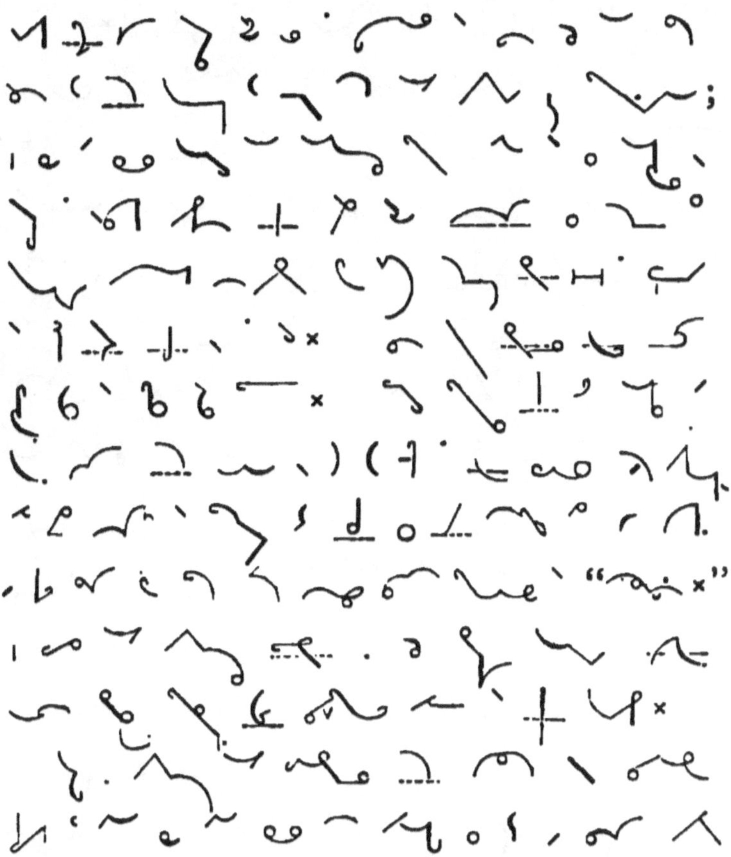

a wilderness of mere words, in search of some thought or fact that could be embodied in the report he was preparing; but sound and sense have been in inverse proportion, and after all his endeavors to obtain a solid residuum out of such abundant material, his work has painfully reminded him of the recipe for Irish workhouse soup—a quart of water boiled down to a pint! Some popular speakers even occasionally deliver themselves of addresses of this character. Called upon, perhaps, at short notice, and having little or nothing to say, they utter a few sentences *ore rotundo* and with such an amplitude of verbiage that the audience is as much impressed as the old lady who derived spiritual comfort from her minister's solemn pronunciation of "Mesopotamia." But once in the reporter's crucible the words speedily evaporate, leaving no more substantial precipitate than the Hibernian article of diet aforesaid.

If then the reporter in the witness-box or elsewhere be henceforth twitted with writing sound and not sense, my recommendation is that he should simply reply, "That depends," and shift the responsibility from his own shoulder to that of the speaker. I know it is sometimes alleged that a

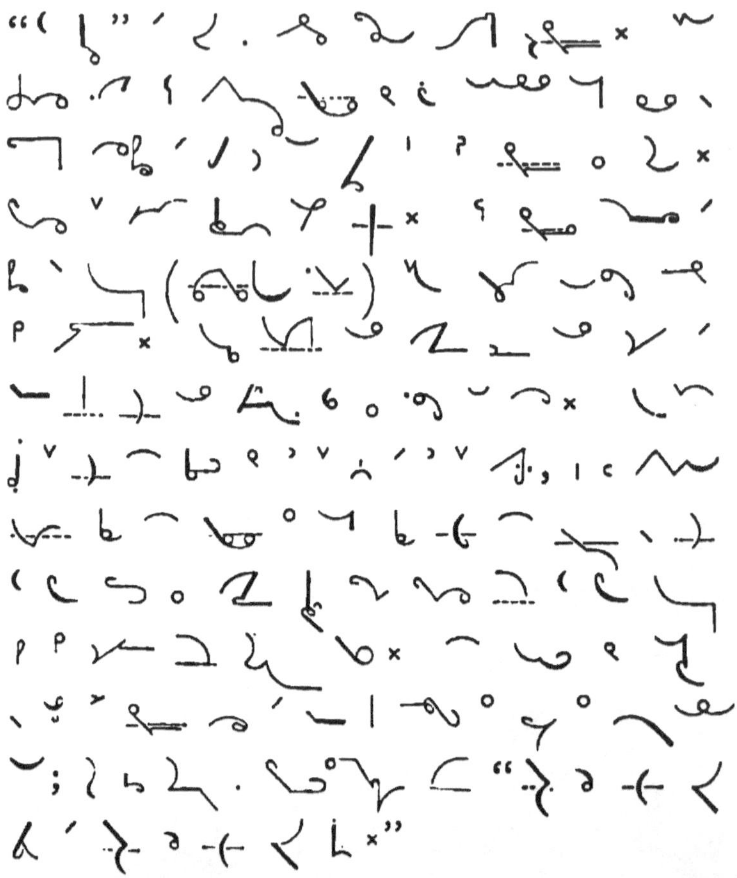

reporter's business is to convert nonsense into sense, to correct misstatements, and generally sit in judgment on what a speaker is saying. For myself I wholly disclaim any such duty. With a speaker's arguments and statements of fact (slips of the tongue apart) I have absolutely no concern except as a recorder. If he is faulty in his logic, weak in his history, and altogether at sea in his geography, that is his concern, not mine. If I am condensing I use my discretion as to what I omit and what I retain; but when reporting fully, it is not my business, as indeed it is not within my power, to see that every conclusion is logically deducible from the premise, or that every fact stated has an historical or scientific basis. My function is to endeavor to understand what the speaker means, and to give it expression as nearly as may be in his own language; so that he may not escape the application of the Scriptural law, "By thy words thou shalt be justified, and by thy words thou shalt be condemned."

www.ingramcontent.com/pod-product-compliance
Lightning Source LLC
Chambersburg PA
CBHW031111020726
47495CB00007B/2151
* 9 7 8 3 3 3 7 3 9 6 6 0 2 *